Praise for Jace Carlton and *Letting Go*

Sigh! I just love how *Letting Go* pulled me in from the very first paragraph! The story Jace weaves from cover to cover and the characters he creates are so authentic! He makes me feel like I'm right in the story, cheering for the heroine and booing the villains.

I love being at the ocean and I want so badly to stay at that beach house! I also love horses and I want to spend time at that guest ranch, as well! PLEASE tell me they're real!

My favorite characters were Nicole and Emma. Nicole, because her fun side is so vibrant and playful, while her serious side is focused and determined; and Emma, because she's just so darn charming! And I definitely can't forget Liam! If any of you know country music just think of Chris LeDoux and you'll see Liam!

Thank you for a great page turner, Jace! Staying up late on those nights was well worth it!

— Caren Ansaldo-Byers Aggas

Oh, my GOSH! What an epic love story! *Letting Go* captured me right from the start and I just couldn't put it down! First *The Reunion*, then *Breaking the Stillness*, and now *Letting Go*! It appears that Jace's way of touching my heart has no limits! This definitely belongs on the top of everyone's reading list NOW!

— Merilynn Campbell

Jace Carlton has done it again! *Letting Go* is a masterful tale of struggle, survival, and love fulfilled! I love his romantic heart! I read somewhere that this is the first book in a series? If that's true, I can't wait for the story to continue!

— **MariAnne Crosby**

What a wonderful new romantic tale from Jace Carlton! I love a story that pulls me in and gives me the feeling that I'm right there witnessing the action firsthand. I cried over Nicole's struggles and wanted desperately to give her a hug to let her know everything would be okay. As a career woman myself I cheered over her strong-willed triumphs (nicely done, young lady)! And finally, I celebrated enthusiastically as her desire beyond her wildest dreams came true! Where does her story go from here, Jace? I need to know!

— **Diana Phillips**

Letting Go is beautifully written and extremely romantic with moments of tenderness climaxing into eternal love! I loved every word in this latest romantic novel by Jace Carlton! He is an extraordinary storyteller. So well done!

— **Megan Michaels**

Letting Go is one of the best romantic novels I've ever read! I so thoroughly enjoyed reading Jace's debut novel, *The Reunion*, and now he's captured my heart again with another wonderful love story! More, Jace, more!

— **Susanne Marshall**

I have to admit I'm not much into love stories (mysteries, thrillers, and non-fiction are much more to my liking), but a friend of mine asked Jace for permission to share an advanced copy of *Letting Go* with me and told me I needed to give it a shot and I'm so glad I did! I know that the vast majority of romance novels are written by and for women, and that's great, but for a man to venture forward into this genre, and succeed like Jace has, is truly impressive. Kudos, Jace! You've done a fine job! I'm looking forward to reading more, so keep these stories coming!

— Cory Marks

Are you ready to read a romantic novel that will draw you in?? Well, here it is!! You will become a part of this incredible and fascinating love story. It's one book I couldn't put down. Enjoy!

— Kari Kauffman

Ralph Waldo Emerson once said, "Life is a journey, not a destination."

How can a very young broken heart be turned into determination and continuous successes only to experience more heartbreak, then ultimate happiness? You'll find the answers with Nicole's journey in *Letting Go*!

— Bruce Sexton

LETTING GO

LETTING GO

a novel

JACE CARLTON

1423
PRESS

Eagle Mountain, Utah

Letting Go
by Jace Carlton

Published by 1423 Press
212 Crossroads Blvd., #184
Saratoga Springs, UT 84045

Copyright © 2023 Jace Carlton

Author note: As with all works of fiction, the characters that an author creates are simply from their imagination. Such is generally true with *Letting Go*. However, a number of characters in this book are based on people I know in my life and I've received their permission to use their first names, and for this I am truly grateful.

Editor: Terrie Dailey Morgan
Cover Painting by: Doreman Burns, DoremanBurns.com
   (Used with permission and publishing rights secured)
Cover and Book Design by James Woosley, FreeAgentPress.com
1423 Press Logo Design by Brianna Rawlings, Fiverr.com/Braidedlady

First Printing, November 2023

ISBN: 978-0-9996855-8-7 (hardcover)
ISBN: 978-0-9996855-9-4 (paperback)
ISBN: 979-8-9894610-0-4 (e-book)
ISBN: 979-8-9894610-1-1 (Kindle)

The Lighthouse logo is a trademark of 1423 Press.

Other Books by Jace Carlton

Novels
The Reunion

Poetry
Sounds of Darkness

Poetry and Lyrics
Breaking the Stillness

Private Edition
Reflections

ACKNOWLEDGMENTS

I'D LIKE TO BEGIN by thanking my technical advisors, Dr. Rachel Valentine, Spencer Hamons, and Debra Hunter Miller. They provided the expertise I needed to keep everything authentic. Rachel provided the veterinary advice, Spencer provided the aviation insights as someone who has flown in and out of Angel Fire/Colfax County Airport, and Debra assisted with information about guest ranches.

Terrie Dailey Morgan was once again my wonderful editor who very patiently went around and around with me over a few technicalities, smiling and laughing all along the way. You are a true gem that gets brighter and brighter over time, Terrie! Bless you!

The book you're holding is the work of my ever-creative book designer, James Woosley, of Free Agent Press. It's been great to work with you again, James! There are many more to come so stay close!

The initial inspiration for this book came when I saw a painting by Doreman Burns titled "Letting Go". I admire his work and how he portrays the women in his paintings with their eyes hidden under wide brim cowboy hats. This truly intrigued me and after viewing his collection on his website, "Letting Go" stood out to me and I asked myself, "Okay, what is she letting go of? Something in her past? Or someone? Or both?" And with that I was off and running! Doreman was gracious enough to allow me to purchase the rights to use the painting on my cover. Thank you, my friend! Let's do this again!

In the early stages of development of the storyline for *Letting Go* it was clear to me that I was going to have to make a personal visit to Angel Fire, New Mexico in order to make sure I "had my bearings right" for the story. Rachel and Carlos Valentine were originally set to be my hosts for my week-long visit until a case of COVID forced a change in plans. Carlos reached out to his friend Conné Kalweit, the Central Reservations Manager at Angel Fire Resort, and I was provided with top-notch accommodations! Thank you one and all!

Many thanks to Jan Mika for taking charge of publicizing my visit with flyers posted throughout the village, along with arranging for an "Author Night" that was held mid-week at the Chamber of Commerce and sponsored by realtor, Annie Jo Lindsey. Jan also gave me a tour of the Moreno Valley and shared some insights of historical significance, as well as intimating about several "scoundrels and ne'er-do-wells" that lived in the mountains for a time in the not too distant past. I made many wonderful new friends that week, both at the Resort as well as throughout the Village, whom I'm looking forward to seeing again on my next visit!

Typically, a statement is placed on the copyright page that states something like the following -

> This book is a work of fiction. Names, characters, places, and incidents are the product of the author's imagination or are used fictitiously. Any resemblance to actual events, locales, or persons, living or dead, is coincidental.

Well, with their permission, my wonderful friends Mike & Kay Robertson, their daughters, Nicole and Ashli, and their son, Kevin, and his wife Maureen were gracious enough to allow me to use their first names for important characters throughout the book. Nicole's husband, Adam, has a minor role. I had actually offered this opportunity online when I couldn't come up with a name for one of the important characters. Nearly one hundred and fifty names were submitted for me to choose from, and after I finally narrowed down my choice in a blind test it turned out that it was Kay who offered the winning name! As my part of the deal I was offering an incentive to the winner of having a character named after them. Author's discretion – I chose to include their whole family!

Also, my friend, Nashville professional photographer, Sheri Oneal, appears "as herself", also with permission.

Two more wonderful family friends were inspirations for characters – Nancy Harris as the piano teacher, Mrs. Harris, and Sandy Morgan as Carli. I think I matched the personalities of both of their characters to a 'T', and I know you'll love them, too!

At the time I began writing *Letting Go* I became a member of the online group *Loves to Read*. I invited the members to submit brief emails if they would like to be a character in one of my future books and why, along with what kind of character they'd like me to portray them as. Many of the characters you'll come across throughout the book are based on about half those who submitted these emails, while others will appear in future books in this series. Only their first names were used, but they'll be able to tell who they are.

I would, however, like to bring special attention to one of these wonderful new friends of mine from the *Loves to Read* group, Brenda Moriniti Riggan. Her initial response to my request really hit a special note with me! I wrote back with more questions so I could get to know her better and she enthusiastically responded, and we've maintained a close correspondence ever since. Her character, Brendy, becomes the best friend and confidant of the main female character, Nicole, from the time they first meet in the story, and she'll go on to play an equally important role in the next book in the series tentatively titled *Searching*. Thank you, Brenda, for allowing me to develop your character in such a way as to make her heart and soul truly shine! I hope you love her!

Another friend I made through *Loves to Read* is Gayle Coy and I'm very thankful for this blessing. Prior to the contest to name that one specific character I ran a similar contest to come up with just the right name for the ranch that became a major location in the book. This time over one hundred seventy-five suggestions came in from nearly one hundred fifty people! I narrowed my choices down to a top fifty, then twenty-five, then ten, and finally I took a look at the top five contenders. I chose Hidden Glory Ranch, and when I looked to see who submitted the name it was Gayle! Many thanks, my friend!

Finally, I wish to thank my beta readers for their helpful comments and wonderful reviews – Caren Ansaldo-Byers Aggas, Kari Kauffman, MariAnne Crosby, Susanne Marshall, Diana Phillips, Cory Marks, Megan Michaels, Merilynn Campbell, and Bruce Sexton.

AUTHOR'S NOTE

INSPIRATION AND IMAGINATION ARE wondrous things! A writer, artist, sculptor, musician, songwriter, or dancer has a flash of inspiration that seemingly comes from out of nowhere and imagination kicks in! Creativity takes over, and before long something never before read, seen, or heard is presented to the world! The creator takes a deep, contented breath of satisfaction, briefly admires the finished work, and then begins the process all over again; always seeking, always desiring to discover something new to share, for sharing is what we truly do! We, the creators, are blessed with a gift, but this gift is not for ourselves … it's for others. And it is up to us to share what we create with others who are seeking what we have to offer.

As an author my inspiration comes from many sources – visual, aural, and spiritual to name a few. I strive to keep my eyes, ears, mind, and heart open at all times to new possibilities, then filter through them to see what I might be able to do with them before the inspiration is gone. Have I goofed up and missed out on some things along the way? Sure! I learned my lesson a long time ago that telling myself "I'll remember such and such until I can write it down later" never works. Ideas are just that fickle. If you don't grab them when they're presented to you they'll leave and find someone else who *will* recognize them and take advantage of that precious moment. My muse, Kiera, can attest to that!

Letting Go was inspired visually. I had been looking at a variety of paintings on Doreman Burns' website and a few stood out as possibilities to inspire a future book or two. The painting titled *Letting Go* was one of those paintings, but the real inspiration didn't come right away. In fact, it took a long time … one year, to be exact. When I first saw it I was in the midst of preparing to launch *Breaking the Stillness*, but I made a note to check his website often just to see which of his paintings might be the one to inspire me enough to consider a new book. Some ideas spring forth quickly, while others just need time. *Letting Go* needed one year.

I *love* the process of creating something new! Words are my colors and pages are my canvas! In the words of my favorite thriller author, David Baldacci, "I can't *not* write!"

I'm an author … it's how I breathe!

Jace Carlton
October 23, 2023

For Debra Hunter Miller

THANKS TO YOU **I** discovered the art of Doreman Burns and a whole new vision for my writing was opened to me. Thank you again for your technical assistance, particularly regarding guest ranches. And finally, thank you for our long time friendship!

S OMETIMES, WHEN LIFE IS going smoothly, so smoothly that you're not really paying close enough attention, something happens to shake up your world. It can be terribly upsetting or it can lift your spirits at a most unexpected moment.

Two people from totally different worlds and completely different paths in their lives find out just what it's like when their worlds unexpectedly come together for a brief moment in time … a moment that just might last forever.

CHAPTER 1

Another Sleepless Night

THE ANXIETY ATTACK STRUCK Nicole out of nowhere. It had been *so* long since she had taken any time off and her mind and body were showing deep signs of stress. She loved her job as an architect, the people she worked with, and her boss, Warren, was beyond amazing. So, if everything was so great at work, why was she feeling so much pressure? After last night's emotional breakdown, she knew she needed to do *something*, but what?

For as long as she could remember she had always been the stable one, not emotionless but cool and calm under pressure. Where did this crack in her polished executive veneer come from, and how long could she keep it to herself? When her executive assistant, Amanda, looked at her, could she see that something was wrong? She prayed she could hold everything together just a little longer, until she could figure out what was going on and how she was going to change it. And was it *what* needed to be changed? Or was it … who?

* * *

It was almost lunch time, but instead of joining a few friends as she usually did on Fridays, Nicole decided to have some quiet time alone. She added some final touches to the notes for her presentation at the staff meeting after lunch and then grabbed her purse from the desk drawer. The weather had become quite pleasant since she had arrived earlier that morning, so she left her coat on the back of the door as she left her office.

"I'm heading out for lunch, Amanda. I'll be back in time to finish my prep for the staff meeting."

"Thanks, Nicole. Enjoy your lunch!"

"Thank you. See you in a bit."

Nicole deftly made her way through the office so as not to attract too much, if any, attention. She especially hoped that Denise would not notice. While she usually enjoyed Denise's company, listening to her rightfully brag about her children and how well they were doing in school, today was different. She needed to think, and that meant going *anywhere* quiet and alone.

Rico's Deli was only a few blocks away. She thought about just walking over there, ordering a sandwich and a drink, then walking across the street and relaxing on a park bench while watching the children play. However, she knew the park would be too noisy. She drove over instead, bought her lunch, and then went to a secluded park up in the hills that she had been to many times before. There were usually plenty of benches under big shade trees to choose from, but she especially enjoyed the wonderful view of the bustling city below and the Pacific Ocean beyond.

As she sat down and placed her lunch on the bench, her phone vibrated. It was just a reminder about the staff meeting coming up in ninety minutes. No problem. She had plenty of time. Another alert would come through in thirty minutes and she would head back to the office.

She unwrapped her roast beef and Swiss cheese sandwich on sourdough bread and sighed heavily as she took in the view. Something in her life was just not right, but no matter how hard she tried she could not figure out what it was. She took a bite of her sandwich, pleased with how cool and fresh it tasted. She closed her eyes, letting her mind wander back to the night before, and the overwhelming confusion that seemed to come out of nowhere, followed by uncontrollable sobbing.

CHAPTER 2

The Night Before

THE WEEKEND WASN'T APPROACHING fast enough for Nicole's liking and she was grateful that she had decided to stay home and relax. She'd been out with Chandler the previous two nights. Tuesday was just the two of them at Chez Lafitte's, a quiet and romantic hideaway. It was such an exclusive restaurant that when Chandler had made the reservations the waiting list was over two months. Last night they had spent the evening with two of Chandler's associates from his law office and their wives. Dinner was elegant and the conversation was lively, although Nicole felt a bit awkward since she and Chandler were not married with kids like the others.

Whenever the conversation shifted to the other couple's children, Nicole felt left out. Chandler was from a large family, with an older brother and sister and two younger sisters. Nicole was an only child and could not relate. It had never really bothered her before, mostly because she had never known any other family dynamic. While her father was busy with his career, her mother had always given her plenty of attention. However, it would have been nice if her father had not been so hard on her so many times. She often felt that he was that way because she knew he had wanted a son. He had made the mistake of saying as much when Nicole was only six, not realizing she had overheard him talking to a neighbor. His comment stung her tender heart then, and now whenever it crossed her mind, it still hurt deeply.

* * *

Since she could not be the son her father had always wanted, she was determined to be the best replacement she could be. She excelled in music by learning how to play the piano vibrantly by ten; her crowning achievement being Gershwin's "Rhapsody in Blue" which she performed in a full orchestral recital ... from *perfect* memory! She was captain of her high school basketball and tennis teams, Homecoming Queen, and her classmates voted her the girl "Most Likely to Succeed". Her cup runneth over as she amassed an amazing number of scholarships on her way to earning the coveted title of Valedictorian of her graduating class. Everything she touched seemingly turned to gold.

She had been recruited heavily by the best colleges and universities in the nation. Most of them that were eager to have her attend were located along the east coast, mainly in New England, including Princeton and Yale. She even gave serious thought to attending the University of Wisconsin–Madison to pay homage to her architectural design hero, Frank Lloyd Wright. However, preferring to stay as close to her friends as possible, one in particular, she had narrowed her choices to the University of Southern California, the University of California–San Diego, and the Art Center College–Hillside Campus in Pasadena. After visiting each of the campuses and meeting with counselors and potential professors she set her sights on USC, and then, to be true to her dream, completed her graduate work at Frank Lloyd Wright's School of Architecture at Talesin–West in Scottsdale, Arizona.

Now, a phenomenally successful architect in her own right, she struggled to separate her work life, social life, and time just for herself; the latter usually receiving little or no attention. The thought of burnout never crossed her mind. Not at her age, and not at this stage of her career. Ignoring the many awards and other accolades that had come her way over the short span of her young career she was still determined to make a name for herself. She felt this intense need to finally prove to her father once and for all that *she* was fully capable of proudly carrying on the family name, not the son he never had. She was *so* determined that she could not afford to even blink. And, when the time came to get married, she was seriously considering having a hyphenated last name.

But tonight … tonight while she was alone with her thoughts, mingled with extreme mental exhaustion, she began to question it all. Everything. Her life. The career she had worked so hard to build. Her future that, by all accounts, *looked* golden. But was it really? Was everything she had, everything *she* had wanted?

* * *

Chandler had called mid-afternoon and again shortly after she arrived home, but she ignored both calls and let them go to voicemail. After the call she had received this evening, she simply shut off her phone. She was in no mood to talk with him or anyone else. She *might* check her messages later but there was no rush. She had enough on her mind and a lot of it was not good.

Chandler Whittingham was a great guy who she had been dating for over five years, although lately he had been dropping hints about the idea of settling down. He had not come right out and said as much, but Nicole easily read between the lines. And last night he had shown a bit too much interest as his friends discussed their lives - their *married* lives - and their children. No. Not for her. At least … not yet.

But when? In a year or two? Or five? She knew that if she genuinely wanted to settle down and have a family she could not wait too much longer. All she knew was that Chandler was not going to talk her into it now. *But why had he started hinting more and more about it lately?* She cared for him, but was caring enough? There was just something missing that she had always believed *had* to be in every deep, loving, and lasting relationship … love. That was it, love! She cared for him, laughed with him, supported him in his career, lifted him up when he was down or angry about something, attended various family, corporate, and social events with him, but did she love him? *Truly* love him?

What role models did she have to lean on or look to for an example of how love should be? Her parents? Perhaps, but while they certainly appeared to treat each other kindly and showed mutual affection toward each other as she was growing up, she had not witnessed that as much these last few years, especially after her father had chosen to retire early. The last time she had visited them at their home in Rancho Mirage, she had waited until her father went golfing before trying to have a heart-to-heart talk with her mother. It did not work out as well as she had hoped. Perhaps she should have called a few days ahead and given her mother a heads up about wanting to chat about something potentially sensitive. What actually happened was her mother sweetly glossed over anything and everything that Nicole may have perceived to be any signs of trouble in paradise. Just great! No help there!

Chelsea, her best friend since grade school, had only been married for two years so she was still in that newlywed stage when *everything* was perfect! No help there either.

So many questions with no answers. She was exhausted, but she still had one more day of work to get through, a busier day than usual that included an important staff meeting after lunch. She believed she was ready for it, although, being the perfectionist that she was, she would review her notes again in the morning and make revisions as necessary. Because of how she lived her personal and business life, she was *always* ready for *anything*. She did not like to be caught off guard by anyone or anything at *any* time. But her head was spinning. If she could only get control of her thoughts, focus on just one thing, *whatever* it might be, she might feel better about herself right now. However, she could not bring herself to do so. And, as she laid her head on the pillow her eyes began to water, then the tears flowed, and moments later she was sobbing uncontrollably. Her life was *not* so golden after all.

The Difference Between Night ...

CHANDLER WHITTINGHAM WAS AN exceptionally handsome man. He stood six feet two inches with dark brown slightly wavy hair, always tastefully styled, and deep brown, engaging eyes. He was always impeccably dressed regardless of the occasion.

One third of his immense walk-in closet was office wear - black, blue, or navy blue pinstriped Brooks Brothers suits. He also had over two dozen starched white shirts and nearly two dozen colored dress shirts, equally starched, all arranged by color and shade, dark to light, left to right. Over one hundred very fashionable ties were neatly rolled and placed in a boxed case that was installed at the end of the wall.

The back third was for casual wear for evenings and weekends – black, navy blue, light or dark grey, brown, khaki, and tan casual slacks and coordinated sports coats in a dozen colors, with nearly three dozen shirts, once again all arranged dark to light.

Half of the remaining third was for short-sleeved Ralph Lauren Polo shirts, and the final half had a dozen pairs of jeans along with over a dozen pairs of shoes in all styles and appropriate colors to fit the occasion or his mood. A door-sized mirror occupied the back of each of the double closet doors. The track lighting was appropriately installed to enhance every angle and nuance of the over-sized closet, including aiding Chandler with the finishing touches to his wardrobe as he tightened the double Windsor knot of his tie and straightened his pocket square each morning.

Chandler grew up in Greenwich, Connecticut where his family lived in a seven-thousand square foot home along the eighth fairway of the exclusive Windsor–Vale Country Club. His father, Charles, had been a highly successful defense attorney in New York City. His office had been located in One World Trade Center, and he and his fellow attorneys and staff were fortunate to escape with their lives just moments prior to the collapse of the tower in the horrific terrorist attack on September 11, 2001.

Physically, Charles survived the traumatic event. However, his mental state was a different story. Not long after the collapse of the towers, he was struck by post-traumatic stress and the effects were overwhelming. He sought and received excellent counseling that helped him begin to deal with the nightmares and day tremors. After his firm had been fortunate to find new office space a month later he notified his partners that he would be taking a three-month leave of absence.

He returned to the office at the end of the three months, but the concentration he needed to effectively fulfill his responsibilities and properly represent his clients had been deeply affected. He met with the other partners, passed along his pending case load for them to disperse among the associates, and then announced he was taking an indefinite leave of absence.

Chandler had always loved and admired his father, but seeing the changes that had come over him post 9/11 worried him deeply. Knowing that he would be going off to college in less than two years, he became more determined to get closer to his father. With Charles around the home more, Chandler made a point of spending as much time with him as possible without neglecting his studies, which he continued to excel in. His overriding motivation was to receive as many scholarships as he could in order to cover as many of his college expenses as possible. This, he hoped, would in turn ease the financial concerns of his parents, as he had an older brother and sister already in college, and two younger sisters in high school.

After an additional six-month leave of absence, Charles attempted to ease back into working fulltime, but the pressure that came upon him, the same pressure that had been no problem to handle with ease prior to 9/11, now caused issues with his concentration. Initially, he cut back to working only thirty hours a week, but by the time Chandler was halfway through his senior year, his father reduced his time even further by going into work just two days a week. Physically, Charles was still strong and healthy, but the effects of his post-traumatic stress had taken their toll.

Chandler graduated from high school as Valedictorian, earning a full ride scholarship to Harvard, at which point Charles and Cynthia looked at their finances and investments, including Charles' quite impressive retirement package. After talking with their financial consultant, Charles decided to call it quits and retired early.

Chandler was grateful that his hard work had paid off, knowing that he had lifted any potential financial burden off his parents. He continued to study hard and found various ways to cover all his own expenses for the rest of his time at Harvard.

Following in his father's footsteps, Chandler graduated with an MBA, and then graduated in the top ten percent of his class from Harvard Law School. After considering offers from law firms in Los Angeles, New York City, Washington D.C., and Boston, he accepted an offer with the prestigious Los Angeles firm of Wade, Harrison, Winston, and Shaw. He was intelligent and ambitious, and determined to become a partner in less than the ten-year minimum track the law firm advised him of during his interviews. He knew that he could probably make partner in five to seven years at many other law firms, but he was willing to wait a little longer to make partner at the Wade group because of the added prestige it would give him for his future.

He did not want to be seen as brash so he kept this goal to himself, concerned that he would alienate the very people who held his future in their hands. Plus, one of the signs of an excellent candidate for partner included getting along well with your associates. Sometimes this had proven difficult, particularly regarding Benjamin Sawyer.

A couple of the partners had been discussing which of the associates to offer a particular case to. One partner suggested Chandler, while another suggested Benjamin. A problem arose when both partners thought that the associate they suggested had been the one that was finally agreed upon, only to find out their mistake *after* the case had been offered to both associates within mere minutes of each other. Both Benjamin and Chandler had been excited to accept the case, as it would most certainly have added a feather to their cap upon its successful litigation. However, once the error had been discovered, there seemed to be an invisible steel wall Chandler had built up between them.

It was Benjamin who had finally suggested to Chandler that, together, they call for a meeting with the partners in question. When the four of them met, and the issue was presented to the partners, a solution was quickly offered with a second high profile case being offered to them. With the ball being thrown back into their court, Benjamin and Chandler were given the opportunity to choose which case they would take on. Benjamin spoke first and agreed to take the newly offered case, and the short-lived animosity between the two men was resolved.

The partners later became aware that it was Benjamin who had made the suggestion that he and Chandler meet together with them. And, when Benjamin quickly agreed to accept the new case offered to both he and Chandler, he was seen by the partners as the associate possessing greater leadership and compatibility skills. That led to him being offered his partnership during the early part of his ninth year with the firm.

Chandler was now well into his tenth year and there had not even been a hint or rumor of an offer until just recently. He wondered, with all the long hours he had put in over the years, all the tough cases he had volunteered for, all the satisfied high-profile clients he had brought into the firm, why had there not been any mention, or even a hint, sifting through the office until now. Then, early one morning, Malcolm Shaw, one of the founding partners of the firm, asked him to be his guest for lunch at the exclusive Los Angeles Country Club on Wilshire Blvd. *FINALLY*, he thought!

Their lunch lasted nearly two hours, and other than the few minutes they took to decide what entrees to order, Malcolm asked question after question about Chandler's experiences as an associate in their firm, and Chandler kept pace with his best answers. When it seemed like things were beginning to wind down, Malcolm hit Chandler with a question he was not prepared for.

"Chandler, I understand you are single, is that correct?"

"Yes, sir." Chandler replied.

"Are you a confirmed bachelor, or is there a young lady that you're currently seeing?"

Chandler was puzzled. He had brought Nicole to several of the firm's events over the last few years, and he had introduced Nicole to many of the partners during this time including Malcolm. *Surely,* at least *one* of the partners would be aware that he was in a serious relationship and would have mentioned it to the others during their discussions about future partners!

"No, sir, I'm not a confirmed bachelor. In fact, I've been seeing the same young lady for over five years now. Her name is Nicole Hart."

"Nicole Hart? Ah, yes, I believe I *have* met her at some point."

"Yes, sir."

"So, what, may I ask, is keeping you from getting serious and taking the next step and marrying her?"

"We both have demanding careers, so we don't see a lot of each other. Two to three times a week, at the most."

Malcolm pondered this response for a long moment and Chandler chose to remain silent so as not to interfere with Malcolm's thoughts.

Malcolm cleared his throat, looked Chandler dead on, and asked, "Do you have any plans for when you're going to ask her?"

Chandler knew that his chance for becoming a partner anytime soon could very well ride on his response. He had heard hints recently that one of the reasons he had not been more seriously considered for partner before was because he was single, and the partners only looked at highly qualified *married* associates, or at least those who were engaged with a specific date for their wedding; something about such a candidate having a more solid and stable character.

"Actually, sir, I'm planning on taking Nicole out this Sunday evening after I get home from the conference. We'll have a great chance to talk about our future then."

Malcolm studied Chandler for a moment. "Fine. That's just fine. Please drop by my office the first thing Monday morning and let me know how it went. I don't think I need to tell you that this could mean a great deal to you and your future, Chandler."

"No, sir. I understand, sir."

"Good. I'm glad to hear that."

"In fact, we just had dinner with Benjamin and Steven and their wives last night, and during the evening the topic shifted to their families, and I think Nicole really enjoyed the discussion. She did not have too much to say because we're not married with a family yet, but she seemed to find the discussion quite interesting!"

"Wonderful! Well, it sounds like you have things in order."

"Yes, sir!"

"That's good, Chandler. Very good. Now, let's head back to the office, shall we?"

"Yes, sir."

Ahhhhh, Chandler thought, *things are* finally *getting serious! It won't be long now! I'll call Nicole this afternoon and make arrangements for Sunday evening. I just* know *she will be* thrilled *to hear all about this, and then we can start to talk* seriously *about getting married!*

... and Day

EVER SINCE SHE WAS a child, Nicole Hart had been bright and enthusiastic, always eager to learn and try new things. As an only child, Nicole had wished that she could have had a large family, with brothers and sisters, like her best friend, Chelsea. Well, at least one sister, older or younger, it did not matter to her. She had been carefree and fun-loving, up until that fateful day when she was six and overheard her father tell their neighbor, Mr. Parkins, that he wished he had had a son instead. In that very moment she had changed. Initially she was crushed, but after crying herself to sleep every night for over a week, she woke up one morning and decided she needed to make a change. She was not sure what kind of change it was going to be, she just knew something needed to be different for her to not completely fall apart.

Normally, when the weather was nice, Nicole's Saturday mornings consisted of watching some of her favorite television shows after breakfast, then helping her mother in the garden, before her play time began. Not today. It was cold and rainy, so playing with her friends outside was out of the question. Instead, after breakfast, she headed for her room, closed her door, took out her diary, and began to write.

Saturday, April 5th

Dear Diary,

What did I do to make Daddy hate me? Was it just being born a girl, and not a boy, like he told Mr. Parkins last weekend that that's what he had wished for? Or have I done something wrong that made him disappointed in me? I sure wish I knew.

If it was something I did or said that made him hate me, then I wish I knew what it was. Then maybe I could apologize so he would love me again.

For now, I guess I will just stay out of his way. At least Mommy still loves me.

It was over a month before she wrote in her diary again. That was unusual for her, because she normally wrote in it three to four times a week, but she had been busy.

Wednesday, May 14th

Dear Diary,

Have you missed me? I'm sorry, but I've been SO busy!

Guess what? I'm taking piano lessons and I'm LOVING it! Well, it is hard sometimes to practice so much, but my teacher, Mrs. Harris, is very nice and is very patient with me too. I'm supposed to practice for thirty minutes every day but I skip Sundays because Daddy is home after golfing early.

Mommy had seen that I was sad and wanted to talk to me one day, but I just could not tell her why. One day after school I sat down at her piano and just started playing a few notes. The keys were harder to push down on than I thought they would be, but I seemed to get the hang of it after a while. I was not playing a song, of course, but just having fun. I was just about to stop when Mommy came in from the kitchen and said,

"It sounds like you are having fun."

I said, "Yeah, kinda. I don't know what I'm doing. It was just a kind of silly thought I had that I could sit down and just start playing a song."

"If you would like to learn how to play the piano, I would be happy to pay for piano lessons for you."

"Oh, I don't know. Maybe another time."

"Okay, sweetheart. Just let me know, okay?"

"Sure, Mommy. Thanks."

"You're welcome, dear."

And then I went to my room to read a book.

After dinner a few days later, I told Mommy that I might be interested in learning how to play the piano after all. She smiled really big and then she hugged me! I sure was not expecting that! I just asked her to not say anything to Daddy about it. She asked me why and I just replied "Because". She looked at me for a minute, and then nodded her head and said, "Okay, sweetheart. I promise I won't tell your father."

While I was at school the next day, she called the music store and made arrangements for me to start taking lessons, and when I got home from school that day, she said that my lessons would start the next day! I was so nervous at my first lesson, but my teacher was really nice. She had the prettiest smile that made me feel so calm. I still get nervous when I go to every lesson because I want my teacher to be happy with me, but it seems to be getting easier.

Time flew by as she continued to practice every day. Mrs. Harris kept telling her mother that Nicole was far exceeding her expectations for a student Nicole's age. Once she had moved on from the standard scales and basic songs, she started practicing for an hour every day. After a few days her mother noticed that she was going beyond her normal half hour.

"Honey, your practice time is already over."

"I know," Nicole replied.

"You know?"

"Yeah, I'm having fun!"

Nicole's mother eyes widened in disbelief. "Okay, sweetheart. I'm not going to stop you from having fun! Especially *this* kind of fun."

Nicole grinned and went back to practicing, knowing that she had made her mother happy.

Because of Nicole's growing passion for the piano, she was advancing rapidly in her abilities. Mrs. Harris was finding it harder and harder to find enough challenging songs for Nicole to practice on. During one lesson, Nicole played the song she had been asked to practice, then surprised her teacher by playing a song from a different, more advanced music book that she had begged her mother to buy. Three months later she was beginning to play songs by ear that she was hearing on the radio!

"Sweetheart," her mother said as they were driving home from another lesson, "please let me tell your father how well you're doing."

"No, please don't, Mom. Not yet."

"But you're doing so well, and I want him to hear you, too."

"Please no."

"But when?"

Nicole hesitated. *Maybe never,* she thought to herself. "Some time. I'll let you know when, okay?"

Her mother sighed. "Okay, sweetheart. I'll wait."

"Thanks," Nicole said softly. What her mother did not know was that Nicole *still* did not think she was good enough for her father to hear her play. Maybe she never would be. For the time being she was just playing for herself. Well, and her mother, who was always so encouraging and supportive. But playing for her father? That was a risk she was not ready to take. She had to get better, a *lot* better, because she just could not bear the thought of him being disappointed in her again.

She had no idea exactly what she could do to make him love her, but she had to keep trying different things, hoping she would know when the time was right. If ever.

She went on to excel with her music, and one day when she was nine Mrs. Harris invited her to prepare for her first recital, but Nicole declined, saying she didn't feel like she was ready yet. Mrs. Harris tried to assure her that she was, but she politely requested to not be included.

Mrs. Harris tried again a year later and was so pleased when Nicole agreed! She finally felt like she was ready for that next step, and on her way home from practice that day she told her mother all about it!

"Mom! You're *not* going to believe what Mrs. Harris told me at the end of my lesson today!"

"What, sweetheart?"

"She said she is going to schedule a recital for all of her students, and she wants me to be a part of it! Isn't that exciting?"

"Oh, my goodness! Yes! When is it going to be?"

"She hasn't set a date yet because she wanted to send out a message to the parents in case there might be any conflict with their schedules, but she said it won't be for another month or so."

"Oh, Nicole, I'm *so* happy for you! I know every time I've asked, you've told me over and over that I can't tell your father, but this is such wonderful news that I really wish I could. Please?

Nicole sat back in her seat and was quiet for a long time.

"It's okay if you don't want me to, honey. I'm trying to understand why you've never wanted him to know about this wonderful talent of yours. I'm sure he would be so proud of you."

Nicole let out a long sigh. "Maybe I'll tell you someday, but not yet."

"But what about telling him about the recital?"

Again, Nicole remained silent for a long time.

"I'm sorry, Mom. I don't know yet. But I'll try to let you know soon, okay?"

"Okay, dear. That will be fine."

"Thanks."

Nicole was wrapped in a tight ball of confusion. She was over the moon excited about the recital, and part of her *wanted* her dad to know, but, on the other hand, what if he didn't like the recital? Or, worse yet, what if he didn't like *her* performance?

The next day, as she sat down to practice, she lacked the normal enthusiasm that usually accompanied every practice since she had started taking lessons. She hesitated as she raised her hands above the keys, closed her eyes, took a deep breath, opened her eyes, and began her normal warm up. For the first time in a very long time it felt sluggish. She stopped, took another deep breath, shook her hands to try to relax, and began again. She felt like she was stumbling through the motions, like her fingers had weights tied to them, making it harder to move them over the keys. Finally, she simply stopped and walked outside where her mother was working in the garden.

"Mom?" Nicole asked timidly.

"Hi, sweetheart!"

As she approached her mother she fought to keep her lower lip from trembling.

"Mom, I'm not feeling well. Is it okay if I skip my practice today?"

"Oh, honey! What's wrong?"

"I don't know, but I don't think it's anything serious. May I go to my room instead?"

"Certainly, sweetheart. Come here and let me give you a hug."

Nicole walked up to her mother, and as her mother reached toward her with muddy, gloved hands, Nicole's eyes widened, and she suddenly pulled back, alerting her mother who quickly pulled her hands back. They both laughed as her mother just as quickly removed her gloves.

"Okay, shall we try that again?" her mother added with a big smile.

Nicole responded with a smile and a slight laugh. Her mother's hug felt surprisingly good, and she held on for a moment longer.

"Would you like to take a short nap before dinner?"

"No, I don't think I need a nap. Maybe I'll just read a book."

"Okay, dear. I'll let you know when dinner is almost ready."

"Thanks, Mom. I love you."

"I love you, too, sweetheart."

As Nicole headed back to the house, Charlotte continued to watch her daughter, a daughter she was so proud of and loved so much. *Playing the piano so passionately for all these years has made her mature so fast. Has it been* too *fast?*

As Nicole entered the house and turned toward her room, she felt the trembling return. As she neared her room, she saw her bed and ran and threw herself face down and began sobbing into her pillow.

What's wrong with me? I can't play, I can't think straight. I can't do anything! What's happening to me?

She laid there sobbing for several minutes until she heard her mother crossing the patio and about to open the back door. She quickly got up and headed to the bathroom and closed the door. She grabbed a hand towel and set it on the marble counter near the sink, then turned on the faucet to let the cold water run. When it felt just right she held her hands under the faucet, filling them with the flowing coolness. Then she brought her hands toward her face, letting the coolness bring a much-needed relief to her reddened cheeks and eyes. She let out a sigh and repeated the process two more times.

Feeling a bit more relaxed, she wiped her face and placed the towel back on the chrome circular towel holder. She opened the door and headed toward her room, but was startled to see her mother sitting on the bed.

"What's wrong, Nicole?" her mother asked gently.

"I'm just not feeling very well."

"Sweetheart, I think it might be more than that," she added lovingly.

"Really, that's all it is, Mom. I promise."

"Then why did I see your comforter all askew, and your pillow with the impression of your head, as well as it being wet as if you've been crying? Please talk to me, sweetheart."

"Oh, Mom—", and she ran into her mother's waiting arms.

They sat there on the edge of her bed for several minutes while Nicole continued sobbing. When her tears began to subside, she looked up at her mom.

"Thanks, Mom. I love you so much."

"I love you, too, sweetheart. When you're ready, I hope you'll come talk to me and maybe together we can figure out why you're so emotional this afternoon."

"Do you think it's possible to figure me out?"

Her mother smiled a knowing smile, "Yes, honey, I truly do."

They gave each other another big hug, and then her mother stood to go and begin preparing dinner.

Nicole remained on her bed for another minute or so, sighed heavily, then got up and walked to her desk. As she sat down, she turned to her right and opened a drawer, reaching for her diary.

Tuesday, July 17th

Dear Diary,

> *I'm so confused and scared. I don't know what's wrong with me.*
>
> *I sat down to practice a little while ago, but I felt such a horrible feeling come over me, and it scared me! I've never wanted to avoid practicing before, but today I just couldn't do it! I tried, I really tried, but I just couldn't do anything right!*
>
> *Oh, no! Have I lost my ability to play? NO!!! PLEASE NO!!!!!!!!!!!!!!!!*
>
> *WHAT'S WRONG WITH ME????????*

Nicole set her pen down and, without re-reading the last entry, she closed her diary and returned it to the drawer. The only thing she felt like doing now was to take that nap her mother had mentioned earlier. She pulled on the side of her comforter, smoothing it out, then laid down, made herself comfortable, and closed her eyes. An hour later her mother awakened her for dinner.

* * *

Two days had passed since her meltdown and Nicole was finally beginning to pull out of her slump. Yesterday's practice was better, but she still had not found her groove. However, this afternoon's effort was much better, and she knew she was getting back to her normal form, but there was still much more work to do. She *had* to be perfect!

When she had first started taking her lessons, she had practiced faithfully for the recommended thirty minutes a day. Once she felt like she was really catching on, and loving to play more and more, she started to practice for an hour every day. Then she had upped it to ninety minutes, and a few months later she made it a full two hours.

Nicole thought back to Mrs. Harris' invitation to perform her first recital. She felt bad that she had turned her down, but also knew she was not ready, despite Mrs. Harris trying to convince her otherwise.

Because her father never arrived home from work until at least six-thirty, she decided it was safe to add more time onto her practice, and was now up to three hours a day.

Despite the results of all her passionate practicing, something was still weighing heavily on Nicole's mind. She thought it might have been how much the meltdown had shaken her, but then she realized it must have been caused by something else. Perhaps it was something deeper, something that, prior to two days ago, had been disguised and kept her conscious mind from seeing exactly what the problem had been all along — she was once again afraid of her father's rejection!

But, with the recital coming up in about a month, she had to make a decision about whether or not to let her mother tell her dad about it. *He's going to have a lot of questions but mom is better at handling those than I could ever be.* After dinner that evening, she quietly asked her mother to come to her room.

After they entered the room Nicole sat down at her desk while her mother sat on the edge of the bed.

"Mom, I need to ask you something."

"Sure, sweetheart! What is it?"

"You haven't told Dad about my playing the piano, right?"

"Absolutely not! I made a promise to you that I wouldn't until you said it was okay. Why?"

Nicole hesitated, then cleared her throat. "Mom, I need to tell you something."

Concern shrouded Charlotte's face as she looked deeply into her sweet daughter's eyes.

"What is it, darling?" she asked softly.

Nicole took a deep breath before letting it out slowly. She interlocked her fingers in her lap, then looked up at her mother.

"Mom, I just wanted to let you know that I've made a decision … I think."

"You think?"

"Yes, because I'm still not sure, but I'm trying to be brave."

'I don't understand, sweetheart. What do you need to be brave about?"

Nicole looked out her window, took another deep breath, then looked back at her mother.

"I need to be brave about you asking Dad to come to my recital."

Charlotte's eyes brightened with joy! "Really, darling?"

"Mom, please don't get too excited."

"But why? This is wonderful news!"

Nicole sighed. "Because … I'm scared."

"Oh, honey, you have nothing to be afraid of."

"Yes, I do."

"What could you possibly be afraid of? I've heard you practicing all these years, and you are *so* ready for this recital."

"Oh, I'm fine about my performance, Mom. Well, I'm a little nervous, but—"

"Then what is it, sweetheart?" her mother asked encouragingly.

"Dad."

Her mother looked at her with a puzzled look. "Your father? But why, honey?"

Nicole looked down at her hands and studied her fingers for a few moments before looking up at her mother again.

"I know he doesn't know I've been playing the piano, because I've made sure he's never heard me practice, but … I'm really hoping that he won't reject my performance."

Her mother's jaw dropped! "Sweetheart, why would you think that he would reject your performance?"

"Because —" Nicole paused for a long time, trying to find the right words without starting to cry like every other time she had rehearsed telling her mother what she was about to reveal.

"Because … I don't think Daddy loves me," and Nicole began sobbing uncontrollably.

"Oh, Nicole! Of course your father loves you!" her mother said in a way to try to allay Nicole's fears and concerns. "Why do you think he doesn't love you?"

Nicole tried valiantly to catch her breath. "It's … it's just a feeling I've had for a while."

"Oh, my gosh, sweetie! I'm so sorry you've felt this way. Did he say or do something that made you feel that he didn't love you?"

Nicole just shrugged her shoulders, afraid to even share with her mother what her father had said about her when she was six. Then, she lifted her hands up to cover her face as her tears began to flow again. Her mother quickly got up from the bed and knelt down next to the daughter she loved with all her heart and hugged her tightly. Nicole then wrapped her arms around her mother who started to cry as well.

After a few minutes Nicole's sobbing eased and her mother brushed the tears away from her cheeks with her fingers.

"I love you, Nicole."

"I love you, too, Mom."

"When did you say the recital is going to be?"

"Probably a little over a month from now."

"Okay, when Mrs. Harris lets us know, I'll find a way to talk to your father about it, okay?"

Nicole sighed. "Yeah, I guess that will be okay."

"I'm *sure* everything will be fine, sweetie. So, in the meantime, please don't give it another thought, okay?"

"I'll try not to."

"Just concentrate on your practicing and preparing for the big day, okay?"

Nicole sat looking at her mother without saying anything.

"Promise?" her mother asked with a wink and a smile.

Nicole began to laugh. "Yes, *Mom!* I *promise!*" And mother and daughter shared a fun laugh.

* * *

With fewer than three weeks to go before the recital, Nicole said she was ready for her mother to let her dad know about it. Then she crossed her fingers and said a prayer, knowing that all she could do at this point was hope for the best.

That evening, after Nicole had gone to bed and her mother knew she was asleep, Charlotte sat down next to her husband in the family room and shared with him Nicole's exciting news.

"A piano recital? How long has she been taking lessons?" Jenson asked incredulously.

"Oh, for a while," her mother replied casually.

"And she's already playing her first recital? It seems a little soon, don't you think?"

"Well, she is pretty good. I think you'll be pleased."

"And why have I not heard her practicing?"

"She always practices right after she gets home from school."

"What about weekends?"

"Well, you're usually golfing when she practices on Saturdays."

"And what about Sundays?"

Charlotte hesitated for a moment. "You don't play as long on Sunday mornings, and she doesn't want to disturb you on the day you're home."

"That's nonsense," he replied gruffly. "If she's going to do well, she needs to practice *all* the time."

"She practices enough, Jenson," Charlotte replied as calmly as she could. "Just come and you'll see."

"When is it?"

"Two weeks from this coming Saturday."

"Saturday? You know I golf on Saturdays."

"That's why I'm asking you this soon, so you can make plans to skip that day."

Jenson pondered it for a moment. "Well, there's no tournament that day, so I guess I can skip it this once."

"Thank you, dear. I'm sure your being there will make Nicole very happy."

Jenson simply nodded his head, which usually meant a nonchalant and noncommittal 'I guess so.'

"And, in the meantime, please don't say anything to Nicole about her practicing or the recital. It'll only make her more nervous than she already is."

Jenson gave Charlotte a look of disbelief.

"Seriously? How do you figure that?"

"Jenson," Charlotte began, then paused for a moment to gather her thoughts, "I don't know what it is, but you just don't seem to be as close to our sweet daughter as I wish you were."

"Why do you say that? I've been a great father for her?"

Charlotte bit her tongue to keep from sharing Nicole's fears.

"I don't know. It's something I can't explain in words. It's just—"

"It's just nonsense, is what it is," and Jenson went back to reading the newspaper.

Charlotte stared at her husband and shook her head sadly as tears came to her eyes. She got up and walked into their bedroom, closed the door behind her, sat down on the bed and cried.

* * *

The day of the recital finally arrived and Nicole was more nervous about what her father was going to think than she was about her actual performance.

She put her heart and soul into her performance of Gershwin's *Rhapsody in Blue!* And she was *so* excited that it was with a full orchestra that had been arranged for specifically for this event! Prior to the recital she had glanced from backstage to see where her parents were sitting, but when she had finished, and amidst the thundering applause, she could not bear to look their way. She could not take the chance that her father was less than enthusiastic. Perhaps telling her mom it was okay for her to invite her father had been a mistake. She would find out soon enough.

Because Nicole's performance had been listed as the last one on the program, she would soon be ready to head home with her parents. In the meantime, she was basking in the wondrous glow of the continuing standing ovation and enthusiastic shouts of "BRAVA! BRAVA!" and "ENCORE! ENCORE!" Even the members of the orchestra joined in the adoration of this amazing young lady! The crowd would just have to wait for another time.

When Nicole finally saw her parents outside the venue, she noticed the big smiles on their faces! She *knew* her mother would be pleased, but it was her father's reaction that made her let out a deep sigh of relief, and tears of great joy began to flow! Were all these years of seemingly hiding in the shadows, afraid of what he might think or say finally over? Had she finally done something that would make him proud that he had a daughter instead of a son?

"My gosh, sweetheart! Where did you learn to play like that? That was *wonderful!*" her proud father exclaimed.

"Thanks, Daddy!" Nicole's heart leapt with excitement! She was *finally* feeling the love she had desired, wanted, needed, prayed, and worked so hard for! She was absolutely glowing as they got in the car and drove home.

While her father could not stop talking about her performance, her mother sat quietly, with a gentle and sweet smile on her face. Did she have *any* idea how important this recital *really* was to Nicole? Had her mother, by chance, read her diary and discovered why Nicole had become so driven? Would this be enough to win back her father's love and attention?

After dinner that night her father asked her to play for him, but Nicole politely declined.

"Preparing for the recital took a lot out of me, Daddy. Maybe another time?"

"Sure, sweetie, sure," he responded, hoping he had masked the disappointment he felt. If Nicole had noticed it she had not let on.

Preparing for her recital truly *had* taken a lot out of Nicole, and instead of watching TV with her parents she decided to read a book in the quiet of her room. A half hour later she put the book aside and sat down at the desk with her diary.

Saturday, August 18th

Dear Diary,

> *Well, I did it! I think!*
> *After what seems like forever, but has only been a little over four years, I think I finally have my daddy back!*
> *He came to my piano recital today and really enjoyed it!*
> *I was so proud of myself, too, and my teacher, Mrs. Harris,*

was also excited that everything had gone so well! She had arranged for a full orchestra to be a part of the event because a few students, including me, were playing major classical pieces. I played George Gershwin's "Rhapsody in Blue", without needing any sheet music! Can you believe that?!

Anyway, I'm hoping this was enough to get my daddy to love me again. I'll just have to wait and see!

* * *

Sunday afternoon told a different story. Nicole's father asked her why she didn't practice on Sundays. She could not tell him the real reason, but instead she explained that she just liked to take a break on Sundays so she would be fresh for the coming week. He gruffly told her that that did not make any sense, that *any* musician, regardless of age, needs to practice *every* day, and, if she expected to become a good pianist she had better change her attitude and do the same. Without saying a word, she got up, went to her room and closed the door.

"Jenson, how can you be so hard on her?" Charlotte demanded. "She's only ten years old, for crying out loud! She doesn't want to be a professional concert pianist, she just wants to enjoy playing. Her teacher told me that Nicole far exceeds any other student she has taught at any other time in her life. She also advised me that we should continue to be encouraging but never demanding. Otherwise, the fire will most certainly go out. Is that what you want?"

"You're just making too much out of this whole thing. Practice never hurt anyone, and if she doesn't practice she'll never get any better."

"Any better? *Any better?!* I just got through reminding you that she's only ten years old, and yet she just played Gershwin's *Rhapsody in Blue* from memory! What other ten-year-old can say that?! Do you have *any* idea how hard and long she has worked to make it this far?"

"No, but that is not important. Besides, that is all in the past, and what counts is right now and the future. That's it."

"You can't believe that!"

"Why not? It's true!"

Charlotte stared at her husband, then got up and went to the bedroom. On her way, she passed Nicole's bedroom and thought she heard something other than the radio. She stepped closer to the door and listened. Nicole was crying. Instinctively she tapped on the door.

"Nicole?"

"What?" Nicole replied through her sniffles.

"May I come in?"

"Not now, Mom. Okay?"

"Are you alright?"

Nicole did not answer for a few seconds which worried Charlotte. The crying stopped and she heard Nicole blow her nose.

"Mom, I would just like to be alone, if you don't mind."

Charlotte's heart was breaking. Whatever had caused Nicole's sadness, especially after such a beautiful day the day before, she just wanted to comfort her daughter and let her know she was loved.

"Okay, sweetheart."

"Thanks, Mom."

As Charlotte walked away, she wondered if Nicole had heard her and her father's conversation, and she shuddered to think this is what made Nicole so upset.

* * *

Sunday, August 19th

Dear Diary,

> *I just can't stop crying!*
> *My dad broke my heart again.*
> *I thought everything was finally okay between us, at least it was yesterday, but today he gave me a hard time about not practicing on Sundays. I tried to explain to him that I've always taken Sundays off, and I especially needed to today because of how hard I had prepared for yesterday's recital. But he got all upset, and demanded that if I ever hoped to be any good at all that I had to practice every day!*

He just doesn't get it! He's so mean! But why? Why can't I be enough? Just me, the way I am?

I know I'll never be the perfect son he always wanted, but why is it so hard for him to realize that I can be the best daughter he could ever imagine? Maybe, deep down, this has all been for him. I've pushed myself and demanded more and more of myself in order to be the best. Yesterday I was, and I was so happy with how everything went! And, for a short time, he thought so too. Or, at least I thought he did. But I guess I was wrong. SO wrong!

Then I just heard him and mom arguing. She has always been so supportive and encouraging about my playing the piano and that has helped me a lot!

I just wish I could do ONE THING RIGHT!

I hate feeling this way!

Maybe I'll just completely forget about trying to please him and just do what I want for me. I know my mom will always be by my side, no matter what, and maybe that's all I need.

I'll find other things to make me happy.

Chelsea plays basketball with her older brothers, and she always looks like she's having a good time, so maybe I'll see if I can join them sometime.

In the meantime, I just feel horrible, and I don't know what to do about it.

I hate my dad!

Moving on from caring anything about or for her father, Nicole soon committed herself to earning the best possible grades, participating in and excelling in sports, and doing her best to fit in among her friends during middle school and high school. A tall order for a young girl, but one that she was completely committed to.

After she turned sixteen, she dated occasionally, and while there were many boys who tried, she did not want a steady boyfriend. That is, until she saw Dusty Clark perform in a school production of *Man of La Mancha* during her junior year. She did not have the chance to meet him until the beginning of their senior year, but after that they were inseparable! They went to so many dances and parties together, occasionally double dated with friends to movies, the beach, and even Disneyland! And then, to top it all off, in the spring they performed opposite each other in the school production of *South Pacific!* And a month later their heavenly senior ball was appropriately named *Some Enchanted Evening!*

Everything about Dusty and her senior year had been magical! That is, until he broke her heart just before graduation. After that she refused to get serious about another guy. Not during college, or even the years before she met Chandler. Even her relationship with Chandler was not that serious. Convenient, yes, but not serious, and as far as she was concerned it would stay that way for a long time to come.

CHAPTER 5

Friday Afternoon

AS EXPECTED, THE STAFF meeting went great. Nicole's presentation of her revised design and model for the new Laguna Beach Museum and Artist-in-Residence facility was very well received by her colleagues, after which they made presentations of their latest projects. The meeting was then adjourned. While gathering her papers Nicole's boss and mentor, Warren Knapp, approached.

"Wonderful presentation, Nicole! Once again, your work not only shows such amazing insight into the culture and environment of the city of Laguna Beach, but also the proposed location where this will be built. The mayor told me just a few days ago that, after all these months of presentations, proposals, and changes the city agencies requested that you make, he and the city council are quite anxious to give their final approval at next week's council meeting." Warren did not notice Nicole's imperceptible cringe when he mentioned the upcoming meeting.

"Thank you, Warren. Your kind words of encouragement always mean so much to me."

"Well, you deserve every one of them and so many more. You are such a wonderful architect, and I'm so grateful to have you as not only an outstanding associate in our firm, but also such a great example and inspiration to others."

Then a sly smile creased Warren's face as he winked. "Even the more seasoned pros hanging around until they decide to retire!"

They shared a hearty laugh.

It had taken everything in her to get and keep herself together for her presentation this afternoon, and normally making a presentation to community leaders would not have caused a moment's hesitation on her part. But last night's breakdown not only surprised her for having come seemingly from out of nowhere, but it left her deeply unsettled; a feeling she had not experienced since she was a little girl.

"Warren?"

"Yes?"

"After I get my things back to my office, would you have a few moments that I might chat with you about something?"

"Of course! Anything for you, Nicole! Take your time and I'll meet with you when you're ready."

"Thank you. I appreciate that. I should be there in just a few minutes."

"Fine with me."

As Warren headed for his office Nicole moved her model to the far end of the conference room, gathered her papers, and headed for her office.

Before her presentation Nicole had turned off her phone so she would not be disturbed. As she was walking back to her office, she turned it back on and saw five messages from Chandler and sighed. *Five?! What on earth could be so important that you keep trying to reach me?*

"How did it go?" Amanda inquired enthusiastically, distracting Nicole from her phone.

"Everyone is excited!" Nicole replied, forcing a smile to hide her anxiety. She set her papers on the desk, flipped open her desk calendar, and scanned the following couple of weeks for appointments and project deadlines. She took a deep breath and let it out slowly, then repeated it two more times. Her anxiety began to ease. She looked at Amanda through the glass panels of her office and gave her a smile. She took another deep breath and then left her office.

"I'll be in Warren's office for a few minutes."

"Thanks, Nicole."

Along the way she passed Martin's office and poked her head in. "Hey, Martin."

"Hey, Nicole! Great presentation today!"

"Thank you. I appreciate that. Say, you know that project you asked me for some help on?"

"The one in Marina Del Rey?"

"Yes, that's the one."

"I'm actually not quite ready for your help yet. I still have a couple of things I need to complete first, but how does later next week work for you? Maybe Thursday? Or even Friday?"

"That sounds good to me. I'll check with you again on Thursday morning and we can go from there."

"Sure! That sounds good! And thanks!"

"Anytime."

* * *

Warren Knapp's spacious office was tastefully designed. He fancied the look of rich burlwood for many pieces of furniture including his desk and two seven-foot-tall bookcases. A coffee table set in front of an eight-foot-long deep-brown leather sofa, along with matching chairs at the far end of his office was also of burlwood. Finishing it all off was the addition of a small round table set in front of his window which he used for more personal discussions with his staff or clients, and offered a beautiful view of the Pacific Ocean.

Framed photos of his wife, family, and close friends were mounted on the walls, as well as set on his credenza and a few shelves in the bookcases.

The paintings throughout Warren's office were dominated by breathtaking scenes of beaches, sunsets, and lighthouses. And finally, a long, weathered piece of driftwood was mounted securely to the wall above the credenza behind his desk.

As Nicole approached Warren's office, his secretary, Maryann, nodded for her to go right in. She entered and closed the door behind her. Warren stood up and motioned for her to join him at the table near the window. His view of the Pacific Ocean always seemed so peaceful, a feeling she needed desperately right now.

"Thank you for seeing me, Warren. I know how busy you are so I won't keep you long."

"Nicole, I have *all* the time in the world for you. I even asked Maryann to hold my calls so you can take as long as you'd like. Now, what's on your mind?"

Nicole sighed heavily as she gathered her thoughts.

"Uh-oh. I'm sensing this isn't going to be a light chat, am I right?"

Nicole noticed that her hands were beginning to tremble. She took another deep breath and then briefly looked out the window before engaging her mentor.

"Warren, something's wrong with me." She caught her breath and Warren fought the urge to say something, choosing instead to just give Nicole time to get her thoughts together before she spoke again. She took another deep breath and looked out the window. When she looked at Warren again, she was looking into the compassionate eyes of the man who had hired her, mentored her, and believed strongly in her and her abilities as an architect. A man who had treated her with great respect from the first time they met. It was the kind of look that she would have welcomed from her father, but never saw.

"I don't know what's happened, but something is wrong with me … with my life."

Warren sat quietly, as if he were listening with the heart of a caring and loving father.

"I'm thirty-two years old. I have been working for you since I graduated from college, and I have been *so* happy here. I have worked hard, I have kept myself on the straight and narrow path in every part of my life, and by all outside observations many would consider me highly successful. Ever since I was six, I have only focused on doing my best at everything I have chosen to do in my life. I have excelled in music, sports, and my education. I have always strived to do my best for you, and along the way the awards and accolades have been wonderful and rewarding. And something else I am incredibly grateful for; you've always paid me fairly and handsomely for my work. But … for some reason, all of that is just not enough."

Tears began to flow, and Warren reached to his right to retrieve a box of tissues and handed it to her.

"Thank you," she responded in between light sobbing. "See? That's *another* thing about you that I'm grateful for … you are always so kind and considerate to everyone here."

Warren smiled but remained quiet.

After dabbing her eyes Nicole sighed.

"Warren … I know this is short notice—"

"Oh, please don't tell me you're resigning!"

"What? Oh, no! Not at all!"

Warren's smile and heavy sigh of relief made Nicole chuckle. "No, I would never drop a bomb like that on you."

"Oh, good! I was afraid that I was about to lose my biggest and brightest star! Sorry to interrupt, Nicole. Please, go on."

With her tears and anxiety beginning to subside, she dabbed her eyes once more before continuing.

"I know this is short notice, but may I take a few days off at the start of next week? Perhaps Monday through Wednesday? Martin has asked me to help him with one of his projects and I promised him I would. I will be back in the office next Thursday. I just checked with him before coming to see you and he said he won't be ready until late next week anyway."

"Sure, I don't see why not. Come to think of it, when was the last time you took some actual vacation time?"

"Never."

"What?!"

"Just kidding, but I honestly don't recall when it was."

"Then it's been way too long. Would you like to take the whole week off? I'm sure Martin can get started on his project without you and you can join him the following week."

"No, I don't think that will be necessary. Besides I have the presentation next Thursday evening."

"Oh, that's right!"

"Between this weekend and the early part of next week I think that should be enough time."

"Okay, but if you change your mind, you just give me a call and the rest of the week is all yours. And I can always call the mayor down in Laguna Beach and reset the date for your presentation. So, if that is an option for you, just let me know. Deal?"

"Yes, Warren. Thank you."

"Absolutely!"

"And thank you for putting up with my tears and craziness. I didn't mean to fall apart on you."

"Nonsense. You're perfectly safe around here, craziness and all." Warren's wink made Nicole laugh, and for the first time in several days she felt a huge weight begin to lift off her mind. And her heart.

CHAPTER 6

Friday Evening

NICOLE WAS GRATEFUL FOR the solitude that greeted her as she closed the door to her condo. After her meeting with Warren, the afternoon had sailed by. Before she knew it, she was saying goodbye to her colleagues and heading out the door and looking forward to a *long* break. She had also taken a few minutes to brief Amanda on a few things she could do in her absence that would help her with the preparations for her final presentation to the Laguna Beach City Council the following Thursday.

Talking with Warren had helped, but she knew she was not out of the woods yet. It was going to take time, but who knew just how long? She kicked off her shoes, set her purse and keys down on the marble kitchen counter, flipped through her mail, set every piece aside but one, and headed to the living room to unwind.

She rested her head against her plush brown leather sofa and slowly closed her eyes. Lifting her legs and resting them on the matching ottoman she let out a long sigh. She embraced the mixture of relief and release, absorbing the stillness, and began to let the tension go that had been building inside for longer than she could remember. Ahhhh … finally. Alone.

As Nicole awoke from an unexpected nap she was momentarily disoriented by the darkness. She blinked twice, trying to read the clock on the wall. *What time is it? How long have I been asleep?* She reached up and turned on the lamp, allowing her eyes to adjust. Half past nine?! Her lightheadedness lasted only a moment, and once she regained her bearings, she noticed the lone envelope in her lap – a card or something from Chandler. She tore open the end of the envelope and removed a card.

I love you, Sweetheart!

Chandler had written on the outside of the blank, but classically designed, notecard. On the inside she read,

> *I'll miss you this weekend. I wish you could have joined me for the conference, but I understood when you explained that I'd be in meetings most of the time and you'd be searching for things to do. But please don't hesitate to call me if you need anything or just want to chat, okay?*
> *Love you, Nicole!*

Chandler

She tossed the card and envelope onto the coffee table, leaned her head against the sofa, and sighed.

Oh, Chandler, what are we doing? Where are we going? And what's with your recent increased interest in talking about settling down? Do you really mean it? Or are you just feeling that it's the next stage in your life? Something you should *be doing, and I just happen to be a convenience? Do you* really *love me? Or are you just used to me because we've been together for so long? Enjoy your weekend. I'll be just fine without you.*

WAIT! I'll be just fine *without you?! Where did* that *come from?*

She began to feel dizzy again, even though she had not tried to stand up yet. Setting her feet back on the carpet, she leaned forward on the sofa. The dizziness subsided but still bothered her. Then she remembered that she had taken an early lunch, followed by a tense afternoon, and now, after waking from an unexpected nap, she was hungry but not in the mood for fixing anything herself.

Her ringing phone distracted her from her hunger. Chandler. She ignored his call and tossed the phone onto the coffee table. It rang again. She ignored it once again, got up and walked into the kitchen. Maybe she would fix something after all.

She found the leftover prime rib from the fancy dinner with Chandler's friends on Wednesday evening and set it on the counter. She took out a head of lettuce, a tomato, two hardboiled eggs, and ranch dressing, then found the croutons in the pantry and set everything on the island. Anything else? She ignored another call, probably another one from Chandler. *I'm just fine, thank you. Now leave me alone.*

She reached for a large mixing bowl, a cutting board, and a sharp knife and began preparing her salad. The phone rang *again*! *That's it!* She charged into the living room, grabbed her phone, and answered it without bothering to look at the screen.

"Chandler, would you please stop calling! I'm trying to—"

"Nicole?'

"Mom?!"

"Nicole, what's wrong, sweetheart?"

"Oh, Mom, I'm sorry. I thought it was Chandler."

"No, it's been me. I've been trying to reach you for several minutes."

Nicole sighed. "Sorry, Mom. Is everything okay?"

"Yes, but I haven't heard from you in quite a while, and I felt like I needed to give you a call just to see if you're all right."

"Yes, I'm fine, Mom."

"Well, it doesn't sound like things are fine with Chandler."

"Oh, it's no big deal."

"Are you sure? Do you want to talk—"

"I'm fine, Mom. Really, I'm fine."

"Well, you know you can always—"

"Yes, Mom. Yes, I know I can always call you, and I can always tell you everything."

Charlotte softly sighed. "Am I that predictable, honey?"

"Well, after thirty-two years I've gotten to know you pretty well," Nicole replied with a smile creasing her lips.

"Yes, I guess you have."

"How are you guys?"

"We're fine. Nothing new going on here." Nicole knew it was not true, but she was not in the mood to press her mother right now.

"That's good. That's good. Well, if everything is okay, I need to go. I'm right in the middle of fixing dinner."

"Oh, I'm sorry, honey. Yes, go ahead. We'll talk another time."

"Thanks, Mom."

"Soon, I hope."

"Yes, soon. Bye, Mom."

"Goodbye, sweetheart."

Nicole sighed as she set her phone down on the island and turned her attention back to prepping her salad. The phone rang again. She froze in a mixed fit of frustration and anger. *I just want to be left alone!*

It was Chandler. She took a deep breath so *if* she decided to answer it, she would not sound as angry as when her mother had called.

"Hey, Chandler," she answered, with little to no emotion in her voice.

"Hi, Nicole! How are you?" Chandler replied excitedly.

"Tired and hungry, and in the midst of making dinner."

"I wish I were there! I would take you out somewhere nice so you wouldn't have to think about doing it yourself."

"It's okay, I don't mind. I'm a big girl and I can take care of myself."

"Hey, is everything okay? You don't sound like you."

"I don't sound like *me*? Who or what do I sound like?" Chandler was just about to step on Nicole's last nerve.

"Oh, I don't know. You just sound … different."

"Well, as I just told you, I'm tired and hungry and I really don't feel up to talking right now. I'm sorry."

"All right. I guess I'll let you go then. I'll call you when I get a chance tomorrow!"

"Sure. If you get the chance. Good night." Nicole's whole attitude was void of any emotion.

"Good night, Nicole. And I lo—" Before he could finish telling Nicole he loved her, he heard the click on his phone. *I wonder what's up? She hasn't really been herself all week. Maybe I shouldn't have come to this conference.*

Before setting her phone back down on the island Nicole turned it off. Enough was enough. She just needed to be left alone.

* * *

After enjoying her dinner and a hot, luxurious bath without any further distractions, Nicole decided to go to bed early. The week and the stress, at least for the most part, were over and she prayed she would not have a repeat of last night anytime soon.

The bath had felt so incredible, and as she laid there, she had sensed every muscle begin to ease ever so gradually. The dozen tealight candles she had lit provided just the right, soothing ambiance. She could not remember a time when a bath had felt that perfect. She blow-dried her hair and generously applied her soothing body lotion.

After slipping on her silky, pink knee length nightgown, she brushed her hair. Then she propped up her pillows and climbed into bed, ready to relax and browse through the cable channels for a movie that would further help her escape. Relief was just moments away.

CHAPTER 7

Making Plans

A s Nicole awoke the next morning, she stretched and realized she could not remember the last time she had slept so well. She began to wonder whether she really needed to take *any* time off at all or just head back to work on Monday after a restful weekend. No, Warren was right, it *had* been too long since she had taken any time off, and, hopefully these extra few days should do the trick. She hoped.

Not expecting to be feeling this much better so soon, she was unsure of what to do with all this available time. She vaguely remembered hearing something about some Airbnb places available along the coast. Having grown up in Southern California she had loved to go to the beach with her friends but she had not taken any time to visit *any* of them in at least a year or two. Any spare time she had on the weekends was usually spent visiting her parents in Rancho Mirage, or doing something with Chandler. For the next few days this time was going to be strictly for herself.

She also remembered that her friend, Royal, was in real estate and wondered if he might know of any short-term rentals. Or perhaps he might know more about the Airbnb market than she did. She decided to call him right after breakfast.

The restful sleep from the night before had not only improved her disposition, but also her appetite. She prepared a plate of four Eggs Benedict, two strips of bacon, two slices of fresh cantaloupe, and a tall glass of cranberry juice. She sat on the patio and enjoyed it all as she watched the city below begin to wake up to another beautiful spring morning.

After breakfast she took a quick shower to freshen up. Then she dressed in faded Wranglers, a pastel yellow short-sleeved blouse, and white Skechers. She debated about pulling her strawberry blonde hair back in a ponytail or just letting it fall past her shoulders. At the moment she felt light and carefree, so a ponytail it was. Besides, chances are, she would be out and about later and did not want to be constantly brushing her hair back from the balmy Southern California breezes.

Looking for her phone to call Royal, Nicole remembered that she had turned it off the night before. She retrieved it from her nightstand and turned it on. It took only moments for it to come back to life, then she checked for messages. Chandler had called late last night and again a half hour ago. He had also left four text messages. She ignored them all and decided that this weekend was truly going to be just for herself, and perhaps for the rest of her time off. Five days? Before this past week she could not remember the last time she had gone more than about twelve hours without chatting or texting with Chandler. What will he think? She just shrugged nonchalantly and looked up Royal's personal number.

His phone rang twice before he picked up. "Hi, this is Royal!" He was always in a good mood, and it was not just because he was in sales.

"Hi, Royal! It's Nicole!"

"Hey, stranger! How have you been?"

"I'm doing great! Busy as ever, but great! How about you?"

"Same here! You timed your call perfectly because I'm right in the middle of a couple of calls to help one of my clients close on a new home this afternoon!"

"Oh, that's wonderful, Royal. I'm happy for you *and* them!"

"Thanks! So, what's up?"

"Well, I'll keep this quick. I know you're primarily focused on sales, but do you have any information on the local short-term rental market or know anything about Airbnbs?"

"No, I sure don't. I'm strictly in the sales arena but, depending on what you're looking for, I might know someone who could help. Are you looking for a friend or—"

"Actually, I'm looking for something for myself."

"Really?"

"Well, this is going to sound crazy, and I know it's short notice, but I'm looking to rent a place along the beach for the next few days. If it can start today that would be amazing. Otherwise, if I could find a place to rent from Monday through Wednesday that would be great."

"Is this just for you, or you and some friends?"

"It's just for me. And I know this also sounds crazy because I don't live *that* far from the beach, but I just need to get out of my place for a few days and check out some place new."

"Okay, any particular area you're interested in?"

"Just somewhere fairly close. Maybe Newport Beach to Laguna Beach, or even Monarch Bay."

"What's your budget?"

"Wide open, but I don't need anything big or fancy because I may not be spending that much time there. I might go shopping or check out some art galleries, and I'll probably eat out for most of my meals. But I also want some place accessible to the beach, so I don't have to drive somewhere just to go for a walk in the sand."

"Wow, that sounds nice! You know, I have a friend who rents a room in her home fairly regularly. Let me give her a call and see if it's available or if she knows of any other places near her."

"That would be great, Royal! Thank you!"

"My pleasure. I'll give her a call right now and hopefully she's in town. I'll call you back as soon as I talk with her."

"Oh, thank you, Royal! I'll keep my fingers crossed!"

"Chat with you soon!"

"Okay, bye!"

Nicole started imagining what kind of place it would be and her excitement began bubbling over! She started walking randomly through her condo and thinking about what she would need for this getaway. She retrieved a couple of bags from the closet in her guest room and put them next to her bed. Then, she started laying out some outfits on her bed, along with an assortment of shoes, but decided to hold off getting anything else ready until after she heard from Royal. If a place wasn't available until Monday, then she was just getting ahead of herself. Out of the corner of her eye she noticed some magazines and a book on her nightstand and couldn't resist. Temptation got the better of her and she placed them on her bed, as well. Her excitement was growing with every passing minute!

Her phone rang and she grabbed it off the bed and answered at the end of the first ring.

"I just got off the phone with my friend, Carli, and it looks like you're in luck!"

"YES!!!"

"Someone was supposed to come into town this weekend, but something came up and they had to cancel at the last moment. So it's available if you want it."

"Oh, my gosh! YES, Royal! YES!"

"I asked her to hold it until she heard from either me or you. I'll send you the link so you can check out all the details online."

"Thanks, Royal! I appreciate this *so* much! Did she happen to mention if it's available into next week?"

"She said that it had been reserved through next Thursday before it was cancelled, and that someone else is coming in next Friday."

"Oh good! I only need it until Wednesday, so let me check it out and I'll get back to you."

"That sounds good, Nicole."

"Thanks for your help, Royal. I really appreciate it!"

"Sure! I hope it works out!"

"Me, too! Bye."

"Talk to you soon, Nicole. Bye."

Nicole checked her email, found the message from Royal, and hit the link for the rental. As the website opened, she could not believe her eyes! *What a gorgeous place! And right on the beach?! Oh, my gosh!* She felt her luck returning!

> *Spacious rental with king bed and private full bathroom with spa jets in the bath.*

Semi-private deck with easy access to the beach.

You also have full use of the kitchen and family room.

*A large variety of restaurants, shops, and art galleries galore
are just minutes away!*

Nicole grabbed her phone and excitedly called Royal back!
"It's perfect, Royal! Thank you so much! I'll call her right away!"
"Wonderful! I'm so glad it'll work out for you."
"Me, too! I can't wait to pack up and drive over there!"
"Think of me when you're sipping a tall, cool one on the deck
while watching the sunset," he added with a chuckle. Nicole laughed
along with him.
"Sure thing! Bye!"
"Take care and have fun! And sometime late next week give me a
call and let me know how it went, okay?"
"Sure! I promise!"
After hanging up Nicole started jumping around her condo like a
teenager who had just been invited to the prom by the most popular
guy in school! She looked at Royal's email again for the phone num-
ber and hit the buttons as fast as she could!
"Hi, this is Carli!"
"Good morning, Carli, this is Royal Davis' friend, Nicole. I'm
calling about a room you have available that Royal just told me about."
"Hi, Nicole! Yes, as I mentioned to Royal, I had a cancellation
last night, so the room is available anytime you'd like over the next
several days."
"Wonderful! I can be there later this morning and I only need it
through Wednesday."
"That's fine! Do you need directions on how to get here?"
"No. I have your address from Royal's email, so I'll be fine."
"Okay, I'll see you then! Drive safely!"
"Thanks, Carli! Bye!"
Before she could set her phone down it rang again. Without
thinking she almost answered it but then saw Chandler's name on

the screen and stopped in her tracks. She sighed heavily. *He must be in between sessions. Just leave a message, Chandler, and I'll check it later. Maybe.*

Nicole hurriedly picked out the rest of the clothes, shoes, and accessories she wanted for her getaway, along with her makeup bag. She packed them all in two large duffle bags and a dress bag. Normally, she would not bother with taking a nice dress, but who knows? Maybe she would treat herself to a nice dinner out. Alone.

Thirty minutes after making the arrangements with Carli she was on her way!

CHAPTER 8

Carli

AS NICOLE PULLED UP in front of Carli's home she was amazed! Real estate in this area was at such a high premium that the homes were built with no yards, front or back, and those that were right along the beach were built perpendicular to the beach. However, Carli's home appeared to be one of a kind because it was built parallel to the beach! The front of the house was set back from the sidewalk by over twenty feet, allowing for a beautiful lawn and landscaping next to the two-car driveway. If the lush landscaping was any indication of what awaited her inside, she might never want to leave! She anxiously jumped out of her car and walked excitedly through the wide courtyard on the meandering flagstone walkway.

Off to her left and in front of windows that appeared to be for two large rooms, were tall and wide bunches of pampas grass flowing gently in the late morning breeze. These were rimmed on the front by a perfectly manicured lawn that extended to the sidewalk. On the right of the walkway and in front of an extended porch were alternating purple and blue Lilies of the Nile in full and glorious bloom. More of the perfectly manicured lawn flowed between the walkway and the driveway. A pair of light dusty-blue wooden chairs and a small, round, matching table in between, held court on the porch, as if to invite visitors to relax and stay a while.

Nicole reached the porch and before she could knock, Carli flung the door wide open, and with one of the happiest smiles

Nicole had ever seen, she was greeted with a bright "Hi, Nicole!", along with a sweet welcoming hug from her gracious and enthusiastic host!

"Hi, Carli! Thank you for letting me come on such short notice!"

"Absolutely! I *love* having company, but I also want to assure you that you'll have all the quiet privacy you'd like while you're here. Let's go into the living room and chat for a few minutes, shall we?"

Nicole followed Carli into the spacious living room, admiring the tasteful beach motif. The walls in the living room were painted robin's egg blue, and on each side of the flagstone fireplace stood a deep sea-blue colored vase with artificial pampas grass that was taller than the mantel. Mounted on the wall above the fireplace was a striking painting of a beach scene with a lighthouse to the right. A late afternoon sun slowly descending toward the edge of the world was on the left, with pampas and plume grass rising from the rolling sand dunes. The pastel blue and sandy beige print pattern of the sofa and love seat blended perfectly with their surroundings, making for a most pleasant and comfortable atmosphere!

"Your home is simply lovely, Carli. I love the colors, and the painting is breathtaking!"

"Thank you so much! And that painting is one that I painted just last year!"

"Oh, my gosh! You painted this?! That makes it even more lovely!"

"Go ahead and sit anywhere. Would you like something to drink?"

"Yes, some ice water would be nice."

"Two ice waters coming up!"

"Your front yard and your living room have taken my breath away, Carli."

"Thank you, hon. It took my late husband and me many years to get it just the way we wanted it, and when we did, there was just nothing that would ever take us away."

"I can understand why. Did the two of you do the landscaping out front as well?"

"Yes, most of it anyway. Here's your ice water."

"Thank you." Nicole replied as she took a brief, but welcome, sip. "Mmmmm, nice and cold. So, I'm really curious, how is it possible for you to have such a large piece of property right here along the beach, when all the other homes are on such narrow lots?"

"We used to have a home just like everyone else in this area, but, sadly, about ten years ago, our neighbor's home burned to the ground. They were out of town, and it started at night, so the fire department wasn't alerted to the fire right away. By the time they arrived it was too late to save it, so they just controlled it as best as they could so it wouldn't spread to any of the other homes nearby. Both our home and the one on the other side had some damage, but not severe. In the end, our neighbors chose not to rebuild. We offered to buy their lot, and they accepted. At first we had thought about adding on to our home, but then my husband had the idea to have ours torn down and a new, wider, ranch-style home built in its place. This way we ended up with the opportunity to create a beautiful front yard, *and* we have an amazing view from across the back of our home!"

"Wow, that's quite a change!"

"It sure is!"

"So, where did you go while all the work was being done?"

"We have friends in Palm Desert who invited us to stay with them for as long as necessary. We put everything in storage and when our new home was finished we moved back and took care of the landscaping ourselves."

"Well, you did a beautiful job!"

"Thank you!" Carli said graciously. "So, are you from this area, or just visiting?"

"I grew up very close to here in Corona Del Mar. I stayed close by for college, did my graduate work in Arizona, but then got a job right here in Newport Beach, and I've been in the area ever since."

"Is your family still in the area?"

"My dad retired a few years ago and my parents now live a little over two hours away in Rancho Mirage."

"Oh, it's lovely out there. I visit my friends in Palm Desert every few months when I want to get away to the desert."

"Really? I would think you'd never want to leave this idyllic location. Especially for the desert."

"Oh, don't get me wrong. I *love* living by the ocean, but it can also get a bit noisy around here from time to time. When I find it hard to concentrate, I just call my friends to see if I can come and visit for a few days. Then I'm all charged up and ready to come home!"

"May I ask what you do where you have to concentrate?"

"As an artist I tend to spend a lot of time in my studio, and — well, in fact, why don't you follow me and I'll show you my studio and your room so you can begin to settle in."

"Wonderful!"

Nicole set her glass on a round cork coaster and followed Carli toward the hallway.

"This first room is my bedroom. Yours is on the other half of the house and nearly as large."

"Oh, my gosh! Really?"

"Yes, I'm sure you'll like it."

"Well, if it's anything like yours I know I'm going to *love* it!"

"This next room is my studio. Come on in and let me show you the latest painting I'm working on."

"Oh, Carli. It's beautiful! I love your choice of colors. Were you inspired by a recent trip to your friends?"

"Yes, as a matter of fact, I was. I usually go there to relax and chat. We go out for dinner at one of our favorite spots, and maybe do some shopping, but the last time I was there I felt such a strong urge to paint! So, I headed over to a nearby art store and picked up all of my supplies, headed back to my friends' home, set up my easel and canvas and this beauty began to come to life in no time! Chances are I'll probably have it finished in the next week or so. Of course, it *all* depends on how much talking *we* do over the next few days!"

The two ladies enjoyed a hearty laugh.

"No, seriously Nicole, Royal explained to me that you were looking for a place to get away from it all for several days, and I intend for you to do exactly that right here."

"Thank you, Carli, I appreciate that. However, this is an unexpected bonus to have a hostess who is not only accommodating, but so warm and friendly as well. I promise to leave you to your painting, and I'm sure I'll have plenty to do to keep me busy, as well."

"Fair enough. Would you like to see your room now?"

"Yes, I can't wait!"

The ladies made their way back to the center of the house and then proceeded down the other hallway.

"*This* room here on your left is yours," Carli said with a waving flair of her hand.

"Oh, my gosh! It's … it's beautiful, Carli," Nicole replied breathlessly as she entered the room and looked around. "This is *so* much more than I ever imagined it might be!"

"And your private bath is over there," Carli added, pointing to the far right corner of the room.

Nicole sighed and paused as she collected her thoughts. "Oh, Carli. I'm *so* excited! Thank you *so* much!"

"Wait! The tour isn't over!"

"There's more?"

"*Much* more! Come this way. You also have full use of the kitchen, living room, and here's the family room. The TV remote is on the coffee table, and a wide variety of movies are on the shelves on either side of the fireplace."

Nicole *did* hear most of what Carli was saying, but her attention was on the view from the picture windows that spanned the full width of the family room.

"Oh, Carli, this view is to *die* for!"

"Open the door and get a better look."

Nicole excitedly opened the door and stepped out onto the deck that ran the full width of the house. She caught her breath with the beauty of the expansive view of the Pacific Ocean.

"Amazing, isn't it?"

Nicole just stood there mesmerized.

"Each room across the back of the house, including yours, has easy access to the deck, and over to your right are the steps that lead down to the beach. The back part of our property is all fenced in and there's a lock on the gate that I'll give you a key for, along with a key for the front door."

"Thank you *so* much. You have *no* idea how much this means to me. This … this is simply too good to be true. And it's all so much more than what I was expecting! Between my room and this wonderful view … everything is breathtaking! I feel sorry for the couple that had to cancel, but I'm also so glad they did!"

Nicole briefly looked away and wiped a tear from her eye before looking back toward Carli.

Carli sensed some pretty strong emotions welling up inside Nicole and reached over and offered her a hug.

"Thank you again, Carli," Nicole whispered.

"You're quite welcome, my dear."

As they stepped back into the house Nicole looked around to get a better feel for the cozy family room. The walls were painted a pastel mint green, and they were made even more vibrant by the early afternoon sun peeking in through the picture windows. The sofa was light blue, and the solid-colored fabric was offset pleasantly by green and yellow print throw pillows in each corner of the sofa. Between the flat screen television mounted on the wall and the nearest picture window was a unique wall hanging. Nicole stepped closer to get a better look.

"How interesting!" Nicole exclaimed, drawing Carli's attention to what Nicole was looking at.

"Thank you! That's something I had toyed with doing for a number of years and finally got around to doing it last summer. It's just small pieces of driftwood in various shapes and sizes, along with a few sand dollars and seashells mounted on a piece of wood. I guess it's my way of bringing the beach into my home, that is, besides the sand I tend to track in all too often," Carli added with a wink.

"Well, I love it! I think it's a great idea!"

Carli nodded her appreciation.

"May I help you bring your things in?" Carli asked.

"Oh, I don't have much. Just a few bags."

"Well, let's go get them so you can get settled and comfortable and start your mini vacation, shall we?"

Nicole certainly could not argue with that, and with just one trip by the both of them, Nicole's bags were moved from her car to her king-sized bed in no time.

"I'll leave you alone so you can unpack and get settled. Take as long as you'd like, hon."

"Thank you, Carli."

CHAPTER 9

Settling In

IN THE MIDST OF unpacking her bags, Nicole gazed excitedly around her guestroom, admiring its beauty and spaciousness. The walls were pastel yellow, complimented by the paisley blue and green pattern of the comforter. The nightstands were the same dusty blue as the chairs and table on the front porch, and these were matched by the accordion-style closet doors. The décor gave her a light and fresh feeling … *just* what she needed for these next few days!

She unpacked her bags, hung up her clothes, and placed her shoes on the floor in the closet. Then she pulled out her makeup bag and placed it on the dark blue-green marble counter in the bathroom. She took special notice of the lamp in the corner of the counter with several seashells, a starfish, and a few sand dollars spread across the wide oval wooden base.

In addition to the king size bed, there was also a plush chair in one corner with a matching ottoman. Standing next to it was a small table with an assortment of magazines spread neatly over the top. A tall, arching floor lamp in brushed chrome rose over the chair, and she noticed a remote control for it on the table.

She unlocked the sliding door to the back deck and stepped out to take in the view of the beach and ocean once again. She breathed in deeply, and the scent of the salty air made her memories come alive from her carefree teenage years and all the fun times she spent with her friends at countless beach parties.

When the weather promised to be hot, they would arrive early, usually right after grabbing a quick breakfast, and then spend the whole day soaking up the sun. On those days when fog greeted them as they woke up in the morning, they would take their time and typically arrive as it was burning off, usually between ten and eleven. Other times they would go elsewhere during the day, often spending several hours at various amusement parks like Disneyland or Knott's Berry Farm, before finishing their day at the beach, and later enjoying the beautiful sunsets. Ahhhhh, those were the days!

A few of her friends had surfboards, including her high school sweetheart, Dusty, who had introduced her to the sport. She had been fairly successful at riding the waves, but beach volleyball was more to her liking. She and Dusty had a deal – Nicole would surf with him for a while if he promised to spend time with her playing volleyball. Generally, the arrangement worked out just fine, but Nicole knew that Dusty was much more interested in being on the water than the hot, dry sand. When she could tell he was beginning to lose interest in the game she would send him off to enjoy his passion.

Nicole wrangled her thoughts back into the moment. While her friends were now scattered and busy with their own lives, she was free, at least for these next several days, to spend her time exactly as she wished. She was determined to enjoy each day to the fullest!

She looked south along the beach, noticing families with children making sandcastles and teens working on their tans. She also noticed an occasional senior, walking alone, perhaps recalling their own memories of when they, too, brought their children to this very same beach. A time when they didn't have a care in the world. She closed her eyes and sighed.

* * *

Nicole remembered that she had left her glass of ice water in the living room so she headed back inside, retrieved her glass and took a sip, and walked toward the family room to check out Carli's assortment of videos. She was impressed with the variety, and made a mental note to spend some of her downtime enjoying several of them. Carli, walking down the hallway from her studio, broke her thoughts.

"I'll be in and out throughout the time you're here so you may or may not see very much of me. And when I'm here I'll probably be spending most of my time in my studio, but if you need anything at all just let me know, okay?"

"I sure will. Thank you!"

"You're welcome. And, whenever you want to watch TV or a movie you just go right ahead. The sounds won't bother me. In fact, I might even come out and join you if it's particularly interesting!"

"Sure! That would be fun!"

Yes, I'm definitely going to enjoy it here!

CHAPTER 10

Sunday Morning

NICOLE FELT LAZY AS she woke up from another restful night's sleep. *Two mornings in a row! How can a girl be so lucky!* She stretched, tossed her covers off, and sat up on the side of the bed. She shook her head to get the mental cobwebs to go away, then reached for her phone to see what time it was. *Eight-thirty?! Well, I guess I needed it!* She looked at her messages, noticed a number of texts from Chandler, then listened to her voicemail. There were three more messages from him! She shook her head in disgust, tossed her phone on the bed, and headed for the bathroom to take a nice, long, hot shower. She needed to clear her mind before starting the day.

With four full days ahead of her Nicole was in no rush to do anything in particular today, so after her shower she put on her Wranglers and a blue, green, and pink pastel print blouse. She decided that since she wasn't planning on going anywhere, at least not for the next few hours, she'd remain barefoot. She made her bed, turned the phone ringer back on, and ventured forth from the bedroom.

The rest of the house was quiet, and with the silence she could faintly hear the crashing of the waves on the beach. She walked through the family room, opened the door to the deck, and stepped out to more fully enjoy the peaceful sound. She closed her eyes and breathed in deeply, enjoying the salty air that had been so much a part of her teen years when she spent as much time as she could at the beach with her friends. She smiled as those wonderful memories came rushing back, like the waves rushing to the shore and the water embracing the sand. Her reverie was broken by the squawk of a nearby seagull.

She stepped back into the house, closing the door behind her, and called out for Carli. Walking toward Carli's hallway she called her name again, but there was no response. *Probably out for a while with friends*, she guessed.

As she entered the kitchen, she saw a note on the counter along with two keys on a keyring with a quarter-sized starfish encased in acrylic attached to it.

Good morning, Nicole!

> *I hope you slept well last night. I'm always an early riser and today I decided to go for a drive and maybe see some friends up in Malibu. If they're home, we'll end up talking until late, so chances are you'll be asleep by the time I get back. Of course, if it gets too late, I may even spend the night up there. In either case, the place is all yours!*
>
> *Oh, I've also left you keys for the front and back doors, as well as the gate to get to the beach. Make yourself at home, and that includes anything I have to eat or drink.*
>
> *Enjoy!*
>
> *Carli*

Okay, so the place is mine? Nice! I'll fix some breakfast, go for a walk on the beach, maybe watch a movie, read a book, or—. Her ringing phone broke her train of thought. She hesitated, and as the ringing stopped, she walked into her bedroom to see who it was. She sighed heavily as she noticed it was Chandler. *Again!*

Reluctantly, she decided to read his texts and listen to his messages. Each of them said how much he missed her and how much he loved her and could not wait to see her. He sounded truly worried in the voicemails he left late last night and earlier this morning, but in the one he just left his mood had changed. Did she detect serious concern in his voice, or … was it anger? She was not in the mood to deal with him right now but knew that she should probably call him soon. After breakfast. Perhaps even after her walk on the beach. She set her phone down next to the keys and opened the refrigerator to see what delights awaited her.

There were a few containers of what appeared to be leftovers, which she decided she should probably leave alone. Then she noticed a wide variety of other items that would work for either breakfast, lunch, or dinner! So many choices! A veritable smorgasbord of delight!

Carli said I was welcome to anything, right? So, she checked out the freezer and noticed three items that made her tastebuds water – a large Ziplock bag of homemade waffles, a large Ziplock bag of French toast, and a bag of ready to heat hash brown patties! Perfect! She was not in the mood to spend too much time in the kitchen, so this would work out great! She found a large plate for two waffles and two slices of French toast and began heating them in the toaster. She also located a small plate for a single hash brown patty which she popped into the microwave. She found the butter and syrup, a knife and fork, a glass for some juice, and set everything on the table. Her breakfast feast was ready in no time.

After she sat down to enjoy her meal, she looked out the kitchen window toward the ocean. *What am I doing?* It took her two trips, but she finally had everything set up outside on the deck table. *Ahhh, this is heaven!*

Her phone, still lying on the kitchen counter, began to ring again. 'Well, it's *almost* heaven.'

* * *

Her breakfast was a delight, as was her stroll along the beach. Within another hour or so the beach would no doubt be crowded, but while she was enjoying the waves rushing over her feet the crowd was just right.

As she walked back to the house, she was not looking forward to the next several minutes. At least she was hoping it would not be any longer than that.

Nicole found a comfortable spot on the sofa in the living room, curled her feet up under her and called Chandler. He answered in the midst of the first ring.

"Nicole! Where have you been? I've been going crazy not being able to talk to you! Are you okay?"

"Ahem. *Hi, Nicole! How are you?*" Nicole answered sarcastically as she rolled her eyes.

"Oh, sorry, babe. Hi, how are you?" Chandler replied anxiously.

"Calm down, Chandler. I'm okay."

"Where are you? I went by your condo last night on my way home from the conference and you never showed up. Are you sure you're okay? Where are you?"

"Chandler, I'm okay," she replied calmly. "I decided to take a few days and get away and—"

"Where are you?' Chandler asked more insistently.

Nicole just let silence hang in the air as she did her best to not explode in anger. After she finally seemed calm enough, she firmly replied.

"Chandler … listen to me." She paused to see if Chandler might try to interrupt or respond in any way. "Are you listening?"

"Yes," he replied tersely.

"Where I am doesn't matter. As I *started* to say, I decided to take a few days off from work and get away by myself."

"Why didn't you tell me you were going away when we talked Friday night?"

"Perhaps because I chose not to. Something is going on with me right now that I'm trying to figure out and—"

"What? What are you trying to figure out? Is it us? Because if it's us, I—"

"Chandler!" Nicole interrupted him angrily and sighed heavily before continuing. "You need to listen to me without interrupting. You need to *hear* what I'm trying to say to you and not keep interrupting and trying to control this conversation. If you can't do that I'm hanging up. Do you understand?"

Chandler, now completely frustrated, responded brusquely, "Yes. Okay, talk to me."

That was it! Nicole's last nerve was on fire! She hung up the phone and ignored Chandler's repeated calls. Finally, after his fifth time calling back-to-back, she fired off an email and then texted him.

CHANDLER, CHECK YOUR EMAIL!

Chandler quickly opened his email app and was stunned by Nicole's message!

CHANDLER!

STOP CALLING! AS IF YOU CAN'T TELL, I'M MAD AT YOU RIGHT NOW! YOU HAVE NO RIGHT TO TALK TO ME THE WAY YOU ARE! I NEED SOME TIME AWAY, COMPLETELY AWAY FROM EVERYTHING AND EVERYONE, INCLUDING YOU! AND BECAUSE OF YOUR INCESSANT ATTEMPTS TO GET OUT OF ME WHERE I AM AND WHAT'S GOING ON, THAT WOULD BE ESPECIALLY YOU!!!!! I'M TAKING THIS TIME FOR ME! JUST ME! PERIOD! GET THAT THROUGH YOUR THICK SKULL AND LEAVE ME ALONE FOR A FEW DAYS, PLEASE! OTHERWISE, WE ARE THROUGH! DO YOU UNDERSTAND?! I HOPE SO, BECAUSE I ABSOLUTELY MEAN IT!

Her phone stopped ringing for a few minutes and she assumed Chandler was busy reading. Relieved that she had finally, at least *hopefully*, been able to get her message across, she got up, put her phone in her back pocket, and walked into the kitchen to find something to drink. As she was reaching for the refrigerator door her phone vibrated. She let out another heavy, very frustrated sigh, then relented and reached for her phone.

Replied to your email.

Nicole sighed again and reluctantly read Chandler's email.

I'm sorry, Nicole. I'll leave you alone for as long as you need. I hope you'll call me sometime soon, whenever you figure out what's making you so upset. Whatever it is, even if it's me, I want to know. I love you, Nicole. Please know that. And if I can help in ANY way, I want to know that, too. Okay? I love you.

Nicole closed her eyes, took a deep breath, then let it out. *FINALLY!*

CHAPTER 11

———

Aftermath

THIS WHOLE ISSUE WITH Chandler, not just this latest conversation, but the past several days had built up to the point that Nicole now had a fierce migraine. It had been years since she had had one but she knew it the moment it hit.

That first migraine was near the end of her senior year at USC. She was excited about her upcoming graduation but still had her senior paper to finish as well as preparing for her finals. Her friends kept inviting her to go places with them to help her relax and not take things so seriously, but she just could not do that to herself. Not with her father expecting perfection from her. Even after all this time she wondered if he was proud of her yet. Would graduating Summa Cum Laude be enough? *Finally?*

The stress and worry had caused serious intestinal issues and then, when the migraine hit, she panicked! Every moment she wasted trying to overcome it was precious time that was eating away at her time to study.

Finally, her best friend and roommate, Chelsea, took her to the emergency room at St. Vincent Medical Center to try to get her *some* kind of help. Her diagnosis was serious but treatable with time. Time Nicole did not have but had to take in order to make it through graduation.

If only my father ... NO! I refuse to go there! She had to put all thoughts of him and the pressure he had put on her all those years ago out of her mind. For her sake, both mentally and physically, she had to try.

Now, recognizing that her father and Chandler were, no doubt, the two major issues causing this stress in her life, she also conceded that these next few days needed to be spent figuring out what she was going to do about them. She could not ignore either of them any longer, at least not and still be able to function in her career. The situation in her personal life needed to change, but she was not sure how that would happen or what the end result might look like. She just knew that changes of some sort were coming, and it might be a bumpy road for a while.

Her immediate need now, though, was to get rid of this migraine. Spotting a bowl of fruit on the counter she reached for a banana, then looked in the refrigerator for something to drink. A bottle of water would do just fine. Despite the beautiful view providing its own offering of peace and comfort, and as much as she hated to, she knew she needed her surroundings to be as dark as possible, so she retreated to her bedroom, closed the blinds, pulled the drapes, laid down on her bed, and faced away from the window. She was not tired, but maybe taking a nap would help. At least she might be able to sleep through most of the pain. Fearing a repeat of her frightening episode from college she began to cry. *Please go away. Please!*

* * *

Chandler paced up and down the lobby outside the conference room, completely dumbfounded. Just days ago everything seemed fine between them, and now Nicole was fighting some kind of demons he did not know about or understand. Not only that, but it appeared like she did not want his help. He wondered if her parents might know what was going on. He thought about calling them but reconsidered when he thought it might make them worry unnecessarily if it were not that serious.

Perhaps it was simply something at work and she only needed a few days to work it out before heading back later in the week. Yes, that must be it. Besides, if it had anything to do with *him,* she could have just told him so, right? Hmmmm, *did* it have to do with him?

Or them? Had he been coming on a bit too strong when talking about settling down? No, that could not be it. After all, they had been together for over five years, so why shouldn't they begin to talk seriously about getting married?

But why had she been ignoring his messages and not returning his calls? That was not like her at all. Was she seeing someone else? Hmmmm, that might explain a *lot*, especially when he asked her about where she was and then becoming so defensive. Who might he call to find out where she went and how long she was *really* going to be gone? Once again he thought about her parents, but, like before, he did not want to bother them. If this truly was between just the two of them then they would just need to work everything out together.

Is she seeing someone else?

* * *

Nicole awoke easily from her nap but laid absolutely still waiting for the incessant pain, nausea, and misery from her migraine to hit. Waiting. Hmmm … nothing? She blinked a couple of times. So far so good. She started to roll over, waiting again for the pain and nausea to hit, but nothing. She laid on her back for a few minutes, taking some deep breaths and ever so slowly rolled back over to her side and sat up on the side of the bed. Ahhh … no pain and no nausea. She cautiously stood and walked to the bathroom, looked in the mirror and into the face that appeared much older than the one she had seen in the mirror earlier that morning. She reached for a towel and set it next to the sink as she ran some cold water to splash on her face. The coolness was refreshing. She dabbed her face with the towel, freshened her breath with mouthwash, brushed her hair, took a final look in the mirror, and considered herself ready to re-enter the human race, even though she had absolutely no plans to go anywhere for the rest of the day or evening.

CHAPTER 12

Sunday Evening

NICOLE GLANCED THROUGH CARLI'S collection of videos and found a Blu-Ray version of one of her all-time favorite movies, *Somewhere in Time.* She curled up on the sofa and smiled and cried like she had a hundred times before. It was such a perfect love story! Maybe one day …

After enjoying a delicious late dinner of barbecued steak and shrimp she took a long walk on the beach at sunset. Grateful that her migraine was gone, she was able to think about how she wanted to spend the next few days. Two days of this break were almost gone, and tomorrow and Tuesday would be her best chance to really work out in her mind where she wanted her life to go from here. Wednesday would be spent wrapping things up, then heading back to her condo and prepping to return to work. She knew she might not make any definitive decision about her future, but if she could just get some concrete ideas to work on, that would be great.

With Chandler agreeing to leave her alone she did not have to worry about any calls or texts to disturb her, *and,* she knew she needed to figure out where she stood in relation to whether she was going to continue to see him or not. She had to admit that, for the most part, their time together had been fun. He had an engaging personality which was one of the things that had attracted her to him from the start. He never spared any expense in treating her to the nicest places and was quite the gentleman. They enjoyed many of the same things such as dining at their favorite restaurants, either just the two of them or with friends, day trips to Big Bear Lake for skiing in both the winter and the summer, and occasionally attending Lakers, Dodgers, or Rams games. A few times a year they'd take a trip out to Catalina Island and, once in a while, she joined him on his deep-sea fishing trips off the Southern California coast. However, Chandler was always more excited about those trips than she was.

But what now? Nicole had a very strong feeling that Chandler was wanting to settle down, but she was not that interested; at least not yet. She had no objection to getting married *some*day. However, she was in no rush. She was still young, had a successful career doing what she had always wanted to do, was happy with her condo, and, with the exception of the additional strained relationship with her father, every other part of her life seemed to be going just fine. So why change anything?

Since Chandler had recently become more focused on marriage it was making her come to terms with what she wanted for herself. The more she calmly and logically thought about it, the more she came to realize that she was going to have to have a long talk with Chandler and explain how she felt. If he wasn't happy about it then she would call it quits and move on and let him find someone else who would fit his timetable. Then, as she came to *that* conclusion, she had another moment of clarity. While she enjoyed being *with* Chandler, she was not *in love* with him. And while she was not looking forward to the process of breaking it off with him, she knew it had to be done, and the sooner the better.

After her walk she turned on the TV again. It took her only ten minutes to find a rom-com she had not seen in years, so she made a big bowl of popcorn, grabbed a soda from the refrigerator, and once again made herself comfortable for the next couple of hours.

It was almost eleven when the movie was over. Carli had not arrived home yet, but would probably be arriving soon, unless she decided to spend the night with her friends. Either way, Nicole decided to call it a night and got ready for bed.

After finishing in the bathroom, she glanced through the variety of magazines on her nightstand before choosing the latest issue of Travel + Leisure. She propped up her pillows and climbed into bed, ready to relax, browse, and daydream about a fantastic getaway. These few days she was enjoying were nice, but maybe she needed to take Warren's suggestion and take some serious time off and go somewhere fun! Besides, even though she could not take off for more than just a few days anytime soon, it was always fun to dream, right?

She took her time perusing pages and pages about cruises to the Caribbean or Alaska. Then came European cruises on the Danube or Rhine Rivers with views of various German castles, or cruising into Norwegian fjords. Yes, *that* might be fun sometime to explore the land of some very distant relatives of hers. Sometime.

Next came the sunny beaches of the Hawaiian Islands or down along the Baja coast, or even trips to exotic lands like Fiji, Tahiti, or the mythical Bali Hai! She smiled as she recalled the lead role she had in her high school production of *South Pacific*. They had such a wonderful cast, and oh, that great looking guy who played Emile De Becque. *Hmmm, Dusty Clark. I wonder where you are now?* And his accent was so genuine after taking three years of high school French! She sighed with just the thought of all those wonderful times in high school, times that now seemed so far away.

Nicole had been *so* in love with Dusty, but that all faded with graduation. Or, more accurately, crashed! Their dates throughout their senior year had been wonderful, and they tried to spend every available moment together. However, studying together did not work out as well because they were just too distracted with each other to get anything meaningful accomplished. With every passing day it seemed their love was getting stronger and deeper.

Their Senior Ball, appropriately named *Some Enchanted Evening*, was beyond dreamy, but when he announced the weekend before graduation that he had recently met with a Marine recruiter, and that he was leaving the week after graduation, her heart was crushed. All her dreams were gone! She could hardly look at him without crying during their last week of classes.

Why had he kept his plans a secret? She had shared all of hers with him! One of the main reasons she had chosen to focus on USC was so they could see each other as often as possible. He had led her to believe that he would be "close," but "close" to him was boot camp in San Diego and then wrapping up his training at Camp Pendleton. Sure, *close*, but not *available* for dating! *So* many hopes and dreams lost *forever!*

That was why she had locked her heart while she attended college. Oh, she had dated on a fairly regular basis in order to break away from the monotony of studying, and to have fun with friends she had made along the way. However, she was not going to let another guy break her heart like Dusty had. And even though she and Chandler had been together for over five years, she had not even let *him* get close to her heart. She sighed softly.

Chandler .... You're a good man, and you've treated me nicely and respectfully, but ... I don't love you, and I don't think I ever will. She sighed heavily and went back to her magazine and dreaming of faraway places.

After the cruises and beach getaways came something she had not heard very much, if anything, about ... vacationing at a guest ranch. *A guest ranch? Like a horses and cows and sheep kind of ranch? No, I don't think so.* But, as she started to quickly flip past that section, one photo caught her attention and she flipped back to the page, opening it widely on her lap. *Oh my gosh!!* Look *at this place!!*

"Hidden Glory Ranch, the perfect vacation getaway you've never tried before!"

Hmmm, quite the headline, she thought. But, she had to admit, it *was* accurate. She read closer.

"More than just a ranch, more than just a fun getaway! Hidden Glory Ranch offers an experience and an adventure like no other you have tried! Whether you spend just a few days, a week, or longer, we have the perfect package for you! Even if you have never been around horses, there are still many other things to enjoy during your stay, and we assure you, you will love it! We stake our name and reputation on

it! Give us a call and let us help you plan the perfect getaway just for you!"

A guest ranch? *Hmmm, it certainly is different,* that's *for sure!* Nicole pondered the possibility, but it was so unusual for her to consider any kind of vacation like that, even for a few days. She tossed back the covers, climbed out of bed, adjusted her nightgown, re-set her pillows, climbed back into bed, turned out the light and laid down. After a relaxing evening, and with three more days of her mini vacation still ahead of her, she pulled the covers up and closed her eyes. The thought of spending *any* time on a ranch began to intrigue her, and she kept turning the idea over and over in her mind until she finally drifted off.

CHAPTER 13

Monday

"CHANDLER?" IT WAS EIGHT forty and Malcolm Shaw was standing at Chandler's office door.

"Sir!"

"I thought you were going to come by my office the first thing this morning." Malcolm stated gruffly.

"Yes, sir," Chandler replied anxiously. "I'll be right there, sir."

"Fine. I haven't got long, so hurry."

Chandler knew he was supposed to have met with Malcolm as soon as he arrived at the office that morning to let him know how everything had gone with Nicole the previous night, but there was nothing to report. This did not look good.

"Sorry, Mr. Shaw. I had a lot on my mind on the way to the office this morning, including the Lowrie case. As soon as I arrived, I hurried into my office to get some quick notes down, and I was going to—"

"That's fine, Chandler," Malcolm interrupted. "I'm meeting with a client at nine, so let's make it fast."

"Yes, sir." Chandler took a deep breath. "I actually have nothing to report because I wasn't able to see Nicole last night as I said I would. I kept trying to talk to her from last Thursday on, but she was busy as well, and then she left Saturday morning for a brief vacation."

"And she hadn't mentioned anything to you before about this vacation?"

"No, sir." Chandler could see the wheels turning in Malcolm's head. *I'm sure he's thinking that I don't know Nicole as well as I think I do, but he's wrong. This was just a momentary, and very minor, mis-step.*

After a long, uncomfortable pause, Malcolm cleared his throat and proceeded. "When do you expect to talk with her again?"

"Soon, sir."

"Soon? You can't do any better than that?"

"Nicole said she would be back in town on Thursday."

"Said? So you *did* talk to her."

"No, sir, it was actually a text."

"A text?" Malcolm weighed this over for a long moment. "Chandler, when was the *last* time you actually had a *phone* conversation with her, or spoke with her face to face?"

Chandler could not tell Malcolm about their conversation yesterday morning. Or … could he?

"We talked briefly yesterday morning before I went into the morning session of the conference."

"And?"

"And, sir?"

Malcolm sighed heavily out of a growing frustration. "*And …* did you set a time to meet with her to discuss your future plans together?"

"No, sir. Not yet. But I will take care of that right after she returns."

"And?"

"And I'll let you know later this week how everything is progressing."

The steel-eyed look Malcolm gave Chandler said everything. Chandler's mission was clear. Get engaged, at any and all costs, and the sooner the better. No matter what.

Malcolm's phone rang.

"Mr. Shaw?" It was his executive assistant.

"Yes, Dorene?"

"Mr. Stevenson is here for your nine o'clock appointment."

"Thank you, Dorene. Give me another thirty seconds."

"Very well, sir."

"Okay, Chandler, let's get on with our day, shall we?"

"Yes, sir. And thank you, sir."

Chandler arose from his chair, and as he exited Malcolm's office, Dorene was preparing to escort in Malcom Shaw's next client.

When Chandler returned to his office, he closed the door behind him, sat down at his desk, and pondered the situation that Nicole had put him in.

What is going on, Nicole? Everything seemed to be fine until last week, but since then you're not the same Nicole Hart that I've grown to love so much over these last few years. What happened? Are you okay? Are we okay? I wish Thursday would get here now!

* * *

As Nicole awoke, she found the Travel + Leisure magazine on the bed next to her and remembered the mental trip she took to the ranch the night before. She stretched and enjoyed the feeling of getting a great night's sleep for the *third* night in a row!

After her shower she decided to wear a pair of shorts instead of her Wranglers, anticipating that she'd be spending some more time walking on the beach and possibly doing some shopping. As she dressed, she heard singing from the other room and assumed that Carli must have arrived home long after she had fallen asleep the night before. She finished brushing her hair and as she opened her door, she heard the singing coming from Carli's hallway.

"Well, *someone's* really happy," Nicole exclaimed as she saw Carli in her studio.

"Good morning, Nicole!"

"Good morning! How was your day with friends yesterday?"

"Oh, it was *wonderful!* We talked and laughed for hours and hours, then we went out for dinner at this really fun Polynesian restaurant. Oh, my gosh! The food was *so* good!"

"It sounds like you had a good time!"

"The best! So, how was your day? Did you do anything fun or go anywhere special?"

"No, nothing much. I just stayed here, had a fight with a guy I've been seeing for a few years which gave me a migraine, so I took a nap, watched a movie, made dinner, walked on the beach, then made some popcorn and watched another movie."

"Wow! What a day!" They had a good laugh.

"Yes, it certainly wasn't what I had been expecting, *that's* for sure."

"I can imagine. Are you okay today?"

"Yes, the migraine was gone when I woke from my nap, and since the rest of the day was so relaxing it stayed away."

"Do you get them often?"

"No. It was only the second one I've ever had. The first was in college. I'm glad, too, because they're horrible. Have you ever had one?"

"No, but I have a few friends who have, and they say they're really miserable."

"I can certainly vouch for that."

"Are you okay about things with your friend?"

Nicole sighed. "Yes, I think so. At least for now. I asked him to leave me alone and stop trying to call or text me while I'm here. I needed this time to get away and his constant calls were annoying me."

"Well, I hope everything will turn out okay."

"Oh, they will, but just not the way he's hoping."

"Oh, I'm sorry to hear that. Well, one way or another I hope *you'll* be okay."

"That's what this getaway is all about."

"Do you think it'll be long enough?"

"I don't know. I haven't taken any serious time off in years. That's why I needed this and, fortunately, my boss was willing to let me have this time on virtually no notice."

"He sounds like a great boss."

"Yes, he's the best!"

"What kind of work do you do?"

"I'm an architect at Warren Knapp Design here in Newport Beach."

"Wonderful! Is there any particular part of that field you specialize in?"

"Well, I like my designs to be both subtle and bold. A lot of my work has been for customers who have property along the southern coast, primarily from Newport Beach to San Diego, but I've also designed some homes for people who live in the mountains. And, I've also designed several commercial projects throughout the south state. My latest project is the proposed Laguna Beach Museum and Artist-in-Residence facility."

"Wonderful!"

"Thank you. I'll be making my final presentation to the City Council on Thursday evening, and I can hardly wait."

"Well, I wish you all the luck in the world."

"Thanks, again."

"I was just about to fix some breakfast. Would you like to join me?"

"Sure! That would be great. May I help you with any of it?"

"No, this is your vacation time. You just make yourself comfortable and I'll get right to it."

"That sounds good. I think I'll go sit on the deck for a few minutes."

"Go right ahead and I'll call you when it's ready."

* * *

As Nicole relaxed on the deck, she closed her eyes and enjoyed the morning sun and salty air. *Mmmm, I could* sure *get used to this!* Her thoughts were infused with distant memories of great times spent at the beach with her friends. She always came home with a beautiful bronze tan that made her friend, Christine, so jealous because it was all *she* could do to not get a lobster burn. *Sighhhhh … such good times.*

Her mind jumbled with thoughts of Chandler, work, and her parents. She had been on this fast track for so long. Was last Thursday night a crack in her veneer? Why had she fallen apart like that? Would something else trigger another one? And if it happened, she could only hope that she would be alone where no one else would witness her falling apart. Tears were beginning to well up in her eyes at the thought.

"Breakfast is ready, dear," Carli called from the doorway.

Nicole sniffed and quickly wiped away her tears, but not in time. Carli had seen it all.

"Oh my gosh, Nicole! Are you alright?"

"Yes, I'm sorry. Don't mind me."

Carli sighed. "Well, if there's anything I can do *please* let me know, okay?"

Nicole let out a long sigh. "You're too kind, but I don't think you can. I think it's just something I need to figure out for myself."

Carli was truly concerned for her guest, but also knew that she needed to respect Nicole's privacy and give her the time and space necessary to work things out on her own.

"Well, sweetie, breakfast is ready. Why don't you come in and have some and maybe it might help? Or, if you want, you can dish up however much you'd like and come back out and enjoy it on the deck."

"Thank you, Carli. I'll be right there."

Carli returned to the kitchen and set out plates, glasses, and utensils for the two of them, poured some juice in their glasses, and set the platters of scrambled eggs, link sausages, bacon, and sliced cantaloupe near their settings. The family room door opened and Nicole came in.

"I'll be right back. I need to go wash my face."

"Take your time, sweetie. Take all the time you need."

They were soon at the table and sharing small talk. A few minutes later Carli noticed Nicole appeared to be staring at something outside the window.

"Is everything okay?"

"Hmmm? Oh, yes. My mind was just wandering."

"I think it's contagious. Living here close to the ocean my mind goes wandering quite often, too."

"I can imagine. So, I have a question for you."

"Sure, hon, what is it?"

"I was looking at one of your magazines last night, the one about traveling and vacations?"

"Yes. That's a wonderful magazine with fun getaway ideas! Are you thinking of taking a cruise or something?"

"No, not a cruise, but ... well, this will sound completely crazy because I've never even ridden a horse, with the exception of when I was a little girl and I took a pony ride at the county fair. However, there was an article about vacationing at guest ranches and—"

"Oh, I think you'd *love* it, Nicole! It's *so* much fun!"

"So, you've tried it before?"

"Yes! I've done it twice and loved it both times. The first time was a bit awkward, though."

"How so?"

"Well, it was after my husband, Don, passed away. I was having a very hard time because he had been my high school sweetheart, and we'd been together for over fifty years. I was *so* lost without him. We'd done *everything* together! I have a friend who'd been on a cruise and offered to go on one with me so I could enjoy the time away, seeing places I'd never seen, and doing things I'd never done and not be alone. But I passed. I just wasn't in the mood to do *anything* or go *anywhere*. I just wanted to stay bundled up in my sorrow in our home. I could still feel him here with me, and that helped, at least for a while."

"Then what happened?"

"A couple of months later that same friend suggested I try going to a guest ranch. I initially thought the idea was crazy because, like you, I'd never been on a horse. But the more I read about the whole experience I realized that just because I was going to vacation at a guest ranch, it didn't mean I *had* to go horseback riding, I could just hang around and do the things I was interested in. I only went for a few days the first time, just to try it out. But after I got home, I couldn't *wait* to go *back!*"

"Where was it located?"

"New Mexico. And what was *really* fun for me was one day during my second trip there they had a lady come from Santa Fe to teach a painting class. You know, New Mexico is so popular with artists. I hear it has something to do with the air or the blue sky or something. They say the sky is different, somehow, from anywhere else and that's why artists love to go there to paint. Some even end up moving there for good, but not me. I love this home and the beach too much to *ever* consider moving."

"Did you paint anything special while you were there?"

"Yes! Come see!" Carli led Nicole to her studio. "Nearly everything I've painted has something to do with the beach, the ocean, or the desert, but this one is actually one of my favorites because it was so different for me!" She pointed to a painting on her wall near the window that Nicole hadn't noticed the other day. "There it is!"

"Oh, my gosh, Carli! It's breathtaking!"

"I have to give credit to the air! There truly is something different, or perhaps even magical, about it!"

Nicole took a closer look. "Why ... hmmm ... why does this painting look so familiar?"

"I don't know, but it's of the main building, or what they called the hacienda, at the ranch where I stayed."

"What's the name of it?"

"Hidden Glory Ranch."

"Hidden Glory Ranch? Wait! *That's* the name of the ranch I was reading about last night in your magazine?"

"Really?"

"Yes!"

"Oh, my goodness! You know, half the time I get those magazines and never really pay that much attention to them."

"So, you've stayed there?" Nicole asked excitedly.

"Yes, and like I said, it was *wonderful!*"

Nicole sighed heavily as the wheels were spinning in her mind. *I wonder .....*

"I also took some photographs of the place if you'd like to see them sometime."

"Yes, I'd *love* to!"

"Okay. It'll take me a bit to remember where they are. I have so many albums in various places throughout the house."

"That's quite all right. I'll still be here for a couple of days."

"I know! Aren't we lucky?"

"Well, I can't answer for you, but I know *I* sure am." Nicole was feeling the earlier tension melting away.

"Believe me, Nicole. I'm lucky *and* grateful that you're here, too."

They returned to the kitchen, continuing to chat while they ate, and afterward Nicole helped Carli clean up.

"The warm sun looks inviting so I think I'll go for another walk on the beach."

"Okay, hon! Enjoy!"

"Thank you. Oh, and thank you for your comments about the ranch. It's given me something to think about."

"Like I said, I truly think you'd love it. It's certainly a lot different from the beach, but I think you should give it a try, at least for a few days."

"Thanks! I think I will. It's just a matter of figuring out when, and then giving my boss a *little* more time to say 'Yes' than I gave him last Friday."

* * *

Nicole made good use of her time throughout the rest of the day. After her walk on the beach, she checked in with Carli to let her know that she was going shopping and would probably get a bite to eat at one of the local eateries. That way Carli would not need to worry about her for dinner. And, since she was planning on dining out, she changed back into her Wranglers.

When she arrived back at the house later that evening, she found a note on the kitchen table letting her know that there was some left-over pasta and meatballs along with some garlic bread in the refrigerator in case she might be hungry. She smiled as she thought about how thoughtful and kind Carli had been. Next to the note was a photo album with a note on top.

> *I'd like you to have the travel magazine with the article about the ranch. I've been there so I don't need to read about it. It's all yours! Perhaps it'll inspire you to give it a try!*
> *Also, you'll find lots of photos of the ranch in here!*
> *Enjoy!*
>
> *Carli*

After a quick shower to wash off the salty spray of the day, she propped up her pillows and climbed into bed. She reached for the Travel + Leisure magazine she had been looking at the night before to re-read the article featuring Hidden Glory Ranch. The more she read, the more she liked the idea of trying something new! Then she looked through the photo album and became even more convinced to go there as soon as possible! *Now* to just figure out *when* she would take this trip! She made a mental note to call the ranch in the morning to find out how far into the future they were booked. Then she would decide.

CHAPTER 14

Tuesday

AFTER ANOTHER WONDERFUL BREAKFAST with Carli, Nicole went online and looked up the phone number for Hidden Glory Ranch. She took a deep breath to calm her nerves. Normally, making any kind of phone call never bothered her, but this one felt different … as if by making this call, she might be taking a big step toward … well, she could not quite find the words to describe it. Regardless, she had a feeling that this was somehow more than just another call.

"Good morning, Hidden Glory Ranch! This is Kay."

"Good morning, Kay. This is Nicole, and I'm calling to find out about availability for your guest ranch."

"Sure, Nicole, are you interested in staying in the hacienda, or in one of the surrounding casitas?"

"Um, pardon my ignorance, but what is a casita? I just read a magazine article about your ranch and they mentioned casitas but I didn't really understand what they are."

"Oh, no problem, A casita is similar to a freestanding apartment."

"Oh, yes! I think I'd like to stay in one of your casitas!"

"Wonderful! They come with one, two, or three-bedrooms."

"I'll just be by myself, so a one bedroom will be perfect."

"Okay, and when did you have in mind?"

"Well, I'm curious if you have any vacancies beginning in a couple of weeks or perhaps a month? Or are you fairly well booked up for a while?"

"You're actually catching us at the latter part of the off season, so I believe we have several openings. Let me just take a moment to look at what we have available."

"Thank you."

"Did you have any particular dates in mind?"

"Well, not this coming Sunday, but how about the following Sunday?"

"Yes, that's available. And how many nights will you be staying with us?"

"Six."

"Wonderful! Would you like to book that now?"

"May I put a temporary hold on my reservation? I'm currently away from my office and I won't be back until Thursday. I'll need to check with my boss before I can confirm."

"I'm sure that will be fine, Nicole. We'll need a deposit to hold the casita, and if that date doesn't work out, we can easily transfer the deposit to a date that better fits your schedule."

"Okay, that's fine." Nicole gave Kay her credit card information and email address, and Kay emailed her the tentative reservation.

"You're all set!"

"Thank you. I'll give you a call on Thursday to confirm that date or make other arrangements."

"That's fine, Nicole. And thank you for the call."

"You're welcome! I'm looking forward to this."

"And we're looking forward to having you stay with us!"

They said their goodbyes and Nicole let out a long, happy sigh. She was excited about this new adventure and could hardly wait to be there!

She had been so focused the night before with making this call that she had not thought about what her plans might be for the rest of the day. She wanted to make it special in some way, because tomorrow would be a combination of wrapping things up here with Carli in the morning, heading back to her condo in the afternoon, and then spending the evening getting ready for returning to work Thursday morning.

Carli was in her studio when Nicole came singing down the hall.

"Guess what?!" Nicole asked, unable to contain her elation!

"Well, guessing by that bright smile on your face, it must be pretty exciting!" Carli replied.

"I just placed a call to Hidden Glory Ranch and made a tentative reservation!"

"Really?! Oh, I'm *so* happy for you, Nicole! I just *know* you're going to *love* it! How many nights are you planning on staying?"

"Six. If I get the clearance from my boss, I'll go a week from this Sunday and spend the week there!"

"What do you want to bet you won't want to come home?"

"Oh, I doubt that. Enjoying a vacation somewhere is one thing, but I love my job too much to even *think* of making a change like that."

"Well, perhaps not permanently, but you never know. You might find it too enticing to return home."

"Hmmm, well, I guess we'll see!"

"Yes, we will!" Carli replied with a twinkle in her eye.

"So, what are you working on today?"

"Oh, I saw this beautiful tiki garden outside of the restaurant we went to Sunday evening and I'm trying to capture it the best I can."

"I've seen a few that were so charming! With those tiki statues and torches, and flowers like bird-of-paradise and gardenias."

"Yes, they're just so lovely and enchanting, aren't they?"

"They sure are! Well, I'll let you get back to it. I'm going to head out for a little more shopping today."

"Do you have plans for tonight?"

"No, not yet."

"Great! Since you're going home tomorrow, I'd love to take you out to dinner this evening to celebrate the wonderful time we've had this week!"

"Oh, Carli, that's not necessary. You've been a wonderful host. More than I ever expected before I came here. *That's* for sure!"

"Well, thank you, but if you truly have no other plans, then I insist. My treat," Carli said.

Nicole stood silently for a moment. "You've been so good to me this week," she replied softly. "*I* should be the one treating *you*."

They simply looked at each other for a long moment, realizing that a unique bond had been forged between them, a special friendship that had not existed only a few days earlier.

* * *

Since Carli had insisted on dinner being her treat, Nicole insisted on driving. Traffic wasn't bad so it was only a twenty-five-minute drive down Pacific Coast Highway to Laguna Beach. The parking lot a short block away was nearly full, but Nicole managed to find a spot not too far from the entrance to the restaurant. As they entered The Sundowner, Carli took note of several heads turning their way, obviously looking beyond her and taking in the attractive young lady behind her. Nicole noticed a few herself but quickly looked toward the hostess.

They were soon seated at a table with a beautiful view overlooking the Pacific Ocean where the sun was glistening off the tops of the gentle waves. Their waitress, Serena, took their drink orders, and returned a few minutes later to take their meal orders. Carli had been there before and knew that their salmon was spectacular. This was Nicole's first time, although she had heard about the restaurant from another friend about a year earlier. She chose the petite filet with lobster tail.

Nicole was looking out at the ocean when Carli noticed something in Nicole's expression.

"Everything okay?"

"Yes, I was just thinking."

"Would you care to share?"

Nicole smiled. "Sure. I was just thinking that it's too bad I have to go back to work on Thursday. These last few days have been *so* good for my soul. I *love* my job, but I have to admit it keeps me so busy, and I even catch myself thinking about it *after* I leave the office. I know I probably shouldn't, and I also know that it's not healthy for me mentally *or* physically, but I just care so much about it that I find it hard to simply sit back and relax most of the time."

"If I may ask, do you have many outside interests or hobbies to take your mind off of work?"

"Not really. I love to read, but then again I don't give myself much time to do that. All of my friends are married, so spending time with them isn't an option. And … there's also that guy I told you about yesterday that I've been dating off and on for a few years. Nothing is serious, but we usually get together a couple of times a week to go to dinner, take in a Lakers, Dodgers, or Rams game, or something else like snow or water skiing. However, part of the reason I needed to get away was that lately it feels like he wants to step things up in our relationship, and frankly … I'm just not interested. And I needed this time away to just *think!*"

"I understand completely," Carli replied reassuringly.

"These last few days could *not* have been *more* perfect! Your home and friendship, along with the fun shopping I've been able to do, and just kicking back and relaxing have been *just* what I needed! Thank you."

"You're so very welcome, my dear. It's been such a pleasure having you stay with me!"

Their meals were delivered shortly thereafter and since they were in no hurry they spent the rest of their time chatting about a variety of things while they enjoyed their dinners. Nicole insisted on paying the tip, and doubled the amount since they had stayed longer than expected.

After they arrived home Carli relaxed with a book in the family room while Nicole went for a walk on the beach, and then relaxed on the deck upon her return.

CHAPTER 15

Wednesday

NICOLE AWOKE EARLY TO enjoy a quiet walk along the beach, but this morning it was anything but quiet. The restless waves seemed to rush angrily to the shore, matched only by the dark, threatening clouds gathering along the far horizon. The portending storm looked vicious, even at a distance, and lightning was flashing like paparazzi following the latest Hollywood starlet. She hadn't paid any attention to the weather all week because it had been so pleasant, but today was different, and she wondered how long this storm would last. She had time for breakfast, then run her errands, and finally to pack and leave. Fortunately, she didn't have far to drive to get home to safety.

The intensity of the storm brought to mind another storm that had been brewing in her life for some time; one that she had tried to get away from all week, and one that she was not looking forward to facing any time soon. She wondered just how long she could put it off, but for today, right now, it would have to wait. She was grateful that Chandler had *finally* gotten the message and had stopped trying to contact her after her angry text on Sunday morning. She cleared her mind of those thoughts to avoid any hint of a headache.

Other thoughts swirled through Nicole's head as she tried her best to prioritize her last day at the beach. She knew she had to allow time for doing some laundry, as well as prep for her return to work tomorrow. At the top of her list once she arrived at the office was to thank Warren for these unexpected days off, then ask him for a week more! After receiving his approval, which she knew would not be a problem, she would check her calendar and then confirm her reservation at Hidden Glory. Finally, she would review the notes for her final presentation to the Laguna Beach City Council and Planning Commission tomorrow night and add anything necessary in order to make it the best it could be. She wanted to knock it out of the park!

In the meantime, though, she still wanted to make the most of *today*! Shopping? Probably, depending on how quickly the storm moved toward the coast. Definitely visiting a few galleries in order to track down a special photo she had her eye on. And she also needed to get back to one of the jewelry stores she had visited on Monday. She had thought about spending a little more time with Carli, but once again it all depended on the storm. Carli's enthusiasm for life had been contagious these last few days, and that alone had made her stay there *so* much more enjoyable than she had hoped for!

As Nicole made her way back toward the house, she could not help but feel mentally refreshed! Work had never been a problem. She thrived on the challenges each day presented! However, the challenge regarding her relationship with Chandler was another thing altogether. In fact, these few days away had given her time to perhaps become clearer about her future, and, being honest with herself, she did not see him in it. That realization alone gave her such a sense of relief.

Nicole was grateful for his silence these last few days; not even a text appeared on her phone. She knew she would keep her promise to let him know when she returned home, but she was in no rush to keep that promise. Maybe Friday? Hmmm … maybe.

An icy wave jolted her from her thoughts, and she instinctively jumped to the side as it returned to the ocean. She felt something lightly bump her right leg and, looking down, she saw a starfish. She picked it up and threw it as far as she could beyond the waves that were rolling toward her. Then the thought occurred to her, *not only have I just set myself free, but I've given that starfish another chance.* She smiled at the coincidence.

Once her decision regarding Chandler was clear, she felt the weight of the world suddenly lifted from her heart. In fact, she became almost giddy as she considered the new possibilities her life might hold! But, there was also the matter of deciding when and how to call an end to it. A text or a letter were simple and to the point, but after five years together, she felt Chandler deserved to hear it face to face. It was something she was definitely *not* looking forward to, and it went right to the bottom of her priority list.

Carli stepped out on the deck to take in the freshness of the morning sea breeze and noticed it was much colder than she had felt recently. That's when she looked out and saw the approaching storm on the horizon. She looked down along the beach in search of Nicole and saw her walking along the shoreline. She almost called out to her, but thought better of it. *What if she's lost in thought like I usually am when I'm walking on the beach?* She straightened up the deck chairs, mentally preparing herself to bring them in later before the storm got too close, and retreated to the kitchen.

Nicole reached the place where she could turn and walk straight up to the house, but turned toward the ocean instead. Except when she was in grad school, she had always lived near the beach. She thought back to her high school days when she would be on the beach with her friends every chance she got. Her strawberry blonde hair always seemed to shimmer brighter after each trip, and her tan seemed to grow deeper, adding to her surfer girl mystique. Those days seemed so far away now, and her tan had gradually faded as the responsibilities of college and her career took her further and further away from those carefree days.

Gazing toward the dark horizon, she sighed heavily, almost as if she somehow knew that a change might be coming that would take her away from all this. She closed her eyes, kept the image frozen in time, then turned and walked up to the house.

* * *

"I've made you a special breakfast to start off your last day here," Carli joyfully exclaimed as Nicole closed the door behind her.

"Oh, Carli, thank you so much! You didn't have to do this. Last night's dinner was special enough."

"*Yes!* Wasn't that *wonderful?*"

"Oh, my gosh! I can't remember a time when the food was so amazing *and* the atmosphere was so enchanting!"

"Not even on a date with someone special?"

"No, not even then. I mean, I've been to some nice restaurants where the food was superb, or the ambience was heavenly, but not both of them together like last night! I need to remember that restaurant so I can go there again *very* soon!"

"Well, I'm sure you'll enjoy it even more the next time."

"And, no doubt, the next time after that, too!" Nicole and Carli both laughed heartily at their silliness.

Nicole set the table while Carli placed the serving dishes between them.

Carli offered a brief blessing on the food, and added an additional request that Nicole would have a good day and a safe return home.

"Thank you, Carli," Nicole said, almost in a whisper because of the lump in her throat.

"You're so welcome, my dear."

They dished up their helpings of scrambled eggs and link sausage, fresh-from-the-oven cinnamon rolls with an overabundance of icing, and crispy bacon. Carli had also placed containers of orange, cranberry, and apple juice on the table.

"It's a good thing I went for my walk early this morning," Nicole said with a wink.

Carli smiled. "Well, I wasn't sure what your plans were for today and I wanted to make sure you had plenty to eat before venturing out."

"Believe me, this will be *more* than enough."

"Good! Enjoy!"

Nicole nodded that she certainly would.

"So, what's on tap for today?" Carli asked.

"Well, there are a couple of galleries I want to go back to. I saw a beautiful photograph in one of them that I liked but I don't recall which one it was. And there's also a pretty bracelet I saw in a jewelry store that I decided I'm going to get as a memento of this week. How about you? Any special plans of your own?"

"No, I'm staying home today. I have plenty to do around here to keep me busy. If I finish in time, I might go for a walk down the beach before the storm hits. Any idea when you might be heading home?"

Nicole was just tearing off a piece of her cinnamon roll but stopped and sighed with the realization that she was really going to be leaving this little oasis in just a few hours. She rested her hands on the table and looked at Carli.

"Do I *have* to go home?" Nicole asked with a half-smile and a wink.

"No! My next guests don't arrive until Friday afternoon, so you can stay longer if you wish!"

"Yes, I *do* wish, but I can't. I have to be back to work in the morning."

"I understand. I just wanted you to know that the offer is available."

Nicole again sighed heavily as she looked out the windows toward the ocean. "It sure has been wonderful here. Thank you, Carli."

"It's been my pleasure, dear." They returned to enjoying their breakfast in silence.

After finishing, they cleaned up the kitchen together with lots of fun small talk between them.

"So, tell me about the bracelet you found."

"It's sterling silver and it's a perfect reminder of my stay here! The charms include a seashell, a starfish, a sand dollar, and a seahorse."

"You're right! It *does* sound perfect! Seahorses are my favorite! And what about the photograph?"

"Oh, it's *beautiful!* It's of a few hot air balloons ascending into a clear, deep blue sky, and the colors are so rich and vibrant!"

"Oh, I *love* hot air balloons! I've always wanted to go to the big festival they have every October near Albuquerque! I've heard it's breathtaking to see all of those balloons rising and floating away!"

"You should make plans to go *this* year!"

"You're right! I should!"

With the kitchen clean, they were both ready to get on with their day. Carli retreated to her studio to continue working on her latest painting of the tiki garden, and Nicole headed to her bedroom to get ready for her brief trip to the galleries and jewelry store.

As she was leaving, Carli caught her attention.

"Nicole? I know you have to get back to your condo and get things ready for tomorrow, and depending on how soon the storm hits, how about a light, early dinner? Just something simple."

Nicole only had to think for a moment, then smiled as she replied. "I'd like that very much. Thank you, Carli."

"Oh, my pleasure! Now, go have a good time looking for your photograph and bracelet."

"Thanks, I will! See you soon!"

"Bye, dear!"

* * *

After visiting two of the galleries she had been in the day before, she finally recognized the one that had the photograph of the hot air balloons. With great anticipation she entered and looked toward the far back corner, but her heart sank as she noticed a different photograph displayed where *her* photograph had been hanging the day before. As she stood there in dismay she was approached by a middle-aged lady.

"Good morning! I'm Mary, and welcome to my gallery!"

"Good morning, Mary," Nicole replied, trying to be cheerful despite her disappointment.

"If I recall, didn't I see you in here yesterday?"

"Yes. We didn't get the chance to talk because you were busy with another customer. I saw a photograph in here yesterday that I came back to purchase, but it's not where it was hanging yesterday."

"Could you describe it for me? Sometimes we move some of our photographs around, so hopefully it's still here."

Nicole's hopes rose considerably. "It was a large photograph of colorful hot air balloons rising into a brilliant blue sky."

"Ah, yes. I know the one you're referring to. I'm afraid we sold it shortly after we opened this morning."

"Oh, no!!!"

"I'm so sorry."

Nicole sighed heavily. "That's okay. I *knew* I should have bought it when I was here yesterday instead of waiting. My loss."

"That particular photograph was taken by a very talented photographer based in Nashville, Tennessee. Her name is Sheri Oneal. She spends a lot of her spare time traveling throughout the southwest and she's had great success sharing her photographs here. I have a few of her other photographs in the next room if you'd like to check them out."

"I guess that would be okay."

Mary led Nicole into an adjacent room and pointed out where Sheri's photographs were featured. They included sunrises and sunsets over the Grand Canyon, ocean sunsets, various shots of the desolation of Death Valley, and, just for fun, there were a couple of photographs of that famous street corner in Winslow, Arizona. Nicole admired Sheri's work, including the whimsical one from Winslow, but her heart had been set on the large, three-by-five-foot photograph mounted on canvas. They spoke for a few more minutes before Nicole left.

The jewelry store where she'd seen the bracelet was not far away. After her disappointment at the gallery, she tempered her enthusiasm about being able to buy the bracelet. However, she was overjoyed to find the bracelet exactly where she had seen it the previous day.

Excited about finding this special treat for herself, she decided to spend a few more minutes glancing around the store in hopes that she might find something special as a gift for her wonderful hostess. It was not long before she found the perfect gift – a six-inch-tall crystal paperweight with a laser etching of a seahorse, along with a lighted rotating base! She asked the clerk if they offered gift wrapping, and the clerk was more than happy to oblige her request.

After paying for her treasures, she excitedly put the charm bracelet on her wrist, then reached for the gift bag with Carli's seahorse paperweight and headed back to the house to pack so she could leave for home right after dinner.

* * *

Carli's dinner that evening was truly amazing! Fettuccini Alfredo with chicken and shrimp, salad with Italian dressing, and hot from the oven garlic bread! They talked and laughed forever, but Nicole had kept a close watch on the time and the approaching storm to ensure she would get home safely and at a decent hour.

In the midst of an all too rare lull in their conversation, Carli reached out and placed her hand on top of Nicole's, and their eyes met in a special moment.

"Nicole, I want to thank you for coming to spend these last several days with me," Carli said softly. "You are such a special young lady, and ..." Carli's voice broke, and as her words went silent her eyes began to well up with tears.

"Oh, Carli," Nicole replied, as she placed her other hand on top of Carli's, "thank *you* for allowing me to stay here! This has been a wonderful experience for me, and it was everything I needed and so much more!"

They squeezed each other's hands and shared this last tender moment in silence.

Carli took a deep breath and cleared her throat. "Well, I should let you finish your packing so you can head back home."

"Actually, I've already finished, so I just need to load up my car and I'll be on my way," Nicole replied with a lump in her throat. "But first!"

"First?"

"I'll be right back!"

Nicole got up and headed for her bedroom where she retrieved the gifts for Carli she had purchased earlier. She returned to the kitchen and placed the gift bag on the table next to Carli.

"What's this?!"

"Just a little something to say 'Thank You' for being such an amazing hostess!"

"Oh, Nicole, you didn't have to do anything for me!"

"I know I didn't *have* to, but I *wanted* to!"

Carli picked up the gift bag to look inside. "Oh, my goodness! It's heavy!"

"Well, one of the packages inside is a partial bar of gold!" Nicole joked with a wink.

Carli laughed. "Yeah, I *wish!* Oh, there's *two* packages in here! Do you have a preference for which one I open first?"

"Yes, the tall rectangular one."

Carli proceeded to carefully unwrap the beautifully wrapped

package as if the paper itself was gold leaf. With the paper removed, she lifted the top of the box, folded back the white tissue paper, and gasped when she removed the contents!

"Oh, my gosh! Nicole, this is *beautiful!*"

"When you mentioned you loved seahorses, I knew I wanted to find something for you that had seahorses, and I found this at the jewelry and gift store where I bought my bracelet."

"Oh, Nicole, thank you! This is so thoughtful!" Just then Carli jumped up to give Nicole a big hug.

"Thank you, dear," she said through her tears.

"You're so very welcome," Nicole replied, as tears streamed down her face, as well.

As they released their hug Carli took a deep breath. "So now the second package?"

"Yes."

"I mean, one was quite enough."

"Well, in a minute you'll see why I bought this one, too."

Curious, Carli reached in the bag and pulled out the other, short but square box. This time she unwrapped it quickly and proceeded to open it, too anxious to see what the contents would reveal.

As she lifted the lid of the box and folded back the tissue paper, she paused for a moment as she looked at the contents, unsure of what it was. However, as she lifted it out of the box she realized it was a lighted display stand that she could rest the crystal seahorse paperweight on, and the light would shine up and make the seahorse glow!

"Oh, Nicole, how wonderful! These are just perfect gifts!"

"From my heart to yours, Carli."

"Yes, I can tell. Thank you *so* much! You're just too sweet and thoughtful!"

"Well, I kind of picked that up from you this week," Nicole replied with a wink.

The ladies sat there for a moment, and then they both got up and gave each other another hug.

"You're the best, Carli," Nicole whispered through her tears.

"No ... you are," Carli whispered as she wiped away her own.

It was obvious to both of them that a special friendship had formed between them over these last few days; a friendship they both knew would last for a very long time.

"Okay, may I help you with your bags?" Carli asked, hopeful for the chance to offer her friendship in yet another way.

Normally, Nicole would have simply thanked anyone else, but she welcomed the chance to have these last few minutes with her new friend.

When the last bags were in the trunk, Nicole and Carli gave each other a long hug and said their goodbyes. Just as Nicole was getting into her car Carli called out!

"Wait one second! There's one more thing I need to get for you!"

"Um, okay," Nicole replied, confused because she knew she had double checked everything before they carried her bags out from her bedroom. A moment later she saw Carli emerge from her home with something large in her arms and got back out of her car to see what it was.

"I want you to have this painting, Nicole, as a special gift from me and as a reminder of this week." She then turned the painting around and Nicole gasped, with tears welling up in her eyes, as she saw it was Carli's painting of Hidden Glory Ranch!

"Oh, my gosh, Carli!" Nicole exclaimed through her tears. "I don't know what to say!"

She reached for the back door and carefully slid the painting in and leaned it against the back seat, then closed the door and turned to give Carli another long hug.

"Thank you, thank you, thank you, Carli! Those truly are the only words I can think of."

"You're very welcome, my dear. This way it will also be a reminder to you of that fabulous ranch after you get home from your special time there."

"Yes! Yes, it will!"

They both sighed heavily, smiled, and gave each other another brief hug. Nicole turned and once again got into her car. They waved goodbye as Nicole slowly backed out of the driveway. As she drove away Nicole looked in the rearview mirror and another tear fell to her cheek.

CHAPTER 16

Returning Home

NICOLE OPENED ALL THE windows in her condo to let the fresh air sweep away the stuffiness that had gathered over the last several days. She wouldn't be able to leave them open for long because of the wicked storm within the menacing clouds that were approaching. The heavy rain would be pelting down any minute. But, for now, she needed to clear the air. She even thought about calling Chandler, but her second thought was a clearly defined *No! Not yet! One storm in my life right now is enough.* She wasn't ready to go there. Soon enough. But not now.

She opened her duffle bags and quickly emptied their contents onto the bed. She took her makeup bag to the bathroom, her shoes to the closet, and the contents of her laundry bag were emptied and sorted.

She opened her dress bag and removed her favorite evening dress, fondly reminiscing about wearing it to the wonderful dinner with Carli. She had noticed only a few of the many heads that turned as she made her way through the restaurant, and again when she exited. Her dress was not revealing in any way, other than to reveal an inner beauty that was certainly equal to her elegant appearance.

The dress had always made her feel special and the timing of wearing it could not have been more perfect. A week ago her emotions were in shambles, but she was feeling much better now thanks to these last few days at the beach. Time would tell how long the feeling would last.

She made another, and final, trip out to her car and retrieved the painting of Hidden Glory Ranch that Carli had so graciously and lovingly given to her. She could not believe her great fortune of having connected with such a wonderful woman who had become her close friend in such a short time. She had promised Carli that, no matter what, she would always stay in touch. She always kept her promises, and the one she made to Carli would be no exception. Perhaps they would meet up at the Albuquerque Hot Air Balloon Festival!

Nicole remembered a promise she had made to Royal a few days ago and reached for her phone.

"Hi, this is Royal!"

"Hi, it's Nicole!"

"Hey, my friend! How did it go?"

"Oh, my gosh! It was *so* wonderful! Carli is just the sweetest person and we became instant friends!"

"That's great! I just *knew* you two would hit it off!"

"We sure did! We'll have to get together for lunch soon and I can tell you all about it!"

"I'd like that! Hey, are you going to be okay with this storm that's about to hit?"

"Yes, I think so. I've been keeping an eye on it all day, and it looks like it's about to start raining any minute now, but as long as there's no damaging hail I should be okay. Thanks for asking."

"Okay, good. Well, if you need *anything* don't hesitate to call, okay?"

"I promise. Thanks!"

"You're welcome. Good night."

"Good night, Royal."

After starting a load of laundry, she finally took a few moments to sit back on her sofa, lift her feet up onto the ottoman, lean her head back against the cool, soft leather, and sigh deeply. The last seven days had been quite a roller coaster and she was glad that the ride was over. A feeling of calm and serenity had replaced piercing and nearly debilitating anxiety. It was time to call her mother to let her know she was back home and safe.

CHAPTER 17

———

Thursday Morning

NICOLE ARRIVED AT THE office early and secured her usual parking place. She had always enjoyed getting a jump on the day. It made her feel like she had accomplished so much more when it was time to close up shop and head home.

A few colleagues were already there, and as she passed Warren's car, she excitedly thought to herself, *I'll be seeing you soon, Warren!*

After placing her purse in the lower left desk drawer, she sat down and flipped open her calendar. She scanned her notes about the rest of her week and looked ahead at the next few weeks. She needed to know if there were any conflicts due to her taking some additional time off. She made a mental note to check in with Martin about his project, then headed to Warren's office.

"Good morning, Warren," Nicole cheerfully called from his doorway.

"Good morning, Nicole!! Come in, come in!" Warren replied, greeting her with his usual, generous smile.

"Thank you, sir."

"Have a seat and tell me *all* about these last few days. Well, at least as much as you might *like* to share. I'm not being nosy. I just hope that taking the time away helped with whatever has been bothering you recently."

"Oh, Warren, it was *wonderful!* I basically escaped from my world; well, I should say what my *normal* world has been."

"Did you go anywhere or do anything special?"

"Yes! I rented a room in a beach house right here in Newport Beach, and it was the *perfect* place for me!"

"That sounds great!"

"It was! I called a friend of mine Saturday morning who is in real estate just to see if he had any connections or information about short term rentals along the beach. It turns out he has a friend who rents out one of her rooms from time to time, so I gave her a call and she had an unexpected opening that I was able to take advantage of!"

"Wonderful! Were you able to get the rest you wanted, or should I say, *needed?*"

"Yes, and no. Initially, I guess, but I started thinking more and more about your nudge for me to take a *real* vacation."

"So, is that in your plans any time soon?"

"I guess that depends on how much notice you want?" Nicole replied with a smirk.

"Ahhh, I see where this is going," Warren replied with a wink and a smile. "What's your pleasure?"

"Well, I'm helping Martin with his project beginning today, and there's a possibility that I may have my part completed by tomorrow afternoon, but—"

"So, would you like to take your time off beginning next week?"

"*Next* week?"

"Sure, why not?"

"But isn't that leaving you short-handed unexpectedly?"

"Nicole, you are my star architect, and that deserves some special privileges that I, alone, can grant. If you'd like to take some more time off beginning next week, then I'm more than happy to support it."

A most appreciative smile beamed across Nicole's face. "Thank you, Warren, but I'll have to make a call first and then I'll let you know."

"Perfect! That works for me!"

"Thank you, Warren," Nicole replied, almost in a whisper.

"You're so very welcome. I have absolutely no problem with that. You deserve it, Nicole. Do you only want to take a week? Because you've certainly earned more time off than that if you'd like."

"No, I think a week should be fine."

"Are you planning on another getaway, or just taking it easy at home?"

"Well, I was looking through a travel magazine at the beach house and it had an article about guest ranches. And the ranch they featured in the article is one that Carli, the lady I stayed with, has been to twice, and she *raved* about it!"

"A *guest* ranch?"

"Yes! Can you believe it?!"

"It sounds like quite a fun experience for a young lady whose second home has been the beach most of her life."

"You're right! I was telling Carli that, with the exception of riding a horse at a county fair when I was eight, I've never been horseback riding. And, I've never been around *any* kind of ranch animals for that matter, so I imagine it will take me a couple of days to get used to the big change. However, I *am* actually looking forward to it. I think some changes are good, right?"

"They sure can be!"

"So, you're okay with this?"

"Absolutely! Go for it, and I hope it's everything you hope it will be, and more!"

"Oh, thank you, Warren! I promise to come back fresh and focused."

"Nicole, I've never seen you any other way. Well, with the exception of last Friday afternoon, but I won't count that."

Nicole smiled. "Thank you, Warren. You're very kind."

"I'll do whatever I can to keep my best architect happy. And, speaking of architect, are you all set for this evening's presentation?"

"I will be in a little bit. I want to go over my notes from last Friday's presentation, add a few more thoughts I came up with on the way to work this morning, and I'll be ready."

"Wonderful. I'm planning on being there as well."

"Oh, thank you! I appreciate that. Your moral support means a lot."

"Oh, sure! But … I have to admit, it's also for a selfish reason. I want to see the looks on the collective faces of the council and the mayor. I have a feeling you're going to see some mighty impressed people there tonight."

"I'll do my best."

"You always do, Nicole. You always do."

Nicole nodded her gratitude. "Well, I've kept you from your work long enough and I better get back to mine."

"Thanks for coming in to see me, Nicole. Now, go have a great day!"

"Thank you, Warren. You have a great one, too."

As Nicole approached her office, she saw that Amanda had arrived.

"Good morning, Amanda! How are you?" Nicole said gleefully.

"Good morning, Nicole! I'm doing well! Welcome back!"

"Thank you."

"How were your days off?"

"Wonderful! Would you like to join me for lunch today? I'll tell you all about it!"

"Sure! That'll be fun! Thank you!"

"You're welcome. Have you noticed if Martin has arrived yet?"

"Yes, we arrived together just a few minutes ago."

"Great. I need to talk with him, but I'll give him a little more time to get settled."

"He mentioned that he's anxious to meet with you this morning as well. He said something about having some new ideas he wanted to run by you for his project."

"I can't wait!" And with that Nicole decided to head directly to Martin's office. The sooner they met, the sooner she would be able to concentrate on checking off the balance of her list.

"Good morning, Martin!'

"Hey, welcome back, Nicole! How was it?"

"Oh, it was just what I needed!"

"That's great! So, are you still up for this project?"

"I sure am! Let's see what you have."

For the next half hour Martin laid out his ideas, and together he and Nicole discussed the best strategy for his project. Martin had been with the company for only six months and was still getting up to speed, but he had a keen sense for exacting detail and a strong desire to always do his best. Nicole was more than happy to assist her passionate colleague. She had once been where he is now and she was still grateful for the mentoring she received early on. It was time to pay it back.

Returning to her office, Nicole closed the door behind her. Her next order of business was to call Hidden Glory Ranch. She closed her eyes for a moment and smiled as she pictured herself confidently riding a beautiful horse through a meadow. Then she chuckled at the thought because that confidence would be a long time in coming since she had absolutely no real-life experience with a horse at all!

"Good morning, Hidden Glory Ranch, this is Kay!"

"Hi, Kay, this is Nicole Hart. I called the other day and made a tentative reservation?"

"Oh, yes, Nicole! How are you?"

"I'm doing great, thank you."

"Wonderful! So, you're calling to confirm your reservation?"

"Actually, I'd like to see if I can make a change. Is there *any* chance at all that I could move my reservation up to start *this* coming Sunday?"

"Really? Wow, you're that anxious to get here, huh!"

"Well, it was really my boss's idea."

"Oh, he's trying to get rid of you?" Kay asked with a laugh in her voice.

"Yes, something like that. I've been under a bit of stress lately and haven't taken any time off in a few years, so he's insisting."

"It sounds like you have a great boss!"

"I really do. I'm very lucky."

"Okay, well I'm 99% sure it won't be a problem, but just let me check."

Nicole heard a few clicks from Kay's keyboard.

"There we go. I'm looking at our bookings now and next week is even better! And I'll even upgrade you to our largest one-bedroom casita at no extra charge."

"Oh, my gosh! Thank you, Kay!"

"It's my pleasure! It's not appreciably larger, but it has a few more amenities that you may enjoy."

"Now I can't wait to get there! Which reminds me, I better check to see if I can get a flight to Albuquerque on short notice!"

"I'll let you go, then. And if I don't hear back from you, I'll assume all is well."

"Great, thank you."

"You're welcome, Nicole! And good luck!"

"Thanks, Kay! Bye!"

"Bye!"

Nicole immediately began a search for a flight to Albuquerque on Sunday morning. Within minutes she found a couple of options. Then, out of curiosity, she also checked on flights leaving on Saturday, and her choices were even better. She immediately called Kay back and asked if she could arrive on Saturday instead, and Kay easily made the switch. Then she returned to the airline's website and booked her flight from John Wayne Airport in Santa Ana to Albuquerque, with a return flight the following Saturday.

When everything was settled, she sat back in her chair and felt a bit dizzy with everything that had happened in just a few short minutes! She was going on a *real* vacation, and leaving in less than *two days*. She could hardly wait!

After catching her breath, she called Kay back and confirmed that she was able to get a flight which would arrive in Albuquerque in the early afternoon. Then she'd rent a car and drive up to the ranch, being able to be there before dinner. Kay confirmed that everything would be ready for her!

The next few minutes were a whirlwind of excitement and emotions!

CHAPTER 18

———

Distractions

NEXT ON HER LIST was to go online to the post office and put a hold on her mail delivery while she was gone.

And finally … finally she needed to text Chandler. She picked up her phone and sighed before punching in her message.

> I can't talk right now and it's going to be a busy day
> but I promised to let you know that I got home safely.

She set her phone down and proceeded with her work on Martin's project.

Chandler responded ten minutes later.

> Hi, Nicole! Sorry, I was in a meeting. So, you're back?!
> Wonderful! How was it? Are you okay?

Nicole noticed his response and picked up the conversation.

> Yes, I'm back, and yes, I'm okay.

> May I see you this evening, or at least call you?

> I have something for work I have to do this evening
> and won't be home until late.

Regardless of what time you're done,
may I come by to see you?

Sorry, not tonight.

Perhaps tomorrow night then?
I really want to see you.

No, sorry. Busy tomorrow night as well.

What? Then, when can I see you?

Soon. I only promised to let you know when I
was back. Things just got complicated in the last
several minutes.

This weekend?

Chandler, no. Sorry, just wait until I text you again,
okay? I'm busy right now.

Sheesh, Chandler! Ease up! Nicole was sorry she had bothered to text him.

Chandler was *not* happy! He had expected that when she called to let him know she was home, that he'd be able to actually *talk* to her and not just text! He needed to *see* her as soon as possible, but now it felt like she was just dangling bait. *Hey, I'm home! Now leave me alone!* And a text instead of a call? He threw his phone down on the desk and headed for the break room to walk off his anger.

When he returned to his office a few minutes later he picked up his phone and re-read her last message.

Chandler, no. Sorry, just wait until I text you again,
okay? I'm busy right now.

So, what's up? Is she trying to avoid me? Okay, just one more text.

Nicole's phone buzzed and she hesitated before glancing at it.

> Sorry I bothered you, sweetheart. Take your time and
> we'll talk soon. I missed you. I love you.

Nicole left this last text hanging without a response, not out of meanness or rudeness, but because she did not want to give Chandler any false hopes. She sighed as she placed her phone on the desk. *I'm not sure if I'm up to any kind of discussion anytime soon, but if not soon, then when?*

She cleared her mind and settled back into her part of Martin's project and before she knew it, it was time for lunch. Amanda joined her, and Nicole filled her in on the wonderful time she'd had at the beach.

* * *

Shortly after they arrived back at the office and were settled into their afternoon routine, a deliveryman approached Amanda's desk.

"I have a delivery for Nicole Hart?"

Hearing her name Nicole looked up. She was definitely curious because she had not ordered anything to be delivered at work. Amanda pointed toward Nicole's office and at that moment Nicole reached the doorway.

"Hi, I'm Nicole."

"Hi, Nicole. I have this delivery for you. Where would you like me to put it."

Nicole looked behind the deliveryman and noticed a very large, thick, rectangular box.

"Oh, my gosh! What on earth …?"

"You didn't order anything?" Amanda asked.

"No, nothing!"

Then she looked at the deliveryman. "Why don't you just bring it into my office."

"Sure!" The young man lifted the box and carried it in.

"Just lean it against these filing cabinets," Nicole directed.

"Would you please sign here?" he asked.

Nicole signed the young man's electronic tablet and handed it back to him.

"Thank you," he replied as he turned to leave.

"And thank *you!*"

"What in the world?" Nicole muttered to herself as she turned and stared at the box.

Amanda anxiously approached Nicole. "What do you think it is?"

"I have NO idea! I haven't ordered anything, so …"

"What's it say on the label?"

Nicole looked closely at the label and gasped!

"What's it say?!"

"Oh, my gosh! It CAN'T be!"

"What?!"

Nicole reached across the desk for her letter opener, slid the blade under the sealed flap along one of the short ends, then tipped the box on its side so she could have better access to remove the contents. As she peered into the box she gasped again and hurried to reach inside!

"The suspense is killing me, Nicole! What is it?!" By now their excitement had drawn a crowd of co-workers outside her office!

Nicole carefully removed the bubble wrapped contents and gasped with absolute joy at the sight of the photographic canvas print of her hot air balloons! She was speechless!

"Oh, my *gosh!*" Amanda replied, her excitement almost as much as Nicole's!

As Nicole removed the layers of bubble wrap and protective cardboard frame corners, she noticed an envelope taped to the back of the frame. She detached it, removed the card, and read

Nicole —

Thank you for being such a lovely guest this week. I know how much you wanted this photograph, and I knew exactly which gallery you had seen it in. I called my friend, Mary, right after you left on your excursion yesterday morning. She confirmed the photograph was still there, so I bought it and asked her to hold it in the back room until I could come

by to add this card before they packaged it up to deliver to you. Enjoy!
Your friend,

Carli

Tears were flowing down Nicole's cheeks as she read it, and Amanda's tears were flowing as well. There were also several sniffles emanating from the small crowd just outside her office. She lifted up the photograph for all to see, and more gasps filled the air.

"That's so beautiful, Nicole!" Amanda exclaimed. "Carli sounds like such a wonderful lady!"

"Yes, she is. In *so* many ways!"

Nicole fanned her face with her hands as she tried to quell the tears that just refused to stop.

"Let me know if you'd like some help mounting it on the wall, okay?" Amanda offered.

"Yes, I will. Thank you." Nicole sighed heavily, reached for a tissue from a box on her credenza, dabbed carefully at her eyes, and took a deep breath.

"Okay, I think that's enough excitement for one day. We need to get back to work!"

Amanda nodded and retreated toward her desk, while the others outside her office did the same.

Nicole walked to the window and looked out toward the ocean, grateful for the view she had been blessed with all these years. *I can't believe you, Carli! I mean … I am truly at a loss for words!* However, she knew she would have to figure out *something* to say to Carli because a thank you note would not be enough; she needed to call her *now!*

She turned, walked back to her desk, sat down, and reached for her cellphone.

"Hi, this is Carli!" Carli's voice was always so cheerful!

"You … are … AMAZING!!"

"NICOLE! How *are* you?"

"I'm *speechless*, that's how I am! I can*not* believe that *you* are the one that bought my balloon photograph! Thank you *so* much!"

"Oh, you're welcome, dear. I just couldn't resist the chance to surprise you."

"Well, it *worked*! Oh, my *gosh*!"

"Wonderful! And I hope you don't mind that I had it delivered to your office instead of to your condo."

"No, that's quite alright! I'm actually glad you did because I seem to spend more time here each day than my condo, so it works out perfectly. But, how did you know where to send it?"

"Remember earlier in the week when I asked you what kind of work you did?"

"Yes, and I said I was an architect."

"Well, that's not *all* you said. You also mentioned the name of the company, and that it was right here in Newport Beach."

"Oh, my gosh! That's right! I had completely forgotten about that."

"Well, I'm actually glad you were so specific because it made it that much easier to surprise you!"

"And you *definitely* did that!"

"Good. Good. Well, enjoy it!"

"Oh, I will! And, between your painting of Hidden Glory Ranch and this photograph, they will be the *perfect* reminders of my time at your home and our friendship!"

"I'm so glad you feel that way, Nicole. It was so much fun to have you here. And, I know you are at work, so I better let you go."

"Sure, that's fine. Thank you again, Carli!"

"Oh, one more thing! Good luck with your presentation this evening! I'm *sure* they're going to love your design!"

"Thank you, Carli. Thank you for *everything*!"

"You're welcome, dear. Goodbye."

"Bye, Carli!"

Nicole sighed joyfully as she set her cellphone down on the desk and gazed across the office to her beautiful photograph.

"Oh, my gosh!"

Tears began to pool up once again as she thought about how blessed she was to have such a wonderful friend who had helped her so much these past several days.

CHAPTER 19

The Stars Are Aligned

NICOLE'S PRESENTATION TO THE Laguna Beach City Council and Planning Commission went amazingly well! In fact, the wonderful reception she received was beyond anything she had ever experienced from any previous presentation. And Warren could not have been prouder and more pleased with his star architect!

The mayor called a recess after her presentation to allow her time to gather up her model and leave, but not before each of the members of the city council and planning commission took the opportunity to personally thank her for her extraordinary work. As she and Warren walked to their cars her spirit was soaring!

"Oh, my gosh, Warren! Can you believe what happened this evening?!"

"Yes, Nicole," Warren calmly replied. "I most certainly can. And you absolutely deserved every one of those kudos they extended to you. I'm *so* proud of you, Nicole! Fine job! Fine job!"

"Thank you *so* much!"

A familiar, but unexpected voice called out. "May I add my kudos as well?"

Nicole turned and saw Carli walking toward them.

"Carli?!"

"Yes, my dear."

"Oh, my gosh! You came to the meeting?"

"I wanted to come and support my new friend, and Nicole, your presentation was *exceptional!*"

"Thank you *so much*, and thank you for coming! What a wonderful and sweet surprise. Oh, Warren? This is my friend, Carli. She's the lady I rented the room from this week. Carli, this is my boss, Warren."

"It's a pleasure to meet you, Carli. Nicole told me all about you this morning, and how grateful she was for your generous and fun hospitality."

"It's so nice to meet you, too, Warren. And Nicole shared very high praise of you this week, as well. It sounds like you're both very lucky to have each other."

"Yes, he's the *best* boss!" Nicole exclaimed.

"And she's my star architect!" Warren effused.

"Yes, like I said … a great team!" Carli responded.

"Excuse me while I put my model away safely."

After Nicole placed the model into the back of her GMC Yukon, she gazed around at her beautiful surroundings, then up at the starlit sky. She was on top of the world! If only her dad could have seen her!

Daddy, I did really well this evening, she thought joyously to herself.

"Are you okay, Nicole?" Warren asked.

"Hm? Oh, yes. Yes, I'm fine. I was just thinking about … oh, it doesn't matter."

"Okay, then, I'll see you in the office tomorrow! Good night, and drive safely!"

"Good night, Warren. And thank you for being here this evening. Your enthusiastic support for my work means *everything* to me!"

"My pleasure, young lady. Good night. And it was a pleasure to meet you, Carli."

"Same here, Warren. Good night."

Warren smiled and waved as he closed his car door.

"And I'm going to say good night as well, Nicole."

Nicole sighed happily. "I can't thank you enough for taking time out of your busy schedule to drive down here this evening."

"I wouldn't have missed it for the world!"

They gave each other a hug, and then Carli retreated to her car.

As Nicole opened her door and sat down, she rested her hands on the top of the leather steering wheel and let out a long, deep sigh.

Wow! She thought to herself. *What an amazing evening!*

She started the car, tuned to her favorite satellite radio station, and cranked up the volume. Then she put the car into gear and took off for a long drive down Pacific Coast Highway. She opened the windows and let the wind blow through her hair. There was no need to hurry home tonight!

She was singing along to a favorite song when the screen on her phone lit up. It went unnoticed, and Chandler left her another voicemail.

CHAPTER 20

Friday Afternoon

As Nicole was putting her finishing touches on the project she had been working on with Martin, she was fighting the urge to allow her mind to wander. In less than thirty minutes she would be out the door and on her way home to finish her preparations and pack for the first real vacation she had taken in years. She was both nervous and excited about her forthcoming trip. However, remembering Carli's comments calmed many concerns she had about this new adventure. Getting away for something different was just what she needed in her life right now. Her few days at the beach had been a nice, short getaway, but it was also safe and familiar. Staying at a guest ranch? Now *that* was going to be quite the adventure!

Amanda's phone rang and Nicole was momentarily distracted, glancing toward Amanda to see what the call might be for.

"Hi, Maryann." The call was from Warren's executive assistant.

"Okay, I'll let her know. Thank you."

"Nicole, Warren would like to see you for a few minutes before you leave, but no rush."

"Thank you, Amanda. I just finished so I'll take these designs to Martin and then stop in to chat with Warren." She carefully rolled up her design plans and carried them to Martin's office.

"Here you are, Martin! All finished!"

"Thanks so much, Nicole! I really appreciate your help on this."

"It's been my pleasure! Best of luck with your final presentation."

"I'm sure it will go smoothly, thanks to you. And I hope you have a wonderful vacation!"

"I hope so, too! It's certainly going to be different."

"I'm guessing you're all set with a new wardrobe of cowgirl dresses and boots?" Martin teased.

Nicole winked and laughed. "Yes, I took an extended lunch break today and went shopping. I picked out a few things but I'm guessing that my trusty Wranglers will be perfect for most of what I may be getting myself into. I even have a pair of boots from when I was in grad school in Arizona that will do just fine."

"It sounds like you're all set! Have fun!"

"Thanks, I plan on it! I need to chat with Warren for a few minutes before I head home so I'll see you when I get back."

"Take care, Nicole."

As Nicole approached Warren's office Maryann looked up and nodded the okay to go right in. She paused at the door first, noticed Warren was looking out the window toward the ocean, and knocked.

"Come in, Nicole!"

She entered and closed the door behind her, then joined Warren at the table near the window.

"It's going to be another lovely evening," Nicole said.

"Yes, it sure is. And I doubt you're going to see anything quite this beautiful where you're headed."

"Well, it will certainly be different, but I think it will have its own special charm."

"There you go, always finding a way to put your own positive spin on things."

Nicole just smiled.

"Amanda said you wanted to see me before I left today."

"Yes! I just wanted to chat for a moment to see how you're doing."

"I'm doing great! My part of Martin's project is complete and I've turned over the designs to him. He'll have it wrapped up next week."

"Wonderful! However, what I'm *really* wondering about is you. How are *you* doing?"

Nicole smiled warmly. "Thanks, Warren. I've always appreciated how you care about your employees. I'm doing fine, at least a lot better than I was a week ago at this time."

"Good. I'm glad to hear that. I'll bet you're excited about this little adventure."

"Excited and a bit nervous, but I think I'm ready for it. At least I *hope* I am," she joked.

"Oh, I'm sure it will be great. Just don't get *too* used to the change. I'm expecting to see you back here afterward."

Nicole laughed again, "Oh, you have *nothing* to worry about. I love it here and wouldn't dream of running off with a cowboy." Warren joined her in a good laugh.

"That's music to my ears, young lady. You are absolutely the star of my company, and I would not know what to do without you."

"That's very kind of you to say, but I'm sure there are plenty of other architects around who could easily fill my shoes."

"Not a chance! You are very unique, and I'm also not anxious to search for another one, either."

"No worries. I'll be back, I promise."

"Thank you, Nicole. That's good to know. It looks like it's almost time to head out, so why don't you slip out a few minutes early and get a jump on the traffic."

"Thank you, Warren. I appreciate that. Don't let anyone steal my office or Amanda while I'm gone! I'll need them both when I get back."

Warren smiled broadly and winked as he shook his head. "Not a chance! Take care."

Nicole said goodbye to Maryann as she passed her desk, and moments later she was back in her office to gather her things before heading home.

"I'll see you tomorrow morning at seven?" Amanda asked.

"Um, pardon me? My mind was somewhere else for a second."

"Yesterday I volunteered to drive you to the airport and then pick you up next Saturday."

"Oh, that's right! Yes, seven will be perfect. Thank you!"

"It's my pleasure!"

Nicole smiled. "And I'm grateful. See you then!"

"Bye!"

CHAPTER 21

Getting Ready

NICOLE DIDN'T WANT TO bother to tell Chandler that she was going away for a week. She could tell he was not taking this time apart very well, but she was not going to make things easy on him, either.

At this point she was about to break things off with him altogether but didn't want to deal with it before her vacation. Perhaps having some time away from each other would do both of them some good. Maybe they could each think a bit more clearly about what their personal goals were. She didn't think it would improve things for the both of them, but she knew this next week would certainly help her.

After preparing a light dinner of pasta and salad she focused on packing for the trip. She laid out her clothes on the bed and proceeded to change her mind several times about which items to include and which she thought might not be appropriate. She reminded herself that she would be in a dusty environment, so something fancy was not going to work. However, plain and simple was also just … well, too plain and too simple.

She read over the general itinerary that Kay had emailed her right after she'd made her reservation – horseback riding, campfires, arena games (whatever *those* were!), a game night in the hacienda, as well as time to enjoy all by herself. So, nothing *really* fancy, but she just couldn't pass up the chance to wear the new western style dusty rose print dress she'd found during her extended lunch break earlier that day. Between that dress, her new leather boots, and short leather vest, she felt like she just might catch someone's eye. She laughed to herself at the thought! *I'm not going there to catch a cowboy, I'm going there for myself and to relax and have a good time.* She set the outfit aside … to wear in the morning.

Less than an hour later everything was packed and ready to go. The only thing left to do now was to call her mother.

* * *

"Hello?"

"Hi, Mom!"

"Hi, Nicole! What a pleasant surprise! Are you calling to tell me you're coming to see us this weekend?"

"No, but before I tell you why I called, I need you to just answer the next question with a yes or no, okay?"

"Um, okay. This sounds mysterious."

"It's nothing like that, Mom. I just want to know if Dad is close by and can hear you talking to me?"

"No, sweetheart, he's on his phone in his office and his door is closed. Why, what's up?"

"Well, I'm taking some vacation time and I'm leaving early tomorrow morning."

"Oh, that's wonderful! Where are you going? On another cruise?"

"No, I'm heading to New Mexico."

"New Mexico?! What's in New Mexico?"

"A really nice guest ranch!"

"A *ranch*? That doesn't sound like you," her mother replied with a merry sound in her voice.

Nicole laughed. "I know, Mom. It's kind of a surprise to me, too."

"What made you choose to go there?"

"I read about it in a travel magazine recently. Then I met someone who had been there and *raved* about it so I decided to give it a shot."

"Well, it sounds interesting, dear, but why don't you want your father to know about this?"

"Oh, I don't know. I guess because it's something that I think he would probably feel is a waste of time and money, and that if I'm going on vacation, it should be some place more worthwhile, like Paris, London, Rome, or Hawaii."

Charlotte sighed. "I know what you mean, dear. He can certainly be so particular, especially when it comes to things pertaining to you and your life. I wish he would just let you be your own woman and not try to influence you so much like he has for so long."

"Thanks, Mom. Yes, it's been hard at times. I think this will be a fun adventure, though, and I'm looking forward to trying something different."

"I hope you have a wonderful time. When did you say you're leaving?"

"I'm catching a flight to Albuquerque about nine tomorrow morning and then I'll be home next Saturday evening."

"Oh, I forgot to ask. What's the name of this guest ranch?"

"Hidden Glory Ranch."

"Oooo, that sounds interesting. I wonder how they came up with that name? Well, I better let you go so you can get some sleep, and then you can tell me all about it when you get home."

"I promise. And thanks, Mom. I love you."

"I love you, too, sweetheart. Have a safe flight and be careful."

"Yes, Mom, I will. Bye."

"Bye, dear."

* * *

Fortunately, Amanda was taking her to the airport and they would only have to deal with the early Saturday morning traffic and not the normal weekday nightmare. Nicole also knew that anything could happen, and quite often did if you were running late. She was determined that was *not* going to happen to her!

As her head hit the pillow she sighed heavily. *Finally! Nine days of vacation! This is going to be so much fun!* She ran through a mental checklist to make sure everything was ready, checked her alarm one more time, and was asleep in less than ten minutes.

CHAPTER 22

A New Adventure

NICOLE AWOKE BEFORE HER alarm, stretched, and excitedly bounded out of bed and headed for the shower. Twenty minutes later she was drying and styling her long, strawberry blonde hair. Still wearing her robe, she headed for the kitchen to fix a hearty breakfast. It was going to have to last her until she could get something to eat after her plane arrived in Albuquerque at a half past one.

Next came her makeup, including a new shade of eye shadow and lipstick she purchased specifically to match her new dress. Then, with her makeup done, she slipped on the dress for the first time since trying it on in the store. She twirled in front of her floor-length mirror and smiled brightly. Next came her vest and boots, and enjoyed the view in the mirror one more time. With the exception of the night Carli took her out for dinner, it had been a long time since she had truly felt this attractive. Her happiness brought a tear to her eye which she quickly dabbed away with a tissue before it could ruin her makeup.

An overwhelming sense of joy mixed with calm swept over her. She had this feeling that something wonderful was about to happen in her life, but she did not understand what or why. She loved her job, and, except for Chandler and the situation with her father, she loved her life. What could be better than what she already had? The feeling lingered for the longest time.

Her reverie was broken with a knock on the front door, and she remembered Amanda was picking her up.

"Hi, Amanda! I can't believe it's already seven!"

"Hi, Nicole! Oh, my gosh! You look *gorgeous*!!"

Nicole blushed. "Thank you. I bought this especially for the trip. Is it too much, though? I mean, I'm heading to a ranch, not a fancy hotel or a resort."

"You look absolutely, perfectly stunning!"

"Nothing like overdoing the compliments!" The ladies both laughed. "Come on in, I'm almost ready."

"I'm a few minutes early and—"

"Oh, that's not a problem. Better a few minutes early than late, right?"

"Exactly."

Nicole headed to her bedroom to get her luggage, then walked through the condo one last time to make sure all was set for her to be gone for the week.

"Okay, ready!"

Amanda led the way out as Nicole locked the door. Then, turning toward Amanda, she let out a long sigh.

"I can't believe this is happening! A whole week off, and I'm spending it at a guest ranch!"

Amanda started the car as Nicole finished putting her luggage in the trunk. As Amanda backed out of the driveway, she noticed Nicole's broad grin.

"I can tell you're happy about this."

"I am! As I was getting dressed, I kept thinking that something … I don't know, um … something different is going to happen, but I have no idea what it might be."

"Well, just be open to anything and everything that comes your way. Including *anyone*," Amanda added with a smile.

Nicole laughed. "*That's* not on the itinerary."

"You never know."

They shared a laugh and Nicole changed the subject.

"So, have you ever been to New Mexico before?"

"No, although I've seen photographs of many of the beautiful places."

"When I was in grad school in Arizona, I had a good friend who was from Santa Fe. She invited me to join her and her family for Thanksgiving and it was perfect timing because my parents were in Europe. So, I got to see quite a bit of the beautiful countryside along the way."

"How fun! I hear Santa Fe is a great city."

"Yes, I loved it! The surrounding area is so beautiful, and there is so much to do and see downtown. Are you familiar with the artist Georgia O'Keefe?"

"Yes! I love her paintings!"

"Her museum is only a five-minute walk from the downtown plaza. We took a tour of it one day and our docent was *so* much fun! When we were telling my friend's parents about our tour that night her mother asked if we remembered the docent's name, but neither of us could. Then she asked if the lady had red hair and we said, 'Yes.' She said, "Oh, that's my wonderful friend, Debra! Wasn't she just a delight?!" We agreed that she was. Then she added, "She's such a lovely lady! We have lunch together about once a month and have the *best* time!"

"It sounds like you have at least one place you can go that will be familiar to you."

"The ranch I'm going to isn't too far away, only about two hours, so depending on what I'm doing during the week I might be able to sneak down to Santa Fe and check it out again."

They continued chatting for the few more minutes it took to get to the airport. Traffic had been fairly light, so Nicole was arriving earlier than she had anticipated, which was just fine with her.

"Thank you so much for getting up early on a Saturday to take me to the airport."

"Oh, it's not a problem. And I'll be here to pick you up next Saturday evening."

"Are you sure I'm not imposing on you too much?"

"Not at all. I have no plans, so I'm glad to do it. And, if you're up to it, we can go out for a late dinner and you can tell me all about it."

"You've got a deal!"

Nicole's phone vibrated but she decided that whoever was calling could leave a message.

"Well, I better stop chatting and let you get checked in. May I help you with your luggage?"

"Thanks, but no. Driving me to the airport was quite enough."

"Okay, have a wonderful time, Nicole!"

"Thanks, Amanda. I emailed you my fight information for next Saturday, right?"

"Yes, your flight arrives just before six-thirty, and I'll be right outside baggage claim to pick you up."

"Thanks." Nicole sighed again as she opened the door. "Okay. Here we go!"

"Have a great time!" Amanda chimed.

"I will," Nicole replied, smiling broadly.

"Send me a postcard!"

"Okay!"

CHAPTER 23

The Arrival

AFTER MAKING ONE STOP enroute, Nicole's flight landed in Albuquerque at 1:20 pm. It had been a full flight and it took a while to deplane and then to gather her luggage. Next, she secured her rental car and, after one quick call to the ranch to let them know her approximate time of arrival, she would be on her way.

"Good afternoon, Hidden Glory Ranch. This is Kay!"

"Hi, Kay, this is Nicole Hart. I've arrived in Albuquerque and, according to the app on my phone, I should be there in about three and a half hours."

"Wonderful! We're so excited about your coming to stay with us!! In case you're interested, we do have a local county airport that you could fly into and save yourself a lot of time. Of course, it's also a *lot* less expensive to just drive."

"Thank you, but no thank you. I'm just fine with flying a large passenger jet, but there's no way you'll ever find me in a small one."

Kay laughed in agreement. "I know exactly how you feel because we think alike. I just wanted you to know you have that option."

"Thank you. I appreciate your thoughtfulness."

"You'll be arriving just in time for dinner, so when you get here just leave your luggage in your car and come right into the hacienda. You can't miss it because we're at the end of the long drive coming in from the highway."

"That sounds good to me! I'll see you then."

Next, Nicole opened up the app for the directions, set the phone on the center console, found a radio station she liked, and in no time was zooming along the interstate.

A little over an hour later she was passing through Santa Fe, and ninety minutes after that she pulled into Taos and topped off the gas tank. She knew she had plenty of gas to get to the ranch, but was not sure what she might find when she arrived. She wanted to make sure she would have enough gas to at least get back to Santa Fe, if not all the way to the airport in a week. She was back on the road in no time, winding her way east through the twisting turns of the Carson National Forest. In fewer than thirty minutes she arrived in the Moreno Valley and turned south onto Highway 434. Within five minutes she turned east and headed up the road to the ranch.

As Nicole drove along the tree-lined road she was enthralled by the expanse of the ranch, at least as much of it as she was able to see at this point. There were two large fenced in areas on her right and a woman in her fifties or so, was working with a horse in one of them. Further away there were several horses grazing in a pasture, and then she saw the beautifully designed stable. They apparently spared no expense to make this guest ranch inviting for one and all, whether it's a city girl who is used to the beach, or a celebrity who simply wants to enjoy a comfortable and quiet getaway.

* * *

Chandler was anxious to talk with Nicole. He knew she liked getting up around dawn, even on weekends, and he had left several messages on her phone already. He tried again a moment ago, and once more it went to voicemail, leading to a distinct and heavy sigh of frustration.

"Hi, Nicole! I have some *great* news to share with you, so please call me back when you get this. I love you! Bye, sweetheart!" By noon he had called two more times. He thought about texting her again, and then thought she may have gone to see her parents for the weekend. A quick call to the desert would solve everything.

"Hello?"

"Hi, Mrs. Hart, it's Chandler," he said excitedly.

"Hello, Chandler. How are you?"

"I'm doing fine, thank you. By any chance is Nicole with you this weekend?"

"No, she's not. May I take a message for her, though?"

"No, I just have something *really* important I need to share with her."

Charlotte hesitated, and then remembered that Nicole had not said anything about *not* telling Chandler where she was going, only her father.

"You said it's really important?"

"Yes, and I've been trying to reach her all morning, but she hasn't been answering her phone. I've left several messages but she hasn't responded to them either."

"Well, um, she's taken a week off from work and she's gone out of state on vacation."

What? A vacation?! She just took a few days off! Chandler did his best to conceal his frustration. "Hmmm, that's funny. She didn't mention anything to me about it. Did she say where she's going?"

"Yes, some kind of ranch in New Mexico."

"New Mexico?! Really? That's unusual for her."

"Yes, I thought the same thing when she called to tell me about it last night."

"Did she mention what ranch she was going to?"

"Yes, just a moment. Let me go find my note."

Chandler's mind was spinning, trying to figure out what was possibly going on with his sweetheart.

"Ah, here it is. The place is called Hidden Valley, oops, no sorry, Hidden Glory Ranch, but I have no other information other than that."

"Hidden Glory Ranch?"

"Yes."

"Okay, thank you very much. Hopefully I can reach her there."

"Would you like me to mention to her that you called in case she calls here?"

"No, please don't. This is really special and I want her to be completely surprised."

"Okay, Chandler. Good luck!"

"Thank you, Mrs. Hart."

"Goodbye."

"Bye."

Hidden Glory Ranch. Hidden … Glory … Ranch. Where on earth *is* that?! He opened up his laptop and started his search. *Okay, here it is.*

> *Hidden Glory Ranch is a beautiful guest ranch located in Angel Fire, New Mexico. The Masterson family has owned the property since 2007, with Luke and Jill Masterson in charge of operations today.*
>
> *Hidden Glory Ranch is a part of a much larger operation, Silverado Springs Ranch, located just a few miles south in the Black Lakes area. The original 500-acre cattle ranch was settled by the Masterson family in 1914, and the succeeding generations continued to add to its size over the years, to reach its present 3,800 acres. The guest ranch facilities were built in Angel Fire by Luke and Jill in 2007.*

He had read enough and scanned to the bottom to get their address and phone number. Then he checked for flights leaving early the next morning. It took a while, but he finally located Angel Fire on a map. *Whoa! Way up north … and east of Taos! That's going to be quite a drive. I can't waste that much time.*

As he scanned down the page he thought he had seen something about a nearby airport. He scanned back up and found it – Angel Fire/Colfax County Airport. After making a reservation for his flight into Albuquerque, he was not successful in finding any local airlines that would fly into Angel Fire and realized he would have to charter a jet. He located a charter company, paid the outlandish fee for a roundtrip reservation, and secured a rental car.

Between the engagement ring he had picked out earlier in the week, the roundtrip ticket to Albuquerque, and the rental car, it came to almost the same amount as he had just paid for the charter, but he didn't hesitate because Nicole was worth every dollar he had just invested in his surprise. Maybe she would even change her mind, cancel the rest of her vacation, and fly home with him so they could celebrate in style! Getting an extra ticket for the return trip to Albuquerque, and from there back home, would *not* be a problem. *Especially*, after she heard his great news!

* * *

As Nicole approached the hacienda, she could not believe what she was seeing! Neither the magazine article, nor the photos she had seen online or in Carli's photo albums were able to properly capture the beauty of this place!

Oh, my gosh! This is heaven! And I get to spend the next week here?!?!

Nicole saw a sign at a split in the road. The hacienda and registration were to the left, the casitas were straight ahead. She looked ahead and noticed a lady about her same age relaxing on a rocker on the beautifully designed stone patio in front of the hacienda. She wondered if she was another guest or one of the staff. She would soon find out.

"Hi, are you Nicole?" a friendly voice called as she stepped out of her car.

"Yes, I am."

"Welcome to Hidden Glory Ranch! I'm Brendy!"

"Hi, Brendy. It's nice to meet you."

"Likewise! Kay told me you would be arriving soon, so come with me and I'll let her know you've arrived."

"Thank you."

As Nicole walked toward the entrance to the hacienda she was in awe of the overall design. She made a mental note to spend some time just walking around the property in hopes of getting some fresh, new ideas that she might be able to incorporate in her work.

Stepping into the hacienda she was amazed at its beauty and spaciousness!

"Kay? This is Nicole."

"Welcome to Hidden Glory Ranch, Nicole. We're so glad you're here!"

"Thank you so much, Kay! I'm really excited about it. And everything is so *beautiful!*"

Kay and Brendy smiled knowingly at each other, and Brendy winked at Nicole. "Well, you're catching your first view of the place at the perfect time of day as the afternoon sun is just beginning to go down over the western ridge. Just wait until you see it tomorrow around noon when everything is hot and dusty. By the way, I love your outfit."

"Thank you. I hope I'm not overdressed."

"No, you're just fine!"

"We're just about to gather for dinner," Kay happily interjected. "Why don't you join us in the dining room, and we'll get you settled into your casita after dinner."

"Oh, thank you! I ate a decent breakfast but I was so anxious to get here after my flight that I only grabbed a quick snack in Albuquerque."

"Well, I'm sure your appetite will be satisfied this evening. You have your choice of steak or chicken with all the extras on the side."

"That sounds perfect."

"Would you like to join me at my table?" Brendy asked.

"Sure! Thank you!"

Luke and Jill Masterson entered the dining room and Kay introduced them to Nicole. They warmly greeted her and she immediately got an exceptionally good feeling about them. Despite the obvious wealth of this property, they appeared to be genuinely down-to-earth people.

Somehow Luke seemed to be familiar to Nicole, but she could not place how or why. There was just something about his appearance. Or was it his voice? And Jill seemed familiar, too. *Movie stars*, she mused. *Wait! Maybe … that's IT!* She figured it out, at least about Luke. He looked like a cross between Sam Elliott and Tom Selleck! Thick, dark, wavy hair, a great looking moustache, a smile that was warm and genuine, and his voice was deep and controlled. And when he looked at you, he looked *into* you, as if he already knew you!

And Jill? She took a little longer to assess, but Nicole finally decided that she looked like one of her all-time favorite actresses, Jennifer O'Neill! *Wow! I'm in the company of stars!* Luke was speaking to her, and she snapped out of her trance.

"Normally the guests don't start arriving until Sunday," Luke commented, "but since you're here early, how would like to join us at our table this evening?"

Nicole hesitated and quickly glanced toward Brendy who was eagerly nodding her head. "Yes! Go ahead!"

She looked back at Luke. "Thank you. That would be wonderful!"

"And we'd like you to join us, too, Brendy."

"Sure! Thank you, Luke!"

"It's our pleasure, young lady."

As they sat down Brendy leaned close to Nicole. "Have you ever been on a cruise?"

"Yes, once."

"Well, being invited to sit at this table is like being invited to eat dinner at the captain's table on a cruise."

"Really? I feel so … special!"

"You should! I have a good feeling that this is going to be an amazing vacation for you."

"I sure hope so!"

Liam, the head wrangler, and his assistant and Kay's husband, Mike, came in, laughing over a joke. Liam walked off to chat with Luke for a minute, and Kay introduced Mike to Nicole.

"Sweetheart, this is Nicole, one of our guests for this next week. Nicole, this is my husband, Mike."

"Hi, Nicole," Mike replied with a friendly smile.

"Hi, Mike! It's nice to meet you."

"Same here! Thanks for coming. I promise you're going to have a great time."

Nicole's smile grew ever wider, "I already am!"

"Good, good!"

Kay turned to Mike. "Are the others coming soon?"

"They should be. I thought they were right behind me."

"Will you please go check? Dinner is almost ready."

"Sure, Kebr."

"Keeber?" Nicole asked, as Mike walked toward the door.

Kay smiled and winked. "It's my initials, K-E-B-R, and he's been calling me that for years."

"Oh, how fun! How long have you two been married?"

"Almost forty-eight years!"

"Wow! That's wonderful!"

"Yeah, the poor guy is stuck with me," she added with a wink and a laugh.

"Well, from the look I saw in his eyes when he glanced at you a moment ago, I think he's perfectly happy with that arrangement."

"Yeah, I am, too!"

Mike returned a few moments later followed by their daughter, Ashli, their son, Kevin, and his wife, Maureen. Kay joined them at the next table.

After Liam finished chatting with Luke, he joined Mike and Kay and their family.

"Hey, Liam," Mike called out, "before you sit down, I want to introduce you to one of our guests for this coming week. This is Nicole. Nicole, this is our head wrangler, and my boss, Liam."

Liam nodded his head. "Pleased to meet you, Nicole. I hope you'll enjoy your stay here."

"Thank you, Liam. I do, too." Nicole suddenly felt a bit light-headed. *What in the world …? Shake it off! You're a guest, and you'll be leaving at the end of the week!*

"If you'll excuse me," Liam said, "I forgot to check on something outside, so it'll be a few minutes before I can join you all for dinner."

"Need my help? Mike asked.

"Thanks, but no. This will only take a minute. You guys go ahead and get started."

"Okay."

Nicole looked at Brendy. "So, what do Liam and Mike do here at the ranch?"

"Liam is the head wrangler, and Mike is his assistant. Mike and Kay's son, Kevin, helps them out quite a bit, but he's also the ranch handyman, so he keeps quite busy elsewhere."

"So, their whole family works here?"

"Yes, Kay is in charge of guest relations, including reservations, and their daughter, Ashli, works with her. And Kevin's wife, Maureen, is in charge of all the landscaping projects for the ranch, as well as assisting Ashli with the various plans and activities for the guests. There are several others on the staff who work behind the scenes who you might not see very often, but we're all one very big happy family."

"You mentioned that Liam and Mike are wranglers? I'm really new to this ranching experience. What does a wrangler do?"

"Oh, you've never been on a ranch before?"

"No. The closest I've ever come to a horse was a pony I rode in a county fair when I was eight."

"Oh, you are going to have so much fun this next week! You'll be riding like a pro before next weekend!"

Nicole laughed. "Ha! We'll see about that!"

"I'm serious! We have some great horses, including many for first-timers like yourself!"

Nicole smiled and nodded her head, not sure if she was really ready for *that* part of this adventure yet. *But, then again*, she thought to herself, *if I don't try everything this place has to offer, I might miss out on something great.*

Jill saw the concern in Nicole's eyes. "Don't worry. They'll take things slowly, so you can get comfortable at your own pace."

"Okay, I appreciate that. So, the wranglers work with the horses?"

"Oh, yes, sorry," Brendy replied. "I got side-tracked for a moment and didn't answer your question. Yes, they're in charge of the horses, as well as assisting the guests with trail rides, although there are others who help out with more of the dirty work, like mucking out the stalls."

"Oh, my goodness! The guests aren't going to have to do that, are they?"

Brendy laughed heartily! "Well, the opportunity *might* be offered to you to participate, but it's strictly voluntary."

"Oh, good!" Nicole joined Brendy in a good laugh.

"Will there be many more guests joining us this coming week?" Nicole asked.

"You're the first one from this next week's group to join us," Jill replied. "The rest will be arriving at various times tomorrow. You're also joining us in the latter part of our off season. It always gets busier during the summer."

"Also," Luke added, "since tomorrow is the usual day for guests to arrive, there's not much planned so that everyone can arrive and get settled in comfortably. So just make yourself at home and relax! The fun begins on Monday!"

Nicole, Brendy, and the Masterson's kept up a lively conversation for the rest of the dinner, and afterward, Brendy helped Nicole get settled in her casita.

CHAPTER 24

———

Sunday Morning

NICOLE WAS WIDE AWAKE before her alarm went off, but she stayed in bed, stretched, and thought about what she wanted to do with the day. She remembered that Luke had said that nothing special was planned for the guests so her options seemed to be wide open. When nothing came to her right away, she decided to get up and get ready for her walk. *Maybe I need the cool, fresh air to help me think.*

It was a lovely morning for a walk and, with the exception of some of the staff members taking care of the horses, her surroundings were quiet. *Ahhhhh. No incessant traffic sounds!* That was *one* thing she was certainly not going to miss this week! By the time she returned to her casita she hadn't thought of anything special to do so she decided to just relax and wander around the ranch after breakfast.

After taking a shower she relaxed in her casita by looking over the guest packet. No cares, no worries. Her mother knew where she was if anything important came up. And Chandler? Eh. She was going to completely enjoy this week to herself and not let anything, or *anyone*, distract her.

As the time for breakfast arrived, Nicole made her way to the hacienda. As she entered the dining room she saw the familiar faces of Mike and Kay and their family. Kay waved her over and invited her to sit with them.

"Good morning, Nicole!" Kay said. "How are you this morning?"

"Good morning, everyone!" Nicole replied in return." I'm doing great, thank you."

"Just wait for later," Mike teased, and Kay kiddingly smacked his arm with the back of her hand.

"Stop it, Mike. You don't want to scare off our guest so soon, do you?"

Mike looked at Nicole, grinned, and then winked as he replied, "Nah, not today. She'll find out soon enough."

Ashli couldn't keep from laughing. "Don't mind my dad, Nicole. He's always teasing everyone in our family."

"Oh, I see. So I'm family now?" Nicole teased back with a wink.

"Sure!" Kay replied.

"So, is there any part of this coming week that you're most looking forward to?" Mike inquired.

"Relaxing," Nicole replied, as she let out a long sigh. "My life has been a bit jumbled recently and I'm looking forward to the chance to uncomplicate it. Know what I mean?"

"I sure do!" Kay replied. "And you've chosen the perfect place to do that."

"Wonderful! Other than relaxing, though, I'm looking forward to going horseback riding."

"That's the favorite activity for most of our guests!" Ashli added.

"I'll bet! As I was arriving yesterday, I saw a woman with one of the horses in the corral nearest the stable, and the horse looked so beautiful!"

"Yes, we do have some fine-looking horses, that's for sure. But, um, the corral you were referring to is actually called a paddock."

"Oops? Really?"

"Yes. Corrals are for cattle, while paddocks, pens, and arenas are for horses."

"Oh, thank you for explaining that to me," Nicole replied, slightly embarrassed.

"Sure! Anytime!"

The friendly conversation continued throughout breakfast and Nicole felt relaxed and welcome.

The dining area was still quite sparse since the rest of the guests wouldn't be arriving until mid-morning at the earliest. The breakfast of Eggs Benedict, bacon, cantaloupe, and juice was refreshing and since it was her vacation, she decided to splurge and have a second helping of everything.

After breakfast Nicole wandered around the property a bit to get a feel for how everything was situated. Looking at the map provided in the guest packet earlier that morning was one thing, but to actually get out and wander around the property was a lot more fun.

She wandered toward the stable but dared not venture in without someone on the staff being with her. She glanced in the west entrance and noticed Liam talking with an older lady near the other end. Was it possibly the same woman she had seen in the paddock the day before? They appeared to be having a casual conversation so she walked on without being noticed.

After a short while she walked back toward the hacienda, where she was able to more fully admire the beautifully designed patio in the morning sunlight, after having dashed over it so quickly upon her arrival the previous afternoon.

Ten polished twelve-inch terracotta tiles formed the depth of the expansive patio that ran the full length of the front of the hacienda. The roof gently sloped out beyond the tiles, supported by eight-inch diameter log poles set in twenty-inch stone bases. In addition to the four rocking chairs, two on each side of the entrance to the hacienda, there were two round tables, each four feet in diameter and surrounded by four leather-bound chairs. Fans with lights extended from the ceiling and Nicole was certain the lights would add a warm and friendly glow for the visitors at night. The fans would provide a most welcome cool breeze when the weather warmed up. Tall plants burst upward from large terracotta urns placed along the front wall of the hacienda. Smaller plants rose from shorter terracotta pots along the front of the patio. Beyond the patio bloomed a wonderfully lush garden, replete with cacti and other plants native to the southwest.

Nicole relaxed in one of the rocking chairs and leaned back, closed her eyes, and breathed deeply. The cool mountain air was so clear and refreshing! *I'm going to really love it here this week!* She opened her eyes as she heard a couple of cars approaching. While she was sitting there, a few guests arrived and she waved to them as they parked their cars and entered the hacienda to check in. She closed her eyes once again and let her thoughts begin to wander. She felt deeply grateful to be so far removed from the life she had just taken a break from. This, right here and right now, was truly a little piece of heaven on earth.

CHAPTER 25

Sunday Afternoon

CHANDLER CAUGHT THE FIRST flight out of John Wayne Airport just before eight on Sunday morning. He changed planes in Phoenix, and arrived in Albuquerque just before one-thirty. He brought no bags, other than his attaché case that had files from the office to work on, so he passed through the airport quickly in order to get to his charter jet as soon as possible. When he landed, he had called the charter's office and confirmed that he had arrived, and they had the jet waiting for him when he boarded thirty minutes after arriving at the airport.

He was the single passenger on the Gulfstream Aero Commander 500, and the flight to Angel Fire/Colfax County airport took just over an hour. When he made the reservation for a rental car, he requested and was guaranteed a Mercedes AMG GT 53, just like the car he owned. It was waiting for him at the airport, having been delivered by Elite Services Agency in Taos an hour earlier.

Not needing his attaché case while at the ranch Chandler locked it securely and left it behind on the jet with a clear directive to the pilot to protect it while he was gone. The pilot stared at him intensely although Chandler was unaware as he had already turned to step down to the tarmac.

A rental car agent was standing next to the Mercedes as Chandler approached. The agent spoke briefly to him, securing his signature on the rental agreement before handing over the keys to the hundred-and thirty-thousand-dollar car. A second agent was also there to drive the first agent back to Taos.

"I won't be long so stick around," Chandler commanded.

"Actually, sir, I need to be getting back to Taos. A different driver will be here later to pick up the car."

"I don't want to deal with anyone else. You're here now, stay."

The agent looked at the second agent, trying to decide what to do.

"Listen, if you're concerned about having to deliver another car somewhere, don't worry about it. Someone else can do that."

Chandler stepped forward to open the car door. As he grabbed the keys from the agent he shoved a hundred-dollar bill into his hand. "Go into town or whatever and I'll call you when I'm on my way back."

The agent took the cash, handed over the keys, and Chandler was on his way.

He had printed out the directions from the airport to Hidden Glory Ranch at the time he made all the other reservations. Just after three-thirty Chandler pulled up in front of the hacienda and headed right for the reservations counter. Ashli greeted him with a sweet smile.

"Good afternoon, sir! Are you checking in?"

"No," Chandler replied, turning on the charm. "I'm here to see one of your guests. May I have the room number for Nicole Hart?"

"Is she expecting you, sir?"

"No, I'm a friend from California and I have a special surprise for her."

"One moment while I see if she's available."

Ashli's call went unanswered.

"I'm sorry, sir. She doesn't appear to be in her room. May I take a message for her?"

Chandler's excitement dimmed. "Any idea where she *might* be?"

"No, I'm sorry, sir."

"Just take a guess."

"I'm sorry, sir. She just checked in yesterday and I met her only briefly last night so I have no idea what her plans are for today or where she might be now."

Chandler tried to hold back his frustration the best he could. He only had a limited time to see Nicole, tell her the great news, propose, and then catch his return flight to Albuquerque so he wouldn't miss his flight home.

"Fine. Thanks!" Chandler replied sharply. Bordering on furious, he turned and walked out the door with an angry cloud following in his wake.

Ashli could easily see Chandler wasn't happy with her responses, but there was nothing she could do about it … except hope that he would leave. His bad attitude definitely spelled trouble!

* * *

After lunch, Nicole debated about going back to her casita and taking a short nap, or wandering around the ranch a bit more. She decided on the nap because the excitement of the trip, plus the traveling, mixed with the higher elevation had begun to take its toll on her. She wanted to be fully rested in order to take advantage of all of the activities that were offered to the guests throughout the coming week.

She awoke shortly before three, freshened up, and ventured into the warm and inviting sunshine. A slight breeze flirted with her hair, and she brushed several loose strands from her face and tucked them behind her right ear.

"Hi, Nicole!" Brendy called.

Nicole looked around, shielding her eyes from the bright sunlight.

"Over here!"

Nicole turned further to her right and saw Brendy walking her way.

"Hey there! You're here already?"

"Yes. Corey is keeping the kids busy with cleaning their rooms, so I decided to slip away a bit early."

"Good for you."

"So what have you been up to today?"

"Mostly just looking around the property and becoming familiar with where things are located. Then I took a short nap after lunch and I just now came out to take another look around."

"Good idea," Brendy replied. "Were you headed anywhere

in particular?"

"No, not really."

"Want me to show you around?"

"Sure!"

"Over here beyond the stable is the barbeque area. It doesn't look like much today, but wait until Friday! This whole area is going to be transformed into one big party!"

"Really?"

"We have a huge party tent that will cover the seating area, and LuAnn and her crew will be handling the barbeque. It's always *so* delicious!"

"That sounds like fun!"

"And we'll also have music provided by one of the cool bands out of either Santa Fe, Taos, or Red River!"

"Wow, you guys think of everything!"

"Well, Luke and Jill have been doing this a long time and they keep coming up with more and more ideas to make it fun for the guests!"

"I can't wait!"

"Let's head over to the stable and I'll show you around in there," Brendy suggested.

"I'd love that," Nicole excitedly agreed.

As they entered the west end of the stable, they noticed the lady Nicole had seen earlier chatting with Maureen and another young lady near the other end.

"Hey there!" the older lady called out.

"Hi, Pat!" Brendy replied. "This is Nicole, one of our guests this week. Nicole, this is Pat. She's our other assistant wrangler besides Mike. She is also our stable master and works closely with Liam, our head wrangler you met last night. And, you met Maureen last night. The other lady is Cindi, one of Pat's assistants."

"Hi, Maureen. And Pat, it's nice to meet you, and it's nice to meet you, as well, Cindi."

"Welcome, Nicole," Pat replied. "We're glad you're here!" Maureen and Cindi nodded in agreement.

"It's great to be here! And thank you!"

"I'm showing Nicole around the different areas of the ranch," Brendy continued, "so she'll know her way around a bit better this week."

"Great idea!" Pat said. "Have fun!" She then went back to chatting with Maureen and Cindi, while Brendy began introducing Nicole to the horses.

* * *

Alright, Nicole, where are you? As Chandler walked out of the hacienda he stopped and looked around, trying to decide where to begin looking for Nicole. He began to walk around the north side of the hacienda, but after hearing several female voices coming from the stable, he decided to head in that direction instead.

As three ladies exited the stable and headed toward the nearby paddock, Chandler noted that one of the women, who looked to be in her late fifties, was giving some kind of instructions to the other two, who both looked to be in their late twenties. They saw him approaching rapidly and stopped talking.

"May I help you, sir?" Pat asked.

"Yes, I'm looking for Nicole Hart. Do you know where I can find her?"

"What was the name again?"

"Nicole Hart," Chandler replied, a bit louder and more forceful, as if he thought she might be almost deaf.

"The name kind of sounds familiar," she replied politely, keeping things on the sly. "Is she one of the guests of the ranch?"

"Yes, she just arrived yesterday."

"Oh, I think I may have seen her last night at dinner, but I haven't seen her around today. I'm sorry."

Chandler's look of frustration was read loud and clear by the women. "Thanks," he replied with a strong layer of attitude before he turned and walked off.

"Man, talk about rude!" Maureen said under her breath.

Pat immediately turned back and headed into the stable to give Nicole a head's up, but she and Brendy had already exited the other end.

"Let's go into the hacienda for a moment. I want to check on something," Brendy said, "and then I'll show you where a lot of the other action besides horseback riding will be taking place."

"Thanks! I appreciate that."

As Chandler was walking away from the paddock a pickup truck passed him, and the driver gave him a long look. *What are* you *looking at,* COWBOY? Chandler obviously didn't like the look the driver had just given him, so he watched intently as the truck slowly drove on, and noticed the driver glancing back at him in the side rearview mirror. The truck continued on a short way before turning down a dusty road beyond the paddocks toward another part of the ranch. The sound of more female voices caught his attention, and as he turned back around toward the hacienda, he saw Nicole walking with another woman about her same age.

"Nicole!" Chandler called out excitedly.

Nicole was startled and froze where she stood, facing the hacienda. Brendy turned quickly toward the stranger.

"Nicole! Over here!" Chandler called out louder.

Pat suddenly emerged from the stable, and she, along with Cindi and Maureen, also watched very carefully.

Nicole's whole body tightened up as if she were about to go into battle. Brendy looked back toward Nicole, noticing her clenched fists, as she slowly turned toward Chandler, who was now walking quickly toward her.

"Nicole." Brendy whispered. "Do you know him?"

Nicole was too furious to reply, but the quick look she gave Brendy said it all.

"Hey there, beautiful!" Chandler exclaimed. "Where have you been? I've been looking all over for you!" Brendy backed away, but not far, keeping a watchful eye on her guest.

"Chandler, *what* are you doing here?" Nicole asked sternly.

"Hey, is that any way to greet your special guy who's just flown all this way to see you? I even chartered a jet to the local airport to get here even faster!" Nicole was *not* impressed. Chandler leaned forward to kiss her, but she stood still and folded her arms. Chandler awkwardly pulled back.

"Oh, *this* is going to be *good!*" Maureen said under her breath to Pat and Cindi.

Brendy looked back and forth between Nicole and the stranger, wondering who he was.

"Sweetheart, what's going on? Why are you here? And why didn't you tell me you were coming here?"

Nicole stood silently for a long moment. She was confused, she was upset, and she was *definitely* angry that he had spoiled the start of her vacation.

"Sweetheart, I—"

"*Don't* call me sweetheart!"

Chandler stared at Nicole, not knowing what to say or think.

"Let me repeat my question, in case you didn't hear me the *first* time," Nicole said through gritted teeth. "*What* are you doing here, Chandler?" The look in her eyes pierced him into silence.

"Well, if you can't answer me, I'm going back—"

"No, please don't go, Nicole. Can we … can we go for a walk?"

"I guess we better, so we don't disturb the guests and staff."

They silently walked up the road toward the farthest paddock. Once they were far enough away Nicole turned and spoke first.

"First off, how did you know to find me here?"

"I tried calling you a few times yesterday morning but you weren't answering."

"I was already in the air."

"Ahh, that makes sense."

"You still didn't answer my question."

"Well, after I couldn't reach you, I thought that you might have gone to see your parents for the weekend, and—"

"And so you called my parents?!"

"Yes," he replied quietly, somehow knowing that he was probably going to catch flak for doing so.

Nicole looked away and sighed. "Great. Just great," she replied, sarcastically. "So, how did you get my mother to tell you where I was?"

"I explained I had something extra special to share with you."

"And this *something extra special* couldn't have waited until I got home?"

"No, it couldn't," Chandler replied enthusiastically. His sudden excitement surprised her, and she looked at him suspiciously.

"Somehow I doubt that."

"Just wait until you hear what it is!" His enthusiasm could hardly be contained, but Nicole was getting more irritated by the second.

"In fact, you're going to fall in love with me even more than you already are!"

Nicole turned and started to walk away.

"Wait, sweetheart! Where are you going?"

Nicole flipped around with fire in her eyes. "I said *don't* call me sweetheart!"

"Is this guy bothering you, Nicole?" Liam asked as he slowed his truck to a stop about fifteen feet away.

"*You* again? No, she's fine," Chandler interjected before Nicole could answer. Her neck snapped sideways as she could *not* believe his impertinence!

She was about to say something when she saw Liam stare down Chandler.

"Excuse me," Liam said calmly, "but I was asking the lady, not you."

"Hey, you don't have to get all uptight—"

"Chandler, *stop it!*" Nicole's look pierced Chandler instantly! "*You* don't answer for me, got it?" Liam watched and waited, just in case.

"Liam, I'm sorry," she replied, her eyes meeting his. All of a sudden, she felt something inside that caught her completely off guard. An instant later she snapped out of it. "He's leaving momentarily."

Liam looked at Chandler for another long moment, then looked back at Nicole.

"Okay, if you say so, but I'll be nearby if you need me."

"Thank you, Liam," Nicole replied kindly, "but I should be all right."

Liam took one more long look at Chandler before slowly driving away.

Looking back at Chandler, Nicole let loose. "I can't *even* believe you! How *dare* you interrupt when he was *clearly* speaking to *me*."

"Who was that guy, anyway? And how come he knew your name?"

"It doesn't matter."

"It does to me! You're mine, and I don't want any other guy getting ideas."

"Excuse me?! Did you just say that I'm *yours?*"

"Yes, I did," Chandler replied confidently.

"Go home," Nicole said in a low but firm tone of voice.

"What?"

"You heard me, Chandler. Go … home. You don't belong here. I don't want you here. I *absolutely* don't *belong* to you! And … you've spoiled the start of my vacation. Leave *now*, before I call Liam back to escort you off the property."

"Nicole, I didn't fly all this way today just to turn around and leave before I could tell you what I came here for in the first place."

Nicole was stunned and fuming! *Oh, for crying out loud! What is it going to take for this idiot to get the message?!*

"You have thirty seconds and then you're gone, understand?!"

"Yes, I'll make it quick, but once you hear what I have to say I just *know* you're going to change your mind."

"Twenty seconds!"

"Nicole! I love you! And I want to marry you!" The shocked look on her face surprised him.

"Are you *nuts?!*"

"No, I'm completely on the level. I want us to get married!"

"Why? Where is this coming from?"

"I'm about to get a huge promotion at work, along with quite a sizable bonus, and my new salary is going to make things so much better for us financially. I want to share it all with you!"

Nicole could not believe what she was hearing!

"Hold on. Just wait a minute!" Nicole was still trying to comprehend what Chandler was trying to tell her. *Marriage? Promotion? More money?* kept spinning around in her mind.

"Is this about love? Or is it about money?"

"What kind of question is that?"

"It's an *honest* question that deserves an *honest* answer!"

"Well, of course it's about love!"

"Seriously? Because I've never really felt like you loved me, really *loved* me. Chandler, we've been together for a long time, and I think it's just been a convenience for both of us."

"A convenience? How can you say that?"

"We've enjoyed each other's company, so we go out together, but that's not love. And besides, with all this recent push for us to settle down I can't help thinking that it has to do with something else. So, I'm asking you again … is this about love, or is it about money?"

"Well, actually, it's both."

"A-HA! *Now* the truth comes out! How is this about money, Chandler? How?! Is someone *paying* you to marry me?!"

"No! Well, not exactly. I mean—"

"WHAT? Oh, *this* just keeps getting better and better! You know what? I don't want to know." Nicole turned and took two steps toward the hacienda, noticing Liam, Brendy and the others still watching from afar.

"Nicole, wait! Let me—"

Nicole spun around. "I said, I don't want to know! But what I *do* want is for you to leave."

"Nicole, I—"

"NOW!"

Chandler stepped back, not sure of what to do or say next.

"WELL? What are you waiting for?"

"Ok, Nicole, I'll leave. I promise I'll leave, but let me just say one last thing, okay?"

Nicole gave Chandler an icy stare, folded her arms, and sighed heavily. "Make it quick."

"Baby—"

"Don't call me baby," Nicole interjected through clenched teeth.

"Sorry. Nicole, I *do* love you, and I'm sorry it's taken me so long to make you aware of just how much. I wanted to share this with you another time and in a different way, but now I have no other option."

"Share what? Get to the point."

"Nicole, I'm up for partner in the firm—"

"So? What does *that* have to do with *me*?"

"Please, if you'll let me finish, it'll all make sense."

"I doubt it," Nicole replied under her breath.

"Pardon me?"

"Never mind. Go ahead."

"As I was saying, I'm up for partner soon. When I get it there'll be a big bonus *plus* a much bigger paycheck, which means you and I will be sitting pretty for the rest of our lives! Isn't that great?!"

Chandler would be dead if the daggers in Nicole's stare had been real.

"Excuse me? You're equating love with money?"

"No, you misunderstood."

"NO, I DIDN'T!"

"But—"

"CHANDLER! STOP! You've given me a *huge* headache and I just need you to go."

In desperation, Chandler tried one more angle.

"Nicole, *please* let me finish. One of the senior partners pulled me aside a couple of weeks ago to tell me that I was being considered for partner, and then asked me if we were any closer to getting married."

Nicole's eyes grew wide in disbelief.

"Sweetheart, he—"

Nicole went ballistic! "STOP CALLING ME SWEETHEART!"

"Sorry. Anyway, he said that the other partners would be more interested in me if I were married, or at least engaged, with a date for our wedding."

"Ahhhhh, it's all beginning to make sense now. All this recent interest in settling down was just *your* way of making sure you get *your* precious partner status and that *big* bonus and those *bigger* paychecks. And *I'm* just supposed to go along for the wild ride, is that it? Well, no thank you."

"But Nicole—"

Her stare bored right through him as she stepped right up into his face. "I … said … no … thank … you. Now go. Leave me alone, and that means for good. I never want to see you or hear from you again. Do you understand?"

Chandler's hesitation pierced Nicole's last nerve.

"DO YOU UNDERSTAND?!"

"Yes. Yes, I do. I'm sorry, Nicole. I never meant for this to happen."

"Frankly, Chandler, I couldn't care less whether you intended for it to happen or not. I'm through. Now leave! Get out of my sight!"

And with that Chandler headed toward his car, with Liam keeping a watchful eye on him. He slammed the door, started and raced the engine, and drove off, kicking up rocks and pebbles, and leaving a cloud of sand and dust behind him.

Nicole turned toward the paddock and leaned on the top rail. She had never been so angry in all her life! *What an absolute jerk!* She was shaking from the adrenaline rapidly pulsing through her.

"Are you okay?"

She turned to see Liam approaching cautiously.

"Yes. I'm fine, or at least I will be in a few minutes."

"Who was that guy, if I may ask?"

"Just someone I've known *far* too long."

"I'm sorry things didn't go so well for you, but it's also none of my business, so please pardon me for butting in before … and now."

"No, Liam," Nicole replied softly. "I'm actually so grateful that you did, both before … and now. It's nice to meet a gentleman, so thank you for caring."

"Yes, ma'am. You're welcome."

Nicole chuckled. "What is with this 'ma'am' thing?"

Liam smiled. "Just being polite, ma'am."

"Well, thank you, but I think I'm too young for you to be calling me 'ma'am'."

"Would you prefer that I call you 'miss'?"

Nicole paused and looked into Liam's eyes, and her words temporarily caught in her throat. "I'd prefer that you call me Nicole," she said softly.

Liam smiled. "Then Nicole it is," and he nodded and touched the brim of his hat. "Are you going to be okay? Would you like me to walk you back to your casita?"

"Thank you, but I'll be fine. I just need some time out here to calm down."

"I'll leave you to your thoughts then. But please don't hesitate to let me know if you need anything."

"Thank you, Liam. I will."

Liam turned and began to walk away.

"Oh, Liam?" He paused and turned around. "Thank you for caring. I appreciate it."

"Anytime, Nicole." He nodded and touched the brim of his hat once again. "Anytime."

Nicole watched him as he turned once again and walked back toward the hacienda.

What a gentleman.

About fifteen minutes later Nicole turned and walked toward the hacienda and sat down in a rocker on the patio. As she sat back, she looked longingly at the peaceful clouds floating overhead. She sighed heavily, then closed her eyes and thought about another chapter in her life coming to an end.

Brendy couldn't help overhearing most of their conversation from across the courtyard and after seeing Chandler drive off, she waited to see what Nicole might do next. When she stayed at the paddock, Brendy decided to leave Nicole alone with her thoughts. After noticing Nicole later walking back to the hacienda and settling into a rocker, Brendy cautiously approached her and sat on a nearby rocker.

"Hey, are you okay?" she asked softly.

"Not yet, but I will be."

"Who was that guy?"

"Someone I wish I'd never met."

"I couldn't help noticing you appeared to be in quite a bit of distress."

Nicole sighed and leaned her head back against the rocker. "Yes, it's been really difficult the last few weeks, but it's all for the best. I guess I was just a convenience to him all along. What a waste."

"Nothing is ever wasted if we learn from it."

Nicole raised an eyebrow as she looked at her new friend. "Well, listen to you. My own personal guru or sage or whatever they call them these days."

"Friend is just fine," Brendy replied thoughtfully.

Nicole looked at Brendy, smiled, and nodded. "You're right. Friend is fine for me, too."

They sat there silently, enjoying the spacious view, and watched as Pat worked with a recently acquired horse in the nearby paddock with Cindi and Maureen looking on.

CHAPTER 26

Oblivion

ON HIS WAY BACK to the airport Chandler called the car rental agent to alert him to be ready. He and the other agent had just returned from visiting the local Lowe's grocery store where they had bought a couple of sodas. As Chandler arrived back at the Angel Fire Airport he got out of the car, tossed the keys to the agent, and headed toward the waiting jet.

"Sir, just a moment, please."

"What?!" Chandler snapped.

"I need to quickly look over the car and then give you your receipt."

"The car is just fine. I've barely driven it, so the gas level is fine, too."

"Just a formality, sir."

"I'm in a hurry!"

"I'll make it fast, sir."

The agent quickly, but thoroughly, looked over the car, and checked off that the gas tank was, indeed, full. As he was finishing up the paperwork he looked up toward Chandler.

"How was the ride, sir?" the agent asked.

"Fine," Chandler answered in an 'I couldn't care less' attitude.

The agent handed Chandler his copy of the paperwork.

"Are we *done* here now?" Chandler spat, glaring at the agent.

"Yes, sir. Thank you for your patience."

Chandler muttered something indecipherable under his breath

as he walked off toward the jet.

The agent sighed, looked over the Mercedes carefully one more time and, noticing everything *truly* was fine, climbed in, nodded to the other driver, and they headed back to Taos.

When Chandler had landed earlier, he had told the pilot to keep the jet ready for takeoff as soon as he returned because his flight back to Albuquerque was going to leave him little spare time to make his flight home. The jet had been refueled and was ready to go.

"Hang on a minute," he commanded the pilot. "I need to make a call."

"Yes, this is Chandler Whittingham and I'm returning to Albuquerque from Angel Fire on one of your charters."

(Listens)

"Yes, that's correct. We're leaving Angel Fire momentarily and I have to catch my flight from Albuquerque to John Wayne Airport that leaves at a quarter to six."

(Listens)

"Right. So, what I need is a shuttle that will take me right to the terminal the moment we pull up in front of the hangar."

(Listens)

"I don't care about that! Just have a shuttle or a taxi or whatever waiting to take me *directly* to the terminal. I want no delays, side trips, or picking up anyone else. My timing is too close for any of that other stuff.

(Listens)

"You're going to *charge* me for that? Fine! I don't care how much it costs, just charge it to the credit card you have on file."

(Listens)

"Right. We'll be arriving in just over an hour."

(Listens)

"Fine!"

Chandler hung up and looked forward toward the pilot.

"Okay, go!"

The pilot rolled his eyes and smiled that knowing smile of someone who is dealing with an absolute jerk, and hoping he doesn't cause any problems in flight.

"Yes, sir. We're all set." The pilot radioed the flight control center and waited for their clearance to proceed to the runway. When the jet didn't immediately begin to move Chandler nearly lost it!

"What's the hold up?!" Chandler angrily demanded. The pilot ignored him, and this pushed Chandler nearly over the edge! He was just about to release his seat belt and charge the cockpit, but a sudden over-the-shoulder look from the pilot froze him in his thoughts so he looked out his window and fumed.

The late afternoon temperature had begun to drop and the slight breeze that had been apparent when they landed had picked up significantly. Downdrafts from the mountain range to the west dictated a northerly takeoff from runway 35 toward the town of Eagle Nest.

The pilot was finally given the clearance to approach the runway where they idled for only a few minutes. Chandler was just about to lose it again when the pilot responded to their clearance to take off. He felt the sudden increase of thrust to the engines and the jet was soon airborne.

As the jet began its ascent, Chandler looked out his window in the direction of the ranch, but it was too far behind him to see. The jet angled toward the eastern mountain range of the Moreno Valley in order to take advantage of the updrafts and make it easier to gain the altitude they needed to clear the mountain ranges surrounding the valley. As they approached Eagle Nest Lake the pilot turned west and then south.

Well, it looks like I'll get one last look at the ranch after all. Chandler released his seat belt and was about to move to a seat across the aisle when the pilot spoke sternly.

"Sir, please take your seat and buckle up. I'll let you know if and when it's safe to release your belt." Chandler glared at him, but the pilot either didn't notice or simply didn't care. Chandler sat back down, but took his time to reach for and buckle up his belt again. Even though he wasn't able to see the ranch below after all, he still looked out the window in that direction.

I don't know what has gotten into you, Nicole, but you've just made the biggest mistake of your life.

As the jet continued its ascent out of the valley with the ranch now far behind him, he shook his head, then leaned it against the seat and, with a heavy sigh, closed his eyes. *Nicole, Nicole, Nicole …* what *have you done?!*

All of his plans for his future had just come crashing down, and he could not understand how it had all happened. Just two weeks earlier everything seemed to be perfect! They had enjoyed a beautiful and romantic dinner at Chez Lafitte's, and perhaps he should have proposed that night. The following evening, they had a wonderful dinner with two of his associates from the law firm and their wives.

Then, out of nowhere, everything drastically changed overnight. That is, *Nicole* changed overnight. She seemed to withdraw from him, became harder to reach by phone, or even texting. She took off without *any* notice for a few days, but when she returned, she *still* seemed bothered by his reaching out to her! And *now,* she's taking *another* week of vacation? Why? *She doesn't need to be here. She* needs *to be home, with* me!

A brief thought came to him and he sat bolt upright! *Could my pending partnership have caused me to come on a little too strong about settling down and getting married? I don't see how. After all, as long as we've been together, it only seems natural that we move forward together. It must have been something else. But what? Something at work?* OR … *someone* else *at work?! That must be it! That's the only logical conclusion! But who, and how did it happen? When she's had* any *free time she's spent it with me! It doesn't make any sense.* WAIT! *What if they were together when she took off for those few days? That* must *be it! But who is it?*

His thoughts continued to tumble heavily in his mind when suddenly something else struck him!

What am I going to tell Malcolm?! He's expecting me to walk into his office in the morning with the good news that Nicole and I are getting married and that we even have a firm date! A harder realization hit him square between the eyes! *There goes my partnership!*

Every ounce of strength suddenly left Chandler's body as he dejectedly crashed back into his seat.

Although the movement was ever so slight, compared to the rest of the movement of the jet, the pilot noticed, removed his headset, and turned his head.

"Is everything all right back there, sir?"

Chandler tilted his head up slightly. "Yes," he replied mournfully.

"Okay, sir. Just checking."

Chandler didn't bother to respond. He let out a long, defeated sigh, closed his eyes, and wished for the pain to stop. Somehow, he managed to doze off for over thirty minutes and was awakened as the jet began its descent into Albuquerque International Sunport. He checked his watch and did his best to estimate how long it would take for the jet to land and taxi to the hangar, and then for him to get to the terminal, get through the TSA checkpoint, and run to his gate. His day was getting uglier by the minute.

Twenty minutes later the jet was taxiing up to the hangar and the pilot could not open the door fast enough for Chandler to fly out, run down the steps, and jump into the waiting shuttle. Somehow, he managed to make it through the TSA checkpoint and get to his gate just before they finished boarding for his flight. He hustled onto the plane, found an empty row near the back, and took a seat next to the window, hoping to send the message that he wanted to be left completely alone.

Due to his mood, the flight home to California was excruciating, and it was made ever more painful with his having to change planes in Phoenix. The only thing positive about it all was that he was back in the air quickly and did not have to deal with a long layover. The bad thing? It was a crowded flight.

After landing at John Wayne Airport in Santa Ana and retrieving his car, he started to head directly home, but then decided to take a detour. Disheartened and overwhelmed with so many questions that had no answers, he drove past Nicole's condo twice. On his second pass he stopped across the street and just stared up at her balcony. *Are we really over, Nicole? Or is your trip to that ranch just a chance for you to clear your head about whatever has been bothering you, and then you'll come home, call me, apologize, and ask if we can start again?*

Chandler sighed heavily, closed his eyes, leaned his head on the steering wheel for several moments, then opened his eyes and drove home, hoping the world would end before he got there.

Chapter 27

Sunday Evening

DINNER THAT NIGHT HAD been busier than the previous night since the rest of the guests had arrived. Once again Nicole sat with Brendy, and they were joined by a couple about their age from Minnesota and an older couple from Nebraska. Both couples were like Nicole, greenhorns to ranching and horses, but excited for the new adventure that awaited them!

Once everyone was seated and dinner was about to be served Luke stood up and cleared his throat.

"Ladies and gentlemen, my name is Luke Masterson, and my wife, Jill, and I own Hidden Glory Ranch, and we welcome you most heartily to our little piece of heaven on earth. We also own another little piece of heaven a few miles down the road that's a full working cattle ranch."

Brendy leaned close to Nicole and whispered, "Oh, my gosh! You *have* to see that place! It's *huge!*"

"Really?"

"Yes. It puts this beautiful place to shame!"

Nicole nodded and whispered in return, "Sounds good to me! But that seems pretty difficult to imagine!"

"Just wait! I'll take you over there sometime this week."

Nicole smiled and nodded.

"As you've hopefully seen in our welcome packet," Luke continued, "we have a wide variety of activities scheduled for you throughout the week. We invite you to participate in as many as you wish, but also feel free to kick back and take it easy. This is *your* time away from work and home and whatever other craziness you've left behind for this coming week."

Light laughter floated among the guests.

"By now we hope you have had the opportunity to meet some of our staff. It's our custom to spread them out among the guests' tables so you can get to meet them on a more personal basis, but I'd like to take a moment to more formally introduce them to you so you can put the names you read in your packet to the faces you'll see standing before you."

Each of the staff members arose, smiled, and nodded or waved as their name was called.

"First off, it's my humble pleasure and honor to introduce my wife, Jill. This beautiful bride of mine of over fifty years not only has my heart, but she's also the heart of our ranch. I may provide some of the muscle around here, and had a hand in building most of what you'll see around you this week, but Jill is the one who makes it so beautiful."

Everyone applauded enthusiastically!

"I'll come and go throughout the week because my main job is running our cattle ranch, but you'll see plenty of Jill because she loves to interact with our guests.

"Our daughter, Kay, runs the guest ranch part of our overall operations, and assisting her is our beautiful granddaughter, Ashli.

"Kay's husband, Mike, is one of our assistant wranglers and Liam is our head wrangler.

"A lady you probably may not see very much of this week, except at our barbecue this Friday evening, is our head chef, LuAnn! She's been with us ever since we opened up our guest ranch, and she and her staff are the absolute *best*! You'll find out soon just how true that is as you enjoy the wonderful dinner she's prepared for us this evening.

"Someone you'll see around the hacienda, as well as making regular visits to your casitas, is our lady in charge of housekeeping, Anna.

"Pat is another one of our assistant wranglers, as well as being our stable master, and her assistants working in and around the stable include my sister, Sonia, along with Brendy, Maureen, Kevin, Shane, Cindi, and the newest member to our staff, Beth!

"Each of you are here to have a wonderful experience this week, and *we* are all here to make sure that happens! All of our staff will see to it to make this week one that you will remember for years to come! I may or may not get the pleasure of meeting and chatting with all of you, because, as I said, my main responsibilities revolve around our cattle ranch, but *if* we do, please remember that my wife and I do not stand on formalities, we're simply Jill and Luke. Now, I've just gotten the nod from LuAnn that our dinners are ready so enjoy, everyone!"

The chatter around the dining room was lively and friendly. The staff members who had not already done so, began to introduce themselves to the guests at their tables, and the guests began to introduce themselves to one another, as well.

After dessert, the ranch hands began to excuse themselves so they could complete their evening duties. The guests were free to mingle around the hacienda, return to their casitas, or wander around the ranch under the stars. Brendy caught Beth's attention and waved her over.

"Beth, I'd like you to meet Nicole. Nicole, this is Beth." The ladies warmly greeted each other.

"How do you like the ranch so far?" Beth asked.

"It's *beautiful!* And everyone is so friendly!"

"Yes, it's one of the reasons I love working here!"

"So, how long have you been here?"

"Just six months, but time has gone by so quickly that it seems like only a month. I was brought on right near the end of the peak season last fall because someone else was leaving and moving out of state. They wanted to get someone on board that they could train over the winter."

"And what do you do?"

"A little bit of everything. I've mostly been helping out around the hacienda, as well as assisting Anna with housekeeping, but I'm gradually gaining more experience working with the horses. Pat and Sonia have been very helpful in showing me the reins, so to speak." The ladies laughed at the unintended pun.

"How about you? Where are you from and what do you do?" Brendy asked.

"I live in Southern California, Newport Beach to be exact, and I'm an architect."

"Nice! Do you enjoy it?"

"I *love* it! I have the greatest boss, and the people I work with are the best!"

"That's wonderful!"

"What about you, Beth?" Nicole asked. "Where did you move from and what did you do before working on the ranch? Or is this something you grew up doing?"

"Oh no, far from it! I'm also from California, but I grew up in the San Francisco Bay Area. My father is in banking and investments, and he expected me to follow in his footsteps when I graduated from college. But, I had my own ideas about what I wanted to do with my life, and I followed my dream and became a freelance photographer."

"Oh, wow, that *is* quite different! How did your father take it when you told him about your plans?"

"Not very well, I'm afraid. He told me I was crazy to try to earn a living that way, and I tried to explain to him that it's what truly made me happy. He just scoffed, and it was hard for me to not take his attitude for scoffing *me* off, as well."

"Fathers can be so hard to deal with sometimes," Nicole commented, reflectively.

"Tell me about it! I don't think he's come to terms with it yet, and he *really* thought I was crazy to move to New Mexico and take a job on a ranch!"

"Hmmm, that's too bad. What did your mother have to say about your being a photographer?"

"She's always been supportive of me. I've had a variety of dreams throughout my life, from wanting to be a prima ballerina when I was 8, an Olympic swimmer or ice skater when I was 12, and being a movie star at 16," she added with a laugh. "I loved the attention I got when I was performing, so I just figured why don't I just become a *star*!" Beth added with a flourish and all three ladies laughed together.

"Did you perform in any high school plays?" Nicole asked.

"Yes! I was Eliza Doolittle in *My Fair Lady*, Marion Paroo in *The Music Man*, Julie Jordan in *Carousel*."

"Oh, how wonderful! You really *were* a star! I'll bet you had a *wonderful* time!"

"I did! I loved every minute of it, even the rehearsals, because I knew what the end result would always be – a great production!"

Nicole noticed the starry look in Beth's eyes and it brought back fond memories.

"How about you, Brendy?" Nicole inquired. "Anything fun and exciting in your past?"

"No, not really. I grew up in a small town, so there weren't enough students for a drama club or theatre. But I played the flute from the fifth grade through my senior year of high school and was a cheerleader!"

"Oh, how fun!" Nicole replied.

"I also loved to play softball and basketball, and I was chosen Miss Brewster in my senior year!"

"Really? Well, now *that's* exciting!"

"It was! I have *so* many wonderful memories from those days! How about you? I imagine growing up in Southern California you had a lot of exciting times!"

"I played piano for a lot of years, and then when I got to high school I quit taking lessons because I didn't have enough time to practice because, in addition to my homework, I got busy with school sports."

"Nice! What did you play?"

"Well, like you I played basketball, but I was also on the tennis team."

"Any school plays?"

"Yes, I was in *South Pacific* when I was a senior, and I enjoyed it a lot."

"It looks like the three of us had a lot of fun in our teens," Beth commented to nodding heads all around.

"I was really lucky when I was growing up," Beth continued. "I was always a big dreamer. Where I lived, a lot of my friends were always going to dance, swimming, or ice skating lessons, but their moms were always pushing them too hard. I was the lucky one, because my mom was encouraging but never pushy or demanding. I ended up enjoying the things I did, while so many of my friends were miserable. I think that's why I ultimately felt confident enough in my choice to become a freelance photographer. When my father started to give me a hard time about it, I was confident enough to stand my ground and not budge. I did it politely out of my love and respect for my father, still hoping at some point to gain his approval, but I made it clear I was not going to change my mind."

"Good for you!"

"Thank you!"

"Have you had success with your photography?"

"The arts are always a tough sell, but I've managed to do all right over the last several years. I had a couple of gallery shows in the Bay Area that went well, and I was grateful for the full support of the gallery owners for their strong promotions that brought out good crowds. I also had a showing in Santa Fe not too long ago that went well, especially since many of my photos were taken here in New Mexico. I did sell some canvas prints of scenes from outside of the southwest, and those customers liked my variety a lot!"

"That's wonderful! I'm guessing the ranch keeps you pretty busy. Do you have any spare time to keep your business going?"

"I look for spare time and take advantage of it when I can. The Enchanted Circle is full of so many wonderful sites—"

"Enchanted Circle? I think I may have read about it in a magazine article, but I don't know much about it."

"Oh, yes! It's the route that runs north from Angel Fire to Eagle Nest at the top of Moreno Valley. It then goes north through the mountains to Red River, west to Questa, south to Taos, and then back to Angel Fire. It's a beautiful drive if you'd be interested in a side trip this week."

"Thank you! I just might do that!"

"We can tell you about some other areas, as well, if you'd like?" Brendy added.

"Sure! I would appreciate that!"

The three ladies continued their conversation as they casually walked around the ranch for the next hour, stopping every once in a while to point something out to Nicole. As sunset was coming, they headed back toward the hacienda to relax in the rockers.

"This is just so beautiful here! This hacienda is so much larger than I expected from the magazine article I saw, as well as some photographs that a friend shared with me. Someday I hope to have a nice ranch style home, spread out in the middle of several acres, and a big wraparound porch with rockers like these to relax on."

"That sounds wonderful! " Beth replied. "You'll have to invite me out there some time!"

"Sure!"

CHAPTER 28

Monday Morning

A BUFFET BREAKFAST WAS SERVED between seven and eight thirty every morning which was fine with Nicole because she was always up early. Even though she was on vacation, she had decided to stay pretty much on her same schedule so it wouldn't be hard to get back into her routine once she returned to work.

Hmmm … work. She hadn't given it a single thought after leaving last Friday afternoon. Maybe she truly *was* on vacation after all! And so far, it felt wonderful! Well, except for the interruption yesterday afternoon, but that was now far behind her.

"Good morning, Nicole!" Brendy called from across the lobby of the hacienda. "Come join me!"

Nicole waved and nodded, indicating that she would be right there. As she made her way through the busy lobby, she glanced at the others milling around and chatting. She recognized a few faces from the night before, but most were still strangers. More would, no doubt, become friends before the end of the day.

"Hi, Brendy!" Nicole said, as she joined her at a table near the expansive windows with a view of part of the ranch and the beautiful Moreno Valley beyond.

"Hi! How'd you sleep last night?"

"Oh, my gosh! That bed is *so* comfortable! However, it still took me a while to get to sleep."

"Something on your mind, or—"

"No, it's so quiet here! I noticed it a bit as I was getting ready for bed the night before, but I think I was so tired from the traveling and excitement of the day that as soon as my head hit the pillow I was *out!*"

"Yes, it definitely gets quiet here at night. It's *so* peaceful!"

"I better be careful."

"Why is that?"

"I just might grow to like it, and then I wouldn't want to go back to work!" The ladies shared a laugh. Just then Beth joined them.

"Good morning, you two!"

"Good morning, Beth!" Brendy and Nicole replied in unison.

"So, what did I miss that was so funny?"

"Oh, I was commenting about how quiet it gets here at night," replied Nicole, "and added that I better be careful or I won't want to go back home."

Beth nodded. "Would that be so bad?" she added with a smirk.

"Well, I *am* beginning to like it here, but I have a career waiting for me."

"You mentioned last night that you're an architect?" Beth asked.

"Yes."

"That's wonderful! Do you design homes or buildings—"

"I do a variety of homes and corporate type buildings and complexes. A lot depends on what our clients want at any given time, and who is doing what in our office. But my favorite, by far, is designing homes!"

"I just have to ask," Brendy interjected. "Living in Southern California, have you ever designed a home for someone famous?"

"Well, not famous like you'd know them from movies or being in the music business or anything like that. However, I did design the corporate headquarters for a bank that has several branches all over Southern California. The CEO loved the design so much that he asked me if I'd like to design a new home for him and his wife!"

"Wow! Did you?" Beth asked.

"Yes. We met together a few times so I could find out what they were specifically looking for in the design, general layout, amenities, landscaping, and so forth. We also took into account the location and terrain and it turned out beautifully! They were absolutely ecstatic!"

"How exciting for you!"

"It *was*! And it led to our firm receiving nearly a dozen requests from some of the board members and executives with the bank."

"I'll bet your boss was happy."

"Oh, he was thrilled!"

Just then Nicole noticed that one of the men who worked with Liam had been watching her a bit awkwardly. She looked away from him and whispered to both Brendy and Beth, asking them who he was.

"That's Shane," Brendy whispered back. "If I were you, I wouldn't get too close to him this week. He can be trouble sometimes, if you know what I mean."

"Yes," Beth added. "I'm not sure why he's still here. He's never done anything serious enough to be fired on the spot, but he's been given a few warnings by Liam, as well as Luke. I just wish they would let him go and get him out of here."

"Thank you for the warning."

"Sure," Brendy replied. "You might also want to make sure you're never completely alone near him, or that someone is at least within eyesight or earshot if you are mostly alone," Brendy warned. "I don't think there's ever been a serious problem between him and any of the guests, at least not since I've been here, but I also hope there's never a first time."

"Good to know. Thank you."

"I don't think you have anything to *really* be worried about. Like, you don't have to worry about him hurting you at all. It's just that sometimes he can be … kind of creepy. Do you know what I mean?"

"Yes, I do. Is there anyone else I need to be cautious of this week?"

"No," Beth replied. "Just Shane."

Brendy looked at Beth. "Um, what about Cindi?"

"Oh, yes." Beth replied, then looked at Nicole. "Cindi is kind of a loner and tends to do minimal work, like Shane. Plus, she likes to hang out with him a lot when she's not here working, or during the ranch events like the barbecues, so they're kind of a bad influence on each other. If you ask me, Shane's the worst of the two. I'm not being gossipy, I'm just sharing what I've seen firsthand."

"I agree," Brendy added. "It's best to try to avoid both of them."

"Thanks," Nicole replied.

"Now, how about if we change the subject?" Brendy asked.

"Good idea," Beth replied.

"Thank you!" Nicole exclaimed with a grateful sigh.

"Are you joining us at the paddocks to meet the horses this morning?"

"I'd like to," Nicole replied. "Do you have some beginner horses?"

Brendy and Beth glanced at each other, smiled, and let out a mild chuckle between them.

"Beginner horses?" Brendy asked, curiously.

"You know, one that someone can ride who's never ridden a horse before."

"Yes, I knew what you were referring to. We'd just never heard anyone call them 'beginner' horses before. They're all 'experienced' horses for guests who range from beginners to experts.

"Ah, *that's* what I meant!" The three ladies all had a good laugh.

"Yes, we have lots of them to choose from. We'll be taking all the guests out to the paddock in a little bit so you can get introduced to them. Who knows? One of them just might pick *you*!"

"Ha! Wouldn't *that* be something!"

"You never know," Brendy replied. "It happens occasionally, so we'll see. Maybe this is your lucky day."

"Well, like you said, we'll see. Listen, I need to head back to my casita for something, so I'll see you at the paddocks?"

"Yes, you will," Brendy replied.

* * *

Chandler was anything but confident as he arrived at work. He headed straight to his office, barely acknowledging any of his associates or staff. He closed the office door behind him, set his attaché case down on top of the credenza, turned and sat down heavily. The prospect of what he was about to do weighed heavily on his shoulders.

He absently looked over his calendar to check on what was waiting for him later, but he knew that every moment he delayed was just going to make everything that much harder. He sighed heavily. *Let's get it over with.*

He nodded at his secretary, Claire, as he passed her desk.

"I'll be back in a few minutes," he said sullenly.

"Yes, Mr. Whittingham."

He walked quickly toward Malcolm Shaw's office, avoiding all eye contact with anyone nearby. Inside he felt like this was nothing more than a death walk. No, he would not be fired, but he also would no longer be in consideration for partner, and it was killing him.

He did manage to make eye contact with Malcolm's secretary.

"Good morning, Dorene," Chandler said, somewhat glumly.

"Good morning, Chandler. Mr. Shaw is expecting you so go right in."

"Thank you."

Malcolm was writing down some notes when he noticed out of the corner of his eye that Chandler had entered his office. He looked up briefly then returned to his notes.

"Close the door and have a seat, Chandler. I'm almost finished."

"Yes, sir."

It felt like an eternity that he sat there looking at one of the founding partners of Wade, Harrison, Winston, and Shaw, but it was merely another thirty seconds until Malcolm had finished and set his notes aside.

"Well, good morning, Chandler!" Malcolm exclaimed brightly. "And how are you on this beautiful spring morning?"

"Fine, sir. Just fine."

Malcolm noticed that this response did not match Chandler's demeanor. His long look made Chandler quite uncomfortable, wishing that he was already dead and buried, just anywhere but here right now. Then he noticed that Malcolm's look turned serious.

"I believe you have something to share with me this morning? And I hope it's good news, for your sake."

Ouch! A knife right to the chest!

"Yes, sir, I *do* have something … but I'm afraid it's not the news you want to hear, and it's *certainly* not the news I was expecting to share with you this morning."

"And?"

Chandler cleared his throat, took a deep breath and let it out slowly.

"Sir, nothing has worked out as I had expected it to."

"I'm sorry to hear that, Chandler."

"Thank you, sir."

"Do you see *any* possibility of the situation improving in the future?"

"No, sir. None."

Malcolm pondered this for a long moment.

"Very well, Chandler. That will be all."

"Yes, sir." Not needing any further invitation to leave, he quickly rose from his chair and left the office. Without saying a word, he nodded sullenly toward Dorene. While he had not been fired, the fact that he was no longer a candidate for partner still made this feel like another death walk.

Chandler was so focused on the demise of his chance at a partnership that he absently ignored his secretary as he walked passed her and closed the office door behind him. His driving motivation to make partner had vanished into thin air. What now? He reached for his calendar once again, this time paying closer attention. His first client of the day was due in only fifteen minutes. He had to get himself together, and fast. And the rest of the day? Booked solid. *How am I going to breathe?*

CHAPTER 29

First Things First

MOST OF THE GUESTS were mingling outside the main paddock as Nicole approached. The rest would soon follow. Liam, Mike, and Pat were in the process of bringing the horses out of the stable and into the cool morning sun. Sonia and Cindi were close behind with more horses. They walked them around the paddock before leading them over toward the guests and tying them to the rails so the guests could become familiar with them.

A few of the guests who were more adventurous, and probably more familiar with horses, approached them and began to stroke their heads and manes, winning the approval of most of the horses. Others, who were most likely seeing a horse up close and personal for the first time in their lives, moved back a step or two. They eyed them closely, probably thinking twice about venturing forth on the horseback riding excursion taking place after lunch. Nicole was one of those who stepped forward because she had come for the full experience, and was *not* going to miss out on a *single* opportunity!

Nicole noticed a young girl, perhaps around eleven or twelve-years-old, who looked like she wanted to get near the horses but was not quite sure.

"It's okay, sweetheart," her mother said as she knelt next to her daughter. "We'll be right next to you the whole time."

"But they're so big. And what if they bite?" the young girl said, leaning back closely into her mother's arms.

Liam was standing close by, calmly stroking one of the horses, and overheard their conversation. Nicole watched as Liam glanced at the father, looking for some sort of recognition. The father smiled and nodded his head slightly, and Liam, waiting for just that signal, responded in kind.

"Hi, there," Liam said as he leaned against the rail. "What's your name?"

The young girl looked up at her mother who nodded that it was okay to respond to the man. "Emma, sir."

"Hi, Emma. I'm Liam."

"Liam? That's a different name," she replied with a cute, but nervous smile.

"It's short for William. Some guys go by William, Willy, Bill, or Billy. I like Liam," he replied with a casual shrug of his shoulders.

Emma's eyes brightened as her smile grew bigger. "I like it, too!" she replied enthusiastically.

"Well, thank you, Emma. So, would you like to meet one of our horses?"

Emma brought her hands up and held them together under her chin and nodded her head shyly.

"Well, good. Emma, this is Luna. Luna, this is Emma. Say hi to Emma, Luna." At Liam's gentle command Luna nodded her big head up and down, making Emma giggle.

"Luna is a twelve-year-old mare—"

"Twelve years old?!" Emma asked, her eyes growing big! "I'm going to be twelve on Friday! Oops! I'm sorry, Liam. I didn't mean to interrupt."

"Really? That's great, Emma!" Liam replied with a big grin. "And I don't mind your interrupting. It's okay to be excited about that."

"Emma has a friend who came here last year and had a wonderful time," her father explained. "Ever since then, all Emma has wanted to do was come here and ride a horse. So, we decided to surprise her with this special birthday trip."

"Hey, that's great!"

"By the way, we're the Stafford's. I'm Adam, and this is my wife, Carolyn."

"It's nice to meet you both," Liam said as he smiled, tipped his head forward, and touched the brim of his hat. Then, looking back at Emma he added, "And thank you for coming here to celebrate your birthday, Emma. I hope this week will be all you hope and wish it to be."

"Thank you, Liam! It's already starting off great!"

"I'm so glad to hear that. Now, Luna is really gentle. Would you like to come up and touch her?"

Once again, Emma looked up at her mother, and then to her father, and they both nodded that it would be okay.

"We'll be right next to you, sweetie," her mother assured her.

Emma took a tentative step, just to see how Luna might react. Luna remained calm, so Emma took another, more adventurous step, and Luna still stayed calm. She slowly moved her hands from under her chin and cautiously reached forward with her right hand, waiting to see if Luna might try to bite her. Liam was holding Luna's reins gently, but securely. As Emma touched the side of her head Luna pulled up slightly and nodded, causing Emma to jerk her hand away.

"It's okay, Emma. That was Luna's way of showing you she likes you," Liam said calmly.

"Really? She wasn't going to bite me?"

"No. Did you notice that she moved her head the same way when I introduced you to her and asked her to say hi?"

"Oh, yeah! You're right! So, you think she likes me?"

"I really do, Emma. Would you like to try again?"

"May I?"

"Yes, you may," Liam replied with a kind smile.

This time Liam pulled down gently on Luna's reins, bringing her head lower toward Emma. She slowly moved her hand toward Luna's head and gently stroked it between her ears, making them twitch, and causing Emma to giggle. She was prepared for Luna to nod in approval this time and Luna didn't disappoint her. Emma squealed with glee!

"She likes me!" Emma exclaimed with joy!

"She sure does," Liam replied. He eased up on Luna's reins and Luna nodded her head several times. Emma couldn't stop giggling.

"I love you, Luna!" The mare nodded again.

"It looks like you've made a friend for life, Emma," Liam said with a wink.

"Thank you so much, Liam," Emma's mother, Carolyn, said warmly.

"My pleasure, ma'am," Liam replied with a nod.

"Now, Emma, how would you like to give Luna a cookie?"

Emma's eyes grew wide in anticipation! "Really?"

"Sure! Just hold out your hand and lay it as flat as you can make it."

"Like this?"

"That's perfect! Now, after I place the cookie in your hand, keep it stretched out flat and raise your hand to Luna's mouth. You won't have to worry about her biting you because she'll take the cookie from your hand with her lips. It'll probably tickle." Emma giggled in anticipation.

Luna leaned down toward Emma's hand and snatched the cookie with her lips, just as Liam had described. As Luna's lips brushed across her hands, Emma squealed and laughed!

"Oh, my gosh! That was so much fun!"

"I thought you'd enjoy that."

"Thank you," Emma's father, Adam, said. "You don't know how much this means to her, and to us."

Liam nodded and touched the brim of his hat. "It's my pleasure, Adam."

The interaction between Liam, Emma, and Luna had attracted the attention of the other guests. Seeing how gentle Luna was, the guests who had been a bit hesitant to be near the horses had begun to move a bit closer to the paddock.

"You're really good with children," Nicole said, as she stepped closer to Liam.

"Thanks."

"Where'd you learn that?"

"What, to be gentle with them? It was a long time ago," Liam replied without elaborating. Nicole was curious, but chose not to press him. At least not now.

Mike, Pat, Cindi, and Sonia were having similar results with the guests approaching the horses they had brought to the rail. Perhaps they would have even more guests choosing to go for the afternoon ride after all.

Nicole watched Liam carefully as he interacted with the other guests. His handsome features, combined with a warm smile and easy-going nature, had attracted her when he was there for her when dealing with Chandler yesterday. The more she saw of him, and the more time she spent around him, the more she felt assured that someday she would find a true gentleman like Liam for herself. But that would still be some time in the future. For now, she would simply enjoy the view.

Chapter 30

Shane

SHANE WAS NOT FARING well on his chores as he was definitely distracted by a certain pretty guest with strawberry blonde hair that shimmered in the sunlight. He did not want to cause any trouble, especially after the intense warning he'd received from Liam a month earlier, but there was no harm in looking, right? Besides, chances were pretty good that their paths would cross at least once during the week. *And,* Shane thought, *the sooner the better. Ya never know what good might come from it!*

With the mucking of the stalls done, and with the guests receiving their briefing about the horses, Shane was busy making sure the saddles, blankets, and tack were ready for the first ride of the week. He always thought that mucking the stalls and paddocks was beneath him. He had applied for the head wrangler job long before Liam showed up, and felt that it should have been his. After all, he'd been working at the ranch for over three years before Liam showed his face around here, so it was only right that he should have been given the position instead of it going to that lousy outsider. By all rights he had *earned* it! He had resented Liam from the day he took over, always bossing him around, and being a royal pain. *Maybe someday I'll ...* he let the thought hang in the air.

While Liam and the others were sharing the ins and outs of being around the horses with the guests, Shane was working behind the scenes. *I do all the work, and* he *gets all the glory and attention. If those folks only knew—*

"Hey, Shane! How's it's goin'?" Cindi asked exuberantly.

Shane was startled out of his thoughts by her question.

"Huh? Oh, good. And you?"

"Doin' okay. Did I catch you lost in thought again?"

"No! I was …," Shane paused as he let out a long sigh. "Yeah, you caught me."

"Where were you this time?"

"Oh, I don't know," he responded with a shrug, trying to hide his embarrassment.

"Are you sure? You had a look on your face like you were upset or angry about something or with someone."

"Dang, lady! When did you become a mind reader?"

"So, am I right?"

"Yeah, I guess so."

"So?"

"So what?"

"So, what's got you all riled up?"

"Nothin'."

"Yeah, right. Come on, spill it."

"I'd rather not. At least not while …," he paused again as he looked quickly toward the paddock and then back toward Cindi again.

"While what?" she pushed again.

Shane let out another long sigh.

"Nothing, okay?!" he replied tersely.

Cindi could see he was starting to get worked up over her line of questioning, so she changed the subject.

"It looks like we have another pretty good group this week."

"I haven't really paid that much attention. They all seem to be the same. They all want the ranch experience without the commitment."

"What's wrong with that?"

"Nothin', I guess," Shane replied dismissively.

"Anyway, they're mostly families and couples, and one single woman."

"Yeah? I hadn't noticed."

"Yeah, right! That's not like you to not notice a good-looking single woman."

"Maybe."

"Oh, come on, Shane! You can't stand here and tell me you haven't noticed her. I know you all too well."

"Maybe I don't care."

"Since when."

"Since I heard about her arguing with some guy yesterday."

"A-HA! You *have* noticed her!"

"So? I'm not going to do anything about it."

"Why not? Is she too much for you?"

"Ha! Guess again."

"Then what?"

"Why do *you* care?"

"Well, first you said you hadn't noticed her, then you said you'd heard about her arguing with some guy yesterday, so now I think she's got you twisted in a knot."

"Not a chance!"

"Oh, yeah? Prove it," Cindi replied smugly.

"Why? Just to prove you're right about your *theory*?"

"Yeah, something like that."

"Well, forget it."

Cindi eyed Shane closely, knowing full well that she'd hit the mark, and that was satisfaction enough for her. For now.

CHAPTER 31

First Ride

AFTER LUNCH, LIAM AND his crew brought all the horses out of the stable and moved them to the arena to get ready for the first ride of the week. The larger area would make it possible for the guests to more comfortably and personally meet the horses.

Nicole was leaning against the rail of the arena admiring one of the nearby horses when Liam approached.

"See one you like?"

"Yes! The one with the kind of silvery reddish coat."

"That's Calypso, and she's a strawberry roan quarter horse."

"A what? What's a roan?"

Liam smiled. "See the white hairs mixed in evenly with the strawberry-colored hairs?"

"Yes."

"That distinguishes it as a roan. And a quarter horse has nothing to do with its size. As you can see it's similar in height to the rest of the horses. And you'll see more in a few minutes when I bring out my horse, Wildfire. Her description as a quarter horse has to do with her speed as a racehorse."

Nicole's eyes got big. "Um, does this mean that Calypso is going to go really fast if I do or say something wrong while I'm riding her?"

"Yes."

"WHAT?!"

Liam laughed and winked. "Just kidding. Each of our horses is trained to be a trail horse, which means that no matter who rides them, adult or child, they'll take everything nice and easy."

Nicole let out a relieved sigh. "Oh, thank goodness! But, you sure had me there for a moment."

"Just a bit of ranch humor," Liam added with another wink and a tip of his hat.

When it looked like all of the guests who wished to join the horseback riding activity that day had gathered, Liam walked toward the center of the arena to give them instructions.

"Good afternoon, everyone. As most of you know by now my name is Liam. I'm the head wrangler, and along with my assistants, Mike and Pat, and Pat's assistants, Cindi and Sonia, we'll be preparing you this afternoon for our first ride of the week.

"We take the horses out each day, weather permitting, and follow different trails here in the valley, as well as up into the mountains to the east. In order for you to get used to the horses and the experience of riding them, especially for the first timers, we'll take the main valley trail this afternoon. I hope each of you have had a hearty lunch, because we may or may not make it back in time for dinner."

The look on the guests' faces and the murmuring was exactly what he was hoping for.

"He's just kidding!" yelled Pat, as Liam cracked a knowing smile. Nicole smiled to herself and took note of another example of his sly humor.

"We'll be opening the gate to the arena shortly and will gradually be bringing each of you in so as not to spook the horses. Please remember as you enter to walk slowly. As you do this, both you and your horse will get along just fine. Does anyone have any questions before we get started?"

"Yes, I have one," said a teenage girl about sixteen.

"Sure," replied Liam, "what would you like to know?"

"This is my first time riding a horse and I'm wondering how safe it is?" As Liam was about to answer he noticed several heads nodding in acknowledgement of her question.

"Excellent question, which, it looks like, is on the minds of several other guests this afternoon." Even more heads nodded.

"Each of the horses you see have been with us for an average of ten years. They've taken hundreds of guests, young and old alike, on each of these trails, so everything is completely familiar to them, and they're used to being around a variety of people.

"As I mentioned a few moments ago, we'll be on the main valley trail this afternoon. We'll take everything nice and easy because we just want you to get used to being on horseback. Does that answer your question?"

"Yes, thank you," the young lady replied.

Liam nodded and gave her a wink. Nicole noticed the young lady smile back through a slight blush.

"Any other questions? Okay, one more thing I want to mention before you join us in the arena. As you walk up to the horses make sure they can see you. They're used to being around lots of people, but it's always safe to be cautious and not approach them from behind. Now, if there are no more questions, then just head over to the gate and I'll have Mike open it and allow you to calmly join the horses." As the gate opened, each of the guests gradually entered, some more cautiously than others. Several seemed to approach and stay with just one horse, while others wandered from horse to horse.

Nicole made her way directly to Calypso, and as she approached, Calypso gave her a double nod.

"Hi, girl, I'm Nicole," she said as she slowly and gently reached up to pat Calypso on the side of her neck. Calypso remained still with the exception of a slight sway of her head and the swish of her long tail.

"We're going to be good friends, okay?"

Calypso nodded her head twice. This made Nicole smile like a little girl!

"She likes you!" Liam said as he approached from behind Nicole, making her jump.

"So, does approaching from the front apply to humans, too? Because you just startled me!"

"Sorry about that. I'll be more attentive next time."

"Thank you," Nicole replied with a sly smile.

"Would you like a few more minutes with her before I help you up into the saddle?"

Nicole looked back at Calypso, meeting her eyes. "Yes, I would. Thank you," she replied without breaking her connection with her horse.

"Very well. I'll leave you two to get better acquainted."

As Liam walked off to talk with another guest, Nicole continued to look into Calypso's eyes. Was it just wishful thinking or her imagination? Was Calypso wishing she could talk to this pretty lady who was about to climb into the saddle strapped to her back? Either way, Nicole felt there was the beginning of a special bond between them, and she would just have to wait to see how the rest of the week went for the two of them.

Over the next half hour Liam, Mike, and Pat went from horse to horse to share basic riding instructions with each of the guests. Cindi and Sonia remained close to assist as necessary. When that was complete, they began helping the guests into the saddles of the horses they had chosen while Liam returned to the stable to get Wildfire ready for the ride. Once that was accomplished they gradually moved each of the guests into a line, Brendy opened the gate, and Liam led the guests out. Emma was sitting tall, proud, and excited, although still a bit nervous, in her saddle on Luna with her parents close behind. Mike took his place near the middle of the group on Rocky, then Pat mounted her horse, Domino. After Brendy exited the arena on foot she closed the gate.

"You're not joining us, Brendy?" Nicole asked.

"Not this time. I have things I need to do, but have a great ride!"

"Thank you! I will!"

As the ride began Nicole looked forward and saw Liam on Wildfire. *Oh, my GOSH!* she thought. *Wildfire is so beautiful!* She sighed and wondered if there might be any opportunity for just the two of them to go for a ride sometime. *A girl can wish!*

Pat pulled in behind Nicole and they were off on a wonderful adventure!

Monday Evening

AFTER ANOTHER WONDERFUL DINNER, Brendy asked Nicole if she might be planning to participate in the Games Night event that would be starting in an hour. When Nicole acknowledged that she wasn't and that her evening was free, Brendy asked if she'd like to take a drive to see the other ranch. Nicole enthusiastically agreed.

As they headed south on Highway 434 Brendy proceeded to give Nicole a quick description of the village of Angel Fire, including where she could get great meals if she wanted to try something different than those being served at the ranch. She also pointed out the local grocery store in case she might need anything she may have forgotten to bring from home. She filled her in on the Angel Fire Resort and the amazing skiing that people come from all over the southwest and beyond to enjoy every winter.

"Luke and Jill started opening the ranch for winter visitors to take advantage of the overflow from the Resort and other facilities in the area. The ranch soon became the talk of the town!"

"That's wonderful!"

"Tell me about it! When Beth first started, she told me she had read up on the ranch before submitting her application, but hadn't heard about how active the ranch was during the winter. She thought that after being hired she would have the winter to learn everything she would need to know before the ranch opens up for our peak season in a little over a week. However, last winter was our first year to offer a winter package for skiers, so she had to work extra hard to catch on. She was amazing!"

"Even though I've just met her, she seems like she could handle anything that comes her way, especially after she described standing up to her father when she chose a different career path than what he wanted for her."

"I agree! She's become a wonderful asset for the ranch. Oh, coming up on the right is the Angel Fire Country Club."

"Nice! If my parents ever decide to come here for a vacation, I'm sure my dad would *love* to check it out!"

"I'm sure he would."

"So how big is the ranch you're taking me to see."

"Oh, my gosh! It's huge! *So* much larger than Hidden Glory. You'll soon see part of the ranch ahead on the right. I'll take you past the main road that leads into the ranch. Then we'll go further to where there's an overlook that gives you a commanding view of the whole ranch."

"I can't wait!"

Nicole was certainly enjoying taking in all the sights as they continued through the mountain pass from Angel Fire heading south.

"Okay, if you look to your right, you'll be able to see part of the ranch up ahead. After another turn or two you'll get an even better look at it."

"Well, from what I can see so far, it looks wonderful!"

"Just wait!"

Brendy smiled broadly in anticipation of Nicole's reaction as they rounded the last turn before the ranch came into proper view.

"Oh, my gosh!"

"Hang on. You'll get a better view of it in a couple minutes when we get to the overlook."

"Really? Well, *hurry!*" Brendy started to laugh and Nicole joined in.

Nicole stared in awe as Brendy continued down the highway, making a right-hand turn at a t-intersection to stay on Highway 434, and finally arriving at the overlook.

"Here we are!" Brendy excitedly exclaimed.

The ladies jumped out of the truck and walked to the edge of the overlook.

"Off there in the distance, you can see the main building where Luke's office is located, and to the right of that are the stable and paddocks. And, of course, the rest of what you see in front of you and over to your left is thousands of acres of grazing land for the cattle."

"This is just too amazing for words!"

"I know exactly what you mean. I felt the same way the first time I saw it. This land has been in Luke's family for generations, and it was Jill's idea to create Hidden Glory Ranch. The story goes that they originally thought about sectioning off a portion of this area for Hidden Glory, but then they discovered the prefect spot for it in the village, and they worked hard to make their dream come true."

"And what a blessing it is for people like me who just need a quiet and special place for a getaway!"

"Yes! And for people like me that love working there!"

"You are *so* lucky, Brendy!"

Her new friend simply smiled and nodded her head in response, taking a deep breath in an attempt to hold back the tears.

"Hey, are you okay?" Nicole asked.

"Yes," Brendy replied with a nod. "Just thinking about all of the wonderful experiences I've had since coming to work there and how wonderful Luke and Jill are to work for."

"You're one very lucky lady."

"That I am," Brendy replied with a knowing sigh.

After several more minutes of gazing out over the beautiful ranch they headed back to Hidden Glory.

"So, what do you think about your special getaway so far?"

"Honestly? I'm speechless!"

"Good! That's what I like to hear! And how was your first trail ride this afternoon?"

"It was fun! I loved the horse I rode!"

"You had Calypso, right?"

"Yes."

"Lucky lady. She's been a favorite of our guests in the past."

"I'm sure the other horses are all wonderful, but there just seemed to be an immediate connection I made with her. I sure hope I can get her for all the rides this week."

"I think that can be arranged."

"Really?"

"I can certainly put in a good word for you to the right people."

"Thank you! I would appreciate that!"

"Anytime."

Nicole continued to be enthralled by the scenery as they continued their way back to the ranch. Pat was standing next to Domino in the paddock as they drove by and they shared a wave. As they climbed out of Brendy's truck, Nicole thanked her for the special excursion.

"You're very welcome! I promised I'd take you down there sometime this week, and I figured this evening would be just as good as any other."

"You're right! It was! And now I think I'm going to relax on the patio for a while."

"Good idea! Mind if I join you?"

"Sure, that would be great!"

Nicole and Brendy relaxed on the patio in front of the hacienda and admired the deep pinks, oranges, and yellows of the approaching sunset.

"I can't believe how gorgeous the sunsets are here," Nicole said.

"Well, I'll bet you see plenty from where you are near the beach, right?" Brendy politely countered.

"Yes, we *do* get some amazing sunsets from time to time, but there's just something different about the sunsets, as well as the sunrises, around here."

"Rumor has it that's why this place is called Hidden Glory Ranch."

"Really? I've been wondering how it got its name."

"Well, I don't know that for a fact, but you can always ask either Luke or Jill and they'll be able to tell you where the inspiration came from for the name."

"Good idea. I'll have to remember that when I see them."

CHAPTER 33

Chandler

A S **CHANDLER SAT IN** the encroaching darkness of his condo, he pondered what was left of his life. Both his partnership and Nicole were gone. The only two things that had mattered to him were no longer in reach.

His intense drive to become a partner at Wade, Harrison, Winston, and Shaw had blinded him to the wonderful partner he had had right in front of him. Now that his relationship with Nicole had ended, he found himself completely distracted that day at work. Earlier that morning, he mourned the loss of his partnership, but as the day dragged on, and the realization had sunk in that Nicole was gone forever, he began to see what an important part of his life she had become.

He also became acutely aware of how much he had taken Nicole for granted. It was clear from how everything had gone between them the last couple of weeks, that she had not been as invested in their relationship as he had been, or ... that he *thought* she had. However, the sinking of his partnership had also made him realize that he had been completely selfish, putting himself first in their relationship instead of truly caring about Nicole and her interests, wishes, and dreams. So, what could he do about it now? Anything? She had made it perfectly clear that she never wanted to see or hear from him again. But, was he going to give up without a fight? After all, it wasn't as if he was competing for her attention and affections against another guy. Or was he? The thought that there might be someone else at work came back to haunt him.

Then Chandler thought about the guy in the truck. But he dismissed the thought because Nicole had only arrived at the ranch the day before, so she wouldn't have had time to get to know him. But maybe that guy had eyes on her and felt threatened when he showed up to talk with Nicole. He couldn't worry about that guy now though, because his thoughts were consumed with Nicole. *Is there* any *chance that I can win you back?*

He pondered what he could possibly do next. Nicole's recent actions had made it clear that calling or texting her would probably just make her angry, *again,* and then there was the question of whether or not she would even bother to answer him. A letter? Hmmm … possible. At least he would be able to take his time and say everything he wanted to say, and she wouldn't be able to stop him mid-sentence. Then, it would be her choice how and when she responded. That is, *if* she bothered to reply at all. But … what did he have to lose, right?

With this last flickering hope, Chandler began to feel up to eating something for dinner before settling in for a long, lonely night. He was not up to fixing anything for himself and decided to eat out. He walked into the closet, scanned from side to side and decided to go with everything Ralph Lauren. He would wear dark gray slacks, a white polo shirt, a navy blue blazer, and black loafers. After dressing, he grabbed the keys to his Obsidian Black Mercedes AMG GT 53 and headed out.

Chandler wasn't exactly sure where he would eat. He drove aimlessly through the better parts of Los Angeles for about an hour, all the while thinking of what he would say in his letter. For inspiration he decided to head over to his favorite Italian restaurant, Cecconi's, located at the corner of Melrose and Robertson in West Hollywood. He pulled over and parked while he called the restaurant to see if he could secure a table.

"Good evening, Cecconi's!"

"Enrico! This is Chandler Whittingham!"

"Mr. Whittingham! It's wonderful to hear from you!"

"And it's great to speak to you! Say, I know it's short notice, but do you happen to have an available table for me? I can be there in about twenty minutes, depending on traffic."

"Yes, we have several tables available, but wait one moment and let me check on something for you. It will take just a moment."

"Take your time. I don't mind."

"Yes, just as I was hoping. We have your special table available, and I will reserve it for you right now."

"Thank you, Enrico. You're a good man."

"You're welcome, Mr. Whittingham. We'll see you soon!."

Chandler hung up, checked his rearview mirror, pulled out into traffic, and headed for West Hollywood. As he had hoped, he arrived twenty minutes later, handed the valet his keys, and headed inside.

"Good evening, Mr. Whittingham," Enrico, the maître d', excitedly replied. "It's wonderful to see you again, sir!"

"It's good to see you again, too, my friend!" Chandler replied, shaking Enrico's hand, and slipping him a sizable tip in the process.

"May I show you to your table, or would you like to visit our cocktail lounge first?"

"My table will be just fine."

As they were approaching Chandler's table, Enrico turned and asked, "Will the lovely Miss Hart be joining you this evening, sir?"

Chandler maintained a smile, doing his best to not show any sign of the deep distress he had been reeling under the last twenty eight plus hours. "No, Enrico, not tonight."

"Very well, sir. Your waitress, Ciara, will be here momentarily."

"Thank you, Enrico."

"My pleasure, sir."

There was no need for Chandler to look at the menu. He had eaten there enough to know exactly what he wanted. Instead, while waiting for his waitress, he let his mind wander back to happier times, when Nicole would be sitting across from him, and they would be chatting and laughing about a variety of topics. But not tonight and, more than likely, never again. He looked down at what was always her place at *their* table, and let out a long sigh.

"Good evening, Mr. Whittingham! It's wonderful to see

you again!"

"Well, hello, Ciara. It's good to see you, as well."

"May I get you something to drink before you place your order?"

"Yes, please. I'd like a club soda with lime. And, if you'd like, I can give you my order now, as well."

"Yes, sir!"

"I'd like the filet mignon, medium rare, with sautéed mushrooms, and roasted potatoes."

"Excellent choice, and as I recall, it's your favorite, correct?"

"Yes, I've enjoyed it here many times."

Ciara smiled and nodded her head. "I'll get your order in right away, and will quickly return with your club soda."

"Thank you, Ciara."

"Certainly, sir!"

As Ciara walked away, Chandler glanced around, remembering happier times. *Perhaps it wasn't such a good idea to come here after all. Everything reminds me of Nicole.*

When Ciara returned with his drink, he thanked her and then asked, "Excuse me, Ciara, I don't know if anyone has ever asked you this before, but I was wondering if you might be able to get me a notepad? I've just had a couple of thoughts come to me and I want to jot them down before I forget."

"Well, no one *has* ever asked me that before, but let me check, okay?"

"Thank you. I would appreciate that."

"I'll be right back!" And with that, Ciara headed to the maître d' station and posed the question to Enrico. Enrico smiled, looked toward Chandler, opened the door to the cabinet in the lower part of the stand, reached in and pulled out a notepad. He handed it to Ciara, who then returned to Chandler's table.

"Here you are, sir!"

"Perfect! Thank you so much, Ciara!"

"My pleasure, sir! And thank you for asking, because after working here for over three years I've learned something new!"

Chandler smiled. "You're welcome!"

As Ciara walked away, Chandler set the notepad down on the table and noticed emblazoned across the top "Cecconi's West Hollywood". He smiled as he once again recalled the many wonderful nights he had dined here with Nicole. He removed the burgundy Montblanc pen from his coat pocket and began to write down thoughts that were flowing that he wanted to be sure to include in his letter to Nicole.

He had written several pages, and had lost track of time, when Ciara arrived with his dinner. The filet was sizzling and the aroma was just as he remembered! So, even though Nicole was not with him, he felt like the night would not be a complete loss. He set the notepad aside and took his time to enjoy his meal.

Even for a Monday night the crowd had been large and quite happy. Since Chandler hadn't arrived until nearly nine, it had thinned out nicely by the time he was halfway through his meal. That also meant it was much quieter, which allowed him to ponder more about his letter to Nicole.

Since it was later and not so busy, Enrico and Ciara came by to check on Chandler a bit more often than normal. They each found some special time to chat with him, renewing the close friendships they had built over the last few years. When he had finished, he tipped them both quite generously, and did likewise with the valet.

Home? Chandler looked at his watch. Ten thirty. He sighed and shook his head. *I wish we were together right now, Nicole.* He decided to take a drive down the Pacific Coast Highway before heading home. Perhaps the drive would be just what he needed to finish his thoughts for Nicole's letter.

After arriving home close to midnight, he pulled out his personalized stationery and poured out his heart. At two-thirty in the morning he addressed, stamped, sealed the envelope, and put it next to his keys so he would remember to take it with him to mail in the morning.

CHAPTER 34

Tuesday Morning

NOW THAT NICOLE WAS aware that the nights in Angel Fire could be ultra-quiet, she was able to fall asleep much easier and slept soundly throughout the night, waking up fully refreshed and relaxed. A nice, brisk walk would be a great start to the day!

She stepped out of her casita, and while going through her normal stretching exercises, looked toward the stable in the distance. She heard some activity, including voices and a few horses whinnying. As she began her walk out toward the highway she paid no attention to the noises, but instead focused on the bright leaves, shimmering in the cool morning breeze. She thought about the various activities that were planned for the guests that day, and was particularly looking forward to something called the 'arena games' which were planned for after lunch.

Halfway to the highway, a pickup truck approached and the driver slowed to a stop and rolled down the window.

"Good morning, Nicole!"

Nicole recognized the voice. "Hey, Brendy!"

"Where're you headed?"

"Just going for a walk."

"Beautiful morning for it!"

"It sure is!"

"I've got to get to the stable, so I'll see you at breakfast!"

"Okay! Save me a seat if you get there first."

"Will do!"

As Brendy pulled away, Nicole noticed Liam's truck just turning off the highway and her heart skipped a beat. She slowed her pace and she could see Liam's smile through the windshield as he pulled to a stop.

"Mornin', Nicole." Ooooo, how she loved the sound of his voice!

"Good morning, Liam," she replied with a smile.

"May I give you a ride?"

"No, I'm just out for my morning walk but thank you for the offer."

"Sure, anytime. Ready for another ride this morning?"

"Yes, I can't wait! And ..." she hesitated for a moment.

"Yes?"

"Well, I was just wondering ... um, what are the chances I might be able to ride Calypso again?"

Liam smiled. "I'll talk to the boss and see what I can do." Then he added a wink.

"Aw, you're sweet. Thank you!"

He tipped his hat and drove on.

Nicole sighed and looked over her shoulder as she watched Liam pull away. She caught herself smiling. Yes, it's *so nice to meet a perfect gentleman.*

Nicole reached the highway a couple of minutes later, glanced around and noticed very little traffic. She started to cross the highway to do a little exploring at a small shopping center, but decided to check it out later in the week. She turned and headed back toward the ranch, and halfway there she heard another, much older sounding pickup truck approaching from behind. She made sure she stayed far to the right to give whomever it was plenty of room to pass. Only, this driver was slowing down as well.

She glanced over her shoulder but didn't recognize who it was. From the sound of the engine, she could tell they were pulling up next to her. The passenger window went down halfway and stuck.

"Mornin' there, Nicole!" It was Shane!

"Good morning," she replied politely as she kept walking.

"I'm Shane," he said excitedly.

"Yes, I know."

"Oh, you do?" he replied hopefully.

"Yes." She was trying to keep their conversation as neutral as possible so as not to give him any ideas about becoming friendly with her at any time during the week.

"Um, can I give you a ride to the ranch?"

"No, thank you. I'm enjoying the exercise."

"Okay, suit yourself," he replied, a bit miffed. "I'll see you around."

Nicole nodded without replying as he pulled away.

She looked to her right to make it clear to Shane, in case he was watching in his rearview mirror, that she was not watching him drive off. This view was much better anyway, as she noticed the various buildings and paddocks. And Liam ... on Wildfire. She stopped to watch him ... and smiled.

* * *

Nicole was one of the first guests to arrive for breakfast, and Brendy wasn't far behind.

"So," Brendy began, "how was your walk this morning?"

"Lovely! The cool, mountain air is so refreshing, and there was a slight breeze blowing through the trees. I love the sound of rustling leaves."

"I guess living here as long as I have, I haven't noticed it, but I can see that it would be something new for you to experience."

"Yes, especially coming from the big city."

Brendy nodded.

"Good morning, ladies!" Beth said as she sat down next to them.

"Hey, there!" Brendy replied. Nicole just nodded as she was suddenly distracted when she noticed Shane staring at her from several tables away. She quickly glanced away, then excused herself and got up and moved to a different place on the opposite side of the table so her back would be toward him.

"Is everything okay?" Brendy asked.

"It is now," Nicole replied softly.

"What's up?" Beth asked.

Nicole paused for a long moment before answering.

"Shane," she said, almost in a whisper.

"What about him?" Brendy asked.

"He was staring at me, and it just gave me the creeps."

"Yes, he has a way of doing that," Beth said. "I don't know if it's intentional, but I've noticed it, too, and I agree, it's creepy."

Brendy and Nicole nodded their heads.

"Plus, while I was returning to the ranch from my walk out to the highway this morning, he pulled up next to me and offered to give me a ride."

"Oh, *that's* not good!" Beth said.

"What did you do?" Brendy asked.

"I just said no and kept walking."

"Smart move," Brendy replied.

Beth nodded in agreement.

"Thank you both for giving me the heads up about him."

"Absolutely," Brendy said with a nod.

At that point they got up and walked over to the buffet tables, made their choices, including selecting juice, water, or milk, and returned to their table where the conversation continued.

"So, what can you two tell me about this afternoon's activity, the arena games?" Beth had just taken a bite of her scrambled eggs so Brendy spoke up.

"Oh, they are *so* much fun! Many of the staff here at the ranch put on a show for the guests at the arena!"

"A show?"

"Yes! Have you ever been to a rodeo?

"No, I haven't."

"Oh, this will be a treat for you! It's not a full rodeo, like you would see in an official setting but it's more like several events we compete in."

"Well," Beth interjected, "it's not exactly a competition because it's just for fun. I guess you could call it more like an exhibition."

"Yes, that's a better word for it!" Brendy agreed. "We do barrel racing, pole bending,—"

"Pole bending? *What* is *that?!*"

"Well, we don't actually bend poles, but it's a course that's set up with six poles, each six feet tall and with a fourteen-inch rubber base. They are placed in a straight line, each twenty-one feet apart, with the first pole set twenty-one feet from the starting line.

"The contestant races straight down one side of the poles, and then returns toward the start by weaving in and out of the poles, hopefully without knocking any over. Then they turn around and go back by weaving through the poles again, and then *race* back to the finish line on the other side of the poles from where they started."

"Wow! That sounds like fun!"

"It is! Beth is our all-time champion with a time she achieved just last week of 26.179."

"I'm guessing that's pretty fast?"

"Well, many of us are in the thirties or higher because you get a five second penalty if you knock down a pole, and if you miss a pole altogether it's a ten second penalty."

"It sounds pretty tricky."

"Oh, it can be! The rider and the horse have to be in perfect sync the whole way in order to have a good run."

"Well, I'm looking forward to watching it! And the other events, too, of course."

* * *

After breakfast most of the guests took time to wander around the different areas of the ranch before gathering for that morning's horseback ride. Both Brendy and Beth had their various jobs to do before joining the ride, so Nicole returned to her casita for a bit to freshen up.

That morning's ride took them in the same general direction of the ride the day before, but then it took a turn and followed a gradual switchback trail. That new trail took them up the mountain to a clearing where the guests could get a better view of the valley, the mountains beyond, and Eagle Nest Lake to the north. There were plenty of ooooos and ahhhhs from the guests, and more than half of them were taking photos to capture the moment. When it looked like they were ready, Liam continued to lead them further along the trail and they gradually made their way back to the ranch. As they entered the arena it was clear by their enthusiasm that they were much more confident in their riding abilities today than they had been the day before. A few were even asking if they could go back out after lunch. Pat reminded them they would all be enjoying the arena games, and their excitement began to grow!

CHAPTER 35

Games People Play

THE ARENA GAMES WERE a fun exhibition of the staff member's skills. They had proven to be such a big hit with the guests since they'd been added to their agenda five years ago that permanent bleachers had been installed. Lately, however, the word had gotten out among the residents of Angel Fire, and the locals were allowed to attend for a nominal fee. There was even talk about some of the local residents being allowed to participate in the various games at some point in the future, and perhaps turning them into a true competition. If the idea was to proceed further than just a general discussion, Luke and Jill were fully aware that they would have to consider moving the event to a larger area that could accommodate the expected larger crowds. They had even begun to consider their other ranch for the new arena.

This week the stands were nearly full, since quite a large number of local residents were in attendance. Luke and Jill had assured the guests that they would be allowed into the bleachers first in order to sit where they wanted. Then the locals were allowed in. Nicole chose to sit near Emma and her parents and the area near them filled up quickly.

The different events were announced and explained to the guests before the staff began their exhibitions. The pole bending exhibition was held first and Beth came close to setting a new personal record with a run of 27.249. All of the others recorded times of over thirty-five seconds, mostly from penalties from knocking over at least one pole.

As the barrel racing event was about to start, Nicole noticed Shane walking up the bleachers and looking for a place to sit. She paid no further attention to him because the area around her was mostly full. She didn't expect him to try to squeeze in nearby, but that's exactly what he did. He sat down in a spot that was in the row behind her and off to her right. It made it easy for him to watch her but she couldn't see what he might be up to. She was about to get up and move when it was announced that Liam was the next one to participate in the barrel race, so she remained where she was.

Shane nudged Nicole on her shoulder with his knee.

"There's your guy."

Nicole turned and glared at him. "What do you mean by *that?*"

Shane gave her a wry smile. "Everyone's seen the looks you two have been giving each other."

"There are no *looks* between us. In fact, there is *nothing* going on between us. I'm simply a guest here this week and Liam is just part of the staff."

"Yeah, whatever you say," Shane replied flippantly.

"How about just minding your own business?"

"Oooo, it sounds to me like I hit a nerve!" he said brashly.

"Not in the least. Now, would you please be quiet so I can enjoy the show?"

"Pardon me for breathing!" he snapped, and then got up and moved over to an area on the far side of the bleachers.

What a jerk! Nicole thought to herself as she shook her head in disgust.

Without paying any further attention to him, Nicole was unaware that Shane had found a place further up the bleachers where he could still watch her. *I sure wish I knew how to break her ice.*

Liam put on quite a show in the barrel racing event, and Nicole cheered him on all the way.

Nothing going on between you two? You just keep telling yourself that, missy.

Frustrated, Shane got up and worked his way down the bleachers and out of the arena area altogether. Before he lost sight of Nicole he turned around and took one last look. *Maybe someday.*

* * *

That night everyone enjoyed line dancing. Some of the guests, like Emma's parents, Adam and Carolyn, were quite experienced at it, while others, like Nicole, had never tried it and needed a few quick lessons. However, there's no better teacher than experience, so all of the beginners got their lessons together right in the dance hall, which, during the day, was the dining room.

While Liam was watching Nicole from one corner of the dance floor, Shane was watching them both from a different viewpoint. *Why is Liam taking such a keen interest in her? She's leaving in a couple of days, so it's not like she's going to care about him one way or another. Maybe she'll blow him off like she did that other guy I heard about. I sure would love to see* that *happen!*

Once it looked like the beginners had caught on, the rest of the guests and staff, including Liam, joined them for the next song. Shane, however, stepped further back into the shadows, biding his time. About thirty minutes later Luke came up to Liam, said something in his ear, and they left together. *Perfect timing!*

As the next song began, Nicole headed for the refreshments where she met up with Beth.

"Hey, Beth!"

"Hey there! You're looking pretty good out there!"

"Thanks! I wasn't sure if I was going to try it, but it looked like so much fun that I just thought what the heck!"

"Well, good for you."

"Where's Brendy? I thought she was going to join us this evening, too."

"She wanted to, but her husband had to drive up to Red River to see a potential client, so she's home with their kids."

"Oh, that's nice. I'll bet she has a wonderful family."

"Oh, they're the best! I met them not too long after I started working here. She invited me to dinner one night at their place and her husband, Corey, is loving and attentive, and their daughter, Rileigh, and sons Hunter and Caiden, are kind and considerate, just like her."

"That's great!"

Another song began and Beth looked at Nicole and said, "Let's get back out there!"

"Sure!" replied Nicole enthusiastically.

Shane noticed Nicole heading back to the dance floor so he weaved his way through the crowd and jumped into a spot behind Nicole so he could watch her moves. When everyone turned toward their left during the song, Nicole caught sight of Shane in the corner of her eye and momentarily froze, throwing off her concentration. She gulped, looked away as the line shifted again, glanced at Beth who saw what had happened, and tried to get back into the rhythm once again. However, she felt too uncomfortable to continue and walked off and headed for the door to leave. Beth was not far behind her.

As Nicole opened the door, Liam and Luke were just coming back in, and she walked right passed them without saying a word. Liam was about to say something when Beth quickly walked passed him in pursuit of Nicole.

"Beth? Is everything okay?"

"I'm not sure, but I hope to find out."

Liam turned and looked at Luke. "You go on in, I'm going to hang out here for a few minutes."

"Okay," Luke replied. Then he glanced out toward Nicole and Beth who appeared to be headed in the direction of the stable. Luke looked back at Liam and said, "Let me know if you need anything, okay?"

"Will do, boss."

Luke nodded and went inside.

Liam noticed that Beth had caught up with Nicole just outside the stable and they were talking. He couldn't hear what they were saying but, from what he could see, Nicole did not look very happy.

As Liam continued to watch, he noticed that whatever Beth may have said, it was apparently enough to calm Nicole. Now they were taking a slow walk up the road past the paddocks. He sat down on one of the rockers on the patio and kept a watchful eye on them, just in case.

Shane appeared ten minutes later, nodding toward Liam as he stood on the edge of the patio and glanced out into the mostly dark surroundings.

"Nice night," Shane said, without looking back toward Liam.

"Yes, it is, " Liam replied, curious if Shane's presence there that night had anything to do with why Nicole had walked out so abruptly with Beth hot on her tail.

"How are things going so far this week with the new guests?"

"Fine, as usual."

"That's good. That's good."

Liam kept his eye on the road, and since he knew Nicole and Beth were out there he could just barely make them out in the shadows. He guessed that Shane might also be looking for them, but since he had no idea exactly where they had gone, Liam figured Shane wouldn't know which direction to look.

"Well, it's been a long day for me," Shane said, "so I think I'm going to head home and catch some extra sleep. I'll see you in the mornin'."

"Yep," was all Liam said.

As Shane walked toward his truck, Liam causally stood up and moved into the shadows. This might give Shane the impression that he had gone back inside, but Liam simply wanted to make sure Shane didn't cause any problems when he would most assuredly see Nicole and Beth on the road.

Just as Liam guessed, a few moments later he saw Shane's brake lights go on, and he leaned forward against one of the log roof supports as if to strain in order to get a closer look. As Shane's truck lingered a bit too long for his liking, Liam started to jog toward his truck. He had just opened the door and was about to step inside and start the engine when Shane drove off. He got out and closed the door, waited silently next to his truck, and could now see the faint images of the two ladies walking back toward the hacienda. As they got closer, but still some distance away, Liam came into the light so as not to startle them.

"Everything okay, ladies?"

"Yes," Nicole replied, attempting to be nonchalant. "I just wanted to get some fresh air, and Beth was kind enough to join me."

"Beautiful night for it, you know?" Beth added as they walked passed Liam. She added a telling wink to signal Liam there was more to it than just a casual walk.

"Yes, it sure is," Liam replied, nodding back at Beth.

The ladies re-entered the hacienda, and Liam wasn't far behind.

A half hour later Nicole told Beth she was ready to call it a night, and Beth offered to walk with her to her casita.

They walked mostly in silence until they were almost to the door of the casita. Then Nicole stopped and looked at her new friend.

"Thank you for coming out and calming me down. It really helped."

"You're welcome, Nicole. And thank you for explaining to me what was going on."

"Sure. I hope I'm not blowing this whole thing with Shane out of proportion. I mean, I've only been here a couple of days, and you and the rest of the staff certainly know him a lot better than me, but—"

"There're no buts about it. I think your intuition was probably accurate, and it was best for you to keep your distance from him. Personally, I wish they had let him go a long time ago. I'm not sure what it is, but I heard there's some kind of connection between Shane and Luke. Maybe one of these days I'll be able to find out more, but, until then, I, for one, am staying as far away from Shane as I can, and you should do the same."

"Oh, believe me, I will!" Nicole exclaimed.

With that, the two ladies said good night and Nicole went into her casita, while Beth returned to the dance.

When Liam saw Beth return, he caught her attention and motioned for her to join him outside.

"Whatever's going on with Nicole it looked like you were able to help her out."

"Thanks, Liam. Yes, some things happened today that made her feel kind of … well, I don't know if I should say anything."

"Does it have anything to do with Shane?"

Startled, Beth looked up at Liam. "Why? What have you heard?"

"Somebody passed the word on to me after the games that Shane had apparently said something to Nicole and then moved away from her in the bleachers before leaving altogether. Then this evening she bolted out of here, blowing right passed Luke and me, looking quite distraught, and then you came out right behind her. A few minutes after the two of you started walking up the road, Shane came out, I'm guessing looking for the two of you, or at least Nicole. Then I watched him get in his pickup truck and drive off, stopping next to the two of you a moment later. I was about to come out to see what was going on when he took off. That's all I know, but I'm guessing it's fairly accurate."

Beth proceeded to explain everything that Nicole had shared with her. Liam thanked her, and promised to keep a sharper lookout for anything else Shane might try to do during the rest of the week. He also assured Beth that he would let Pat know, since she worked with Shane more directly than he did.

"Thank you so much, Liam. I really appreciate that."

"Anytime, Beth. Anytime."

At that point they both decided to call it a night, and headed to their respective homes.

CHAPTER 36

Friday Morning

DURING BREAKFAST THAT MORNING, Jill approached Nicole and asked her if she would come by the office after she finished. Puzzled and curious, Nicole agreed. As Jill walked off, Nicole looked at Brendy and Beth.

"I wonder what she wants to see me about?"

Brendy and Beth tried to hide their smiles.

"What? Do you two know?"

"No, not me," Brendy replied, still trying to hide her smile, but failing miserably.

Nicole looked at Beth. "Okay, what's going on? Do you know why Jill asked to see me?"

Beth looked at Brendy who winked back, and her wink didn't go unnoticed.

"Come on, you two, fess up."

The other ladies looked at each other and nodded.

"Nicole," Brendy began, "we've really enjoyed having you stay here this week."

"And we hope you've had a great time!" Beth added.

"Yes, it's been a lot of fun," Nicole replied, "and you two have really made it special for me."

"Well," Brendy continued, but then hesitated as she looked at Beth again. Beth gave her the 'go ahead' nod.

"Well, what?!" Nicole anxiously asked.

Brendy took a deep breath. "Nicole, there's an opening here at the ranch that Luke and Jill haven't been able to fill for a couple of months, and—"

"And," Beth excitedly interjected, "we talked with both of them yesterday and recommended that they talk to you about it."

"What? Really? But I have a wonderful job already, and I don't know anything about actually *working* on a ranch!"

"Well, wait until you hear what Jill has to say," Brendy replied. "Maybe you'll change your mind."

"But—"

"Just meet with her and have an open mind," Beth added. "You never know, maybe she can sway you to our way of thinking."

"But ... oh, I don't know about this. What's the job?"

Both Brendy and Beth shook their heads imperceptibly.

"Just wait until Jill explains it all to you," Brendy replied.

"Aw, come on. Not even a hint?"

"Nope!" Beth responded with another smirk.

Nicole looked back and forth at her friends and shook her head. "Well, I don't know what you guys have cooked up, but—"

"Just say you'll listen to Jill."

"Okay, but I'm *not* promising anything."

"Fair enough."

Nicole smiled, shook her head, and sighed heavily. "You two ..."

"Yes?" Brendy and Beth replied in unison, and then all three of them had a good laugh.

* * *

The door to Luke and Jill's office was open, but Nicole stopped and knocked on the door frame anyway.

"Come in, Nicole! Come in!" Jill said excitedly.

"Thank you, Jill."

"Have a seat!" Nicole walked toward Jill's desk and sat down on one of the plush, high-backed brown leather chairs facing Jill.

"So, we really haven't had much of a chance to chat all week, at least not since dinner last Saturday evening. Have you had a good time so far?"

"It's been wonderful! All of the activities have been fun, and your staff is so friendly!"

"Yes, we have a good crew here. I've noticed you've been spending a lot of time with the horses. Have you had some good rides?"

"Oh, my gosh, yes! Early on I wasn't sure how things would go, but we were all given the chance to ease into our experiences with the horses and I did just fine, especially with Calypso! It's actually been my favorite part of the week."

"That's wonderful! We always hope that our guests go home with at least one really good experience, and it sounds like being around the horses will be yours. And Calypso is a real treat. She can be so sweet and loving, but she can also be pretty sassy."

Nicole laughed. "Yes, she sure can! And you really have a beautiful layout here. The view across the valley is wonderful, the trails are so beautiful, and Liam's been a great guide."

"Yes, we were lucky to get him. He was in high demand three years ago when we started our search for a new head wrangler just before our last one retired. It almost became a bidding war between us, a ranch in Montana, and one in Colorado, but we offered him a couple of things the others couldn't."

"What were they, if I may ask?"

"A complete change of scenery and variety. You see, he'd grown up on a large cattle ranch in Montana, and he'd also worked on one in Colorado. Even though we couldn't compete on salary, and heaven knows he's worth every penny the other ranches offered him, we gave him a chance to try something new – this ranch located in this breathtakingly beautiful valley, and the opportunity of working with a variety of people. Since we're a guest ranch we have folks coming and going all the time. The others were just cattle ranches. Well, I shouldn't say *just* cattle ranches, because they were quite large and he had heavy responsibilities. However, he was looking for a change, and our offer matched what he was looking for. That's why we were so fortunate to get him!"

"It sounds like you're both lucky. You have yourself an all-star wrangler, and he found something he was looking for. He mentioned to me on one of our rides this week that he considers this area a piece of heaven."

"Liam said that?"

"He sure did!"

Jill smiled contentedly, but her smile faded with the commotion she heard from the lobby as Mike rushed in.

"Sorry to interrupt, Jill, but we need to call the vet. It looks like Rocky might have colic."

"What?! Okay, I'll call him now."

"Thanks, Jill."

"Excuse me for a minute, Nicole, while I take care of this."

"No problem."

While Jill placed the call, Nicole began to look around the office and noticed a variety of photos on the walls, many of them of celebrities who had spent some time at the ranch.

"Hi, Dusty, it's Jill at Hidden Glory. When you get this message would you please call me back? I was just notified that Rocky is having a serious problem and we think it might be colic. Thanks, Dusty."

At the sound of the vet's name Nicole froze for a moment, remembering her high school boyfriend who had crushed her heart just before graduation. *It can't be the same guy. Could it?*

"Sorry for the interruption, Nicole, but the health of our horses is paramount around here."

"Oh, I understand completely. So colic is rather serious for a horse?"

"Oh, yes. Unlike babies that get colic for a few different reasons and may last for a few hours, there are several forms of colic in horses, and they have to be treated as quickly as possible. If it's torsion colic, or twisted gut, it can be fatal. Oftentimes surgery is required."

"Oh, my goodness! That *is* serious!"

"Yes, it is. Fortunately, we've never had one of our horses have that serious of a condition, but we also hope there's not a first time."

"I hope not, as well."

"Now, where was I?"

"You were talking about how lucky the ranch is to have Liam."

"Oh, yes. He's such a fine man and a hard worker. I guess growing up on his family's ranch really got into his blood because he's such a natural."

Nicole nodded in agreement.

"But, I didn't ask you to come in to see me this morning to chat about Liam. I'd like to talk about you."

"Excuse me?"

"I'd like to know a little bit more about you, your background, your career, your dreams, that sort of thing."

"Well, I was born and raised in Southern California and graduated from USC with a degree in Architectural Design. Then I moved to Arizona for grad school at the School of Architecture at Taliesin that was founded by Frank Lloyd Wright. Just before I graduated, I was offered a job with Warren Knapp Design in Newport Beach, so I moved back to Southern California where I've been ever since."

"And you must like your job since you've been at it for a while."

"Yes, I was very fortunate to get this job. My boss has been a wonderful mentor and my colleagues are the best. Plus, I'm close to the beach! Of course, my work keeps me from going as often as I'd like, but I have a view of the ocean from my office *and* my condo, so that helps!"

"That sounds wonderful!"

"It is. I've been very blessed."

Jill paused for a moment before continuing, collecting her thoughts regarding what she was about to say next.

"Let me ask you this ... would you ever consider a change of scenery?"

Nicole was puzzled. "Pardon me? Like, what kind of change are you talking about?"

"We'd like you to come to work for us!"

Even though Nicole had had a heads up from Brendy and Beth, unintentional though it was, it was still a bold question to be coming from a co-owner of the ranch!

"Really? But ... what would I be doing? I mean, I don't know anything about working on a ranch!"

"Neither did many of our staff before they came on board. They simply wanted the experience of working here because they'd heard it was a great place to work and make friends. We hired them more for their desire than for their experience. Skills can be taught, and experience comes with time, but a burning desire comes from within, and having that kind of desire to do something makes *all* the difference in the world in whatever you do. Wouldn't you agree?"

"Oh, absolutely! I believe that's why I chose to become an architect. I saw some photos of several homes and buildings designed by Frank Lloyd Wright and something about them really intrigued me. I began to do some research and the more I learned about him and his very unique designs, the more I loved what I saw and believed that I could do the same. Well, perhaps not as well as Mr. Wright, but I believed in myself enough to give it a try."

"Exactly! And that's what we've seen in you this week, as well! You've stood out from the rest of the guests we've had here this week. In fact, more so than anyone we've had here in a very long time."

"Really?"

"Yes, absolutely! The same passion that you've apparently applied to your career, you've applied here this week. The way you approached the various opportunities and challenges afforded the guests, the way you got along with everyone, even the way you calmly handled that situation with Shane."

Nicole caught her breath. "You heard about that?"

"Nicole, nothing happens here that Luke and I don't know about. Now, don't get me wrong. We don't spy on everyone. We just have a well-connected system where the staff stays aware at all times of how our guests are doing in order to assure them the best experience possible. The word got back to us about his behavior at the arena games, plus how uncomfortable he made you feel that night at the dance, so Luke met with him and told him to pay more attention to his job and not the guests. He got the message."

"Well, truth be told, I had fair warning about him from both Brendy and Beth at the start of the week. I certainly wasn't looking for any trouble, but when things got a bit testy with him, I was prepared."

"And you showed a lot of class in the process, young lady."

Nicole smiled. "Thank you, Jill."

"You're most welcome! Now, how about our offer?"

"Well, I have to admit, Brendy and Beth kind of spoiled your surprise because they hinted what this meeting was about after your invitation this morning. They didn't tell me what it was for, only that you and Luke haven't been able to fill the position for a few months."

"Yes, it's true. We've actually had the opening since the end of our peak season last fall, but we didn't post it anywhere until a couple of months ago. There are two reasons why we didn't try until recently. One, it was our off season, so the *need* to fill it wasn't there until now, and two, Luke and I and a few of our staff wanted to find the all-around *right* person to fill it, and we all agree that after seeing you around the ranch this week, *you* are the one we want!"

Nicole just looked at Jill with a stunned expression on her face for a few moments, then blinked, smiled, and said, "But you still haven't told me what you'd like me to do here."

"Well, to begin with, you'll be a generalist, which simply means we'll train you to perform a variety of duties around the ranch. Depending on our needs at the time, we'll either start you off working with Kay and Ashli in Operations or with Brendy and Beth tending the horses. Part of *that* responsibility isn't too glamorous; you may have seen them mucking out the stalls during the week."

Nicole chuckled. "Yes, I noticed." Jill winked.

"Like I said, it's not glamorous, but it *is* an important part of running the ranch."

"Yes, I can see that."

"And then you'll have the wonderful opportunity to work with our grand horse lady, Pat. She works closely with Liam and Mike, and you'll learn some things from her about handling the horses that will really benefit you as you assist our guests. Pat has been hinting for the last couple of years that she may be wanting to cut back a little in her work due to some minor arthritis that acts up from time to time. Both Brendy and Beth have been easing her load a bit, but the two of them *really* want you to be part of the team, too. Now, I know this is a lot for you to consider —"

"Yes, *that's* an understatement!" and both ladies laughed.

"Right, especially since you're *so* in love with your job in California," Jill added with a wink.

"And it's the only *real* job I've ever had, other than several part-time jobs to help out with my college expenses."

Jill's phone rang and Dusty's name appeared on the caller ID.

"Hang on one sec, Nicole. I need to take this."

"Sure."

"Hi, Dusty, thanks for calling back. Can you come out to the ranch as soon as possible? Mike just informed me a couple of minutes ago that Rocky may have colic.

(Listens)

"Yes."

(Listens)

"Okay, that will be fine. I'll let them know."

(Listens)

"Yes. Thanks, Dusty. See you soon."

Jill sighed. "Good, our vet will be here in about fifteen minutes."

"He's a good vet?"

"The best! We've been able to count on him every time, especially with emergencies like this. Give me just another moment while I call Mike to let him know."

"Sure, take your time."

"Hi, Mike. Dusty will be here in about fifteen minutes or so."

(Listens)

"Okay, that will be great. I appreciate it."

(Listens)

"Okay, I'll be over there soon."

"Do problems like this come up very often around here?" Nicole asked.

"Fortunately, no. Dusty makes regular visits to the guest ranch as well as the larger ranch we have just south of here. He tries to stay on top of everything, but every once in a while an emergency comes up. I'm just glad he wasn't somewhere outside the valley. He also has clients up in Eagle Nest, Red River, Questa, and over in Taos. He even has a rancher over in Cimarron that just came onboard. Now *that's* quite a drive!"

"I'll bet."

"But that also proves just how good he is!"

Nicole's curiosity got the best of her. "Has Dusty been your vet for long?"

"About five years. Our previous vet retired and moved to Colorado Springs to be closer to his family. Before that, Dusty worked near Durango for about three years, and before that I don't recall. Why?"

"Oh, no reason. Just curious, I guess."

"Okay. Now, let's get back to you, shall we?" Jill continued excitedly.

"Sure," Nicole replied cautiously, still unsure about what to think about Jill's offer.

"I know careerwise you'd be coming into a brand new environment, something you haven't been trained to do or, for that matter, even *thought* about doing in your life. However, I promise that you'll find it quite a refreshing change from anything you've ever experienced before."

"This week has sure been proof of *that*!" Nicole quipped, and they both laughed. "But seriously, it *does* sound intriguing."

"So, does that mean you'll think about it?"

Nicole paused and looked directly at Jill. Then, with a bright smile she replied, "Yes. Yes, I will."

"Wonderful!"

Just then, Brendy and Beth burst into Jill's office!

"YES!" they exclaimed in unison, startling Nicole!

"Sorry, Jill, we couldn't help but listen in from the hallway." Brendy explained.

"We were hoping you'd think about it," Beth added. "Now, just think about it *hard*, and then choose to come and join us!"

Nicole was overwhelmed by their enthusiasm and started to cry.

"Oh, my gosh! You two are *so* wonderful!"

Then, turning back around toward Jill, she said, "I can't believe how wonderful everyone has made me feel all week long. Thank you. Thank you *so* much!"

"It's our pleasure. We're family, and we want you to be a part of it."

Nicole sighed happily as tears continued to flow.

"I just wish there was some other way I could say thank you."

"No need to," Jill replied. "It's written all over your face."

"Come on, Nicole!" Brendy said. "Let's go talk with LuAnn to see what we can do to help her prepare for the big barbeque later today."

"Sure!' Nicole replied, as she wiped the tears away.

CHAPTER 37

Dusty

"**H**EY, BEFORE WE HEAD to the kitchen, let's go check out the barbeque area," Beth said excitedly.

Mike and Kevin had worked diligently earlier that morning to set up the large canvas tent for that evening's traditional barbeque for the guests. They also set up tables and chairs to accommodate everyone. Liam would certainly have been a part of the crew, but he had been with Rocky in the stable, as he waited for Dusty to arrive.

Shane had also made an appearance and acted like he was involved, but it was more for the opportunity to be noticed by the guests, making it *seem* like he was truly a part of the hard working and dedicated ranch crew. But everyone, including the guests who passed by the area, could see he was just doing it for the glory and not because he truly cared.

As the ladies approached, Mike walked over to chat with Brendy for a moment. Shane made eye contact with Nicole, but she quickly turned away. There was *no* way she wanted to give him *any* idea that she might be interested in him. Shane looked away and muttered something under his breath, which Kevin was close enough to hear. He advised Shane to watch was he was saying. Shane glared at Kevin as if to say, 'You can't tell *me* what I can and can't say!' Kevin cracked a smile, turned his back, and walked back toward Mike and the ladies, making Shane even more mad. At that point he walked away.

Mike noticed Shane heading toward the stable and called out to him.

"Hey, Shane! Where are you going? We're not done yet?"

"*I* am!" Shane replied defiantly.

"Fine," Kevin said under his breath to Mike. "You're worthless to us anyway." Mike smiled and nodded in agreement.

With her chat with Mike over, Brendy had returned to Beth and Nicole, and they resumed the discussion they had earlier in Jill's office. Brendy and Beth kept telling Nicole how excited they were about her great meeting with Jill.

"Hey, ease up a bit. It was just a meeting," Nicole replied cautiously. "I haven't decided anything yet."

"Yes, but you *are* thinking about it, right?" Brendy excitedly asked with a wink and a broad smile.

Nicole smiled in return and let out a short sigh. "Yes, I'm thinking about it."

"YES!" Brendy and Beth yelled together. Their effusive excitement drew the attention of some of the guests who were walking nearby, and Nicole blushed.

"Sorry," Beth said. "We're just excited about something to do with our friend." The guests nodded, smiled, and walked on.

"So, changing the subject," Nicole began, "you two have been here for quite a while, right?"

"Well, I've been here for three years, and Beth has been here for six months," Brendy replied.

"And I'm guessing you've seen the vet come from time to time?"

"Dusty? Sure! In fact, he was just here a few weeks ago to perform his regular check up on all the horses. He's really nice. Why do you ask?"

"Well, while I was meeting with Jill, she was on the phone with him about Rocky—"

"Hey, speaking of Dusty, he's just driving up!" Beth exclaimed.

Nicole froze for a moment, her head beginning to spin. *Get a hold of yourself! The chances of it being the same man—*

"Hi, ladies!" Dusty called toward Brendy and Beth as he got out of his truck. "How are you today?"

It *was* him! Dusty Drake! Without turning to see for sure, she could tell by his voice, that smooth-as-butter voice that was *so* unmistakable! *What do I do?!*

"Hi, Dusty! We're fine," Beth replied. "Thanks for coming. Liam and Pat are in with Rocky."

"Thanks, I'll see you later."

Brendy glanced behind her toward Nicole and noticed her rubbing her eyes.

"Hey, are you okay?"

"Yeah, I think some dust blew up a moment ago and I'm trying to get it out of my eyes."

"Get the ol' tear ducts going to help clear them out, right?" Brendy asked.

"Yeah, that happens every once in a while around here. You'll get used to it." Beth added with a wink.

Nicole finished wiping her eyes and blinked a few times to 'clear' them.

"There, that should do it. Now," looking at Beth, "what was that remark about I'll get *used* to it?" Nicole asked with a slight smirk.

"Just that once you move here from California, you might get some dust in your eyes once in a while. I'm *sure* that's not as bad as sand in your eyes from the beach!"

"Once I move from California, huh?"

"Yes," Brendy replied. "We *know* you can't resist an offer like Jill's. You'll go back, start to work again, and one day you'll realize that this is *exactly* where you belong. Right here with us!"

"You're pretty sure of yourself," Nicole replied with a smile.

"*We're* pretty sure of *ourselves!*" Beth added.

Nicole could not help but smile and shake her head. "You guys are too much." The ladies laughed as they continued on their way to see LuAnn.

* * *

As Brendy and Beth were chatting with LuAnn about the plans for the barbeque, along with a surprise for a certain someone, Brendy noticed that Nicole was hanging back a bit. She also seemed unusually quiet. She took a few steps back toward Nicole.

"Hey, are you alright?" Brendy asked quietly, as Beth continued the conversation with LuAnn.

Nicole snapped out of the daze she was in. "Hm? Oh, yes, I'm fine."

"You just seem to be lost in another world or something."

Nicole thought fast to cover up for the fact that she had been incredibly distracted by the ranch's vet being her former high school sweetheart! "I was just thinking."

"Anything you want to share? Remember, this is your friend, Brendy, here."

Nicole chuckled and shrugged her shoulders. "I guess I was just thinking about Jill's offer."

"And?" Brendy asked excitedly.

"Just … *thinking*," Nicole emphasized with a smile.

"That's okay. I know that making a change like this, leaving a successful career and starting something completely different, is a big decision. Of course, we're all hoping you'll come to work with us, but you have to do what's right for you. We'll still be friends no matter what. And, you'll always be welcome here. So, if you *do* decide to stay in California, please know we'd love to see you back here as often as you can come!"

Nicole's eyes began to tear up, but she took a deep breath to try to stem the flow. "Thank you, Brendy," Nicole whispered, then let out a long sigh. "I think I need to go back to my casita for a bit."

"Sure, whatever you need. We'll see you around, okay?"

"Okay."

"You *will* be joining us for the barbeque later, right?"

Nicole laughed softly. "Yes, I'll be there. I just need to be alone for a little while."

"I totally understand," Brendy replied with a friendly nod.

No, you don't *understand.* Nicole nodded in return, then turned and walked toward the door.

Beth and LuAnn could not help but notice something was up with Nicole.

"Is everything okay?" Beth asked.

"Yes, she just has a lot on her mind after this morning."

"Ahhh, I get it. I've been there myself."

"Me, too."

"And look how *we* turned out!" The ladies shared a good laugh!

* * *

As Nicole headed toward her casita her curiosity got the better of her. She paused for a moment, looked toward the stable, then turned back and continued toward her casita. Halfway there she stopped and took a deep breath. *I can stay back in the shadows … where he won't see or hear me.* After a long sigh she turned back toward the stable and slowly walked closer, all the while questioning her motivation … and sanity. *This is crazy! I know it's him, so why am I even bothering to do this? And what if he recognizes me?* But she couldn't resist, even though she knew she would probably regret it later.

Rocky's stall was near the far end of the stable, away from the road that led to the hacienda. Nicole figured that she could get close enough to the stable door to be able to listen without actually entering. That would eliminate the possibility of being seen by Dusty.

"So, what can we do for him now?" Pat asked.

"With spasmodic colic he needs to be kept upright and walked around casually," Dusty replied. "The muscles in his abdomen need to relax, and light exercise will help with that. But, no more water for him for at least an hour. And definitely no food because proper hydration is important for him to process his food."

My gosh! He really knows his stuff! How did he become interested in this *kind of work? And when and why did he leave California?*

"Hey, Nicole!' Brendy startled her as she approached with Beth.

"Oh! Hi! You caught me by surprise!" Nicole whispered.

"Yeah, it kinda looks that way," Brendy replied with a smile. "Why are we whispering?"

"I was just listening to them talk about Rocky, but I didn't want to disturb anyone."

"Oh, you won't. Come on in and I'll introduce you to Dusty."

Nicole's eyes widened! "Oh, no! Um … that's okay. I should just head to my casita."

As Nicole hurried away, Brendy and Beth looked at each other and shrugged.

"What was *that* all about?" Beth wondered.

"Hmm, I have no idea."

They entered the stable, approached Rocky's stall and listened in to the conversation between Dusty, Liam, and Pat. As the conversation was ending, they walked past the other horses just to see how each were doing.

The horses apparently sensed that one of their own was in trouble, because they had all gathered at the front rail of their stall, as if they were trying to listen in on what was happening with Rocky. Brendy and Beth took their time with each of them, stroking their heads, talking softly, and sharing some love just to assure them that Rocky was going to be just fine.

As Dusty was completing his visit, Beth talked Brendy into walking over toward Dusty's truck so they would "just happen to be passing by" and could say goodbye as he left.

Brendy was married, so whether she said goodbye to Dusty or not made no difference to her, but Beth was single and had been keeping an "interested" eye on Dusty from a distance, of course, for quite some time. As far as she was concerned, he didn't come around often enough!

As Dusty was getting into his truck to leave, he noticed the ladies approaching. "Bye, ladies!" he said, tipping his hat.

"Bye, Dusty!' Beth replied, hoping she didn't sound flirtatious.

"Take care, Dusty," Brendy added, sounding more business-like. "And thank you for coming. We all really appreciate it."

"Anytime, ladies, anytime." He tipped his hat as he put his truck in reverse and backed up, and while Brendy headed back into the stable, Beth watched as Dusty drove away. *Come back soon, handsome!*

* * *

I can't believe it! Nicole muttered to herself as she entered her casita. *Dusty Drake is a vet! And after almost fourteen years he's back in my life! Well, not really* back, *but … What are the odds that he would have to be called to the ranch during the* one *week that I'm here?! I'm just so glad he didn't see me.*

Nicole sat on the edge of her bed, looked down at her hands, and noticed they were shaking slightly. *Now what's going on? I'm so over him! The way he crushed my heart, I could never forget and forgive him for that! With Rocky going to be okay, at least I won't have to worry that I might see him again.*

CHAPTER 38

Shane

LIAM WENT HUNTING FOR Shane, but Pat had a better feeling about where Shane would be and was already with him when Liam arrived. Leaning against the rail at the far end of the second, and largest paddock, Shane stood with his arms folded defiantly across his chest. Pat was giving Shane a fierce piece of her mind.

"That was *totally* irresponsible, Shane! I thought you knew better than that! This is the *second* time you've put one of our horses in danger! What were you thinking?!" Pat demanded.

"I'd like to know that myself," Liam added.

"Oh, great!," Shane snapped. "It's bad enough I have to deal with *one* of you about this, but now it has to be *two?!* What the—"

"Stop right there, Shane! You're in the presence of a lady." Liam firmly advised.

Shane glared at Liam and remained silent for a long moment.

"Well?! Are you going to answer Pat's question?!"

Shane looked from Liam to Pat, back to Liam, and back to Pat. He then let out a long, frustrated sigh. He hung his head low and under his breath said, "I don't understand what the big deal is!"

"WHAT?!" Pat replied.

"I SAID—"

Liam pounced! "We *heard* what you said, Shane, we just can't believe that *you* believe it!"

"Let me finish, will ya?"

The last ounce of patience was rapidly draining from both Pat and Liam's cups of goodwill.

"As I was *starting* to explain, I just wasn't thinking when I brought Rocky back to the stable this morning. I had a lot on my mind, and I forgot to put him through his cool down."

"How could you forget something like that, Shane? That's so basic!" Pat was over the top frustrated.

"I know! I was distracted!"

"Distracted? By what?"

Shane paused, let out a long sigh, unfolded his arms, and stuck his thumbs into the side corner of the front pockets of his Wranglers.

"I just had a lot on my mind."

"That's it?" Pat asked.

Shane hung his head again. "Yeah, that's it," he replied with little energy.

"Well," Liam replied, "since you apparently have *so* much on your mind, take the rest of the weekend off."

"WHAT?!"

"You heard me, Shane."

"But why?"

"We could have lost one of our best horses today because of your negligence!"

"But we *didn't!*" Shane snapped back defensively.

"We were lucky today, Shane. The next time one of our horses may not be so lucky. Go home, take the weekend to think over what you *should* have done this morning, and also take care of whatever it is that made you so distracted. Then come back Monday morning and try again. *But ... *"

Shane glared at Liam, waiting angrily for what was coming next. "But *what?*" he snapped.

Liam glared right back at Shane, counted to ten, then cleared his throat.

"But consider this your *last* warning."

Shane, visibly angry, began to speak, but Liam put up his right index finger and pointed it directly into Shane's face.

"*Don't* say a word, Shane. You *know* you've been walking a tightrope ever since last summer's fiasco at the Independence Day barbeque. That was your first strike, and today is your second. It *would* have been your last and you'd be gone by now, if Rocky's condition had been more serious. So, just take the weekend to work out whatever it is you need to take care of, and be back here Monday morning."

Shane glared at Liam, shook his head in disgust, then walked away without looking at Pat or saying another word.

CHAPTER 39

———

Friday Evening

AS NICOLE WAS GETTING ready to attend the barbeque and dance, she was trying to decide what to wear. She had been in her Wranglers, boots, and various blouses all week, but she thought tonight called for something different, something more … special. She opened her closet and removed her new dusty rose print dress she had worn when she had arrived at the ranch the previous Saturday. She also removed her new, short leather vest and laid them both on the bed. She then reached for her new leather boots, placed them on the floor beside her bed, and headed to the bathroom to finish with her hair and makeup.

Thirty minutes later she was looking at herself in the floor length mirror and she smiled. It hadn't been appropriate to wear this outfit until now, but she closed her eyes and thought, *now it's perfect!* At least she hoped it was perfect enough to catch the eye of a certain head wrangler, and maybe he would ask her to dance. She was ready for a good two-step, but she would prefer a 'hold me close in your arms' slow dance.

What a week it had been! It began with her feeling like she was escaping something in her past, and realizing that it was actually some*one* that she was now *so* glad to be rid of. Then, quite unexpectedly, someone *new* came into her life that, in another place and time, she could see herself falling for quite easily, given the chance.

But was she kidding herself? She barely knew him, and she was heading home tomorrow. Yes, she had been offered a job here at the ranch, but how could she leave her career? Career? Liam. Liam? Career. She sighed heavily and shook her head. *It's been so wonderful here this week, and I'm not ready to go home, but I need to get back to work. Liam has also been wonderful, and he's treated me like I've wanted to be treated for so long. I'd love to get to know him better, but how?* She felt her emotions racing and tears brimming in her eyes, so she took a deep breath, gently dabbed her tears away before they ruined her makeup, drank some cold water, and took another deep breath. She decided to just go out and have a good time this evening and not worry at all about the future. At least not until tomorrow.

* * *

From all the laughter and polite revelry, Friday evening's barbeque appeared to be a huge success. Throughout the week the guests had had the opportunity to bond through many various activities. The daily horseback riding ventures had been a major hit, but they had also enjoyed Monday evening's game night, Tuesday's arena games during the day and line dancing that night. Wednesday was the bonfire and story night by the staff, and last night was the hayride. Tonight they were looking forward to another fun dance. And Tuesday's barrel racing exhibition had been a special treat for Nicole, since she was able to see another, quite intense, side of Liam racing around the barrels on Wildfire!

As dinner time was winding down, and the anticipation of a surprise dessert had everyone's mouths watering, Luke and Jill came forward.

"May I have your attention, everyone?" Luke called out. A hush fell over the crowd instantly out of respect for the owners who had treated them so wonderfully all week.

"Thank you! Jill and I would like to thank each of you for coming to stay with us this week. We hope you've enjoyed your stay, and will consider joining us again in the future!"

"We loved it!" came a voice from the back of the crowd, followed by nodding heads and many more voices of agreement.

Luke and Jill smiled broadly. "Thank you, everyone. Thank you very much. Now before we get things started for the dance, I'd like to turn the time over to my sweetheart, Jill, as she has a special presentation from all the staff here at Hidden Glory Ranch."

"I'd like to add my thanks to Luke's for each of you staying with us this week," Jill said. "To see the smiles on your faces at the end of the trail rides, and enjoying each other's company during our various activities and meals has been so heartwarming. And to see you spending some of your free time just wandering around our property has made us feel like you made this your home for this week."

Jill teared up as she looked out over the guests and everyone was nodding. She noticed a few guests dabbing at their eyes.

"As many of you know, one of our favorite horses became quite ill this morning and we had to call in our vet, but I'm very happy to report that Rocky's illness was only temporary and he's going to be just fine!" The guests all cheered and clapped.

"We ended up keeping our vet rather busy today, because shortly after he left here we had to call him again to head over to our working cattle ranch a few miles away. But, before Luke tells you about that, I'd like to announce that we have a special guest here with us this evening." Jill paused for special effect, noticing the crowd looking around to see if they might be able to figure out who it might be. "May I have Emma Stafford come up and join Luke and me?"

"That's *me!*" Emma exclaimed, as she popped up from her chair and excitedly made her way through the tables. Luke and Jill were smiling broadly as she approached.

"Emma, we understand today is your birthday," Jill stated joyfully.

"Yes, it is!" Emma replied gleefully.

"Well, we have something very special to announce."

"Emma," Luke began, "earlier today we had something wonderful occur at our other ranch."

Emma's eyes grew wide in wonder, not having a clue how that might have anything to do with her birthday.

"Emma … a brand new filly, that's a baby female horse, was born today on your birthday!"

Emma jumped up and down, grinning from ear to ear, and clapping her hands wildly.

"Emma … naming a new foal is something we take very seriously, but it's also a lot of fun, and for your birthday we'd like to give *you* the opportunity to name our new filly!"

"Really?!" Emma eyes grew wide with surprise, as the crowd erupted in cheers and clapping!

"Absolutely! And we'd like you and your parents to join us after breakfast tomorrow morning and we'll take you to meet the filly in person!"

"Oh, my gosh! I'm so happy! Thank you! Thank you!"

"It's our pleasure, sweetheart!"

"Now, we have one more surprise for you, Emma!" Jill announced. "Our wonderful chef, LuAnn, has been working on something special for you all day! LuAnn?! It's time!"

And with that cue, LuAnn began to push out a cart with a huge, three-layer birthday cake with twelve candles burning brightly.

"Oh, my gosh!" Emma exclaimed.

Just then, the crowd clapped and cheered enthusiastically as LuAnn wheeled the cake in front of her.

"Mom! Dad! Look! They did this for me!" she exclaimed, with tears rolling down her cheeks.

Adam and Carolyn were wiping their own tears away as they watched their sweet daughter surrounded by so much love.

"Okay, everyone! Let's sing Happy Birthday to Emma while she makes a wish and blows out the candles!"

Emma was beaming from ear to ear as everyone sang to her. When they were done she looked at the cake, scanned over all the candles, and looked out toward her parents who were smiling so happily at her. Then she closed her eyes, took her time to make her special wish, and then popped them open and blew out all twelve candles in one big breath!

The crowd erupted in cheers and applause, and Emma hugged Luke and Jill tightly.

"Thank you both *so* much! I can't believe you did this all for me!"

"Happy birthday, Emma," Jill replied. "We're so happy we're able to do this for you!"

"Thank you! Thank you!" Emma said, with happy tears flowing

down her cheeks. She then turned and walked back to be with her parents.

As the cheers began to subside Luke spoke up.

"Ladies and gentleman, in addition to LuAnn's special cake for Emma, she also prepared a few more cakes so there will be plenty for each of you to enjoy a nice ranch-sized helping, along with plenty of ice cream!" More cheers and applause greeted LuAnn's staff as they carried out the additional cakes and set them on the serving tables.

As everyone was enjoying their dessert, the band arrived and began to set up for the dance. LuAnn personally cut and delivered pieces of her cake to Emma and her parents, and they all thanked her for her kindness.

Another wonderful week was coming to a close for Luke, Jill, and their staff, and with everyone's smiles it was apparent to one and all that it had been a very good week indeed.

CHAPTER 40

Sunset Ride

THE MID-APRIL SUN WAS beginning to set, with hints of oncoming brilliant hues of pinks, blues, and oranges in the western sky. The weather all week had been ideal, and Nicole acknowledged to herself that she had been fortunate to be able to book her reservation during the cooler part of the year, and not during the hotter, dustier summer.

She was sitting with Brendy and Beth and listening to the great band, when Liam approached, leaned down close to Nicole's ear, and asked her to dance. She leaned back, smiled, and gave him a slight nod. He reached out his hand to escort her to the dance floor.

"Do you think …?" Brendy asked Beth.

"I don't know. I guess it's possible, but he's always been so careful around the guests, always focusing so completely on his work."

"True, but tonight we're all kicking back and enjoying ourselves a little."

Beth didn't reply. She just nodded as they watched Liam and Nicole enjoy a beautiful slow dance, under the emerging stars and a soon-to-be-seen full moon.

From a distance it appeared they were having a pleasant conversation. Liam was probably just asking Nicole if she had enjoyed her stay at the ranch, and she was probably replying in return that she had. He, no doubt, asked her what her favorite parts of the week were, and she was sure to have told him about the trail rides, line dancing, and the staff's horsemanship exhibition at the arena. Liam's smile seemed reserved, almost cool, while Nicole's was more open and friendly, but they seemed to be getting along just fine.

Brendy noticed Adam dancing with his daughter and pointed it out to Beth. They smiled and chatted about how sweet Emma was and how much she had seemed to enjoy the whole week. Each new day had brought its own special new surprises into her young and innocent world.

Beth looked back toward the dance floor.

"Hey, Brendy, do you see Liam and Nicole?"

Brendy looked, but couldn't see them.

"That's funny," Brendy replied. "They were just there a second ago."

"I know. Maybe they went to get something to drink."

They looked toward the refreshment table but didn't see them there, either.

"Hmmm, interesting," Beth replied.

"Yes, *very* interesting," Brendy added.

* * *

Liam had not been trying to be sneaky, he had simply asked Nicole if she wanted to go for a sunset ride and she had agreed. As they left the dance, she asked Liam if he would excuse her for a few minutes while she went back to her casita to change. He smiled and nodded. Liam headed to the stable to saddle the horse Nicole had enjoyed riding all week, Calypso, and then saddled Wildfire. He was leading them out of the stable when Nicole joined them.

They followed the same trail that began each ride that week before Liam took a turn and led Nicole up the mountain in a gentle switchback pattern. They soon arrived at a landing that was perfect for watching the final whispers of the breathtaking sunset. They dismounted and tied the horses to a nearby tree. Liam then untied a large blanket from the back of his saddle and spread it out on the ground.

"After you," he offered, sweeping his hand in front of him.

"Well, thank you, kind sir."

As he joined her, she glanced over at him and noticed him looking at her.

"What?"

"Oh, nothing," he replied casually.

"Keeping secrets from your guests isn't polite," she replied with a wink and a sly smile.

"Is that right?"

"Yes, that's right. It's even written in the guest's guide in our rooms."

"No kidding," Liam replied with a chuckle.

"No kidding!"

They sat there in silence, each smiling at the other, and neither one saying what was on their mind.

Nicole broke the moment, looking out toward the sunset.

"So pretty!"

"Yes, you are."

"Pardon me?" Nicole replied with wide eyes.

"You said the sunset was pretty, and I agreed."

Nicole looked cautiously at Liam.

"That's not exactly what I heard," she said, barely in a whisper.

Liam didn't respond but maintained a slight smile on his face as his gaze shifted from Nicole to the sunset. She kept looking at Liam. Thinking. Wondering.

What's on your mind, Liam? I'm leaving tomorrow morning, and I don't know if I'll ever be coming back. I've had a wonderful time this week, and you're certainly a big reason for it. You are such a wonderful gentleman. I saw that from the start. And this evening, the way you held me when we danced, it felt so … so lovely! But I'm on the rebound from a horrible mess of a relationship and I'm not ready to even think of someone else for a long time. Although … I could certainly think about you, and …… I no doubt will.

Liam glanced toward Nicole. "I loved the dress you wore this evening."

Nicole was caught off guard by his lovely compliment. "Thank you," she replied shyly.

"You were wearing that dress when you arrived last Saturday."

Nicole was stunned! "You remember?!"

"Yes," Liam replied simply.

Now she felt *really* off guard and her mind began to spin! *What else does he remember?*

Liam shifted from looking toward Nicole to looking out toward the sunset. He shifted again to lie on his back with his hands clasped behind his head. He looked up at the stars that were just beginning to show through the thin, wispy clouds, and then glanced at Nicole who was looking out toward the deepening colors of the night.

"Have you had a good time this week?" he asked softly.

Nicole was grateful Liam had changed the subject and turned and looked down at him and replied in kind, "Yes."

"Good. I'm glad."

Nicole smiled sweetly.

"What did you like the best?"

You, she thought, but knew she couldn't say it. "It was *all* so special, but I think … I think it may have been when you were talking with Emma on Monday morning."

"Really?"

"Yes. You were so kind, patient, and playful with her. You made her feel so special. And I watched her parents watching the two of you, and I could tell how much they appreciated you for how you treated their daughter."

"Aw, it was nothing, really."

"How can you say that? You took a little girl who wanted so desperately to be near a horse but was too frightened to do so, and you had her feeding Luna, stroking her head, laughing and giggling while she gave her a cookie. I mean, that was special! *You* are special to be able to do something like that."

Liam just smiled and looked back up at the stars.

"You truly are really good with children."

Liam smiled a half smile and shrugged his shoulders.

"When I asked you Monday where you learned to do that you just said, 'it was a long time ago'. Would you tell me about it?"

Liam looked over at Nicole, and then back up at the stars.

"There's not really much to tell."

"Please?"

Liam hesitated for a long moment, and then began.

"When I was in grade school there was a girl in my class that some of the other students made fun of. I don't know why, but it seemed like they saw her as different or weak or something. Once, one of the guys teased her during recess and made her cry. That made some of the other students laugh, so he did it again. Then, I guess to get their own laughs, a couple of other students started to tease her, and they got what they wanted – laughs from the other students. But all along this poor girl cried. It was so painful to watch.

"After school that day I stayed behind to talk with our teacher. I told her what was happening and she asked what I thought she should do. I thought for a moment, and then said, "Is it possible that you could rearrange some of the seats of the kids in class? Move the teasers away from her, and allow me to be one of those that sit next to her?"

"What did she say?"

"She said it sounded like a good idea, and that she would think about it overnight. When we came into class the next morning, everyone had their names on different desks. There was some confusion as the students tried to figure out what was going on, but we eventually figured it out and sat down in our new places. I was right next to Penny, the girl they teased so much."

"Did the teasing stop?"

"Not right away. During the first recess a different girl came up to Penny and started teasing her, but I had made it a point to be nearby, just in case, and I walked up to her and asked her to please stop teasing my friend. She got all huffy and asked, "Who's gonna make me? You?" And I said, "Yeah. Me!" I stared at her, and she backed away. A couple of the boys who had been teasing her before saw what was happening, and I stared them down as well. They walked off and Penny was never teased again."

"Were you scared that one of the boys might beat you up for taking away their fun?"

"No. But, then again, I was the tallest boy in my class, so I guess that may have counted for something."

"So, it truly was 'a long time ago'."

"Yes, it was."

"Where did you learn to stick up for the little guy?"

"I don't think it was so much about sticking up for the little guy, as much as it was about just doing what was right, and that's something that just came naturally in my family."

"You must have grown up in a very loving home."

"I did. My parents were firm but fair."

Nicole pondered what Liam had just shared with her, then laid down on her back to join Liam's stargazing.

"You were truly blessed, Liam. And I'm guessing Penny wasn't the first one to receive your kindness and compassion. Or the last."

"I don't know. I've never thought about it."

What an amazing gentleman! Oh, Liam, you are truly one in a million!

CHAPTER 41

Stay!

AS NICOLE AWOKE SATURDAY morning, she felt a very strong sense that she needed to stay one more day. But why? What difference would it make to stay one more day? Everything was set for her to leave the ranch right after breakfast. She would load up her car, say her goodbyes, then stop at the Shell station on the highway to gas up before heading through the mountains. She would travel to Taos, then head south through Santa Fe and on toward Albuquerque, topping off the gas tank near the airport before turning in her rental car. Finally, she would check her luggage with a curbside skycap, go through the TSA checkpoint, and on to her gate in plenty of time to relax a while before boarding her flight home. Step by step, all in order. It's just the way she was. Or … at least it's the way she *had* been, so why change anything now?

She fought the feeling at first because her ordered mind had a schedule to keep – go home today, relax tomorrow, get back to work on Monday. Altering that might have consequences she had not planned for, or even thought might be necessary. Back-up plans had never been necessary. She made the most of whatever cards were dealt to her each day. That's the way it had always been … at least since she was six.

But the feeling wouldn't leave her alone, no matter how hard she tried to block it out of her mind. The harder she fought it, the more persistent it became. *Stay. One more day. Just stay.*

She closed and locked the door to her casita and breathed in deeply the fresh, crisp, early morning mountain air. She took a couple of minutes to perform her obligatory stretching and then began her walk. Looking around the ranch, taking in the view of the other casitas, the hacienda, the barbeque area where everyone had had such a wonderful time the night before, the long stable—WAIT! *Is that Liam and Pat with the horses?*

Just then Liam heard a noise from outside the stable and turned to see Nicole walking by.

"Excuse me, Pat, I'll be right back." Pat gave Liam a knowing wink, and Liam smiled back.

"Hey, Nicole," Liam called as he jogged out of the stable.

"Hey yourself, Liam!" Nicole responded brightly.

"Taking your morning walk one last time?"

"Um, yes. I … I think so."

"You *think* so?"

"Well …" Nicole sighed and looked away, trying her best to hide her confusing thoughts. Or … or was it conflicting *feelings?*

"Something wrong, Nicole?"

"Oh, no! Nothing is wrong!"

"Oh, good! I was afraid that after last night—"

"No, last night was *wonderful!*"

Liam smiled, and nodded ever so slightly. "Yes … yes, it was," he replied softly.

Nicole blushed.

"Um, I think I'd better get on with my walk."

Liam, wishing Nicole would stay a moment longer, nodded.

"Sure. Maybe I'll see you at breakfast?"

"Maybe!" Nicole replied with a wink, then turned toward the road and headed out toward the highway.

Liam watched as she walked away. *Come on, Liam, she's going home in a few hours and you'll never see her again. Shake it off and get back to work.*

* * *

What is going on? Nicole thought as she continued her walk. *Why am I feeling so confused? Everything is supposed to be so simple. I have a career! Fly home and get back to work! Simple, right? Right?!*

Stay. One more day. Just stay.

I can't.

Yes, you can!

But why?

Because!

Nicole stopped! *What?!?!*

Trust me. Stay.

Nicole turned around and, scanning from her right to her left, she looked at the ranch, taking it all in – the arena, the paddocks, the stable, the hacienda, everything. She let her eyes drift from one to another, over and over. *Is this where I'm* supposed *to be??*

Yes!

WHAT?! WHY?!

Stay one more day.

How will staying just one more day help? How?!

Just trust your heart.

My heart?!

Yes.

Nicole let out a long and deep sigh, then, without having reached the end of her walk at the highway, she headed back to the ranch, picking up her pace as she went.

As it came into view, she took in the full vista of the place she'd called home for the past week. The arena, the paddocks, the stable, the hacienda … everything, each moment came rushing back to her, filling her with a sense of joy and peace – a quiet feeling she had not felt since … well, she could not remember the last time she felt this way.

Stay.

The feeling came back stronger than before.

Stay!

But that means changing my flight, that is if I can, then calling Amanda and seeing if she can change her plans, and—

Stay. Just stay.

She let out a long sigh. *So … why do I need to stay?*

That was the question that continually tumbled over and over in her mind as she walked down the road, past the paddocks and the stable, and back toward her casita. It had certainly not been the carefree walk like she had enjoyed every other morning this week.

Before heading to her casita, she decided to stop at the hacienda to see if either Kay or Ashli might be at the reservations counter. She would see if she might be able to stay one more night. As she walked in the front door, Kay looked over at her and greeted her with a warm smile.

"You're up bright and early!"

"I like to go for a walk early every morning, and I've kept it up even while I've been on vacation."

"That's a great habit to get into."

"Yes, I've been doing it for years, and whenever the weather hasn't been conducive, there's a mall not far from my condo. I can go there and walk around inside for an hour and then head home. However, I certainly haven't needed it this week!"

"Yes, the weather has been gorgeous, but, then again, you joined us near the end of our off season when winter is typically long gone and spring is beginning to show off its colors."

"Lucky me!"

"And lucky us! We've loved having you here this week!"

"And I've loved being here, too!"

"So, I guess we'll be saying a sad goodbye sometime today?"

"Actually, and you're probably going to think I'm strange, but is there *any* chance that I might be able to stay just one more night?"

"Really?! Oh, wow, I think so! Let me check." Kay brought up their current reservations on the screen and checked when the next guests were arriving. All of them were scheduled to arrive the next day, and Kay smiled as she gave Nicole the good news!

"Yes! You're more than welcome to stay one more night! You just can't let go of us, huh?" Kay added with a wink and a smile.

"It's the funniest thing. I went to bed last night with clear plans to leave right after breakfast this morning, get back to the airport in plenty of time to catch my return flight home early this afternoon, but … when I woke up this morning I had the strongest feeling come over me that I needed to stay one more night."

"Really?"

"Yes! It was so strange, especially because I can't figure out why. The prompting just keeps telling me to stay."

"Maybe it's trying to tell you to stay for *good*."

Nicole laughed. "Maybe, but I don't think that's it, because I just had the impression it was just for one more night, and then I can head home tomorrow."

"What about your flight?"

"That's another thing! I have to get back to my casita and call the airline to see if I can switch my flight until tomorrow. If I can't, then all of this is for nothing."

"Well, then I'll let you go, and I'll keep my fingers crossed that you *can* make it happen!"

"Thanks, Kay! I'll see you at breakfast!"

"Okay, see you then! Good luck!"

"Thank you!"

* * *

With a quick call to Southwest, Nicole was able to change her flight to leave the next day, and the timing was *so* much better, too! Originally, she would have had to leave no later than eight-thirty that morning in order to get to the airport and get her rental car turned in. Then she needed to get checked through TSA and settle in at her gate before boarding her flight before one-thirty. However, her options were much better for the next day. Now she didn't have to leave the ranch until right after lunch in order to make her flight just before five-thirty Sunday evening. Plus, it turned out it was the fastest flight home out of the whole schedule, even with having to change planes in Phoenix! Bonus! Now, one more call!

Nicole picked up her phone again, dialed Amanda, who answered on the second ring.

"Hello?"

"Hi, Amanda. It's Nicole!"

"Hey, good morning! How's it going?"

"Wonderful! And that's why I'm calling. Instead of picking me up at the airport this evening, would you be available to pick me up tomorrow night instead?"

"Um, yes. I think so. About what time?"

"My plane lands just before eight."

"Sure, I can do that. Is everything okay?"

"Yes, it's wonderful, and I'll explain it all when you pick me up. At least, I'll *try* to, anyway."

"That's fine. I'll see you tomorrow night at eight?"

"Thanks so much, Amanda! I owe you big time."

"Not to worry. See you then!"

"Bye!"

Nicole let out a big sigh. *Mission accomplished!*

She was so excited she did not even bother calling Kay, but decided to walk over to the hacienda instead and tell her in person. Then she headed to the dining room to wait for breakfast to be served.

She sat at a table near the windows that looked out over the ranch and took it all in. She reflected upon all she had done and seen throughout the week, and it brought a gentle smile to her face. She had not felt this relaxed in years. She heard a familiar voice coming from the lobby and turned to see Brendy enter the dining room. She waved as Brendy made her way through the tables and sat down next to Nicole.

"Good morning, Nicole!"

"Hi, Brendy!"

"So, today is the day, huh? Are you all set to head home?"

"Actually, no."

"What?"

"I was telling Kay a little while ago that I woke up with the strangest feeling that I needed to stay one more day."

"Really? Why?"

"I have no idea, but the feeling was very strong and insistent."

"So, what are you going to do with your extra time here?"

"I'm not sure, but I thought I might check with Pat to see if I can spend some time with Calypso, and maybe even Rocky. Maybe groom them or something like that?"

"I'm sure Pat would welcome your assistance."

"Good."

"Hi, you two!" Beth called as she approached their table.

"Hi, Beth!" Nicole replied.

"Hey, there!" Brendy added.

"Last day, huh?"

"No, actually," Brendy replied. "We get her for another day!"

"Really? How come?"

"I was just telling Brendy that I had this very strong impression when I woke up this morning that I needed to stay one more day."

"Cool! We're getting to you! I predict you're going to get home, quit your job, and we'll see you back here in a week!"

"Ha! Yeah, I don't think so. I *do* love it here, but I love my job, as well. It's going to take a lot to get this California girl, who's used to the sun and beaches, to trade all of that for dust and cowboy boots."

"Well, it looks like we have our work cut out for us then, eh, Brendy?"

"Right, we sure do!" Brendy agreed.

"You guys are too funny!" Nicole replied with a big smile on her face.

"Well, we're both a little bit more than just funny. You watch. We're going to gently coerce you to make that move. In a friendly sort of way, of course."

"And you won't be sorry you did!" Beth added.

Nicole looked at her two special friends and began to fight back a tear or two.

"Thank you both for caring so much," Nicole whispered.

"We do," Brendy replied softly, and Beth nodded in agreement.

Nicole took a deep breath and let it out in a rush. "Okay, enough seriousness," she replied as she fanned her face.

"It looks like LuAnn has the buffet ready," Beth advised. "Shall we get some breakfast?"

"Yes, I'm starving!" replied Nicole.

CHAPTER 42

Face to Face

AFTER BREAKFAST NICOLE WALKED to the stable with Brendy and Beth and saw Pat tending to the horses.

"Good morning, Pat!" Brendy called out as they entered the stable.

"Well, good morning to each of you! How are you ladies this morning?"

"We're good!" Beth replied.

"We have a favor to ask," Brendy added.

"Sure! Ask away!"

"Nicole is spending one more day with us and she was wondering if she could spend time with a couple of the horses. Is there anything she can do that would be helpful for you?"

"Sure, that would be wonderful! Is there anything special you'd like to do, Nicole?"

"Actually, if I may, I'd like to spend some time with Calypso, because she and I have been together all week on our trail rides. Maybe I could also spend some time with Rocky?"

"I'm sure they'd both love the extra TLC. Why don't you come over here and I'll get you started with Calypso?"

"Thank you!"

"We have a few things we need to do, Nicole," Brendy said, "so Beth and I will catch you later."

"Okay, see you then!"

Pat spent a few minutes showing Nicole how to properly groom

Calypso and then watched as Nicole gave it a try. Once she saw that Nicole had it figured out, she excused herself to return to care for some of the other horses.

As Nicole was grooming Calypso, she began to see memories of their trail rides in her mind.

"Thank you for being such a wonderful companion for me this week, Calypso."

As if she fully understood Nicole, Calypso nodded her head in agreement. This sent a shiver over Nicole!

"Do you understand what I'm saying to you?

Rocky was in the next stall, and while she continued to groom Calypso, she looked over to Rocky.

"How are you doing, boy? You gave everyone quite a scare yesterday, you know? Fortunately, you received some great care. Are you doing okay today?"

Rocky nodded.

"Do you understand me, too?"

"I think it's the soothing sound of your voice," came a voice from behind her that startled her. She turned and looked straight into Dusty's eyes.

"Nicole?!"

"Dusty?!"

"Wha— ... what are you doing here?"

"I ... I've been staying here this week."

"Really? Oh, my gosh! So, were you around yesterday when I was here tending to Rocky?"

"Yes, I was off in the distance."

"Why didn't you come up and say hi?"

"Well, like I was saying, I was off in the distance, and ... and I didn't want to disturb you."

"Gosh, it's so good to see you, Nicole!"

"You ... you too, Dusty." Nicole replied nervously.

"How are you doing?"

"Fine, actually. Just fine." Although she knew she wasn't at that moment.

As Dusty looked deep into Nicole's eyes with wonder and

excitement, she felt uncomfortable, nervous, and very apprehensive.

"So … how have you been?" she asked.

"I'm doing great!"

"That's … nice to hear. How long have you been a vet?"

"About seven years. After I got out of the Corps I went to college. My roommate there was working at some ranch. One day he mentioned they needed some extra help and wanted to know if I'd be interested in applying. I wasn't sure at first, but I went with him just to see what it was all about. It looked kind of interesting, dusty and dirty, but still interesting. So I applied, and I went from having no particular major to wanting to be a vet! And, as they say, the rest is history!"

"That's … that's wonderful, Dusty."

"Thanks." Then Dusty noticed Nicole's distracted attention. "Hey, is everything okay?"

"Yeah. I … I guess so. Um, would you excuse me?" Nicole dropped her grooming brush and rushed out of Calypso's stall and out of the stable.

"Nicole?" Pat called. "Nicole, is everything okay?"

Nicole ran quickly passed her and didn't look back.

Pat walked toward Rocky's stall and saw Dusty standing there.

"Hi, Dusty! I didn't know you were coming by this morning."

"I just wanted to come by to see how Rocky's doing and he looks great!"

"Yes, thanks again for your help yesterday."

"My pleasure."

"So. Were you just talking with our guest, Nicole?"

"Yes! We were high school sweethearts!"

"Hmmm, and am I to guess that things didn't end well?"

"Yeah, I was a jerk and broke up with her just before we graduated. I didn't really have a choice, though, because I'd joined the Marines and was heading off to boot camp the next week."

"And you two lost contact after that?"

"Yeah, looking back I should have written, but boot camp really put me through the ringer!"

"Yes, I've heard some tales in my time."

"I'll bet you have."

"So … Rocky is looking okay to you this morning?"

"Yes, he's looking great."

"Good. We gave him the day off yesterday after his scare, and Liam and I were in early this morning to check on him."

"That's good. I think he's fine now. Some good exercise today and tomorrow and he'll be ready to go on Monday."

"Thanks, Dusty."

"Do you need me for anything else?"

"No, we're good."

"Okay, I'm going to head over to Silverado to check on that new foal."

"We had some excitement here last night in relation to that foal?"

"Really?"

"Yes, one of our guests turned twelve yesterday, and to make it special for her, Luke and Jill invited her and her parents to join them this morning when they head over to Silverado. They'll get to meet the foal, and they told Emma she gets to name her!"

"Hey, that's wonderful! I'll bet she's excited!"

"Oh, you should have seen it! It was such fun to see her jumping up and down with excitement!"

"Ha, that's great! I can't wait until I have some kids of my own."

"Well, you're going to have to wait until you find the right girl to settle down with."

"Yes, I know. I had one once but I was stupid and let her get away."

"Maybe it just wasn't the right time."

"Yeah," Dusty lamented while looking out toward the end of the stable where Nicole had exited so hastily. "Maybe you're right."

Chapter 43

—

Emma

"**G**OOD MORNING, EMMA!" JILL called as she and Luke were approaching the table where Emma and her parents were just finishing their breakfast.

"Hi!" Emma replied with a beaming smile.

"How are you this morning?"

"Happy!"

"Well, that's wonderful to hear! And why are you so happy this morning?"

"Because I get to go see the new horse and give her a name!"

"That's right!"

Looking at her parents Luke asked, "Where abouts do you live?"

"We're east of Denver, in Aurora," her father, Adam, replied.

"Oh, that's nice and close!"

"Yes, less than four hours away."

"Good. Good. Well, whenever it's convenient for you and your family, Jill and I would like to chauffer you over to our other ranch a few miles away so Emma can see our new foal. We're hoping she can come up with just the right name for her."

"That would be wonderful! Thank you!"

"We have a big double cab pickup that can accommodate all of us in a little bit of style, so whenever you're ready, just let us know. If we're not in our office we won't be far away, and someone will find us."

"After breakfast we were just going to head back to our casita and finish packing, so we should be ready to join you in about forty-five minutes or so?"

"That's sounds perfect. We'll see you then!"

* * *

"I can't wait to see my baby horse," Emma exclaimed as they rode down the highway toward Silverado.

"Sweetheart," her mother, Carolyn, said cautiously, "you do understand that the horse isn't really yours, you just get to name her, right?"

"Oh, right, that's what I meant. But wouldn't it be *so much* fun if I could have my *own* horse someday?!"

Her parents smiled at each other with raised eyebrows.

"Yes, sweetheart, it would be," her father, Adam, replied.

"It's not far now," Jill said. "You'll be able to see it up ahead on the right after just a couple more turns."

Emma bounced up and down in her seat with excitement.

The morning was overcast but no rain was predicted. The sun had been fighting to break through, but had yet to find its way.

"Do you have any names in mind that you might want to name her?" Jill asked.

"Not yet! I think I need to see her first, and then maybe I'll have a better idea."

"That's a *very* good idea."

Emma smiled and continued bouncing.

"There it is!" Luke said, pointing to the lush, green valley that had just come into view up ahead on the right.

"Is all of that *yours?*" Emma asked in amazement.

"That's just part of it. You'll be able to see more of it coming up on the right just beyond these trees."

A moment later their view was filled with the beautiful Silverado Springs Ranch. There were tree-covered mountains behind it and to the north, and a lake toward the southern end.

"Oh, my gosh! It's *beautiful!*" exclaimed Carolyn.

"Thank you," Jill replied.

"How many acres do you have?" inquired Adam.

"Just for our ranch alone it's over thirty-eight hundred. That's for winter grazing. During the summer we work in conjunction with seven other ranches and it's considerably more than that."

"Impressive!" Adam replied.

They turned off the highway and headed for the main building housing the office. Along the way they passed the stable, paddocks, and corrals. Beyond that was the arena, and it appeared from this distance to be even larger than the one at Hidden Glory! Off to the left they saw hundreds of cattle grazing between where they were and the lake to the south.

Emma was smiling from ear to ear anticipating her moment to see the filly. As soon as the truck pulled to a stop in front of the main building, Emma popped out of her seat belt and bounced out of the truck!

"When can I see the baby horse?"

"We'll head over to see her in just a minute or two," Jill replied. "Luke needs to check on something in the office first. Then we'll head over there."

Emma looked up at her parents. "Ooooo, I can't wait! I can't wait!"

"It'll be just a moment, sweetie. Please be patient," Carolyn softly assured her anxious daughter.

Emma let out a long sigh, but maintained the excited smile on her face.

"My husband will be done very quickly, Emma," Jill replied with a wink and a smile. "I promise!"

Just then the office door opened, and Luke came out talking with his foreman. They paused at the bottom of the stairs for a moment before the foreman turned toward his truck, climbed in, and headed for the highway. Meanwhile Luke turned toward the anxious Emma and swept his hand toward the stable. "Shall we?"

"YES! Yay, I'm going to see the baby horse!"

Luke and Jill led Adam, Carolyn, and Emma through the stable. They arrived at the nearest paddock where the foal and her mother were given plenty of room. This was also done to allow the mother to be as calm as possible if unfamiliar people came close.

"THERE SHE IS!" Emma ran to the railing surrounding the paddock to get a closer look at the filly who was standing next to her mother just past the center of the paddock.

"Oh, my gosh! She's so *beautiful!*" Carolyn said.

"Yes," Jill replied. "With her light golden coat she looks so much like her mother."

"Can I go in and pet her?" Emma pleaded.

"No, I'm sorry, Emma," Jill said kindly. "Her mother is being very protective of her. If she were a week, or even just a few days old, then you might, but it's best that we just look at her from here."

"Okay, I understand," Emma replied in a sweet, caring voice. Then she turned back to look at the filly and her mother.

"What's her mother's name?" she asked.

"Misty."

"Misty? That's a cool name! How did she get *that* name?"

"Well, when she was born six years ago it was a cool, misty morning, so it just seemed to fit."

Emma nodded her head as her thoughts were tumbling over and over to come up with just the right name for the filly.

Then, after fighting so long to break through, the clouds began to part, and sunlight enveloped the paddock and surrounding area.

Emma gasped! "I'VE GOT IT! I know what I want to name the baby horse!"

"What's the name?" Jill asked.

"SUNSHINE! Or you could also nickname her Sunny!"

"Sunshine it is!" Luke declared.

"Congratulations, Emma!" Jill exclaimed. "You've named a horse! That's a very special honor!"

"Hi, Sunshine! I love you!" Emma said, as happy tears began to stream down her soft cheeks. She remained standing at the railing as her parents chatted with Luke and Jill for another few minutes.

"Emma?" her mother asked.

"Yes, Mom?"

"It's time to go, sweetheart."

"Oh, Mom, just a few minutes more? I don't want to leave Sunshine."

"I know, dear," Carolyn replied gently, "but we need to get back to the other ranch, pack the car, and get on the road to go home."

Emma let out a long and sad sigh.

"Okay, Mom."

"That's my girl." Carolyn put her arm around Emma's shoulders as they walked toward the stable. Just before they entered the stable, Emma turned toward the paddock.

"Bye, Sunshine! I love you!"

As if she already knew her new name, Sunshine turned toward Emma and nodded her head which made Emma squeal with joy!

"Mom! Sunshine knows her name!"

"Yes, it looks like she does, sweetheart."

Emma held her gaze on Sunshine a moment longer before turning toward her parents. "Okay, we can go now!"

CHAPTER 44

Why?!

*S*TAY, *YOU SAID, JUST STAY! I didn't understand it, but I did it. I changed my reservation here at the ranch, my flight, what time for Amanda to pick me up tomorrow, everything! And for what?! To have Dusty thrust back into my life?! How* dare *you! Whoever you are! I've been having such a wonderful time this week, at least since I got rid of Chandler, and then you go and pull a stupid stunt like this! Why?! WHY?!*

Nicole was fuming as she paced through her casita! What she really wanted was to go on a long ride on Calypso all by herself, but she knew she wouldn't get permission. Pat or Liam would have insisted that someone go with her, but that wouldn't work because she needed to be alone. Completely alone. So, into the casita she went.

One long sigh after another! *So* many questions and absolutely *no* answers! And it was too late now to change her flight, so she was stuck here. At least she took consolation in knowing that Dusty wouldn't be here the rest of the day and, hopefully, not tomorrow. *Anytime* near him was too long!

She sat down on the end of her bed, put her hands to her face and wept. In a flash, all the pain she had buried years ago came flooding back. The memories came back in brilliant technicolor. All of the amazing times they spent together. Her dreams, and yes, even her plans, for their future. After the first man in her life had broken her heart when she was child, she had protected her heart with great vigilance. That is, until the fateful night she had seen Dusty in that play. All of a sudden her world was rattled. What was that feeling that took over her mind and her heart? It couldn't be love. She tried her best to quash the feeling but it just wouldn't go away.

With mixed emotions she kept her distance for the rest of her junior year, hoping the feeling would fade. Summer came soon enough, and spending time with friends did wonders for her state of mind. However, as her senior year was about to begin, she steeled herself once again, preparing to do emotional battle to protect her heart. But it was a battle her heart soon lost because Dusty ended up in three of her classes.

Nicole had to admit that she liked him a lot and he seemed like a good student and a nice guy. However, she still preferred to remain off his radar. Before the first week of classes had come to a close, though, he had approached her. With a charming smile he said 'hi' to her after class one day, and the barriers she had built up around her heart seemed to vanish in the blink of an eye. Or was it in the wink of his eye?

Before long they had begun dating, and she couldn't resist the feelings in her heart any longer. Someone cared about her like she had longed to be cared for. Dusty was funny, kind, considerate, and was the perfect gentleman around her friends. So, where was the flaw? Where was the chink in his shiny armor? When would she finally see the *real* Dusty Drake? But the more time she spent with him, the more she began to see that he *was* the real deal, and she gave her whole heart to him.

Her best friend, Chelsea, often commented about how envious she was of Nicole, and wished she could find a guy even half as charming as Dusty. He treated Nicole like a lady, never doing or saying anything disrespectful, and she reveled in the glow of his love.

When he came to pick her up for their first date, he had met her parents. Her mother was friendly and gracious, while her father was more reserved but still polite. After she arrived back home that night her father wanted to know if he had treated her right. Nicole assured him that Dusty had. On the other hand, her mother was more genuinely curious. She told Nicole she thought Dusty seemed like a nice young man, and Nicole assured her that he was.

As time went on and it appeared to her parents that their relationship was getting more serious, her father started asking a lot more questions. Nicole knew where he was headed with his inquiries and always did her best to allay his concerns.

Taking a sincere interest in her daughter's emotional welfare, Charlotte regularly asked questions about their dates as well as their friends. Nicole didn't mind, and actually found it reassuring that her mother loved and cared for her enough to do so.

Her mind relived the wonderful experience of their starring together in their school production of *South Pacific*. Much to her mother's dismay, Nicole had set aside her interest in the piano when she started high school. She realized that in order to reach her personal goals she was going to have to sacrifice her three hours of practicing the piano every day. One of her new goals was to become class valedictorian, and it had paid off handsomely!

However, she had not set aside her musical interests altogether, as she was a member of the school choir, as well as the elite chorale ensemble. Those experiences helped her develop her voice to such an extent that when it came time to audition for the lead role of Ensign Nellie Forbush opposite Dusty's Emile De Becque in *South Pacific*, she was instantly chosen for the role!

Acting and singing opposite her boyfriend was a dream come true, and she realized more than ever before just how deeply in love she was with Dusty.

The theme of their senior ball, *Some Enchanted Evening*, seemed to have been chosen especially for them. Dusty had even taken her to a Polynesian restaurant before the dance just to add more enchantment to the evening! They had such a wonderful time dancing the night away. When the dance was over, he whisked her off to the beach where they walked barefoot for hours, talking, laughing, and kissing under the stars. It was truly the *best* night of her life!

They were about to graduate and have the whole world at their feet, ready to take it on and conquer it together. So, what made him shatter her heart the way he had?

Perhaps she should have read the signs when she was talking about college, even discussing her options with Dusty, and ultimately choosing to stay in Southern California. Her choice was not just to be as near to him as possible, but she had chosen what she considered to be the best architectural engineering school in the nation that was *also* close by! Yes, she was deeply in love, but she was also deeply committed to becoming an architect.

However, she had been so focused on her own goals that she hadn't realized Dusty had not been sharing any of his. That is, until that fateful Sunday evening, just four days before graduation, when he told her he had enlisted in the Marine Corps and would be leaving for boot camp in San Diego the week after graduation.

At first, she could not believe what she was hearing, as if it were some kind of bizarre nightmare. Then it began to sink in and his voice became muffled. Her eyesight blurred and she realized she wasn't breathing. In the moment that she managed to catch her breath, she looked around to try to understand where she was and what was happening. Then she saw Dusty and an instant later everything became crystal clear! Her heart had just been shattered! Dusty was the one she had given her whole heart and soul to, the one she had completely trusted, the one she had seen a beautiful future with.

"NO! What are you saying?!" Nicole remembered screaming.

Dusty was startled! "Please, calm down, Nicole."

"Calm down? CALM DOWN?! NO! Just take me home NOW!"

"But Nicole—"

"NOW!"

Dusty didn't say another word. He just started his car and drove Nicole home.

She remembered them pulling up in front of her home and her bolting from his car and running into the house. She raced down the hall to her bedroom, slamming the door behind her, burying her face in her pillow and crying uncontrollably. All the while her mother was knocking on the door begging to come in.

She cried so hard and for so long that her stomach began to cramp. She doubled up into the fetal position and felt like she just wanted to die. Not getting a response from her daughter, Charlotte had quietly opened the door and sat down on the bed, resting her hand on Nicole's shoulder. She tried her best to console her grieving daughter, even if she did not understand the cause for Nicole's pain. But nothing could stop the flow of tears.

And nothing could stop them now, nearly fourteen years later.

It was bad enough yesterday when she'd heard his name, then his voice after he arrived to care for Rocky. She'd managed to keep her distance in the shadows, so he wouldn't have a clue that she was near. And once he was gone she breathed a sigh of relief, knowing, *knowing*, she wouldn't see him again.

Then today, there he was, right there. When their eyes met, she could tell he was caught completely by surprise. It caught her between breaths, and she nearly passed out after almost not being able to catch her breath in time. Somehow, she had managed to keep a smile on her face while the knife was being plunged deep into her heart again. And again. It seemed relentless.

Is this *why I was supposed to stay? To see Dusty again? Whoever you are, how cruel can you be?!*

Her tears were never-ending. She leaned back on her bed, then rolled to her side and crawled up until her head rested on her pillow. And the tears flowed.

CHAPTER 45

This is Why

MOST OF THE GUESTS had already checked out by the time lunch was ready to be served. Half of the staff, including Brendy and Beth, had arrived early, with the rest gradually beginning to arrive. Liam, Pat, and Mike came in laughing after one of them had apparently told a pretty good joke. Liam looked around, saw Brendy and Beth, and headed toward their table.

"Hey, Nicole hasn't left already, has she?"

"No," Brendy replied. "In fact, she changed her reservation and her flight and she's not going home until tomorrow."

"Really? Did she say why?"

"Something about her having a feeling that she should stay another day."

"Hmmm, okay. Thanks."

"Why?"

Liam shrugged. "Just wondering. I just haven't seen her around since breakfast."

"You're right, I haven't seen her either," Beth added curiously. "Maybe she took off for a little adventure on her own."

"Yeah, maybe."

"Would you like us to give her a message for you when we see her?"

"No, that's not necessary. If she doesn't show up for lunch, maybe I'll see her at dinner."

Brendy nodded as Liam began to walk back to join Mike and Pat.

"Yeah, it's kind of strange that Nicole didn't mention anything about taking off," Brendy said, "but then again our guests are free to do what they wish while they're here.

"She didn't even hint about any excursions at breakfast," Beth replied. "Oh well, I'm sure she's having fun."

* * *

A half hour after falling apart Nicole got up, went to the bathroom and washed her face. It would be a while before her puffy eyes returned to normal, but she re-did her makeup anyway. Then she sat back down on her bed to decide what she was going to do next. She remembered that Beth had mentioned a nice drive called the Enchanted Circle. She checked it out on her phone and decided to get away for a while, believing that the change might do her good. She managed to avoid making contact with anyone as she walked to her car. She hoped to avoid being seen by Liam as she drove past the stable and paddocks. As she reached the highway she paused for a moment, took a deep breath, turned right, and headed north toward Eagle Nest.

Not far north, on the left, she passed the Vietnam Veteran's Memorial, then Eagle Nest Lake on her right, and she finally entered the village of Eagle Nest. She turned off Highway 64 and followed Highway 38 toward Red River. As she was approaching the town, she began to look for a place to get a bite to eat. The sign for Old Tymer's Café caught her eye. She wasn't disappointed because she enjoyed one of the best cheeseburgers, onion rings, and French fries that she had eaten in a long time!

Back on the road she headed west toward Questa. She wasn't very far out of Red River before she decided to stop where the river came close to the road on the left. She parked her car and wandered through the trees, crossing the river on a small bridge, enjoying the clean, refreshing, mountain air!

She sat down on a log, closed her eyes, and simply listened to the quiet sounds of the forest. She said a silent prayer for understanding, a prayer to help her figure out what to do about the wonderful job offer from Luke and Jill. She also tried to understand the voice that had come to her so strongly that morning, urging her to stay one more day. It *couldn't* have been just so she could see Dusty and talk with him again, could it? She hoped it was for something much different, but what?

She also wanted to know what she was going to do about Liam. Would she write to him after she was home? Would he ask for her number so he could call her once in a while? She had to admit that even though it was against her better judgment to be interested in someone so soon after calling it quits with Chandler, she was intrigued by this cowboy who was beginning to sweep her off her feet. *If only you weren't going to be nearly a thousand miles away from me!*

She opened her eyes, took in the beautiful scenery, thought about Carli painting this very setting, let out a long sigh, and then began her trek back to her car.

Part way there, she looked down as she was stepping over a small log and something caught her eye. She stopped, bent over, and picked up a small, rough, blueish-green stone that stood out from all the mostly gray round stones surrounding it. A particular shade of blue, and special shade of green were two of her favorite colors, especially together. She put the stone in her pocket and proceeded back to her car. Once again on the road, she continued on her way through Questa and on toward Taos.

Just a week ago she had been in a hurry to get through Taos and make the turn toward Angel Fire and the ranch. But today she wasn't in any hurry, and as she approached the town from the north she became aware of the rich Native American and Spanish influences in the architecture around her. She just *had* to stop! *How could I have missed all this beauty before?*

She wandered around for about an hour, occasionally stopping in an art gallery to take in the local talent. A variety of restaurants were everywhere, and if she hadn't enjoyed such a wonderful and filling meal in Red River she certainly would have had plenty of delicious choices in Taos! She could have stayed there for many more hours but decided that she should probably head back to the ranch.

She took her time driving through the Carson National Forest, noticing much more than she had the previous Saturday. When the highway ended as it opened up to the Moreno Valley, she once again took in the beautiful vista that lay before her and sighed. *This could possibly be my new home soon!* She turned right onto Highway 434, but as she approached the turn for the ranch, she decided to keep heading south to take another look at the other ranch.

A few more miles down the road another breathtaking vista opened up on the far right. *There it is!* Nicole drove on, following the split in the road to the right, and arrived at the overlook that Brendy had stopped at earlier in the week. She got out of her car, stepped to the edge of the overlook, and took in the spacious view that included well over a hundred cattle grazing. *Oh, my gosh! This place is so beautiful! And Liam used to work on ranches like this? Oh, wow!*

Her mind began to wander. *What would it be like to …* and then too many questions came upon her all at once. She shook her head, bringing her wandering thoughts back into the moment, let out a long sigh, got back into her car and headed for Hidden Glory.

* * *

As Nicole was driving up the entrance to the ranch, she noticed Liam and Pat off to her right. She waved, and they returned the gesture. As she was parking her car, Brendy was coming out of the hacienda and noticed her friend.

"Hey there!"

"Hi, Brendy!"

"We haven't seen you since shortly after you were in the stable with Calypso this morning. Everything okay?"

"Yes, thank you! I just drove the Enchanted Circle and spent some time in Taos."

"Oh, wonderful! How did you like it?"

"It was *so* beautiful! I stopped in Red River for lunch, then spent a little time near the river where it comes close to the highway. Then I stopped in Taos to enjoy the beautiful architecture, and before coming back I headed further south down the highway to check out Silverado Springs Ranch again. Oh, my gosh! It truly is *so beautiful!*"

"Oh, I'm so glad you were able to see it again, and also to take that wonderful drive."

"Yes, it was exactly what I needed!"

"Needed?"

Nicole caught herself before she said anything to Brendy about Dusty. "I … I just have had a lot on my mind, and the drive helped me to calm down so I could enjoy the rest of my stay." *I hope she buys that and doesn't ask any more questions.*

"I know what you mean. When things get crazy at home, which, with three teenagers, it often does, Corey and I like to take a long drive. The Enchanted Circle is one of our favorites, but we also like to head out toward Cimarron, as well."

"Is that the same Cimarron that I used to see in old western movies?"

"One and the same!"

"Oh, how fun! If I decide to take the job, I'll have to put that on my bucket list to do on one of my days off!"

"*IF* you decide to take the job?" Brendy asked with a wink and a sly smile.

"Ha-ha, yes, *if.*"

"Okay, just checking."

"You don't give up, do you?"

"Not when something just feels so right."

Nicole pondered Brendy's reply with a smile, but without responding.

* * *

Before dinner Brendy headed home to spend the evening with her husband and family. She wasn't due back until late Sunday afternoon, in time to help welcome the new guests. Beth had plans with a few friends in Taos and had invited Nicole to join them. With all of the excitement of the week, Nicole chose to bow out and just hang around the ranch.

As she was heading to her casita after dinner, she heard Liam call her name. She turned and saw the handsome wrangler walking her way with Wildfire and Calypso.

"What's this?" Nicole asked with a sweet smile.

"I just thought you might like to go for one more ride before you head home tomorrow."

Nicole felt a rush of excitement flow over her.

"Thank you, Liam," she replied, almost in a whisper. "This is very thoughtful of you. Yes, I would love to go for another ride with you."

Liam helped Nicole into her saddle, and then mounted Wildfire.

"You've been on a variety of trails this week. Is there one in particular you'd like to ride again?"

"Actually, can we take the one we rode last night and watch the sunset again?"

Liam smiled. "I was hoping you'd say that."

Even in the dimming light Nicole's blush didn't go unnoticed.

"I didn't see you around earlier today. Brendy and Beth thought you might have gone for a drive?"

Nicole remained quiet and Liam turned to see if she was okay.

"No," she replied softly. "I was here, at least for a while. Then … then I went for a drive."

The way Nicole replied gave Liam the impression that perhaps she did not want to talk about it, so he remained quiet.

"I … I wasn't feeling well, so I laid down in my casita for a while. I fell asleep and missed lunch."

"Then I'll bet you were pretty hungry when dinner time rolled around, huh?"

Nicole allowed a smile to cross her lips. "Actually, after I woke up I took the Enchanted Circle drive and stopped in Red River for lunch."

"How was it? The drive, I mean."

"I'm glad I went. The drive was beautiful, and along the way I was able to clear my head of a few things, and that helped."

"Are you feeling better now?"

"Yes, thank you."

They rode on in silence as they worked their way up the switchback to the landing where, like the previous night, they dismounted. They tied their horses to a tree and Liam untied the blanket he had brought with him. Nicole helped him spread it out, and they sat down together. They remained silent while looking at the sky which looked as if it was on fire that evening.

"So," Liam tentatively broke the silence. "What do think of Angel Fire?"

Nicole felt her emotions begin to catch in her throat as she thought back on the past week.

"It's beautiful, Liam. Truly beautiful," she replied softly.

"As Luke and Jill like to say, it's our little piece of heaven on earth."

"Yes, it is. I had read what I thought was a pretty extensive article in a travel magazine, and checked out the ranch's website, but neither really prepared me for the experiences I've had."

"I'm glad. That's the kind of impression we hope all our guests go home with. Hopefully, many will return in the future."

"It's worth returning to, that's for sure."

"Do you think you might?"

"I'd like to ... someday."

"Good."

"May I ask you a question?"

"Certainly," Liam replied as he turned to face Nicole who remained looking out toward the sunset.

"Why do they call it Hidden Glory Ranch?"

"There are lots of stories about that, but the best people to ask are Luke and Jill. Luke's family has been running the big cattle ranch down at Silverado Springs for generations prior to them buying this property and developing it into a guest ranch. I'm sure they had a special reason."

Nicole nodded but didn't reply.

"May I ask *you* a question now?"

Hesitant, Nicole held her breath for a moment before nodding her head. "Okay."

"I know that Luke and Jill extended a job offer to you. Is there any chance you might accept it?"

Nicole remained silent for a long moment, then let out a long, but gentle, sigh.

"I'm not sure."

"I guess it's really too soon to get a grasp on the changes that it would bring into your life."

"*That's* for sure!" Nicole replied, and they both laughed. "Except for the couple of years I spent in Arizona for my graduate studies I've always lived in Southern California, and always near the beach. I've never imagined living anywhere else."

"Is it at least intriguing enough that you'll give it some thought?"

"Yes, I think so. Although I have no idea how soon I'll know one way or the other."

"That's fine. Taking your time is important for something as big as this."

Nicole nodded.

This time it was Nicole who laid back first, while Liam remained sitting up. She reached up and lightly touched his shoulder.

"Liam, I apologize if I'm not very good company this evening."

"Oh, you're fine, Nicole. Why would you say that?"

"I'm just not as talkative as I have been this week, especially compared to last night."

"It's perfectly okay. I'm guessing you have a lot on your mind. One of the reasons I asked if you'd like to join me for a ride this evening was to get you away from the ranch and give you a chance to relax, unwind, and think. And I thought that being up here where you can enjoy the sunset and listen to the night sounds might be just what you needed."

Nicole sighed lightly. "Yes," she softly whispered. "It's perfect. Thank you."

Liam laid down near Nicole and together they remained silent, simply enjoying the calming sounds of the night.

And in the silence Nicole felt something different, something … reassuring, come over her.

Was this to be their last time together? She closed her eyes as a tear rolled down her cheek.

This is why you were supposed to stay. This. Right here. Right now.

CHAPTER 46

Searching

THE DINING ROOM FELT deserted as all the previous weeks' guests had departed for home the day before, but Beth was there to greet Nicole and join her for breakfast. About a third of the other staff had also come in for a brief bite, but she had yet to see Liam. She hesitated to ask about him, not wanting to give away her secret desire to see him one last time before she departed. *Just one last time, please?*

Brendy surprised her by joining them, even though she wasn't due to start work until later that afternoon. "I told my husband that I needed to see you once more before you left in order to put in one final plug for coming back and working with us!"

Nicole smiled and shook her head. "You two just won't quit, will you?"

"Not when we've seen who we want to have work with us!" Beth replied excitedly. "The three of us would make the perfect team!"

They *did* manage to talk about other things besides Nicole's potential employment, including Beth's sharing about her night out with friends at a couple of clubs in Taos the night before.

After their dishes were cleared the three ladies remained at the table to chat. Luke and Jill came by to thank Nicole for coming, asking if her experience had been all she had hoped.

"Oh, yes!" she exclaimed! "*SO* much more! I'm going home with so many wonderful memories, and I've made new friends, and you both were the perfect hosts!"

Luke smiled his reserved smile, pleased that they had another satisfied customer.

"We sure loved having you stay with us, Nicole," Jill replied.

"And," Luke added, "Jill and I are serious about our job offer. You would be the perfect addition to our staff. We've waited a long time to fill this position with just the right individual, and we both agree that you're the perfect person."

"I do, too!" Brendy added.

"Me, too!" Beth nodded in agreement.

Nicole was overcome with emotion. She had never felt so much love from so many people who, just a week ago, were complete strangers.

She stood up and faced Luke. "Would you mind very much if I gave you a hug?"

Luke chuckled. "I would be delighted."

After that she gave Jill a hug, too.

* * *

Nicole's flight from Albuquerque would not depart until almost five-thirty, so she had time to stay a little longer. She wanted to allow at least four hours for the drive, including time to return her rental car. She hadn't seen Liam at breakfast like she had hoped, and after breakfast she walked over to the stable to see Calypso one last time.

"Hi, Pat!"

"Hi, Nicole! Heading home today?"

"Yes. It's hard to leave, but I need to get back to work."

"I understand completely."

"I came to see Calypso one more time, and—"

"Well, look at that! When she saw you walk in she immediately came to the front of her stall!"

"Hi, Calypso!" Nicole said as they walked toward her.

Calypso nodded her head up and down several times and swished her tail.

"Hi, girl! Thank you for being so good for me this last week!" Nicole stroked Calypso's head and neck. "I'm going to miss you!"

Calypso nodded again, convincing Nicole that she was able to understand her.

"There you go! You've made yourself a friend!" Pat replied with a bright smile.

Nicole looked deep into Calypso's eyes and leaned her forehead against Calypso's head. "I'm *really* going to miss you." Was it just Nicole's imagination, or did Calypso let out a long breath that sounded just like a sigh? They looked at each other, eye to eye, not saying a word ... but somehow, they each knew that, one way or another, they would see each other again.

Nicole stroked Calypso's head and neck again, gave her a hug, then reluctantly looked away.

"Have you seen Liam this morning?"

"He called earlier and said he wouldn't be in until late morning at the earliest."

Nicole took a deep breath and valiantly fought back the tears that had started to come.

"Thank you for everything, Pat. I had a wonderful time, and I appreciate everything you did for me during my stay."

"Oh, you're so welcome, Nicole. I really hope we'll see you again, if not as an employee, then at least as a guest."

"Something tells me that I *will* be back, but I just don't know yet in what capacity. But even being a guest again would be a lot of fun!"

"Yes, it sure would. Have a safe trip home!"

"Thank you, Pat. Bye!"

"Goodbye, Nicole."

As she turned to leave she glanced back toward Calypso one more time. They shared another special look, then Nicole turned and walked toward the end of the stable. Just as she reached the wide door Calypso whinnied, and she burst into tears.

Nicole tried everything to hide her deep disappointment that Liam was missing in action. *I want to see you just one more time, Liam! Please?* And now, after those special moments with Calypso, her heart strings were being pulled tighter and tighter.

She walked back to her casita to make sure everything was packed, and that the room was left neat and clean. She dabbed her eyes with a wet washcloth, and as she headed toward the nightstand next to her bed to turn off the lamp, she noticed the guest card that she had postponed filling out from the previous day.

To our wonderful guests!

We hope you have enjoyed your stay with us here at Hidden Glory Ranch, and we would love to know about your experience. We would appreciate it if you would leave us a message to let us know if there is anything we can do to improve our future guest's experiences. Hope to see you again soon!
Thank you!

Luke & Jill Masterson

Nicole sat down at the table near the window with a pen and a page of the ranch stationery.

Dear Luke & Jill —

I hardly know what to say or where to begin! This week has been a once-in-a-lifetime experience for me! Between your wonderful accommodations, staff, meals, and activities, how could I have NOT had a great time! A thousand times THANK YOU!
And … I have a very good feeling that I WILL be seeing you again!
Love,

Nicole Hart

She left the note on the table for Anna to see when she came later to clean the room and get it ready for the next guests. Then she opened the door and carried her luggage out to the car. She took a deep breath, then walked into the hacienda to finally check out and say her goodbyes.

Jill, Kay, and Ashli had all watched as Nicole loaded her car, and then, as she opened the door to the hacienda, all three stepped out from behind the reservations counter and approached her. As she saw their smiles Nicole burst into tears once again.

"My gosh, why am I so emotional?!"

"Because," Jill began, "You don't want to leave, and we don't want to see you go." She gave Nicole a big hug, followed by Kay and then Ashli.

"Thank you all so very much! I can't describe to you how wonderful my week here has been. And Jill, thank you to you and Luke for your job offer. I promise to pray hard for the right thing to do."

"We know you will, Nicole. We're hoping you'll accept, but we also know you'll do what's right for you, for now *and* your future."

"Thank you, Jill. That means the world to me."

Nicole took a step back and looked at all three ladies. "Okay, I better leave before I call my boss and resign over the phone!" she said with a wink and a smile.

All the ladies laughed.

Turning toward Kay she asked, "And, would you do me a favor?"

"Sure," Kay said. "Anything."

"Would you please tell Liam goodbye for me? He was really sweet and treated me so kindly this week. I really appreciated it."

"Oh, you haven't seen him this morning?" Kay asked.

A lump caught in her throat. "No, but Pat told me a little while ago that he had called and said he would be in a little later."

"Oh, we're so sorry you missed him."

"Yes ... me too."

"Well, yes, of course we'll tell him," Kay replied.

Nicole took a deep breath to stifle a tear, both from missing seeing Liam before she left, as well as how hard it was to say goodbye to these wonderful ladies.

"Bye, everyone!" Nicole said with a lump in her throat.

"Bye, Nicole!" the ladies replied together.

As Nicole exited the hacienda she looked toward the spacious and beautiful front patio to her right and paused. She thought of how welcoming it looked for the guests and remembered the many times she had enjoyed there during the week. So relaxing and peaceful.

As she stepped out toward her car she was surprised to see Brendy waiting for her.

"Hi, Brendy!"

"Hi, there! I just couldn't let you leave without seeing you more time."

"Oh, thank you so much. That's very kind and thoughtful of you."

"Nicole, I know between so many of us we've been encouraging you to come back and work here, and believe me we're all praying that you do, but I also know you should do what is right and best for you."

Nicole began to tear up and her reply stuck in her throat so Brendy continued.

"Take your time. Think it over. This would be a big change for you, I'm sure, so don't do this alone. Pray earnestly, and I know He'll guide you to make the right choice."

By now Nicole's tears were flowing and Brendy couldn't help but join her as they gave each other a hug. As they separated Nicole let out a long sigh.

"Oh, my gosh. I don't know where to begin." Nicole paused and took a deep breath.

"Thank you for all you've done for me this week. Your friendship *truly* means the world to me. Between you and Beth and I, I can't think of a better vacation that I've ever had in my life! And when I, *oops! IF* I return—" Nicole and Brendy both laughed at the slip. "If I return to work here I can see us having *many* more fun times, in addition to the work we'll do together."

"I do, too! It would be amazing!"

"I know!"

Nicole paused and then let out another long sigh.

"Thank you, my friend. Thank you for the unexpected blessing you have become in my life. Whether I return or not I *know* we'll always be friends."

"*Best* friends!" Brendy emphasized joyfully.

"Yes! *Best* friends!" Nicole replied with a bright smile.

They gave each other another hug and then Nicole walked toward the door of her car. As she reached for the door handle she paused and turned back toward Brendy.

"Would you do me a big favor?"

"Absolutely! Anything!"

"I also asked Kay for this favor a few moments ago, but … when you see Liam," Nicole forced back tears, "would you please tell him thank you, as well? He's quite a special man, and I enjoined the little time I was able to spend with him. He made me feel special and … I *truly* needed that this week."

Brendy knew more than what she was able to say to Nicole at that moment, and she fought back tears as she shared what she could.

"Yes … I promise to tell him. Many of us noticed that something had happened to him the night you arrived. He was *different* at dinner that night. Not dramatically so, just … well, his demeanor seemed to change. He was a bit more reserved than usual, like he had something on his mind."

"Really?"

"Yes. And then, throughout the week, we noticed other things about him we had never seen before. It didn't take us long to figure out why. It was you."

Nicole couldn't reply because of the lump in her throat, but it was accompanied by an overwhelming feeling of peace, joy, excitement, and elation.

"Thank you!" she whispered.

"You're welcome. And it probably won't be the moment I see him, but I'll look for a quiet time when I can tell him privately."

"That would be nice. Thank you." Nicole briefly looked away to compose herself and then turned back. "Okay, before I become more of a basket case than I already am, I better leave."

Brendy smiled as she wiped away her tears. "Okay, Nicole. Take care and drive carefully."

"I promise!"

Nicole started the engine and lowered the windows to enjoy the cool morning air. As she began to back up, Brendy stepped back and waited to wave goodbye. They shared more goodbyes and waves, and then Nicole began her long drive toward the highway, *wishing* she could have seen Liam just one more time.

CHAPTER 47

Tumbling Thoughts

A S NICOLE MADE THE drive toward the highway, she fought desperately to hold back the tears welling up in her eyes. What she had just experienced over the past week was definitely *not* what she had been expecting. Sure, Carli mentioned that it could, and possibly *would*, be life changing, but OH MY GOSH!

As she was nearing the highway she was momentarily blinded as the sun burst through the trees to her left and caused a bright glare on the windshield. It took a moment to regain her vision, but when she did, she was stunned and *thrilled* by what she saw up ahead! At the end of the road Liam was there on Wildfire! She slowed as she drove closer.

"Mornin', Nicole," Liam said in his strong, confident voice as he tipped his hat to her.

"Hi, Liam!" she replied excitedly. "I looked for you at breakfast and again just before I was leaving, but Pat said you had called and wouldn't be in until later. I thought I was going to miss seeing you, and—"

"Easy, Nicole. Slow down." Liam said with a wink and a smile.

"Sorry, I'm just so happy to see you before I leave. How long have you been here?"

"It doesn't matter. What matters is that I was able to see you one more time before you left."

Nicole blushed. "Gee, do you send all of your guests off this way?"

"No," Liam said softly. "Just you."

Nicole's blush grew brighter.

"I … I don't know what to say," she replied softly.

"Just say you'll be coming back."

"Now I *really* don't know what to say." She looked away, trying to regain her composure.

"Well … I know you have quite a drive ahead of you, so I won't delay you any longer."

"Thank you, Liam. And … thank you for this past week. I really had a *wonderful* time."

"I'm glad to hear that. And I did, too. It's … been a long time."

"Really? How so?"

"Oh … it doesn't matter."

Nicole felt like it was something Liam preferred to not talk about. *But why mention it then?*

"Do me a favor?" Nicole asked.

"Sure, anything!"

"Think of me if you happen to take any rides up to our spot on the mountain. I'm going to miss our quiet time together."

Liam smiled and responded softly. "I promise. I'm going to miss them, too."

The two of them looked at each other without saying another word, even though they both had so much more they *wanted* to say.

"Liam, I … I can't thank you enough for how you made this week so special for me."

"It was my pleasure, ma'am," Liam replied as he dipped his head and touched the brim of his hat.

"Ma'am?! I thought we settled that last Sunday!" Nicole said, laughing.

Liam chuckled. "Yes, we sure did. I just wanted to tease you. I love seeing your smile."

"Stop it! You're embarrassing me!"

"Why? Because I complimented you for your smile?"

"It's … it's just that … oh, now you have me all worked up."

"Good!" Liam replied in a smart aleck sort of way.

"What?!"

"Well, maybe I've given you something to remember me by."

"Oh, believe me, you did that long before this moment."

'Yeah?"

"Oh, yeah, mister!"

"Mister? Well, look who's getting formal now!"

The emotional tension was broken as they both enjoyed a good laugh.

"Well, m'lady, it's probably time that I bid you adieu."

"And I, you, my handsome sir."

They laughed again as Liam tipped his hat to Nicole and she winked back at him.

"Drive carefully, Nicole," Liam said in a more serious tone.

"I promise. And you take care, Liam."

"I promise."

"And do you *always* keep your promises?" she asked with a wink.

Liam smiled. "Always."

And with that, Nicole began to ease onto the highway, noticing in her rearview mirror the handsome man sitting tall in the saddle. Amazingly, it was only a week ago that he was a complete stranger.

Who are you really, Liam? Maybe someday I'll have the chance to find out. And, oh how I wish I could bury myself in your arms right now!

One last look in her rearview mirror. Liam was dutifully watching her, and she noticed Wildfire nod his head, followed by a long whinny. Then she completely lost it.

* * *

Nicole stopped at the Shell station in the village and filled up the tank of her rental car. Before pulling back onto the highway she drove to the back of the lot, got out of her car, and looked back toward the ranch. It seemed like Hidden Glory Ranch was glowing, but it was probably just her imagination. Imagination or not, it made her smile. Other than the silent prayer she had sent up to heaven the day before while she was sitting on a log near the Red River, she had already been seriously pondering Luke and Jill's offer. She would pray again that night after she was settled back into her condo where there would not be a single distraction. That is, with the exception of her memories of the past week ... and one tall, handsome, quiet cowboy.

She stood there for several minutes as memories flashed before her of each day, and each new friend she had made, especially Brendy and Beth. *If I do* decide *to make this change, at least I'll have some friends ready and willing to help me make the transition.*

And Liam. She sighed heavily, but joyfully, and smiled warmly. Watching him work throughout the week was such a pleasure. He was handsome, strong, confident, polite, self-assured, and … perfect? Well, he *seemed* to be, but everyone has their weaknesses, flaws, and perhaps a secret or two; she just hadn't seen a single one. *Just wait. You'll find one. Wait!! Does that mean I'm coming back for sure? Hmmmm ……..*

She had definitely *not* been looking to fall for someone, especially after her confrontation with what's his name a week ago. And Liam was just Liam, all week long. He never went out of his way to get her to notice him. He just went about performing his duties like anyone else who truly cared about their work. However, there was just something about him … and her thoughts drifted to the few times she was alone with him. She smiled and let out a long sigh.

Nicole finally shook her head and brought her thoughts back into the moment. She walked back to her car, started the engine, and reluctantly pulled back out of her spot. She proceeded to drive up to and onto the highway, heading north toward the turn to head west that would lead her to Taos.

Before making the turn, she glanced back over her right shoulder, saw the ranch in the distance, and smiled. *See you again … soon.*

Despite the ranch and her friends on her mind, including the job offer, Nicole did her best to pay attention to the twists and turns as she made her way through the forest. The weather was clear, the roads were dry, and the traffic was light. However, she still needed to pay attention, because around any bend there could be any number of obstructions that would cause her to have to slow down or stop; a slow semi being one of them. Or a deer. Both of which she had encountered on her way to the ranch a week earlier.

Less than forty minutes later Nicole reached Taos and made the turn south onto Highway 68 that would take her to Española. There, she switched over to Highway 285 south toward Santa Fe.

Before reaching downtown Santa Fe, she branched off onto Highway 599 that would take her to I-25, and then on toward the airport in Albuquerque. As she approached the interchange with Interstate 40, she took an offramp and headed for another Shell station. She needed to top off the tank so she would be ready to turn in her rental at the airport. Back on the freeway, she continued heading south and took the Sunport Boulevard offramp that took her right into the airport. Total elapsed time from the ranch – less than four hours.

Nicole's drive to the airport in Albuquerque was uneventful, just as she had hoped. It had given her plenty of time to seriously think about Luke and Jill's wonderful offer. It truly was only the beginning. There was just so much to consider! *And* pray about.

Her return flight to John Wayne Airport would board in just over ninety minutes so she had time to get a quick bite to eat.

* * *

Amanda was waiting for Nicole near baggage claim and helped her load her bags into her trunk.

"Would you like to stop and get something to eat on our way home?"

"Normally I'd say absolutely, but I'm pretty tired so how about if we just head home?"

"Sure! Whatever you'd like."

"Thanks. I appreciate the offer, though."

"Oh, sure!" And with that, Amanda pulled away from the curb and they were on their way.

Amanda was full of questions and Nicole had all the answers. Other than the normal heavy Southern California interstate traffic, the drive home was uneventful.

Nicole didn't mention anything about the job offer because she did not want Amanda to worry unnecessarily. She was not concerned about Amanda saying anything around the office. She just felt it was wise not to say anything to anyone until she had had time to truly think, and pray, about the offer. If she ultimately decided to turn the offer down, then no one needed to know. But, if she *did* decide to accept it, there was a proper procedure to follow in order to make the transition with as little hassle as possible. However, that time was not now.

After arriving at Nicole's condo Amanda insisted on helping her with her luggage. Once inside, Nicole walked across the living room and opened the door to her deck. She walked outside to take in a deep breath of ocean air. Amanda did the same, but had nothing to properly compare it to.

"Ahhhh, I've missed this!" Nicole said as she let out a long breath.

"I'll bet," Amanda replied. "But I'm guessing the mountain air was also refreshing, wasn't it?"

"Oh, my gosh, yes! When was the last time you went camping?"

"So long ago that I've forgotten," Amanda replied wistfully.

"Well, you should go! And soon!"

Amanda smiled at her friend and boss. "I will, I promise. Now, I should take off so you can get unpacked and settled in."

"Thanks again for the ride, Amanda!"

"You're welcome."

"And I'm sorry if my change of plans messed up your weekend."

"Oh, not at all. With the exception of doing some shopping it was a quiet and relaxing weekend and I enjoyed it.

"Good, I'm glad."

"See you bright and early in the morning!"

"I'll be there!"

As Nicole closed the door behind Amanda, she turned and picked up her luggage and carried it to the bedroom. She worked swiftly to put things in their places, and started a load of laundry. Her stomach growled, reminding her that she hadn't eaten dinner! She walked to the kitchen and looked in the freezer, but nothing looked appealing that could be defrosted quickly. She reached for her phone and placed an order for a large Canadian bacon and mushroom pizza to be delivered. While she waited for it to arrive, she finished unpacking and then headed out to relax on her deck.

A slight, but warm, breeze was blowing in from the ocean as Nicole relaxed. Her pizza arrived fifteen minutes later. She grabbed a soda from the refrigerator and headed back to the deck, setting everything down on a table. Dusk had settled in so she lit a tall glass jar candle, opened up the pizza box and enjoyed the aroma. As she took a bite of her first slice, her mind wandered to Angel Fire. *I wonder if he's on our mountain and enjoying this sunset?*

CHAPTER 48

Monday

NICOLE'S COMMUTE TO WORK Monday morning felt like it had taken her twice as long as normal. It was probably just the dramatic change from her more relaxed time at the ranch the previous week. Since she hadn't been on a real vacation for way too long, she had nothing more recent to compare it to. She was happy to be back, but she knew she would need to talk with Warren right away, and was not sure how he would react. She still had not made up her mind completely, but, surprisingly, she was leaning quite strongly toward accepting Luke and Jill's offer.

She loved her career, her boss, and her associates. She also loved her condo. If she went ahead with this change, she would miss her friends, and being able to see her parents as often as she had become accustomed to. But, change is good, right? Right?

After pulling into her parking space and gathering her purse, she locked the car and walked to the door of her office. As if going through a mental car wash, her whole demeanor changed as she walked through the door. The old, cheerful, "attack at dawn" Nicole was back! However … how long could she maintain the façade before the veneer cracked.

"Good morning, Amanda!"

"Good morning, Nicole! Ready to get back at it?"

"As ready as I've ever been!" she replied as cheerfully as she could to mask her thoughts.

"Great! I made sure to keep your schedule light for today to give you a chance to get back into the groove as smoothly as possible."

"Thank you! Remind me to put in a good word for you when it comes time for your next review."

"I certainly will!" The ladies had a good laugh and Nicole walked into her office, sat down at the desk, and put her purse in the lower desk drawer. She looked over at the canvas photograph of the hot air balloons that Carli had gifted her. It immediately gave her a feeling of lightness and freedom!

Carry me away!!

She opened her calendar, reviewed the notes Amanda had left for her, and took a deep breath. Then she swiveled in her chair, got up and walked to the window, and took in the morning view of the beach and the ocean.

Am I really ready for this change? This company has been so good to me, and for me! Warren has been an amazing boss and mentor, and I have to admit he's also been a wonderful father-figure. Heaven knows I've certainly needed one. But something is telling me that I've been offered a very special opportunity and would be a fool to pass it up. True, I could always come back, but that's not like me. I've always given all of my heart to everything I've tried to do in my life, with the understandable exception of Chandler, so if I'm going to do this I'm going to give it everything I have! No safety net!

Nicole let out a long and deep sigh. *What to do? What to do?*

What Nicole realized she *needed* to do was to see Warren right away and thank him for allowing her to take this wonderful vacation on such short notice. But, before she headed to Warren's office she had one phone call to make. She picked up her cellphone, turned and walked back toward her beautiful view, and made the call.

"Hi, this is Carli!"

"Hi, Carli! It's Nicole!"

"Oh, my gosh! Hi, Nicole! How are you? And how was your vacation? Did you go horseback riding? Did you meet anyone fun?"

"Whoa, Carli! Slow down!" The ladies shared an excited laugh.

"Sorry, Nicole. I'm just so anxious for you to tell me all about it."

"Well, actually, that's why I'm calling! By any chance are you free for lunch?"

"Yes! In fact, why don't you come to my place and I'll fix us something fun!"

"That would be nice, Carli! Thank you!"

"My pleasure!"

"So, is noon okay?"

"That's fine with me! I'll be home all day so come whenever it's convenient for you."

"Okay, thank you. I'll see you then!"

"You're welcome! Bye!"

Nicole turned and walked back to her desk, set her phone down, and smiled. *I have a feeling I know what advice Carli will give me, but I just have to hear it face to face.*

With that taken care of Nicole headed for Warren's office.

"I'll be back in a few minutes, Amanda!"

"Okay. I'll hold down the fort," Amanda said with a wink and a smile.

Nicole smiled and shook her head. *I'm going to miss her.*

She took a couple of deep breaths to calm her nerves. Nicole had not prepared what she was about to share with her boss, and she was not much for just winging it, so she prayed that whatever was about to come out of her mouth would make sense.

"Hi, Maryann!"

"Good morning, Nicole," replied Warren's executive assistant. "Did you have a nice vacation?"

"Oh, it was wonderful!"

"That's great to hear. Warren had a feeling you might be coming by to see him early, so you can go right in."

"Thank you, Maryann."

"Is that my superstar architect I hear coming through my doorway?"

"Ha-ha, you flatter me, Warren!"

"No, just speaking the truth! Come in and take a seat!"

"Thank you." Nicole shut the door behind her and then crossed the spacious office and sat down across from Warren at his desk.

"So, how was your vacation?"

"It was *wonderful!*"

"Do you wish you hadn't waited so long to take a whole week off?"

"Well, yes and no. I love my job, so until just recently I never thought much about taking any real time off, but it sure felt good to just get away and do something totally different than I've ever done before!"

"So … are you back for good, or have I lost you to a new and fabulous adventure?"

"Boy, you don't waste time getting right to the point," Nicole replied with a sense of surprise in her voice. *I definitely wasn't prepared for* that*!*

"No, I don't," Warren replied with a twinkle in his eye that totally disarmed Nicole.

"Okay … well, I'm going to be completely upfront with you—"

"Uh-oh!" Warren interjected, maintaining his broad smile.

Nicole sighed and paused.

Warren leaned forward and intertwined his fingers as he set his hands on the desk. "It's okay, Nicole." His gentle smile had completely caught Nicole off guard.

"Warren … I was offered a job at the ranch," Nicole replied, followed by a long sigh.

"Oh, my gosh! That's great!"

"It is?!" Nicole asked in complete wonderment.

"Yes! It means that someone else has discovered how amazing you are besides me!"

Nicole's jaw dropped for a brief moment before she caught it and closed her mouth before speaking again.

"Warren, you have caught me completely … well, I just don't know what to say."

Warren smiled as Nicole shook her head.

"Nicole, Nicole, Nicole … you are one very special lady, someone I consider myself very fortunate enough to have hired many years ago. You have done wonders with your career, and I could not be more proud of the superior architect that you have become."

Nicole began to blush and took a deep breath.

"You could stay here and have a very successful and fulfilling career, perhaps even take over the company when I retire, but do you know what?"

"What?" Nicole asked as she tilted her head slightly to one side.

"I've also always seen something else in you."

"What would that be?"

"A spirit that comes alive with a new challenge!"

"Really?"

"Yes! I've seen your eyes light up when we're discussing new projects in our staff meetings, and on a fairly regular basis I could tell exactly which ones you wanted to tackle!"

"Are you serious?"

"Yes! Your eyes would light up and you would sit a little straighter. You get an eagerness in your eyes as if you can't *wait* to get started on it!"

"Oh, my gosh. I had no idea I was that obvious!"

"Well, I don't think anyone else noticed, but it's my responsibility to nurture all my employees so that they can excel in whatever they do. That includes reading body language, and I've never been wrong with you."

"Warren, I … I don't know what to say."

"Well, let me share something else with you."

"Okay," Nicole replied curiously.

"I had a feeling that this vacation was going to be good for you in more ways than just getting away to relax. You were going to be doing something different, something active, something that would get you involved with something new and challenging, and I wondered how you might feel about it after it was all over.

"And then, as I overheard you chatting with Maryann a moment ago, I *knew* something special had happened at that ranch."

Nicole smiled and briefly looked down at her hands, and then met Warren's eyes again.

"You are *so* perceptive."

"So I'm right? Something *did* happen last week?"

"Yes, more than one thing."

"I *knew* it! Nicole, I'm *so* happy for you!"

"But … what about my job here? I've loved working here with

you, and you've been an amazing mentor."

"Nicole, you have to grab the reins of opportunity when they're handed to you!"

Nicole smiled. "A little ranch humor?"

Warren thought for a moment. "Oh! Right! Reins and horses! Ha! Good catch!"

"Well, you're the one that said it."

"I guess I must have subconsciously had ranches and horses on my mind because it just slipped out."

Warren's congenial mood had definitely put Nicole at ease. All of her worrying about how he would take the news that she was considering moving to New Mexico and taking a new job was apparently all for naught.

"I haven't made up my mind for sure yet—"

"Why not? Go for it!"

"Really?"

"Yes! How soon do they need you?"

"Soon. They said they've had the position open for quite some time, but it was also their off season so there wasn't really a *need* to fill it until now."

"Okay, fine! Make me a list of everything you've been working on, the status of each project, and who you would recommend I turn them over to."

"Really? Are you sure?"

"I'm positive! Can you have that list for me later today?"

"Yes, I believe I can. But … can I be candid with you, Warren?"

"Absolutely!"

"Well … it almost seems like you're trying to get rid of me," Nicole said with a twinkle in her eye.

"Nicole, if I could, I'd keep you here forever. However, I'm wise enough to recognize when one of my employees would blossom even more in a different environment, even if it means losing them."

Nicole sighed. "What did I ever do to deserve a boss and mentor like you?"

"Well, to begin with, you studied hard and became a shining star in your field before you were ever employed. And, when you applied to work here, and we sat down face to face for your interview, I saw something unique in you that I hadn't seen in any man or woman I've ever employed. I'm not quite sure how to describe it, but there was just something different about you. Perhaps it was a piercing type of determination that I saw in your demeanor. It was like a perfect blend of passion, complete focus, with an equal part of an easy-going attitude, as well. You've performed your job with excellence, and now I think it's time for you to show the world what else you can do."

Nicole was overcome by Warren's candid assessment of her, and it took her a moment to regain her composure.

"You really are the best, Warren," she said, almost in a whisper.

"I know you said that you had not made up your mind about this job offer yet, but I personally believe it's just what you need. Yes, I'm going to hate to lose you, but one day I'll be saying, 'I knew her when.'"

"Thank you, but I don't aspire to be any great cowgirl winning belt buckles at rodeos and such."

"You never know what special opportunities might come your way somewhere down the line. Just keep an open mind and a watchful eye, and I believe something special is yet to present itself. Something that you are uniquely qualified to do that is going to make a world of difference to others. Just remember to always be yourself."

"Thank you, Warren. I appreciate you more than words can possibly say."

"You're welcome, Nicole. Now, go make up that list for me. And let's go ahead and plan on this Friday being your last day, shall we?"

"Are you sure? Only one week's notice?"

"Yes, I'm sure. With your dedication and how hard you've worked for me since your first day on the job, you absolutely deserve it."

Nicole smiled a very grateful smile, rose from her chair, reached across Warren's desk and firmly shook his hand. Then she took a deep breath and let it out in a brief burst.

"Okay. Here we go!"

"Onward and upward, young lady."

She gave Warren a deeply genuine smile, then turned and walked toward his office door. She paused for just a moment, then firmly gripped the doorknob, opened the door confidently, smiled at Maryann, and headed back to her office.

CHAPTER 49

One More Step Forward

AS NICOLE PULLED INTO Carli's driveway she had barely opened her car door before Carli was bounding out the door to greet her!

"Oh, my gosh! It's so wonderful to see you, Nicole!"

"And it's great to see you, too, Carli!"

The ladies gave each other a friendly hug and Carli lead Nicole into her home.

"The weather is so beautiful that I set up everything on the deck!"

"That sounds good to me!"

Before settling into her deck chair, Nicole took in the view and breathed the salty air deep into her lungs.

"Ahhh, I missed this!"

"I'll bet! But I'll also bet you enjoyed the clearer mountain air just as much, right?"

"It was certainly a nice change, and it was so beautiful there, too! But then again, I'm not telling you anything that you don't already know."

"True. True. I *loved* it there! And I'm guessing you saw some amazing sunsets?"

Nicole hesitated for a quick moment as she recalled the last couple that she had shared with Liam.

"Yes, they were most definitely different than I had ever seen before."

Carli leaned backed and sighed as memories of her own visits came back to her.

"So, let's dig into these sandwiches and then you can tell me all about your week!"

"That sounds good."

For the next hour Nicole shared everything she could think of, with the exception of when Chandler surprised her and she summarily sent him packing, as well as her special times alone with Liam.

She told Carli about the two ladies she met and became friends with, and Carli mentioned that she remembered Brendy who was relatively new when she was there the second time. Nicole also asked if she had met the head wrangler, Liam, but Carli said the name was not familiar. When she asked Nicole to describe him and she mentioned he was in his mid-thirties or so, Carli shook her head and said the one she'd met was older, in his sixties.

Nicole also shared her interesting news about her job offer, curious what Carli might think of it. Not surprisingly, Carli was excited for her and encouraged her to go for it! And when she related to Carli what Warren had said, Carli completely agreed.

They talked about other experiences they had each had at the ranch, then, noticing the time, Nicole said she needed to get back to the office. She helped Carli clear the table and return everything to the kitchen counter. Carli then followed Nicole out to her car where they shared another hug and Nicole was on her way.

Her mind began to wander a bit as she drove back to the office. After her mind had been spinning during the flight home, and all night and early that morning, Nicole was now even more clear about what she was going to do. With the wonderful encouragement she received from Warren, along with the excited support she felt from Carli, she was about to make one of the biggest decisions of her life!

CHAPTER 50

The Call

"HI, AMANDA!"

"Welcome back, Nicole! Did you have a good lunch?"

"Yes, I went to see Carli, the lady who gave me the hot air balloon photograph."

"Oh, nice. I'll bet you had a good time!"

"We did! Um … would you mind coming into my office for a moment?"

"Sure!"

"And please close the door behind you."

Nicole led Amanda to her table near the window. As they sat down Nicole took a deep breath and let it out slowly.

"I have something special I want to share with you."

With the word *special* Amanda's eyes lit up, waiting anxiously for Nicole to share what she had to say.

"When I met with Warren this morning, I shared with him what I'm about to share with you."

"Oh, so I'm not the *first* to know, huh?" Amanda teased, and they both laughed. Nicole relaxed a bit as Amanda's comment eased her nervousness.

"Actually, you're the third to know, since I also mentioned it to Carli a little while ago."

Amanda sighed with a wink and a smile. "That's okay. Being third isn't bad."

"Not at all! In fact, you're hearing this from me before I even mention it to my parents."

"Whoa! Then third *really* isn't bad at all. So, what's this something special you want to share with me?"

Nicole took another deep breath and paused before she could speak.

"I've been offered a new job."

Amanda's eyes grew wide and her jaw dropped!

"What?! On, my gosh! Where?"

"At the ranch I was visiting last week."

Now it was Amanda's head that was spinning, and she was nearly speechless. "Um … really? So you're not going to be an architect anymore?"

"That's correct."

"Oh, my gosh. Oh, my gosh! I'm … I'm so happy for you, but … oh, my gosh!"

Amanda sat back, shaking her head as she tried to comprehend what her boss had just shared with her.

"I know it's something you may have never thought you'd hear from me—"

"That's for sure! Wow! Um … so, how much longer will you be here?"

"Friday is my last day."

"What?! Oh, wow! So soon?!"

"Warren asked how soon they needed me, and I told him as soon as possible. I had expected that I would be giving him the normal two weeks' notice, but he encouraged me to wrap everything up as quickly as I can this week and then take off into my future."

Amanda sat stunned, still trying to comprehend everything she was hearing, and let out a long sigh.

"I'm *so* happy for you, Nicole. I really am. But … this has just caught me by surprise."

"I know. This has all happened so fast for me, too."

"I'll bet!"

"When I arrived at the ranch last weekend I was simply looking forward to a nice week where I could relax and take advantage of some of the various activities they had to offer. Early on, I met a couple of ladies near my age that work there and we really hit it off.

"Then, Friday morning, one of the owners, Jill, came up to me during breakfast and asked to see me after breakfast. I had *no* idea why she might want to see me, but both Brendy and Beth, the two ladies I just mentioned, had smiles on their faces, like they knew what was going on. Long story short, they had convinced Jill and her husband, Luke, that I was the right person for a position that had been open for quite some time."

"Really? Doing what?"

"Well, initially I'll be trained to do several different things around the ranch, sort of a generalist. But Jill told me that Pat, the lady who is in charge of stable operations, is going to be retiring soon. Jill didn't say who would be taking Pat's place, but, according to Jill, both Brendy and Beth asked her and Luke to seriously consider me to be a part of their team. So, there you have it!"

"I'm … I'm so happy for you, Nicole! This … wow … I mean, this is just amazing! And you're going from being a topflight architect to working on a ranch?!"

"Yes, I'm still trying to wrap my head around the whole idea!"

"I'll bet!"

"Now, I need to go see Warren and give him my decision that I *am* going to accept the offer so we can proceed to finalize everything for my final week. Then, I'll need your help this afternoon to make a list of my projects and their status for Warren."

"Sure, I'll be glad to help you with that!"

"Great! I knew I could count on you."

"Always!"

* * *

After Nicole met with Warren, she returned to her office, closed the door, and sat down at her desk. She took a deep breath, then picked up her phone to make her life-changing call.

"Good afternoon, Hidden Glory Ranch! This is Kay!"

"Hi, Kay! This is Nicole Hart!"

"Hi, Nicole! This is a pleasant surprise!"

"Thank you! By any chance do you know if Jill is available?"

"Let me check. May I put you on hold for a moment?"

"Sure!"

"Thank you!"

While she was on hold Nicole took a deep breath and let it out ever so slowly. *You can do this, Nicole. It's the right thing to do!*

"Hi, Nicole! It's Jill!"

"Hi, how are you?"

"I'm doing wonderfully! And, I hope to be doing even *better*, depending on the reason you're calling."

"Well … I'm calling to let you and Luke know that I'm going to accept your offer!"

"Oh, that's *wonderful*, Nicole! You've just made our day!"

"Thank you! I'm so glad you feel that way!"

"And I can't wait to tell everyone! The possibility of your accepting our offer has been on everyone's lips since you left."

"Really?"

"Yes! We just had no idea how soon we might hear back from you, and this was fast!"

"Well, I have to admit that I haven't been thinking about much else since you made the offer, and by this morning, I was leaning fairly strongly toward accepting it."

"So, I'm guessing you've already talked to your boss about this?"

"Yes! And I was stunned by his reaction!"

"Was he happy for you?"

"Yes! He asked me how soon you needed me and I said 'soon'. He then completely threw away the idea of my giving two weeks' notice, and said my last day here could be this Friday!"

"Oh, that's amazing, Nicole!"

"I had to laugh as I told him it almost felt like he was trying to get rid of me, and he laughed, too. But he's always been such a wonderful boss and he's so happy for me to take on a new adventure in my life. In fact, listen to this. He told me, 'I personally believe it's just what you need. Yes, I'm going to hate to lose you, but one day I'll be saying, 'I knew her when.'

"Then I replied, 'Thank you, but I don't aspire to be any great cowgirl winning belt buckles at rodeos and such.' To which he replied, 'You never know what special opportunities just might come your way somewhere down the line. Just keep an open mind and a watchful eye, and I believe something special is yet to present itself. Something that you are uniquely qualified to do that is going to make a world of difference to others. Just remember to always be yourself.'

"Oh, my gosh, Nicole! You *do* have an amazing boss!"

"I know, and that's just one reason why it's going to be so hard to leave here."

"I'll bet."

"However, in the brief time I got to know you and Luke last week, as well as many of your staff, I *know* that I'm going to feel right at home there."

"And your last day is this Friday?"

"Correct. And I have *so* much to do this week to get ready for the move. Oh, that reminds me! Do you have any suggestions on where I might find a place to live once I arrive?"

"Yes! To begin with you can stay in one of our casitas, even the one you stayed in last week if you'd like. That will give you a chance to get somewhat settled in until you're able to find a place for yourself somewhere in the area. And I'm sure Brendy and Beth will have a few suggestions for you as well."

"Oh, thank you, Jill. May I ask a favor? Since I'll be bringing quite a few things with me, may I have a 2-bedroom casita instead? And I'll be *more* than happy to pay for it, as well."

"Sure! I'm certain we can work that out, so just plan on it. We can discuss the financial arrangements after you get here and get settled."

"That sounds perfect. Thank you, Jill!"

"You're welcome! And, by the way, speaking of Brendy and Beth, may I have your permission to share the good news with them?"

"Yes! Please do! I just wish I could see their faces when you tell them."

"Well, I have an idea about that."

"What is it?"

"Well, I'm presuming you have a computer handy, right?"

"Yes."

"Great! Let's set up a Zoom call for thirty minutes from now and I'll get them in here but won't tell them why."

"Hey, that's a great idea! But you might want to check with Kay first, since she initially took my call and transferred me to you. She may have already seen them and spilled the beans."

"Good point! I'll check with her, and then I'll email you the link and we'll chat in thirty minutes."

"Sounds good."

Nicole checked her watch and made a mental note to be ready to connect with the ranch on time. Then she checked with Amanda about pulling together all of her current projects and notes from her meetings. Returning to her desk, she pulled out a notebook to begin making notes about the various things she was going to have to do in order to be ready to move that coming weekend!

This weekend?! How on earth am I going to pull this off? Friday might be my last day here, but I may have to take another week just to prepare for the move! Nicole sat back and let out a long sigh.

As the minutes ticked away, her list continued to grow. The time was passing quickly and before she knew it, she was on the computer and clicking on the link for the meeting. Once her connection was complete, she saw Jill and smiled and waved. Jill returned the gesture, including holding a finger to her mouth to give the sign to Nicole to not say anything. Nicole nodded.

"Hi, there! I have Brendy and Beth in the office with me, but they don't know why."

Looking across her desk to the other ladies Jill said, "Would you like to join me over here?"

With that invitation both Brendy and Beth walked around Jill's desk where she was holding up two manila folders, side by side, to hide who was on the screen.

"Okay, mystery person, we're all here!"

"Hi, ladies!" Nicole said excitedly, and with that Jill dropped the folders.

"Oh, my gosh!" Brendy exclaimed. "Hi, Nicole!"

"Hi, Nicole," Beth added, equally excited to see her friend. "How are you?"

"I'm doing great! And it's fun to see you!"

"I know! This was Jill's idea!"

Jill looked at both Brendy and Beth. "She has something to share with us."

Brendy's and Beth's eyes lit up in great anticipation!

"Okay, Nicole. Go ahead!"

"I'm coming back to join you!"

"What?!" Brendy screamed. "Oh, wow!"

"Oh, my gosh, Nicole! YES!!!" Beth exclaimed.

"As you can tell we're all so excited!" added Jill.

"Yes, I can see! And believe me, I am too!"

"How soon?" Brendy asked.

"I'll arrive early next week!"

Nicole watched as her friend's jaws dropped.

"That soon?" Beth excitedly asked.

"Yes! As I was talking with my boss this morning he became really excited for me. He told me to go ahead and wrap up everything this week and take care of any personal things I need to handle. That way I can get there as soon as possible."

"Oh, my gosh! We can't wait to see you!" Brendy exclaimed.

"And I can't wait to see all of you!" Nicole replied in kind.

By now tears of joy were flowing down the cheeks of all four ladies.

"Well," Jill said, "we better let you go. You have lot to do to get ready to join us."

Nicole rolled her eyes. "I know! But before you go may I ask a favor?"

"Anything!"

"Please tell Luke 'thank you' as well for this opportunity. I appreciate this so much!"

"I sure will! We're excited to have you join us. Just take care of what you need to and we'll see you when you get here next week."

Nicole was still fighting back the tears. "Thank you, Jill. And bye Brendy and Beth!"

"Bye, Nicole!" they responded in unison as they waved.

Nicole waved back to everyone and then clicked out of the meeting.

She reached for the box of tissues near her desk, took two, and dabbed her eyes and wiped her nose. She took a deep breath and looked out toward Amanda who was busy working on the project list for her. Then she swiveled around and got up and walked to the window.

Oh, my gosh! What a day!

CHAPTER 51

The Next Call

ON HER WAY HOME Nicole stopped at the post office to pick up her mail. She also let them know they could continue delivering it for the rest of the week, but starting the following Monday she would be moving. She was handed a small stack of mail with a rubber band around it, along with a change of address form to complete. She slipped the mail into her purse, filled out the form, returned it to the clerk, and was on her way.

Knowing that her refrigerator was virtually empty, as was her freezer, Nicole tried to decide what to pick up for dinner on her way home. With her impending move, she didn't need to buy too many groceries. She decided to make a quick stop to buy enough for just that night, and then go out again tomorrow after work for more.

After arriving home, Nicole set her purse and groceries down on the kitchen counter and opened the patio door to let the faint ocean breeze freshen up her condo. She took an extra moment to enjoy the view and sighed as she realized she had taken this beautiful view for granted. She had always assumed she would be close enough to the ocean to at least see it, if not actually visit it often. How quickly her life was changing!

Nicole returned to the kitchen, put the groceries away, moved her purse to the island and took out her phone and the mail. She set them down before heading into her bedroom to change into something more relaxing for the evening. She brushed her hair and pulled it back into a ponytail, then returned to the kitchen. As she flipped through the mail, she began separating the bills from the —*WHAT?!* Chandler had written her a letter?! She let out a long, frustrated sigh. *Just what I* don't *need right now!* She threw his letter down onto the island and flipped through the rest of her mail – two bills and the rest was junk. And, as far as she was concerned, Chandler's letter could just as well go with the latter. *He's probably begging me to give him a second chance so he can get his* precious *partnership! Well, sorry.* Not *interested!*

Nicole needed a distraction to take her mind off the letter and noticed her phone sitting nearby. She was not particularly looking forward to the call she was about to make, but knew she had to bite the bullet and get it over with. She took a deep breath, let it out slowly, picked up her phone and walked through the living room and out onto her deck. She hoped that just looking at the waves crashing on the distant shore would bring her the calm she was seeking so desperately right now. One more deep breath, exhaling as she hit speed dial. She bit her lip and closed her eyes.

"Hello?"

"Hi, Mom."

"Hi, Nicole! How are you?"

Nicole let out another deep sigh. "I'm doing okay," she replied unconvincingly.

"Nicole, what's wrong?"

"Mom, is Dad there?"

"No, he's golfing but he's due home soon for dinner. Why? Did you need to talk to him?"

"No! No, I want to talk to you, but I was just hoping he couldn't hear the call."

"Sweetheart, what's wrong?"

"Oh, nothing is *wrong*. I just wanted to let you know that I'm … moving to New Mexico."

"What?! Oh, my gosh! Why? Where? I mean, this is so sudden! What's going on?"

"I've been offered a job at the ranch where I stayed last week."

"Oh, Nicole! Really?"

"Yes. I'm nervous about this change, but I'm also *so* excited!"

"Wow! What a change! I mean, this seems so sudden. Did you really give this a lot of thought?"

"Yes, I did. I know this *does* seems quite sudden, but it also feels so right."

"Well, if it feels right to you, then that's good enough for me."

"Thanks, Mom. I was hoping you would say that."

"Of course, dear! Whatever makes you happy will make me happy."

"Now, if I could just get Dad to see it your way."

"You just leave your father to me."

Nicole thought about this for a moment. "Mom, I really think I need to talk to him myself."

"Sweetheart, as big a change that this is going to be for you, it's going to be even bigger in your father's mind. We both know that he hasn't always been there for you when it was most important. I'll find the right time and the right way to break the news."

"Are you sure, Mom?"

"I'm *very* sure, dear."

Nicole sighed. "Thank you."

"Absolutely. So, when are you planning on moving?"

"Early next week."

"So soon?"

"They need me there to fill a position that's been open for quite a while."

Charlotte sighed heavily. "Will you have a chance to come see us before you leave?"

"Yes, I'd like to come on Saturday and spend the night."

"That would be wonderful, dear!"

"I couldn't leave without seeing you both. Plus, I won't be that far away. I can fly home to see you, and you guys can always come to visit me! It's a beautiful ranch!"

"Oh, that might be fun!"

"And you can stay for as long as you'd like. A weekend, a couple of days, or a week. Whatever you'd like."

"I'd sure like to come and see what you're going to be doing, and I hope your father will join me."

"Me, too, Mom. Me, too."

"Well, I'm sure you have many things to do to get ready, so I'll let you get back to them. I look forward to seeing you this weekend."

"Okay, Mom. I love you!"

"And I love you, too, dear."

Nicole sighed in relief. *That went better than I thought it might. At least my dad wasn't there. I can only imagine how he's going to take the news. Good luck, Mom.*

With that over, Nicole could now concentrate on thinking about everything else she needed to take care of before she moved and her mind began to spin. First on her list would be to contact Royal and make arrangements for him to sell her condo. Then she would need to decide carefully what to pack to take with her. Later she would fly home and rent a truck to move what she'd left behind to her new place in Angel Fire.

But first, dinner. And then … the letter.

Chapter 52

The Letter

NICOLE ENJOYED HER DINNER on the deck while taking in one of her final coastal sunsets. She let her mind wander over the various stages of her life, some happy, some not so much. She had to admit the good times far outnumbered the bad, but sometimes the bad had been so intense that she could barely deal with them. However, she always managed to see her way through to better times, and, as far as she could tell, even better times were just ahead!

Then she remembered Chandler's letter, and grudgingly brought her dinner dishes inside, rinsed them off, and placed them in the dishwasher. She picked up his letter from the island, walked into the living room, turned on the lamp next to the sofa, and sat down. She ripped open the end and slid the letter out.

Dear Nicole,

I'll begin by apologizing for my completely uncalled for visit to the ranch. I was just so anxious to see you and I couldn't wait until you got home to share my good news. It was clearly uncalled for and I'm deeply sorry.

During and since my flight home I've done a lot of thinking and soul-searching. I can now see that we have not really been on the same page in our lives for quite some time, and I had also been seriously taking you for granted.

We always seemed to have such a good time together, and as I was gradually getting more serious about us, at least in my mind, I can also see that you weren't feeling the same. If I had been more aware, more sensitive to you and your feelings, I'm sure I would have been aware of that as soon as you began to be disengaged in us.

I always felt we had a wonderful thing going, and I can also see now that I was spending too much time focused on my career and not enough on us, or more especially, on you.

The partnership in my firm is gone, and I only have myself to blame. I completely misplaced my priorities, and now I'll deal with it the best I can. I was so anxious and excited to share this new adventure in my life with you, but I'm now aware that it wasn't financial security you're wanting, but someone to share your whole life with, completely.

Nicole, I can still be that man. I can still be the one person you will always be able to turn to, to trust, to confide in, the person who will love you purely and forever, and to give you all that you could possibly wish for.

Sweetheart, sorry, I know you don't want me to call you that now, but I truly mean it from the depths of my heart when I say I love you. I don't care about the partnership anymore. It's no longer important to me. What is important is that I love you with all of my heart, and if there is any chance that you could find it in your heart to give me a second chance, I promise I'll never hurt you or let you down again.

Believe me, I'm not hoping for a quick reply. I know this may be a lot for you to think about right now, so take all the time you need. I'll be here waiting only for you.

I love you with all of my heart, Nicole.

Love,

Chandler

As Nicole finished reading the letter, she noticed a tear rolling down each cheek. She set the letter down and quickly swiped her cheeks with the backs of her hands and let out a sigh. She laid her head against the back cushion of the sofa and stared at the ceiling for a long moment, then got up and walked out onto her deck and leaned against the railing, looking out toward the horizon.

Letting the words of his letter roll over and over in her mind, she began to mentally compose her reply. She was sure he would not like it, but at this point she no longer held any animosity toward him, only a sense of relief that she had made the decision to move on in a new direction in her life. And even though she didn't know exactly where this new direction would take her, she truly felt it was the right choice for her.

After a few more minutes, Nicole went back inside, folded up Chandler's letter, put it back in the envelope, and placed it on the coffee table. Her priority now was to sit down and finish the list of tasks she needed to complete, by day, to prepare for her move in less than a week.

CHAPTER 53

Bittersweet

NICOLE'S LAST WEEK IN sunny California was a whirlwind! Between wrapping up everything at the office, meeting with Royal to prepare to put her condo on the market, doing some shopping for a new, more appropriate wardrobe, and saying goodbye to her closest friends, she was exhausted. She spent her late evenings separating the more important things she would need to pack and take with her. The other things she would leave behind until she could return and work out her future moving plans.

Her mother had promised to call Nicole after she had broken the news to her father, so in the meantime she tried not to worry about how she was going to handle the fallout from that nuclear blast. She just prayed that the blast wouldn't trigger a 10.0 earthquake on the San Andreas Fault!

Nicole was grateful that she had already ended her relationship with Chandler, even as messy as it was at the end. While the letter she had received earlier that week had been conciliatory, and she felt his feelings and intensions were genuine, it was definitely time to move on and she would tell him so. She had not heard from him after that. *Just let me move on with my life.*

***

Friday had arrived all too quickly! Royal had come by after work on Tuesday, and they had made plans to put her home on the market on Wednesday of the following week. He assured her that she would not have to bring in anyone to "stage" her condo for two reasons; her furnishings were in excellent condition and quite modern, and the demand for housing was so great that she would probably receive multiple excellent offers within the first twenty-four hours!

She had spent her lunch breaks taking care of all her wardrobe shopping, and on Wednesday evening she had a wonderful but tear-filled dinner with Carli. She was now packing up the last items she would be taking with her on Monday morning. Her secretary, Amanda, had made arrangements to come into work late that day so she could help Nicole load her car. Then she would stay behind and give Nicole's condo a top-notch cleaning as a going away present. She then would meet with Royal later in the day to pass along Nicole's extra keys to the condo.

* * *

Nicole's last day at the office was spent packing up her personal items, making arrangements for her beautiful photograph from Carli to be properly packed up and delivered to her at the ranch, and taking an extended lunch hour to treat Amanda to a special lunch at their favorite restaurant, Olive Garden.

After lunch she took time to write thank you notes to each of her co-workers and delivered each of them personally while trying her best to hold back tears. She finished with a special note for Warren. They had a sweet, but brief, conversation after which he wished her well.

"I know you're going to be amazing in your new adventure."

"Well, I don't know about *amazing* but I'm certainly going to try."

"Don't underestimate yourself, young lady. Your new bosses saw something unique in you after your being there for only a few days. You'll be just fine, I know it!"

"Thank you for your confidence, Warren."

"Absolutely! Oh, by the way, your final paycheck should have already arrived at your bank."

"Oh, thank you! With all of the craziness going on this week I had not even thought about that!"

"Somehow that does not surprise me. I've also authorized a special severance package for you."

"Really? You didn't have to do that, Warren."

"Yes, I did, because you deserve it. And as part of that package, I've made arrangements for you to maintain your insurance package with us for the next three months. Plus, you'll see a little extra in your bank account to help you get settled."

"Warren, you are just too good to me."

"Nonsense! As I said, you deserve it."

Tears began to pool in Nicole's eyes which she quickly flipped away with her finger.

"Thank you so much for everything, Warren. You're the best."

Warren just nodded and smiled. *Is that a tear I see in the corner of his eye?*

Nicole stepped forward and gave Warren a warm and grateful hug.

"I better be getting back to my office to finish packing and write a few more notes."

"By all means. Thank you for coming in to see me."

Nicole nodded as she choked back more tears.

As she left Warren's office she could only nod and share a tearful smile with Maryann, and as she approached her office, she avoided looking at Amanda, afraid that she would lose it altogether. She walked into her office, closed the door, and reached for some tissues on her way to stand in the window to look at the view one last time. *This is so much harder than I thought it would be!*

* * *

The office was quiet as Nicole came in after loading the last box into her car, but it didn't particularly stand out as unusual. As she entered her office, she walked to the window to catch one last look of the view she had enjoyed for so many years. She sat down at her desk and reached out her hands and laid them flat, sweeping them side to side, feeling the coolness of the rich oak desktop. Then she rose and walked to her designer's desk and sat on the stool, closing her eyes and picturing in her mind all of the various buildings and homes she had designed over the years.

She rose from the stool and looked over her office one last time and was about to say goodbye to Amanda, but noticed she wasn't at her desk. *She's probably in the ladies room. Maybe it's just as well. I'm not sure I could handle another tearful goodbye. Besides, I'll see her again Monday morning.*

As Nicole walked to Warren's office to say goodbye to him for the last time, she noticed something odd … the office was surprisingly quiet. Maryann wasn't at her desk and Warren wasn't in his office. *This is just strange*, she thought. *Where is everyone? No one around? Not a sound throughout the whole office?*

"Hello? Anyone here?" She listened intently but heard nothing. "Okay, what's going on? Hello??" Nicole sighed heavily and slowly walked past her office and toward the office foyer. As she turned the corner toward the front door an easel was standing in her way that had not been there several minutes before. The message on a poster read, "Nicole, please join me in the conference room. Warren."

She stood there for a moment trying to figure out what was happening. She headed toward the conference room, surprised to see the blinds pulled shut on the hallway glass panels, and no light coming from within. As she reached for the doorknob, she paused for a long moment, took a deep breath, and slowly opened the door. It was so dark inside.

"Hello?" she asked almost timidly.

"SURPRISE!" Nicole jumped backward as the lights went on!

"Oh, my gosh! What??? What's going on?"

Warren stepped forward from the near side of the room.

"There was just no way we could let you go without having a little party in your honor, and to be able to tell you how much we love you and how excited we are for this new adventure in your life!"

"Oh, Warren, I don't know what to say. This is all just so …" Nicole fought back the tears that she promised herself earlier that morning she wouldn't let flow as she left today. No such luck … they were flowing.

"Take a look!" Amanda called from across the room, pointing to the conference table in front of her. There was a full-sized sheet cake decorated on top with a replica of the first home Nicole had designed after being hired. A punch bowl with cups were next to the cake, and further down the table were over a dozen presents! The tears kept flowing!

Over the next several minutes Nicole made her way around the room and thanked everyone for their kindness and friendship. Warren stepped up to the table and cut the cake, serving the first piece to Nicole.

As the excitement was calming down, and her colleagues were getting ready to head out for the weekend, Warren cleared his throat.

"May I please have everyone's attention?" The staff hushed quickly.

Warren sighed deeply before continuing. "Nicole, this is a bitter-sweet moment for me—"

"And me, too!" Amanda interjected.

Similar comments were heard from around the room, with everyone's heads nodding in agreement.

"Okay, let me rephrase that … Nicole, this is a bittersweet moment for *all* of us—"

"Me, too," Nicole added with a wink, causing laughter to filter throughout the room.

Warren smiled. "You're not making this any easier, young lady," Warren replied with a wink and a smile. Everyone laughed.

"Ahem! Okay, enough with any kind of long, drawn-out speech I may have come up with. Let's let Nicole be on her way. EXCEPT …" Warren looked at Nicole, "not until we share with you this one last gift of thanks and best of luck from the whole office." He handed her an envelope, and as she accepted it her tears began to flow once again, and her hands began to tremble. Warren leaned toward her and put a fatherly arm around her, and she turned and cried into his shoulder.

"We love you, Nicole!" Martin shouted from the far end of the room.

"We're really going to miss you!" added Maryann.

"You're welcome back anytime," Warren whispered in her ear.

Nicole caught her breath and looked around the room. "Thank you all so very much! I'm really going to miss each of you."

Warren cleared his throat once again, doing his best to hold on to his own emotions.

"There's one more thing. The content of this envelope comes with one condition."

Nicole looked hesitantly at Warren, then glanced around the room and noticed everyone was smiling. "Do you all know what's in here?" she asked. Everyone nodded.

Warren winked, "Go ahead and open it."

Nicole took a deep breath, trying to calm her nerves. She opened the envelope and pulled out a check and nearly fainted. She looked at Warren and the astonished look in her eyes was all he needed to see.

"Read the memo on the check out loud."

Nicole glanced down. "For your new saddle, tack, and accessories." Overcome with emotion, she held the check to her breast and mouthed a breathless "thank you" to everyone, then looked at Warren.

"But I don't even have my own horse yet!" she exclaimed, and everyone laughed.

"You will, soon enough," Warren replied. "And when you do, you'll be ready to put the best looking gear on it." Everyone began cheering and clapping and Nicole sobbed with total joy.

"Thank you, everyone, so *very* much! You have *no* idea what your kindness means to me."

"We want to see lots of photos of that horse and saddle, too!" Martin shouted, and everyone laughed and nodded.

As her co-workers were leaving, Warren and Amanda helped Nicole load her presents into her car. Once the job was done Nicole gave them each a tearful hug and said goodbye. As she approached the exit to the parking lot she took a deep breath, turned onto the street, took one last look at the wonderful office she had called home for nearly ten years, and headed toward her condo.

* * *

After arriving home and unpacking the boxes and presents from her car, Nicole walked out onto the deck, leaned against the railing, and looked out toward the ocean. She closed her eyes and did her best to block out the sounds of the nearby traffic. She imagined she was walking along the beach, and the only sounds she could hear were of the crashing waves. Ahhh, so peaceful!

After several minutes of enjoying this reverie, Nicole opened her eyes, took a deep breath, and walked back into the condo. She glanced at the stack of boxes, then headed toward the kitchen to see what she might find for dinner. Knowing she would be moving soon she had not done any serious shopping. She had picked up a few things earlier in the week which she had already prepared for dinner on Tuesday evening and last night. Even her freezer was mostly bare, with the exception of a hand packed half-gallon of her favorite ice cream from Baskin Robbins, World Class Chocolate. For a brief moment she thought about just going ahead and splurging, but then decided against it. She ordered a large pizza to be delivered instead.

While she waited for the pizza she went downstairs and retrieved her mail. As she returned to the condo, she remembered that she needed to respond to Chandler's letter. It would not take long and she decided to take care of it while she waited.

As she walked back into the condo, she separated the mail on the island into bills and junk. She set the junk mail aside to shred, and then retrieved her laptop to pay the bills, as well as to notify those companies of her new address.

With the bills paid, Nicole walked into the bedroom, retrieved her stationery from the middle drawer of her desk, and returned to the kitchen. As she sat down on a high stool at the island, she paused to think about what she wanted to say to Chandler. She then applied pen to paper, and within a few minutes her note was ready to be put into an envelope which she would then mail the next morning.

By the time she was finished, she had a feeling her pizza would be delivered soon, so she took out a large plate, some napkins, and a tumbler for a soda. Five minutes later she was sitting on the deck, enjoying her pizza and the view.

* * *

The excitement of the week was catching up to Nicole, and she was feeling beyond exhausted. Instead of worrying any more about packing for her move, she decided to take a long, hot bath to unwind, and then get to bed a little early.

Forty-five minutes later she slipped between the cool, soft sheets and laid her head on her pillow. As her thoughts drifted over everything that had happened during the past week, her eyes became heavy, and she slipped into a well-deserved and restful sleep.

CHAPTER 54

Saturday

NICOLE WAS AWAKE BEFORE her alarm and excitedly jumped out of bed. The thought of a new beginning had her spirits soaring!

She dressed quickly and completed her pre-walk stretching a little quicker than normal. Just before leaving, she picked up the note she had written to Chandler the night before from the island in the kitchen, and was out the door and on her way! However, after dropping the note into a blue postal collection box a block away, she felt a strong impression that she needed to slow her pace and look around her a little bit more. She no longer had to concentrate about anything at work, and she did not need to think about what was coming up for her in a few days. She just wanted to take in this moment for all it was worth.

She didn't really see anything new that she had not seen before, but she noticed sounds that she could not remember being aware of in the recent past. As early as it was, there was still the normal sound of traffic, but she also heard birds chirping in the trees as she walked along. A dog barked from a nearby house, and she looked and noticed it standing in the plate glass window with its tail happily wagging. A cyclist rode by on the opposite side of the street and they nodded to each other.

Part of her walk always took her out of her neighborhood and into a small business district. The aroma of fresh bakery goods wafted passed her and she wondered how she could have missed that before! She was ever so tempted to stop, but continued on her way. However, before she reached the end of the block she turned and went back. *I'm leaving in a few days,* she reasoned, *so why not treat myself to something yummy?* Her choices were too numerous to count, but she was drawn to the fresh, warm cherry turnovers the baker had just placed on the shelf and bought two!

She continued to take in the sights, sounds, and aromas for the next couple of miles and then took her normal turn to head back home. She did her best to stay in the moment and not think ahead to the long list of chores yet to be completed before her move.

After she arrived home, she showered and dressed comfortably for the day ahead and, while standing at the island in her kitchen, she enjoyed her cherry turnovers. She reviewed her list, checked off a few items that she had already completed the night before, turned on her laptop and logged into her favorite Sirius/XM channel, and the work commenced.

* * *

Nicole and Royal had decided that she would simply clean her condo and straighten everything before it was open for visitors the following Wednesday. She had focused on one room each night over the past few days so as not to have too much to do all at once. Around noon she stopped and scanned each room to see what needed to be taken care of and realized that she was nearly finished. The living room and kitchen were the last on her list and within an hour the last item had been checked off. She grabbed a bottle of water from the refrigerator, walked out onto the deck, and sat down for the first time since she had arrived home from her walk. She completely relaxed as she sat back, closed her eyes, and enjoyed the warmth from the sun and the scent of the ocean breeze.

I can't believe that I'm leaving all of this! My condo, the beach, everything to see and do in Southern California ... my work. Am I really doing the right thing? Nicole took a long pull of her water and looked around once more. She let out a long sigh before heading back inside. Even though the question was still hanging in the air, she felt an overall calm and peace about her decision. She smiled to herself and a chill suddenly ran through her, making her feel even that much more confident. *Let's* do *this!!*

* * *

The rest of the afternoon passed quickly and before she knew it Nicole found herself sitting at her parent's dining room table. She enjoyed a delicious dinner of one of her favorite dishes, Chicken Cordon Bleu. Her father had been golfing when she arrived, and her mother explained that she had not had the chance to break the news of her moving to him yet. Nicole began to wonder again if she should just go ahead and bring it up over dinner, but then had second thoughts, not wanting to take the chance of ruining what would be their last dinner together for quite a while. She hated to leave it to her mother to break the news, knowing the potential fury that would ensue.

Deciding not to mention anything to him turned out to be a wise choice, as her father was not in a good mood when he arrived home. He had lost a sizable wager on the course that day, paying the price for his ego.

Nicole also thought about bringing it up after dinner while they sat on the patio enjoying the light pinks, blues, and oranges of the slowly approaching desert sunset. However, her mother saw her in deep thought and read her mind, shaking her head imperceptibly. Nicole nodded in kind. The silence was broken by her father's question that caught her completely off guard.

"So, how's work going? Working on any big, new projects?"

Nicole felt a lump catch in her throat and fought to clear it as quickly as she could. "Work has been fine, Dad. Just fine."

"Good. Good. My old friend Warren still treating you fairly?"

"Yes, he's been a wonderful boss and mentor."

"Well, he better be. Otherwise, I'll have to have a talk with him."

"Um, that won't be necessary."

"Good."

Nicole looked desperately toward her mother for some help, and her mother took her cue and changed the subject.

"I was talking with Gwen Stevens today, and she and Ralph are selling their home and moving."

"What?!" Jenson replied somewhat harshly. Nicole was taken aback by his tone.

"She said they have been thinking about it for a while and a few days ago they decided it was time."

"I wonder why he didn't say anything to me while we were golfing last weekend."

"Maybe because they hadn't decided anything yet and just wanted to keep it to themselves until they knew for sure."

Jenson let out a long, disgusted sigh. "Did she say where they are moving to?"

"Yes, Texas."

"Texas! What's in Texas that would make them do something crazy like that?"

"They have a daughter who just got a divorce so they decided to move to be near her and their grandchildren."

"Couldn't they just fly down to visit them once in a while?"

"What's wrong with them wanting to be closer to them?"

Jenson didn't answer, he just shook his head.

Not wanting to be a part of her father's bad mood any longer, Nicole stood up and headed toward the patio door.

"I'm going to the kitchen. Would anyone care for something to drink?"

"Nothing for me," her father answered in a gruff tone.

"I'd like some iced tea, sweetheart."

"Sure, Mom. Coming right up."

A moment later she handed her mother a glass of iced tea, and when her mother noticed that Nicole did not have a drink of her own, she asked, "Aren't you having anything, dear?"

"I already had some ice water. And now I think I'll go for a walk."

"Where to?" Her father asked intensely.

"Just around the neighborhood," she responded casually.

"Well, don't be gone too long. It's getting dark."

Nicole rolled her eyes, knowing that there would still be plenty of light an hour from now. Her mother tipped her head toward the house as her signal to just get going.

"Enjoy your walk, sweetheart."

"Thank you, Mom. I will."

As Nicole walked through the palm tree lined streets, plenty of thoughts were spinning in her mind, most of them surrounding her father. She wanted him to know about her plans before she left for her new adventure so they would have a chance to talk things over. She wanted to explain her choice to move on from the successful career she had worked so hard to establish. She didn't want her mother to take the brunt of what, Nicole knew, was going to be a strong backlash, but her mother had insisted. While her dad was golfing that afternoon, her mother shared with Nicole the approach she would use to ease into the discussion. However, it still didn't make Nicole feel any better.

Again she wondered if she was, in fact, making the right decision. Sure, on the surface it appeared to be a good choice, but was it the *right* choice for her, especially at this point in her life? She had been highly motivated, and had worked so hard to get to this point in her career to just throw it all away on a whim. But, was it just a whim? Or could this be leading her toward a more challenging and rewarding future? Only time would truly answer that question, but *when* would she know? Patience was not always a virtue in her basket.

This was truly a leap of faith, one that she was confident enough in to at least give it a try. She had Warren's assurance that her place would always be open should she decide to return. While that was a generous offer on his part, she knew that she needed to burn as much of this bridge as possible in order to fully focus on her future. She needed to stand on her own with no crutches of any kind.

Another question tumbling over and over was *what*, exactly, had attracted her so much to making this change? While the mountains, trees, and ranch were most certainly a dramatic change in scenery to what she had grown up around, there was also a strong sense of ... mystery. She was walking away from dresses, business suits and heels, business meetings, and client presentations. Also, a varying night life of restaurants, Lakers or Dodgers games, movies or concerts. She was now stepping into a world of Wranglers and boots, horses and dust, breathtaking sunsets, and quiet starry nights. *Okay,* she thought, *if you put it that way … let's do it!* Besides … what was the name of the ranch all about? Hidden Glory Ranch? Another mystery.

Her pace picked up as she returned to her parent's home. As Nicole walked through the front door her mother immediately noticed a change in her countenance.

"Hi, sweetie, did you have a good walk?"

"Yes, it was wonderful!"

"Wonderful, huh? Care to share what made it so *wonderful?*"

"Well, you know, the weather is perfect, and the sunset is so gorgeous right now."

"Yes, I noticed. Anything else?" she asked with a wink.

Nicole glanced around, checking to see if her dad was within earshot range.

"Yeah," Nicole whispered excitedly. "I'm excited about my move!"

Her mother's eyes lit up with joy for her daughter! "That *is* wonderful, Nicole! I'm so happy for you!" her mother whispered back.

"What's so wonderful?" Jenson asked, causing both ladies to jump as it appeared their gentle conspiracy had been discovered.

"Oh!", Charlotte replied. "Um, Nicole was just telling me something that had to do with her job." Nicole gave her a nod as a signal of *Good one, Mom!*

"Well, tell me about it," Jenson replied as he looked back and forth between his wife and daughter.

"Another time, sweetheart, okay?"

"Well, why not now?"

"Because," Nicole replied, "not all of the details have been worked out."

"Details? For what?"

"Dear," Charlotte interjected, "I said we'll talk about it later, okay?"

Jenson was used to getting his way but it was clear that he was outnumbered this time.

"Okay," he groused under his breath as he walked away.

Nicole gave her mother a thumbs up. "Thanks, Mom!" she whispered, softer this time.

"You're welcome," her mother whispered with a wink.

CHAPTER 55

The Last Day

JENSON WAS UP EARLY Sunday morning and on the golf course at sunrise. Nicole and her mother enjoyed a leisurely breakfast on the patio.

"That was a close call last night, Mom."

"Yes, it sure was, dear. I'm actually surprised your father gave up so easily." They both laughed.

"Mom, are you sure you don't want to let me talk to Dad about my plans?"

"Sweetie, you and I both know that it's best that I'm the one to break the news. We know he will be upset, mostly because he wasn't a part of the decision-making process, but also because he has always tried, in one way or another, to influence your plans and decisions. I don't want him to make you feel like you've made a wrong decision. This is *your* life, not his, and he has absolutely *no* say in how you live it. I'll know when the time is right, so don't think any more about it, okay?"

Nicole paused and smiled sweetly at her mother. "I love you, Mom. You're the best."

"I just know what's best for my little girl."

"Yes, you do. Thanks."

Charlotte reached over and placed her hand on the back of Nicole's arm. "Anytime, sweetie. Anytime."

"I do have one question."

"What's that?"

"Should I listen for a sonic boom when you tell Dad?"

Mother and daughter had a *big* laugh over *that* one!

"I know I should probably be heading home soon to make sure everything is ready before I leave tomorrow, but it's likely going to be quite a while before I can see you and Dad again, so if it's okay with you I'm just going to hang around here a while longer."

"Well, you know that's perfectly fine with me. I'm not sure when your father will be home, but I think I heard him say something about playing just one round this morning."

Nicole didn't reply, she just nodded her head. She *was* going to miss seeing her dad, even if he *had* always been hard to be around. He *was* her father, and he deserved a certain level of respect for that.

"Mom, are you sure I can't tell him about my new job?"

"Oh, I'm positive, sweetheart. Try thinking back to when you were playing the piano and had done so well at that recital. Initially, he was stunned and excited at how well you performed, but by the next day he fell back into that mode of needing to control you."

"Yes … I remember," Nicole replied sullenly, letting out a long and knowing sigh.

"Fortunately, you had matured enough by then that you refused to let him stop you from striving to achieve anything and everything you set your heart and mind on."

Nicole smiled as she looked out across the patio. *Yes … I had, and I did!*

"So, you just let me take care of your father. And I'll make sure you're long gone and settled into your new job in … in … what's the name of the place again?"

"Hidden Glory Ranch."

"Right, right. That's such an interesting name! Do you know why they call it that?"

"No, not yet. I asked a couple of people while I was there, but they didn't know. They just told me I should talk to the owners, Luke or Jill, to find out for sure. I will, soon, and I'll let you know."

"Sure, that's fine, dear."

"I think I'm going to go lie down and take a short nap."

"Are you feeling okay, dear?"

"Oh, yes! I've just been so busy this last week trying to get everything ready, that I haven't fully rested that much while I've slept. Too anxious and excited, I guess."

"I can imagine. Sure, go enjoy a nice nap. What time would you like me to make sure you're awake?"

"How about no later than two-thirty? That way I can casually make my exit and get back to my condo early enough to have a productive, and yet relaxing, last evening in California. Oh gosh, that sounds so strange!"

Charlotte sighed. "Oh, my gosh. It's really happening," she replied with a trace of a tear forming in her eye.

Nicole sighed, as well. "Yes, it looks like it really is."

They gave each other a long, tight hug.

"Okay, dear. Go enjoy your nap."

"Thanks, Mom. I love you!"

"I love you, too, sweetheart."

* * *

As exhausted as Nicole was, it took her only a few minutes to fall asleep. Talking with her mother always seemed to calm her. With her mother's reassurance that she believed her sweet daughter had made the right choice, Nicole was able to let go of any other immediate concerns and just relax into a deep sleep.

She awakened three hours later feeling fully rested and glanced at her watch. *Thirty minutes ahead of time. Nice!* As she sat up on the bed, she heard her father and mother talking in the other room. She listened carefully. *It sounds like he's in a better mood than yesterday. Good!* She smoothed the comforter on her bed, packed up her overnight bag, and ventured into the other room.

"Hi, there, sleepyhead!" her mother called.

"Hi, Mom. Hi, Dad."

"Hi! How's my little girl?"

"Wow, you're in a good mood," Nicole replied cautiously. "I'm guessing things went better on the golf course today?"

"Yes! Not only did I have one of my best rounds ever, I also pocketed a nice bit of spare change."

Nicole simply nodded.

"Nicole is headed back to the coast in a little bit," her mother said.

"Oh, that's too bad! Well, when will we see you again?"

Nicole felt a twist in her stomach.

"I'm not sure. Things are going to be busy for a while, but I'll keep you posted."

"Fine, fine! Well, drive carefully and work hard!"

"I will, Dad. Thank you."

Nicole could not get over her father's exuberance. This just was not like him!

She gave her mother a big hug, holding it longer than usual. As they separated, her mother reached up and touched the side of her face with the palm of her right hand.

"Take care, sweetheart." The look in her eyes conveyed what her lips could not, and Nicole read her message perfectly.

She then stepped toward her father and gave him an extra-long hug.

"I love you, Dad."

"You, too, Nicole." It wasn't the warm, cozy feeling that she had hoped for, but then again … when was the last time he had been sincerely caring toward his daughter. She stepped back a bit hesitantly.

"Is everything okay?" her father asked.

"Yes, why?"

"Oh, I don't know. Your hug just seemed a little different this time."

"No, everything is fine, Dad."

"Okay, just checking." *There he goes again. Does he* really *care? I'm so confused!*

"Don't forget your bag!"

"Oh, right. Thanks, Mom." Nicole turned and walked to her bedroom, retrieved her bag, and headed for the front door.

"Bye, dear," her mother said as Nicole walked out the door. "Drive carefully!"

"I promise."

* * *

The drive home was uneventful. The weather was pleasant and the traffic fairly light until she reached Beaumont. From there it was busier but still moved along at a decent pace. Nicole knew that if she had left an hour later this area would be jammed and moving at a snail's pace until she reached the coast. Instead, she was able to make it home in just a little over two hours.

As she walked into her condo, she set her overnight bag down and headed for the deck. She sighed heavily as she looked out over the beautiful view.

"I'm going to miss this so much!" Nicole softly said to herself.

She went back inside, retrieved her bag, and headed for the bedroom. She kicked off her shoes, changed into shorts and a t-shirt, gathered together the few remaining items that needed to be washed, and started a cycle.

She found her laptop and turned it on, found her favorite channel on Sirius/XM, grabbed a bottle of water from the refrigerator, and walked out onto her deck. She slowly scanned the view, not looking for anything in particular. She sat down, leaned back, crossed her legs at her ankles, closed her eyes, and, with a contented smile on her face, got lost in her thoughts.

CHAPTER 56

Monday Morning

NICOLE WAS WIDE AWAKE before her alarm. She laid there for several minutes with her head spinning with excitement. *I did it! I really did it! This is the day my new life begins!!*

There was no debate about whether to go for one last morning walk. After all these years, why stop now? She had plenty of time. She had already plotted her route to Angel Fire. If she drove straight through she would be there in just over sixteen hours, taking into account stops for gas and meals. But there was no need to push it. Besides, that would mean she would arrive in the middle of the night. No thank you! Instead, she would be spending the night just over halfway to Angel Fire, in Winslow, Arizona.

At the time she started her walk, it was overcast with a chilly breeze. She stopped at the bakery along the way and bought four cherry turnovers so she could share them with Amanda. By the time she had returned to her condo the sun had broken through the clouds, but it was still a bit early to feel its warmth. She set the turnovers on the island and headed for the shower.

* * *

As she was packing the last of the clothes from her closet, Nicole set out two outfits, one to wear today, and the other to wear tomorrow. The day was going to be sunny and warm, so she chose her Wranglers, a short sleeved white on white blouse, and sandals. The other outfit she tucked neatly away in her overnight bag. Her long strawberry blonde hair and makeup were done to perfection, as if she were heading back to work this morning and not hitting the road for the new adventure that lay ahead.

Having already been given permission by Warren to come in late that morning, Amanda arrived at seven to assist Nicole with packing her Chevy Tahoe. Sure, it was not *that* big of a job, but it gave them a few final minutes together. Amanda had been Nicole's efficient and indispensable assistant from the start, having been hired just one week after Nicole. They had become more than just office associates. Over the years their friendship had grown to the point where they would often confide in each other over nearly everything. Now a separation was coming that neither of them was looking forward to.

As Nicole answered the front door Amanda's jaw dropped.

"Oh, wow, girl! You look amazing! I thought you were heading to New Mexico today, but you look more like you're heading to a fun party!"

Nicole laughed. "No, I just want to dazzle the truckers I'll be flying passed on my way." The ladies had a good laugh as Nicole stepped back and waved her friend in.

"I picked up some cherry turnovers from a bakery this morning. Care to indulge yourself with me?"

"Sure! I love cherry turnovers and it's been a while since I've had one."

"Then you're in luck, because you get to enjoy *two* this morning!"

"How lucky can a girl get?!"

"Would you like yours warmed up a bit?"

"Yes, that would be nice. Thank you."

As they sat on stools at the island Nicole filled Amanda in on her travel plans, and let her know she would be staying at the ranch while she got settled in. She also thanked Amanda for her offer to give the condo one final quick cleaning to make sure everything was ready for Royal and his clients on Wednesday.

"I'm curious what kind of offers Royal might receive."

"Might? Nicole, there's no *might* about it! Think about it. Your place looks great, it's in a nice neighborhood, close to everything, *plus* it's not only close to the beach but you have an *amazing* view! I guarantee you're going to have your pick of offers on the first day."

"I sure hope so. I'm taking everything with me that I really *need* to get started in a new place, with the exception of my furniture, so hopefully things will move quickly, and I'll be able to fly back in a month, pick up a rental truck, pack up and make my final move."

"And I'll come to help you with it all"

"That would be wonderful. Thanks, Amanda!"

"Sure! I wouldn't miss an opportunity to see you again!"

Nicole smiled, wiped her face with a napkin, finished the last bit of milk in her plastic cup, and tossed it and the napkin in the garbage.

She let out a long sigh.

"Ready?" Amanda asked.

"Let's do it!"

It did not take them long to carry Nicole's luggage and boxes down to her car and get it loaded. Together they made sure it was packed right and tight, assuring that Nicole would still have full vison out of all the windows. Then they walked up to the condo one last time.

Amanda stood near the door while Nicole walked from room to room, making sure everything was done and that she had not left *anything* behind that she was going to need right away. As she walked down the hallway she smiled and said, "Okay, Amanda. It's time."

"One more thing."

Nicole tilted her head. "What did I forget?"

Amanda's eyes looked sideways toward the deck.

"You need to take in that view one more time."

Nicole smiled. "Yes! Yes, I do!"

Amanda remained where she was so her friend could enjoy this special moment alone, and for as long as needed.

Five minutes later Nicole wiped happy tears from her eyes, walked back into the condo, and closed and locked the door. She avoided eye contact with Amanda while she walked toward the front door.

"Are you okay, Nicole?"

Nicole sniffed, and reached for a tissue from a box on the counter.

"Yes. Just thinking."

"Memories?"

"Oh, my gosh! *Yes! So* many memories!"

"I know. I know. But … just think about all of the *new* memories you're about to make!"

"You have always been so good at looking for everything good and positive in life, Amanda. Thank you."

"Always, my friend. Always."

Amanda opened up her arms and they shared a wonderful hug.

"Oh, one more thing! I need to call my new boss!"

Nicole grabbed her phone, brought up the number of the ranch and hit 'dial'.

"Good morning, Hidden Glory Ranch! This is Ashli!"

"Hi, Ashli! It's Nicole Hart!"

"Hi, Nicole! How are you?"

"I'm excited because I'm on my way to see everyone again!"

"Yes! And we're so excited that you're joining us!"

"Thank you! Do you know if Jill is handy?"

"She and Luke are over at Silverado right now. May I take a message?"

"Yes, please tell her I'm on my way. I'll be staying in Winslow, Arizona this evening, so I should be there at the ranch about mid-afternoon tomorrow."

"Oh, how exciting! Okay, I'll let her know!"

"Thank you, Ashli! Bye!"

"Bye, Nicole!"

Nicole let out a big sigh.

"Okay. It's time," she declared with a confident smile.

Amanda followed Nicole down to her car where they briefly hugged again. She then watched as Nicole started her car, pulled out, and drove away. They waved to each other one last time and then Amanda returned to the condo.

Nicole had done such an excellent job of cleaning that Amanda was finished and locking the door less than hour later. She dropped off Nicole's extra pair of keys with Royal on her way to work.

CHAPTER 57

Life is a Highway

NICOLE HIT HEAVY TRAFFIC immediately but took it all in stride. Once she reached I-15 just east of Corona and headed north it improved a bit, but she was waiting for just the right moment. That moment came as traffic coming northwest on I-215 from San Bernadino merged with I-15. Just after the merge, the traffic eased enough for her to hit the gas and get into the fast lane. Once she reached Barstow, she would change over to I-40 which would take her right into Winslow.

She opened all the windows, and with her hair flying behind her she popped a mix CD into the player, cranked up the volume, and listened as Rascal Flatts blasted out the perfect road trip song, "Life is a Highway"! Without a care in the world she sang along to her heart's content!

The weather was perfect, and the traffic was now light enough that she was able to make it to Winslow in eight and half hours, including the necessary stops along the way. She had made a couple of sandwiches for lunch, eaten a half dozen orange slices, and finished it all off with a bottle of juice. She also had a half dozen bottles of water in a cooler strapped to the passenger seat. She was not much for snacking while driving long distances, so she was definitely hungry for a decent meal.

Following the GPS directions, Nicole drove past her hotel and proceeded to head downtown. It did not take long for her to find the famed corner in Winslow that the Eagles had made famous with their song. There was even the flatbed Ford parked along the street a short distance away. Despite her growing hunger, she pulled over, parked her car, and paid a visit to the gift shops located across the street and kitty-corner. An hour later she was back in her car with three bags of souvenirs. They included a couple of t-shirts, a Route 66 bandana, a baseball cap, and a sixteen-ounce glass with the image of the statue of a man with a guitar standing on the corner of the street on one side, and the lyrics to "Take It Easy" on the other.

The grumbling in her stomach reminded her of her priorities, so she drove around until she found what appeared to be an old-style diner. She parked where she could keep an eye on her car, and upon entering the diner she felt like she had been transported back to a time before her parents were born! The floor was made up of large black and white tile squares and the booths had red leather seats, as did the chairs surrounding smaller tables throughout the diner. The tables had red Formica tops, and each booth had an old-style tabletop jukebox. She listened and heard a song that she remembered hearing her mother playing on their stereo when she was a child. She truly *was* in a time warp!

Nicole ordered the All-American Burger with a side of French fries and onion rings and a large chocolate malt. She was not normally a big eater, but today, right now, she was starving! Maybe she would reconsider her rule of not eating snacks on long road trips. While she waited for her meal, she enjoyed listening to the oldies and looked over the list of songs posted on the flip pages inside her tabletop jukebox. Most of the songs were unfamiliar to her, at least by name, but she just *knew* her parents would know them, or at least her mother would. Her waitress brought her meal, and she was thrilled to see her leave the larger malt mixer container with the extra malt that did not fit in the tall glass! She was most *definitely* going to get her money's worth with *this* meal!

When Nicole had finished, she was pleasantly full and declined her waitress' offer for dessert, even though the chocolate fudge layer cake and the hot fudge sundae in a *huge* goblet looked *so* tempting!

She left a generous tip, not only because her waitress was so attentive throughout her meal, but also because she knew that waiters and waitresses typically never earned what they deserved, even with tips. She had always made it a point to be more generous to them. She thanked her waitress and the manager for the wonderful 'experience', and then headed for her hotel.

As Nicole checked in, she asked for a wake-up call for six a.m. She was not on a set-in-stone schedule, but she wanted to make sure she didn't ignore her alarm and oversleep. Angel Fire and Hidden Glory Ranch were calling! She asked for a room on the first floor and since it was a Monday, and not during the summer, there was no problem with granting her request. She was handed the key card for room 114 and advised that there was a continental breakfast available between seven and eight thirty a.m. She thanked the manager and headed for her room.

She was able to park directly in front of her room, so she felt fairly comfortable about leaving most of her belongings in the car over-night. She thought about just bringing in her bag with a change of clothes but then thought better of it and brought in all her suitcases. They were easy to retrieve and, would likewise, be easy to re-pack in the morning and allow her to quickly be on her way.

With her outfit for tomorrow hanging in the closet, and every-thing else settled in her room, Nicole sat down on the side of her bed and let out a deep sigh. *It's been a good day!* She laid back on her pillow, not wanting to go to sleep but just to unwind. As she lay there, her mind flashed on the crazy whirlwind of the last month and she had an idea. She got up, walked over to her overnight bag, withdrew her laptop, and sat down at the table in front of the window.

Monday, May 1st
Winslow, Arizona

Dear Diary –

It's been too long. I know, no excuses. I'll just get right to the point.

I've recently made a monumental decision, actually two monumental decisions, and in a way I'm both scared and elated!

The first decision, of much less consequence for sure, was to let go of a relationship that I probably should have ended years ago, because it was simply a friendship of convenience. Enough said.

The second decision, of much greater consequence and significance, was to walk away from a career that I worked so hard to establish, a career that I was very successful at, and that I loved immensely. I've chosen to move to New Mexico and work on a ranch! Can you believe that?! I don't know if I can, at least not yet! But here I am, in Winslow, Arizona, more than halfway to my new home in Angel Fire, New Mexico! I know, this is crazy, but I'm also so excited!

On Wednesday my condo goes on the market, and Royal has assured me that it will go quickly, and probably for more money than what I'm asking. I know that with the outrageous prices of real estate in California, especially in Southern California, once it sells I will no doubt have enough to buy a mansion in Angel Fire. But that's not me. I'm a simple girl, and maybe that's why I feel so attracted to this job and this new place to work! Yes, I think that just might be it!

With the exception of when I was in grad school south of here, near Phoenix, growing up in Southern California is all I've known! The sun, the beaches, so many things to do and places to go … it was dizzying! But spending a week at a guest ranch definitely had a powerful effect on me. I began to see things differently - my life, my priorities, everything — and I just felt I needed to make some changes.

Of course, it didn't hurt that I was offered a job at the ranch! Can you believe that?! Me, working on a ranch?! And a guest ranch, no less! Every day is certainly going to be an adventure! HA! Can you see me mucking out horse stalls?! Because I'm almost sure that will be one of my many and varied responsibilities!

And then ... sighhhhh ... then there's Liam! I know, I should not get my hopes up about any kind of a new relationship, but there's just something different, something ... well, I don't think I can describe it yet. I feel ... I feel safe around him. I feel ... well, I better not go there yet. Time will tell where our friendship will go, if it goes anywhere at all. But it sure doesn't hurt to dream.

Nicole closed her laptop, then looked for the ice bucket, and went for a walk to find the ice machine. Next to the machine was a soda machine. She popped in some spare change and selected a can of root beer and headed back to her room. She removed the cellophane wrapper from a plastic cup she found on the bathroom counter, scooped some ice out of the bucket, poured in the root beer, and walked over and reached for the TV remote. She sat down on the bed, propped up the pillows against the headboard, and sat back and got comfortable. She flipped through the channels looking for something interesting to watch and found a movie that she had been wanting to see for a while. She readjusted her pillows as the movie began, and wished she had a large bucket of buttered popcorn.

CHAPTER 58

The Reply

AFTER CHANDLER'S LAST APPOINTMENT of the day, he debated about leaving or working late. He certainly had nothing to go home for, so he decided to bury himself in his work in order to deal with his not having heard back from Nicole yet. Was that a good or bad sign?

Perhaps she was taking him up on his suggestion to take her time, to think long and hard about the possibility of a future together, and now she was trying to come up with the right words to apologize and ask him to take her back. Or not. *That* was what was eating at him. *What if she blows me off for good? That we truly* are *over? What then? What if it* is *someone from her office that she's interested in now? How did* that *happen? And when?* All his mind could do was spin until he heard from Nicole one way or another. *IF,* in fact, he ever heard from her again.

He looked through the files on his desk, trying to decide which one had the highest priority, but in his state of mind *each* was screaming 'Me first!' He pushed his chair back in disgust and walked out of his office and headed for the break room. He'd only eaten half his sandwich for lunch, so he grabbed the rest of it from the refrigerator and headed back to his office.

Dorene was just getting up from her desk as he approached. "Good night, Chandler."

"Good night, Dorene," he replied in a distracted tone.

"Are you going to work late again this evening?"

"Yes."

"Okay. Well, um, good luck and I'll see you in the morning."

"Thanks," Chandler replied without looking at her. He slumped into his chair, set his sandwich off to the right, reached to his left to pick up his cellphone, but then stopped himself. He realized that he was about to call Nicole and knew he couldn't do that. At least not yet. Perhaps never again. *Am I* ever *going to hear from you again?* He let out a long sigh as he pulled his hand back, then reached for his sandwich, took a bite, set it down on the wrapper, and reached for a file.

* * *

Chandler arrived home after nine-thirty and tossed his keys in a dish on the front hall table. He walked into the kitchen to see what he might have in the refrigerator to eat for dinner only to find it nearly empty of anything fresh. There were only a couple of plastic containers with leftovers, one of which didn't look very healthy. That one he tossed in the garbage, plastic container and all. Then he opened his freezer, only to find a couple of partial half gallons of ice cream and a half dozen frozen waffles. He slammed the door shut and walked out of the kitchen, turning off the light behind him. He walked into the living room, and sat down heavily on his black leather sofa.

He sat there in the dark for over ten minutes before remembering he had not yet retrieved his mail. He debated about getting up and walking out to get it. *What's the use? There's probably nothing but junk anyway.* Then he remembered that there might be a letter from Nicole, and he moved a bit faster to get out the door than he had when he first arrived home.

He flipped quickly through the flyers, bills, a weekly grocery store ad, and THERE IT WAS! Nicole's letter! His heart went from pure excitement to a more tepid hesitation since it appeared more like a note because the envelope was small and thin. Nevertheless, he hurried back into the condo, tossed everything but her letter onto the hall table near his keys, took out his knife to slice the envelope open, and walked quickly to the living room. He sat down on the sofa and leaned over to turn on the lamp. Then he reached into the envelope for the letter.

Dear Chandler,

I'll admit that your letter was a surprise. I believe you're sincere in your apologies, but by the time you read this I'll be on my way to New Mexico. I was offered a position at the ranch and accepted it. Warren was excited for me and wished me well, and then offered me the opportunity to leave with little notice, so I took him up on it.

We had a lot of wonderful times together, but I believe you'll agree with me that we were perhaps nothing more than a convenience for each other, two friends who enjoyed doing a variety of things together. If we had both been truly serious about a future together it would have happened a long time ago. As it is, I've chosen to take a different path in my life.

I wish you well, Chandler.

Nicole

So, that's it then. We're officially over. Nothing more than a convenience for each other? Chandler let out a long sigh. He looked absently around his living room and set Nicole's letter next to him on the sofa. He turned off the light, laid his head against the back of the sofa, and sat in the dark. *I wish you well, too, Nicole.*

CHAPTER 59

No Looking Back

NOT BEING FAMILIAR WITH the area Nicole chose to skip her morning walk. She didn't feel like she was breaking any kind of streak, she was simply being prudent. She showered, put on her makeup, dried and attempted to style her hair. It was not wanting to cooperate so she pulled it back in a ponytail. She put on the outfit she had chosen for the day: Wrangler shorts, a short sleeved pastel blue blouse with a pastel yellow and pink print design, and leather sandals. Then she decided to see what the continental breakfast had to offer.

She was pleasantly surprised to see more than the usual offerings of cereal, fruit, toast, and juice. She also had her choice of freshly made waffles, sweet rolls, fresh blueberry muffins, and hot chocolate. She chose a cherry sweet roll and blueberry muffin, and warmed up both in the microwave oven. She also chose apple juice. It was not much, but it was enough to get her started, and she planned to stop for lunch in Albuquerque.

On her way out, she just *had* to drive through downtown Winslow one more time to see their famous intersection. She thought about stopping to see if she might want any more souvenirs, but decided to just hit the road. With her windows down she merged onto Interstate 40, popped her CD into the player, cranked up the volume, and once again sang along to "Life is a Highway"! She replayed it two more times before letting the CD just play through the rest of the songs she had burned onto it.

Nicole felt so free and excited! That afternoon she would arrive in Angel Fire to begin a new life, and she could not *wait!* She had faith that whatever lay beyond was what she was supposed to do and where she was supposed to be.

CHAPTER 60

Home

IT WAS MOSTLY CLOUDY as Nicole exited the Carson National Forest and saw the Moreno Valley stretched out before her. A wave of excitement washed over her whole body, and she found a place to pull over on the side of the road. She stepped out of her SUV and took a few steps forward to survey the beautiful landscape. She looked to her left toward Eagle Nest, then slowly scanned the valley until Angel Fire came into view on her far right. Her eyesight then scanned back to the left ever so slightly until she could see Hidden Glory Ranch.

Ever since Nicole made the decision to leave her job, she had held a prayer in her heart. She had felt mostly confident that she had made the right choice. However, there was still a sliver of doubt that was nagging at her. Any final hesitation vanished in the next instant as the clouds broke, and a bright ray of sun shone down on the ranch and Angel Fire. She choked up and tears flowed freely. *This is where I belong!*

She took a deep breath and returned to her SUV where she reached for a tissue and dabbed the tears away from her eyes and cheeks. She pulled out onto Highway 434, heading toward the village. As she approached the Shell station on her left where she had stopped on her way out of town just ten days earlier, she slowed and pulled in, circling the station to where the restrooms were located. She parked her SUV and removed the makeup kit and hairbrush from her overnight bag. She entered the ladies' room, grateful for its cleanliness, and proceeded to wet a paper towel to dab her eyes. She hoped no one at the ranch would see she had been crying. Satisfied that her eyes looked almost normal, she touched up her makeup and pulled the rubber band from her hair. She brushed and fluffed her hair for a couple of minutes until she had it just right, then walked back to her SUV and drove on toward the ranch.

Turning left down the road to the ranch her emotions began to get the better of her again. She took deep breaths and fought back the tears. *I can do this! Just keep it together a little longer!*

She slowed down as she approached the paddocks up ahead on her right, and looked to see if she saw any familiar faces. Pat, Cindi, and Sonia were standing just outside the stable. Then she looked further to her right and hit the brakes! With the afternoon sun shining down from behind him, Liam looked *so* handsome on Wildfire as he was coming down the trail toward her. Of course, he had no idea what kind of car she drove, and she hesitated to try to get his attention, but she just couldn't drive on. She put her SUV in park, stepped out, and walked to the back, shielding her eyes from the sun to get a better look.

Liam suddenly pulled back on Wildfire's reins, looked directly at Nicole, and as soon as he recognized her, he launched Wildfire into a full gallop! Nicole's heart leapt!

"Hey there!" Liam called as he reined Wildfire to a halt and jumped down.

"Hey there, yourself!" Nicole replied as Liam approached with Wildfire's reins in his hands.

Neither one wanting to be too forward, they gave each other a brief hug. Pat and her assistants had seen the commotion and looked on, approvingly.

"You got here earlier than I expected you might."

"I flew low all the way because I couldn't *wait* to get here!" *And to you!*

"Well, I'm glad you made it safely."

"Me, too!" Nothing could erase their broad smiles.

They stood just looking at each other for a long moment before Liam broke the silence.

"Well, I, uh … I better let you go so you can see Jill and the gang and get settled in. I have some things I need to finish before dinner, so, uh … I'll see you later?"

"I'm looking forward to it, Liam!" They looked into each other's eyes, then gave each other another brief hug.

Liam mounted Wildfire, but remained on the side of the road and watched as Nicole drove off toward the hacienda. He let out a long sigh, and with that big smile still on his face, he rode off to finish his chores.

Looking on from inside the stable, another pair of eyes took notice that Nicole had returned. Doing his best to shake his attitude, Shane turned and walked further back out of sight.

* * *

When Nicole had called yesterday and spoken with Ashli, she asked her to keep her arrival time a secret, and also asked her to tell Jill the same thing, because she wanted to catch as many people by surprise as she could. And it worked beautifully! Hearing the commotion caused by Kay and Ashli, Jill came out from her office. The guests relaxing in the lobby were treated to quite a show of joy between the four ladies!

They stood talking for several minutes before Ashli returned to the reservations desk to assist a guest with a question. She returned holding the keycard for Nicole's casita, and after a few more minutes of excited conversation, Nicole said her goodbyes for now and headed to her SUV. Just before she got in she looked back to the stable, but wished she hadn't. There, standing just outside the stable, was Shane. She quickly turned away, climbed into her SUV, shuddered with the realization that she had forgotten he worked here, and did her best to shake his image from her mind. Flashbacks of the times he had approached her before came on strong. Now that she was here as an employee and not a guest, he better not try to start anything again.

Nicole drove her SUV around the hacienda and parked it near the door of her casita so she could unload her luggage and boxes. She was about one fourth of the way along and in the back bedroom when she heard a knock on the frame of her front door.

"Hi! Anyone here?" came a familiar voice.

"Back here!" Nicole called. And with that Brendy and Beth hurried down the hall.

"Welcome back, Nicole!" the ladies called out in unison.

"Hey! My buddies!" The ladies gave each other a big group hug.

"We heard you were here and had to come and say hi!"

"Gosh, it's so good to see you!"

"And you, too!" Beth added.

"Can we help you unload your things?" Brendy asked.

"Oh, that would be wonderful. Nothing is really heavy and there are no breakables. Everything like that is still at my condo."

"Okay, we'll start unloading things and you just tell us where you want them."

"That sounds like a plan!"

Brendy and Beth worked quickly and, less than ten minutes later, Nicole's SUV was unloaded, and every box and piece of luggage was exactly where it needed to be.

* * *

That evening at dinner Nicole was welcomed warmly by the staff who hadn't yet seen her since her arrival. By now the guests had become aware that they were in the presence of someone quite special. They couldn't miss the amount of attention being showered on her. Tomorrow she would begin her training as the newest employee of Hidden Glory Ranch, but tonight she was treated like a guest.

After dinner, Brendy took off to spend the evening with her family, and Beth corralled her with question after question about how things had gone at home with her job, her friends, and her parents. Nicole excitedly explained how supportive her boss was about her starting this new phase of her life, and how great everyone at work was, including their going-away party and the amazing check they presented to her before she left for good.

Then Nicole explained how she gave her mother the news, but that her mother had insisted on informing her dad about the change *after* she was already at the ranch and out of range of the expected blast. Beth's eyes grew large for a moment, and noticing her reaction,

Nicole added, "Believe me, you have *no* idea how hard he is going to take this news. I kept asking my mother if she was sure she wanted to be the one to tell him, but she insisted. So, I guess we'll see."

"Good luck with that," Beth replied.

Beth continued to pepper Nicole with more questions until Liam came into view. Nicole stopped mid-sentence and just stared.

"You might want to close your mouth, Nicole," Beth whispered.

Nicole began to blush as she realized that the sight of Liam had caused her to drop her jaw. As she watched him walking toward her, it felt as if everything was moving in slow motion. The sun was to his back and this handsome cowboy was walking toward her, perhaps to ask her if she would like to run away with him. The thought made her laugh out loud, catching Beth's attention.

"What's so funny?"

"Oh, my gosh! Did I just laugh out loud?"

"Yes. What's up?"

As Liam drew even closer Nicole whispered, "Maybe I'll tell you later."

"Hi, Nicole."

"Hi, Liam!"

"Um, Beth, I hope you don't mind, but may I steal Nicole away from you for a while?"

"Absolutely! You two have fun!"

"Thanks!" Liam and Nicole replied in unison, then looked at each other and laughed.

"Hi, Liam! So you want to steal me away, huh?"

"Yes, something like that."

"What did you have in mind?"

"Well … how about we saddle up the horses and go for one of our sunset rides?"

A wave of excitement washed over Nicole as Liam took her hand to help her up. Then they walked together toward the stable.

"I think Calypso is excited to see you back."

"CALYPSO! Oh, my gosh! I was going to stop at the stable and see her right after I arrived, but everything happened so fast that I completely forgot!"

"Well, I'm sure she'll forgive you."

"I sure hope so!"

Nicole had her answer a moment later as they entered the stable. Calypso caught sight of Nicole, whinnied excitedly, and immediately jumped toward the front of her stall and started dancing!

"Calypso! Hi, girl! Did you miss me?"

Calypso nodded her head up and down rapidly, causing Nicole to laugh and cry at the same time as she leaned over the gate of the stall and gave Calypso a big hug.

"See? All forgiven." Liam replied.

In the hope and anticipation of being able to persuade her to go on this ride with him, Liam had already saddled up Wildfire. He assisted Nicole in putting on Calypso's bridle. Then Nicole led Calypso out of her stall where they slipped on her blanket and saddle. When they finished, they led the horses out of the stable, then mounted them and headed for their favorite spot on the mountain to enjoy another special sunset.

"I'm glad you came back," Liam said casually, doing his best to hide the excitement he felt inside.

"Me, too," Nicole replied with a warm smile.

Their eyes lingered on each other for a few more seconds as their horses faithfully took them up the mountain.

CHAPTER 61

Wednesday Morning

AFTER BREAKFAST **N**ICOLE **REPORTED** to Jill's office to begin her official orientation to the ranch. Luke was there, as well, as he had not yet left for Silverado. The three of them spoke together briefly, with Luke and Jill once again sharing their joy that Nicole had accepted their offer. Nicole, in turn, shared how grateful she was that they had chosen her. Luke then left for Silverado and Jill proceeded with the orientation.

She went over the list of responsibilities that Nicole would have, some to do on a daily basis, while others would be as-needed. At this point it was highly unlikely she would stay in any one area for a full day simply because of the large variety of jobs that needed to be completed around the ranch at any given time. Sometimes she might be assisting directly with the guests, while other times she would be working behind the scenes preparing for future events. Regardless of what she would be doing at any given time, it was clear that she would keep quite busy, and she liked that!

When they were finished, Jill asked Nicole if she had any questions.

"Yes, who will I be training with?"

"I hope you don't mind, but I've asked Brendy to be your trainer."

"Mind? No, not at all! That will be fun!"

"I noticed the two of you really hit it off from your first day here a few weeks ago. So I thought it would be a good match."

"Absolutely! Thank you!"

"I'm sure you have a cellphone, right?"

Nicole chuckled. "Yes. I can't live without it."

"Well, you won't need it very often here at the ranch," Jill replied, reaching into the top draw of her desk.

"Here's your new flip phone that will fit easily into any pocket. It has full voice and texting features, and the phone numbers for all of our employees are already entered into it, so you can reach any of us at any time.

"Thank you! This is wonderful!"

"I've already let Brendy know you'll be reaching out to her, so why don't you go ahead and text her now and let her know you're ready to begin."

"Sure!"

Nicole sent the message and Brendy replied a few moments later. "On my way!"

Nicole and Jill were sharing small talk when Brendy arrived.

"Hi, again! Ready to get started?"

"I sure am!" Nicole replied excitedly.

"Okay, let's go!"

"Have fun you two!"

"Thanks, Jill," Nicole replied. "We will."

Over the next few hours Brendy proceeded to give Nicole an in-depth orientation to every aspect of the ranch. She explained much more of the behind-the-scenes action than Nicole had privy to during her vacation. They also stopped and spoke with some of the guests who were casually walking around, taking in the beauty of their surroundings.

Afterward they sat in the barbeque/picnic area and reviewed Nicole's overall training schedule. She would definitely be kept busy, but she was anxious to dig in and do her part.

After lunch they spent some time in the stable where Pat went over the general duties she would have with the horses, and, of course, that included how to properly muck the stalls. Nicole jokingly rolled her eyes, but gladly accepted her fate, knowing that it was all a part of the full ranch experience. Besides, everyone was expected to carry their own weight in order to make the ranch run properly as well as to make it the best possible experience for the guests.

CHAPTER 62

Wednesday Late Afternoon

J ENSON HAD ARRIVED HOME from another round of golf in an exceptionally good mood. Charlotte was ready for the 'discussion' about Nicole, but she waited until he had completely settled in and was relaxing in his recliner.

"Honey, I have some wonderful news about Nicole!"

"Does it have anything to do with what the two of you were talking about last Saturday night?"

"As a matter of fact, yes!"

"Great! Tell me all about it!"

"Now sweetheart, promise me you'll stay calm and let me share everything with you, okay?"

"Why? If it's good news, why should I have to stay calm?"

Charlotte paused and took a deep breath. "Because Nicole has chosen to change jobs."

"WHAT?!"

"Dear, please stay calm and listen to me!"

"What do you mean she's changed jobs?! Is she *nuts?!*"

"Jenson, why do you have to be this way? This is *her* life, and she can choose to do whatever she likes. And she doesn't need our, or especially *your*, permission."

"And you knew about this on Saturday?"

"Yes."

"Then why didn't you tell me before now?!"

"Think about it, Jens. You've never *really* supported Nicole in achieving her dreams *unless* they fit *your* ambitions for her."

"That's not true."

"Yes, it is."

"This is *nuts!* Why didn't she tell me herself? Why did *you* have to be the one to dump this on me?"

"*Dump* this on you? Honey, this is *wonderful* news, and a wonderful opportunity for our daughter!"

Jenson didn't respond, he just sat there fuming.

"Dear, Nicole wants us to be happy for her. Is that too much to ask?"

"What is she going to be doing now?" Jenson asked in a surprisingly subdued manner.

"She'll be working on a guest ranch," Charlotte replied cautiously, waiting for the explosion that was sure to come.

Jenson sat there stunned, while Charlotte waited for Mount Vesuvius to erupt.

Jenson did erupt, right out of his chair!

"Is she NUTS?! She's thrown away her career to work on a stupid *ranch?!*"

"It's actually a very beautiful ranch, dear."

"But she's *not* going to be an architect, right?"

"No, she's not."

"That's it!" Jenson replied and stormed off.

"Where are you going?"

"To my *office!*" Jenson headed down the hallway and slammed the door to his office behind him.

* * *

"Warren Knapp Design. Warren Knapp's office. How may I help you?"

"This is Jenson Hart and I need to speak with Warren."

"One moment, Mr. Hart, and I'll see if he is available." Maryann put him on hold immediately before he could respond.

"Warren? Jenson Hart is on the line for you."

"My old friend, Jenson? I haven't spoken to him in a long time! Sure, put him through."

"Before I do, sir, I should warn you that he does not seem to be in a good mood."

Warren thought for a moment. "Okay, Maryann, thank you for the heads up. Go ahead and put him through."

"Yes, sir."

"I'm connecting you now, Mr. Hart."

"Thank you," Jenson replied gruffly.

"Jenson?"

"Hello, Warren! How are you?"

"Fine, just fine! How about you?"

"I've been better."

"It's been a long time! So, what do I owe the pleasure of chatting with you today? Are you going to try to entice me into retiring and joining you out in the desert?"

"Well, that's *always* a standing offer, but no, I'm actually calling about Nicole."

"Ahhh, Nicole. An *amazing* asset to my company. I seriously couldn't have been more blessed to have found her and hired her."

"Then what's this I've heard that she's left your company and completely walked away from her career?" Jenson asked pointedly, trying to quell his anger. "We've been friends for too long for you to not have given me a call to alert me to what's going on in her life. When you hired her—"

"Hold it right there, Jenson," Warren interrupted firmly. "First off, I didn't hire her because she's your daughter. I hired her because she was the most dynamic architect I'd *ever* met! And, she has designed circles around even the most experienced architects I've ever known. Secondly, Nicole's decision to make this change in her life was based on things beyond this office!"

"What's *that* supposed to mean?!"

"Why are we even having this conversation? You should be talking to Nicole yourself."

"Maybe I'll do just that!"

"Maybe? Jenson, there's no *maybe* about it."

"Wait, are you telling me *you* know what's behind this?"

"Jenson, all I'm saying is that despite her amazing career with my company, there were other things that apparently weighed so heavily on her mind that she chose to make this change. And not only did I wish her well in her new adventure, I even gave her my blessings!"

"You *what?!*"

"You heard me, Jenson. And, quite frankly, that's all I'm going to say about it."

Jenson slammed his phone down without even a thank you or a goodbye. *Some friend* you *are*, he muttered under his breath. He sat at his desk fuming for several minutes before walking to the kitchen to get a drink.

"Who were you talking to, Jenson?" Charlotte asked calmly.

"Nicole's boss, well *ex*-boss, Warren Knapp. Some friend *he* is!"

"Why? What did he say?"

"He told me she left because of things in her life *outside* the office, and then he told me I needed to talk to *her* myself to find out what those are."

"So, call her."

"I'm too mad right now. I need to calm down first, so I don't blow up on the phone."

"What are you so *mad* about?"

Jenson sighed heavily, looked out the patio doors, and avoided eye contact with his wife.

"Jens, what are you mad about?" she asked more slowly, but firmly.

"I just expected better from her."

"Excuse me? *You* expected better from *her*?

"You know what I mean," Jenson replied, attempting to brush off Charlotte's remark.

"No. No, I don't, Jenson. Why don't you explain it to me?"

"I don't have time right now."

"Why not? You weren't in a hurry to go anywhere a few minutes ago."

"Oh, never mind. I don't want to talk about it right now."

"Why not?

"Charlotte! Will you please stop?!"

Charlotte didn't respond, but her piercing glare said more than words could ever say, and he knew he was in for a lot more.

"Look what she's accomplished! She has excelled in everything since she was a child! Music, sports, her education, and her career! And look where it's taken her, right to the top in her profession!"

"Well, that's all well and good. Those are all things she *wanted* to do," he replied flippantly.

"She didn't choose to do those things because she *wanted* to. She excelled because she *had* to."

"What are you talking about? Nicole didn't *have* to do *anything*! All of this was her own doing. *She* chose to learn how to play the piano. *She* chose to participate in sports in high school. *She* chose to earn her way to be valedictorian. Now, she may not have chosen to be Homecoming Queen, or voted Most Likely to Succeed, but her classmates liked her enough to make it so. And look at all the awards and scholarships she earned! Even in college she was the best. So why do you say she *had* to do all those things?

"To win your approval."

"What?!!!"

"Nicole chose to learn how to play the piano and dedicate so much of her time and energy to do so well at such a young age to win your approval. She chose to participate in those sports in high school and play her heart out to win in order to also win your approval. She chose to excel in her classes so she could have a chance to be the class valedictorian to win your approval. Now, you're right, she may *not* have chosen to be Homecoming Queen, or be voted Most Likely to Succeed, but her classmates *admired* her for the great young woman she was back then, and it paid off handsomely with all the awards and scholarships she earned. And yes, in college she *was* the best. And she did it *all* just to win your approval."

Jenson stood there scowling with his arms crossed defiantly across his chest.

"Did you ever *tell* her how wonderful you thought she was doing? Did you ever *tell* her how proud you were of her back then?"

"She knew."

"No, she didn't."

"Of course, she did! I told her all the time!"

"Oh, really? When?"

"All the time."

"Tell me *one* time you told her you were proud of her. One time, *specifically*."

"Why are you grilling me like this?"

"Don't avoid the question. Tell me *one* specific time when you told her you were proud of her."

Jenson stood silent, reaching for and gripping his glass, furious that his wife would question him like this.

"Well?! Tell me!"

"Charlotte," he began, with a lower timber than he had previously been speaking to her. "How dare you question my love for my daughter."

"Excuse me? *Your* daughter? She's *our* daughter, Jenson. And I haven't even gotten to the question about when the last time was that you told Nicole that you *loved* her."

"I told her I loved her before she left here on Sunday."

"No, you didn't."

"I most certainly did! She said, 'I love you, Dad' and I replied, 'Same here'."

"That's not the same, Jenson," Charlotte replied calmly.

"Of *course* it's the same!"

"No. it's *not*, and you *know* it! You haven't said 'I love you, Nicole' since she was a very little girl."

"How do you know? I could have very easily said it when you weren't around!"

"Did you?"

"Of course I did!"

"When?"

Jenson was furious with Charlotte over her questioning his love for his own daughter, but he was at a loss for how to stop all of her questions.

"Charlotte, you *know* I love her, and you *know* I'm proud of her."

Charlotte sighed heavily in desperation.

"Jenson, this isn't about whether or not *I* know. It's about whether *Nicole* knows. Don't you get that?"

Jenson looked into Charlotte's eyes with frustration and then looked away once again.

Charlotte eased her tone a bit. "Jens, when was the last time you talked with Nicole, just the two of you?"

"I don't know."

"Well, then it's been too long."

"Why don't *you* give her a call and talk to her? She always talks to you. Find out what's going on."

"No, this isn't about me and my relationship with our daughter. This is about *you* and *your* relationship with our daughter."

Jenson looked out through the patio doors again.

"Where is this ranch where she's going to be working?"

"New Mexico."

"*New Mexico?!* Why New Mexico?!"

"Because she went there for vacation a couple of weeks ago, spent a week there and loved it. It turns out they loved her, too, and offered her a job."

"Along with a huge cut in pay!"

"It has nothing to do with money, Jens."

"She is absolutely *crazy* to walk away from her career like this *and* lose out on a great income. She'll see the light and come back. I just hope Warren will take her back when she does."

"Did you happen to think that perhaps she has already 'seen the light', and that's why she made this change?"

"You're not making any sense, Charlotte."

"Maybe I'm making *perfect* sense."

Jenson studied the melting ice in his glass. "What's the name of this ranch?"

"Why?"

"Because I'd like to find out more about it."

"It's called Hidden Glory Ranch."

Jenson just stood there shaking his head.

"And when is she supposed to arrive there?"

"She texted me last night to let me know she had arrived safely a few hours earlier, and that she would be starting her new job bright and early this morning."

Jenson took a drink of his ice water and thought for a long moment. "So, what are we supposed to do now?"

"Nothing."

"Nothing? How can we sit back and do nothing?"

"Jens, Nicole is a grown woman, *quite* capable of making her own decisions for her life without *any* input *or* interference from either of us. This is *her* life, and she needs to be able to live it exactly the way she wants to. If, at some point in her future she decides to make another change, so be it! We need to let her live her life *her* way, *and* with our love, support, and blessing."

We'll see about that! Jenson thought as he got some more ice water and returned to his office.

When he went to bed later that night, Jenson informed Charlotte that he had some business to take care of in Los Angeles the next day and that he'd be leaving early and would not be home until quite late. This was not unusual for him, as he went there every couple of months to meet with investment counselors and other business connections he'd known prior to retiring.

Before she fell asleep Charlotte checked her phone for messages and saw one that had come in from Nicole an hour earlier.

Hi, Mom! Quick question. Have you told Dad yet?

Charlotte held her breath, debating about whether to answer right then or wait until the morning. She decided to go ahead.

Yes. He was over-the-top upset at first, but he seems to be resigned to it now. How was your first day?

Nicole's phone alerted her that a new message had arrived.

Thanks, Mom! I love you! My first day was GREAT!
Thanks for asking!

Wonderful! I love you, too, sweetheart!

I'll chat with you tomorrow, Mom!

                                        Okay, dear. Good night.

Good night.

CHAPTER 63

The Offer

NICOLE WAS JUST GETTING ready for bed when her phone rang. It was Royal!

"Hello?"

"Hi, Nicole, it's Royal! I'm sorry to call you so late—"

"It's not a problem. I wasn't really expecting to hear from you until maybe tomorrow."

"I couldn't wait!"

"You have some good news for me then?"

"*Good* news? Try *great* news!"

"You're kidding! I got some offers already?"

"Are you sitting down?"

Nicole turned and sat down on her bed.

"I am now."

"Okay, here we go. You are about to become a very rich lady," Royal said in as calm and understated a way as he could.

"Um, really?"

"Yes."

"How so?"

"Well, first off ... you have *six* offers on your condo!"

"What?! Oh, my gosh!"

"That's not even the *best* part."

"Well, stop stalling and give it to me!"

"In all my time in real estate, I've *never* seen an offer like this!"

"Royal!! Stop teasing me! What's the offer?!"

"All the offers were for more than our asking price, but—"

"ROYAL! PLEASE stop teasing me!"

"The top offer came from a couple that wants to buy your condo *exactly* as it stands right now, including *all* of the furniture … for *three* times your asking price—"

"WHAT?!"

"AND … they hope you'll be agreeable to accept cash."

Nicole's jaw dropped and she was speechless.

"Nicole? Did you hear me?"

"Y-yes, I think so. Did you say *three* times my asking price *and* they want my furniture, too? And they're paying cash?"

"Yes! And … they want to close in two weeks!"

"Oh … my … GOSH!!! Is this a dream?"

"Nicole, this is a dream come true!"

"But *three* times? I can't believe that! With the prices as crazy as they are in that market, I was just hoping to get my asking price. Or, perhaps, a little more."

"It was crazy. I had people in and out of your condo all day. They ALL loved it, and there was a bidding war going on for a while, until that one couple came along and made that offer. At that point I closed the bidding and told everyone that I needed to speak with you before anything else would happen."

"This is crazy! I can't believe it!"

"And, to top it all off, that couple handed me a cashier's check for $100,000 as earnest money!"

"And they want *everything*?"

"Well, they said that if you wanted things like your plates and silverware, pots and pans, etc. that would be fine. *And* they offered to have everything boxed up and delivered to you at *their* expense!"

"Who *are* these people?"

"They're an older couple, I'm guessing in their sixties. They said they have other homes in other parts of the country and, apparently, they travel a lot and were looking for a place in this area. The timing of you putting your condo on the market was apparently just right for them. They are *so* excited!"

"But for *three* times my asking price?"

"Yes, and cash."

"Oh, my gosh! What am I going to do with all of that money?"

"Well, I'm guessing with the *huge* difference in the real estate market between here and where you are in New Mexico, you'll be able to afford to buy a mansion, or buy a huge piece of property and have a custom home built exactly to your liking."

"Oh, Royal, Royal, Royal … I can't thank you enough."

"Not a problem!"

"I'm guessing *you're* pretty happy yourself, considering your commission."

"Yes, you could say that." They both shared a good laugh.

"My gosh, I am *sure* going to sleep well tonight, *if* I can get to sleep at all!"

"I'm sure you will, Nicole. And with that I'll say goodnight and I'll be in touch to wrap up this deal."

"Good night, Royal, and thank you again. Oh, wait!"

"What is it?"

"I don't think I formally told you whether or not I accept their offer!"

"And?"

"I DO!"

"Wonderful! I'll let them know!"

"Thank you! Good night!"

"Good night, Nicole!"

Nicole debated about calling or texting her mother again to give her the exciting news, but decided to wait until after work the next day. Besides, her head was *still* spinning, and she needed time to fully comprehend the magnitude of it all before sharing her amazing news with anyone else.

CHAPTER 64

Armageddon

JENSON'S CHARTER JET FROM Albuquerque landed at the Angel Fire airport and taxied toward the rental car he had arranged for the night before.

"I won't be long," he arrogantly advised the pilot as he stepped down from the jet. "I'm just here to pick up my daughter, so make sure we're fueled up and ready to go when we return." The pilot angrily pursed his lips and nodded without a verbal reply.

Jenson approached the rental car. He had paid extra to have it delivered to the airport from Taos. He double-checked the paperwork that had been handed to him by the agent, making sure the agency had done it correctly, then signed it.

"Don't leave. I'll be back shortly." He opened the door to the Cadillac CT5-V Blackwing and reached above the driver's visor to retrieve the key. He turned on the engine and drove off in a cloud of dust. The pilot observed everything and shook his head in disgust. The agent did the same.

Following the map he had printed out, Jenson made his way toward the ranch. He was anxious to find his daughter, get her packed up, and fly her back home where she belonged.

As Jenson drove under the tall, wooden arch proclaiming the property to be Hidden Glory Ranch, he wondered how long it would take to find his daughter and talk some sense into her. By the time they returned to the airport the charter jet would be refueled and ready to fly back to Albuquerque with *two* passengers, instead of just the one it arrived with. As for her car, he'd hire someone to drive the car back to California for her.

He could *not* believe *his* daughter would do something so outrageously idiotic as to quit her wonderful job and walk away from an amazing career as a star architect. *What* could have possibly possessed her to do something like that? He was so proud to be able to drive around and see the various buildings and homes his daughter had designed! What would his friends think *now*?!

As he drove along the tree-lined road he noticed the paddocks along with the stable and other buildings to his right and in front of him. He slowed as he thought he caught a glimpse of a tall strawberry blonde who looked a bit like his daughter, but he couldn't be sure because he'd never seen his daughter in such a dusty place. Besides, whoever it might be, she was leading a horse toward the stable so there was no chance to see her face.

He parked his car in front of the hacienda and decided to walk back to the paddock and take a closer look. As he walked along the side of the paddock, approaching the entrance to the stable, he paused a moment as he heard his daughter's familiar laugh coming from just inside the stable. It *must* have been her he saw a moment ago!

Nicole and Brendy were just exiting the stable when Nicole froze!

"Father?! What are *you* doing here?"

"Now, is that anyway to greet your father?"

"Well, I had no idea you were coming." She then turned toward Brendy.

"Brendy, would you please excuse me? It appears I have an unexpected visitor."

"Sure thing. I'll catch up with you later."

"Thank you."

Turning back toward her father she continued. "Where's Mom?"

"Your mother is at home."

"I don't understand. And I will ask again, what are you doing here?"

"I'm here to ask you the same question, young lady?"

Before Nicole could say anything else, her father took charge.

"So, what's this I heard from your mother about your quitting your job just to work out here in the middle of nowhere? Are you crazy? And why did I have to hear it from your mother and *not* directly from you?"

Nicole did not answer her father immediately but stared at him coldly.

"Did you fly all this way just to berate me?"

"No, I flew all this way to knock some sense into your head."

Nicole folded her arms across her chest and let out a very discordant sigh.

"I can't believe it. My father, the great controller, is here to knock some sense into me, huh?"

"Don't get smart with me, young lady. I'm here to tell you to grab your things and then I'll take you back home where you belong. Then you'd better hope and pray that Warren will take you back."

"No," Nicole said simply and calmly.

"What did you just say?"

"You heard me."

Her father's anger was reaching nuclear meltdown.

"Pack up your things *now*! You're coming with me!"

"No," she replied, more defiantly than before.

"That's it! Nicole, if you don't—"

"Stop right there! If you're going to talk to me like this, you can turn right around and go home!"

"Not on your life! Not until I get some answers!"

"I don't owe you *any* explanation for *my* choices."

"Yes, you do! You're still my daughter, and I can't believe you've made such a rash decision to leave your wonderful career! How could you do something so senseless? Have you lost your mind?"

Liam overheard the commotion as he was exiting the stable and interceded.

"Mr. Hart, I presume?"

"Yes!"

"Nicole isn't going anywhere."

"Liam, please. This is my battle to fight."

"Yeah, *cowboy*! Get lost!"

"Don't talk to him that way!" Nicole demanded.

"I'll talk to him any way I want to!" Jensen shouted.

"MR. HART!" Liam roared in order to be heard over Jensen's rage. His fierceness momentarily startled Nicole. "I *demand* that you apologize to your daughter, right now!"

Jenson started to interrupt, but Liam stepped closer and held up his hand close to Jenson's face.

"I *demand* that you apologize to Nicole and respect your daughter's decisions. And, if you don't do that, if you *can't* do that … then you aren't worthy to be called her father! Nicole made up her *own* mind to change things in *her* life, and for *her* own reasons. She doesn't need anyone else's permission, *including* yours, and you had better accept that *fact*! Yes, she's your flesh and blood, but you don't control her, her life, or her choices. Only Nicole can do that, and if you can't accept that … then you can—"

"Liam, please," Nicole pleaded as she stepped forward and lightly touched his arm.

Liam glanced at Nicole momentarily, acknowledging her concern.

"So … what's it going to be?"

Jenson stood there speechless.

"Well?!?! Answer me!!"

"First off … just who do you think—"

"Father!" Nicole yelled.

"Shut up, Nicole! This is between me and this *cowboy* here."

"Father! Stop! Stop it right now!"

"Nicole?!" Jenson angrily took a step toward her, but Liam stepped between them.

"What?!" Liam hissed between his teeth. "What were you thinking of saying or doing to your daughter."

"That's none of your business, *cowboy*."

"Yes, it *is* my business."

"Father, stop! Please!"

Jenson pointed a threatening finger past Liam's arm, but Liam grabbed Jenson's wrist and squeezed it as tight as he could as he ever so slowly raised Jenson's arm up high, then brought it down ever so slowly between them as he gave Jenson an ice-cold stare. Jenson had fire in his eyes, but he knew this wasn't the time or place to continue this conversation with his daughter.

"Sir, I believe I asked you a question," Liam said in a lower, but still intense tone of voice.

Jenson stared back at him, rubbing his wrist.

"Well?"

"This isn't over, mister," Jenson replied, with his own steely stare. "I don't know who you are, or who you *think* you are, but *you* have *no* business getting into *my* business with *my* daughter."

"Oh, I believe I do."

"Oh, yeah? Who died and made you sheriff?" Jenson replied with a smirk.

"Father, *please* stop this *now!*"

"And just why should I?" Jenson snapped at his daughter.

"Because … Liam is my boss and I respect him. And that's a *lot* more than I can say about you."

"He's your *what?!*"

"You heard me loud and clear, Father. Now, stop *all* of this right now, and I want you to leave this ranch immediately, and I never want to see you again. Do you hear me? *NEVER* again! You never really loved me. I was always a disappointment to you because you wanted a son."

"That's not true, Nicole."

"Oh, yes, it is."

"No, it's not! And I *do* love you, Nicole. I always have."

"Oh, really? Then why did you tell our neighbor, Mr. Parkins, that you were *so* disappointed that you didn't have a son."

"I never said that!"

"Yes you did, Father. I was six years old, *six years old* when you said it. Do you have *any* idea how that made me feel? I was *crushed!* At that very moment I knew you didn't love me, and perhaps you never had, but I was determined to try to make you love me by making you proud of me for everything I tried to do after that. I did everything I could to be the best so that *maybe* you might notice, but you were always too busy with your career to notice. Mom was the *only* one who cared, the *only* one I knew loved me. She was always there for me, no matter what, but not you! No, not you."

"Nicole—"

"*I'm* not finished!"

"Nicole, *please*!"

"Father, *stop*! You need to listen to me, and listen to me *now*!"

Jenson stood there and folded his arms across his chest in disgust.

"I'm sorry for having to speak to you like this—"

"You *should* be!"

Nicole froze as her father had just stepped on her last nerve. She felt so much rage at that moment that she lost control and swung her hand to slap him, but her father grabbed her wrist before she connected. In a flash, Liam grabbed Jenson's wrist with so much pressure that Jenson instantly released his daughter's arm.

"I wouldn't do that if I were you," Jenson said with a menacing look.

Liam stared him down, forcing Jenson to retreat three steps. Then, while still maintaining a barrier between Nicole and her father, he released Jenson's wrist.

Nicole backed away, rubbing her wrist. All of the pent-up thoughts, feelings, and emotions she had repressed for over twenty-six years were right below the surface, ready to explode. The fury in her eyes spoke volumes, and her father's bullheadedness made Nicole realize that she was finally through with her father. She turned and walked away.

"We're not done here, Nicole!"

Nicole kept walking.

"NICOLE!"

She froze, slowly turned, her fists clenched by her side, and took two steps back toward her father.

"That is the last time you will *ever* raise your voice to me," Nicole replied in a controlled but fierce voice. "After the way you've treated me all of my life, and *especially* right now … I am disowning you as my father, and you are now dead to me."

Jenson stood there, stunned.

"Nicole, stop. Let's talk about this." Nicole ignored him and retreated toward the stable.

Jenson didn't know what to say or do next. He looked toward Liam and his expression once again turned to extreme anger.

"And as for you, *cowboy*—"

"You need to leave, Mr. Hart," Liam calmly interrupted.

"*You* don't tell *me* what to do" Jenson replied with a sneer.

"You need to remember that this is not your property. I seem to recall that Nicole told you to leave, so that would mean you're now trespassing."

"Cowboy, if I were thirty years younger, I'd—"

"You'd *what?!* Hmm? *What* would you do?"

Jenson stood there speechless. He wanted to smash Liam's face, but he remembered that he wasn't as fast or as strong as when he was in his thirties.

"That's right, Mr. Hart. I think you're beginning to realize that you've not only lost this battle, but also the war, so it's time for you to leave. And, if I were you, I'd never come back."

"You have *no right* to—"

"Actually, yes I do. But more importantly, so does your daughter, because she lives and works here now, and as her supervisor, I, too, have the right to ask you to leave. So, we can make this clean and quiet, or I can call the sheriff. It's your choice."

"Are you threatening me, *cowboy?*"

"You seem to be using that term as if I'd take it as an insult. Well, I don't. I'm actually quite proud to be a cowboy. Always have been. Now, are you going to leave, or am I calling the sheriff?"

"Stop threatening me, or—"

"Not a threat, simply a promise."

"You haven't heard the last of me."

"Yes, I believe I have."

"What's going on, Liam?"

"Who are *you?*" Jenson growled.

"The name is Luke Masterson, and this is my ranch, and from what I've heard while walking out here, I'd say you don't belong here. I'm going to have to ask you to leave."

"I'm not leaving without my daughter."

"Mr. Hart," Liam interjected, "you no longer have a daughter.

Nicole made that crystal clear a few moments ago when she disowned you."

"Ah, you're Nicole's father?" Luke inquired.

"*Was* Nicole's father," Liam added, "and he's about to leave."

Jenson was just about to speak when Luke interrupted.

"Before you say anything else, Mr. Hart, I'd listen to Liam. Before you get yourself into any more trouble than you're already in, starting with trespassing and disturbing the peace on my ranch. Now turn around, get in your car, and leave. And … you're *not* welcome back. If I ever see you on my property again, I'll place you under citizen's arrest until the Sheriff arrives to haul you away."

"Do you have any idea who I am and who I know? One call and I can have your ranch shut down with the snap of my fingers!"

"Last time, Mr. Hart. One more threat and you'll be under arrest right here and right now."

Jenson stood there seething for several moments, while Luke and Liam waited calmly, but alertly, for his next move. He had *never* been so insulted in all his life! And by a couple of lousy, dirty *cowboys*, no less! He gave them one more sneering look, then turned and walked back to his car. Thirty minutes later the charter jet was airborne. With just one passenger.

CHAPTER 65

Aftermath, II

INSTEAD OF RETURNING TO the stable, Nicole headed for her casita. She was fuming as she entered and closed the door hard behind her! *What was he thinking?! That I would simply pack up and go with him without a fight?! That does it! I'm through! I never want to see him again!*

Nicole's adrenaline level was spiking and she began to tremble with fury, followed by breaking down into uncontrollable sobbing. One minute she had been so happy, and the next minute everything came crashing down! The *last* thing she needed right now was another migraine, like the one Chandler had caused just a couple of weeks ago. She fought valiantly to keep the oncoming pain at bay.

How could he do this to me? And why?! Why can't he stop trying to control me?

Her sobbing continued for several minutes until she thought she heard a knock on her door. She held her breath for a moment and heard it again.

"Nicole?" It was Liam. "Nicole, are you in there?"

"Yes," she replied weakly.

"Are you alright?"

"Just a minute."

"Okay."

Nicole reached for several tissues to wipe away her tears and blow her nose. She knew she probably looked like a mess and wished Liam didn't have to see her this way, but right now she needed him more than she needed her dignity. She took a deep breath and opened the door.

"Hey," was all Liam could say before Nicole dove into his arms.

"Oh, Liam!" and the tears began to flow again.

He held her tight and didn't say a word.

Nicole leaned back and looked up into Liam's eyes.

"Come in, please." Liam followed her into her casita, but he left the door ajar.

Nicole reached out and took Liam's hands.

"Liam, I'm … I'm *so* sorry for what just happened out there."

"There's nothing for you to be sorry about."

"I'm *so* embarrassed that my father came here and caused such a scene in front of everyone. I just hope Luke and Jill won't regret hiring me after that."

"I'm sure you have *nothing* to worry about. Remember, Luke stepped in to support you. He's on your side."

"Maybe in that moment, but what about when things begin to settle down. He'll obviously share what happened with Jill, and they might get a different impression of me—"

"No, this incident reflected on your *father* and the type of person *he* is. You stood your ground, you rightfully defended your choice, and I'm sure Luke was quite proud of you for doing so. If anything, I believe that moment made it clear in his eyes that they made a *great* choice in hiring you."

"You really think so?"

"Absolutely!"

Nicole leaned in and hugged Liam tightly.

"You know … you really impress me," Liam said softly.

"I do?"

"Yes! You're driven, focused … strong."

Nicole heard that last word and paused before responding.

"I had no other choice," she replied softly.

Liam understood completely.

"Hey, I want you to wait right here for about thirty minutes, okay?"

"But I have to get back to work," Nicole protested.

"I'll take care of that. I have something I need to do and then I'll be back, okay?"

"Are you sure?"

"Yes, it'll be fine. I'll see you right here in thirty minutes."

"Okay, I'll be here."

"Great! I'll see you then."

* * *

Nicole gently closed the door behind Liam. *How lucky can a girl get?* She returned to sitting on her bed, let out a long, heavy sigh, and reached for her phone to make a call.

"Hello?"

"Hi, mom."

"Nicole! Hi! How are you?"

"Well, I had originally planned on giving you a call tonight to share some amazing news, but now I'm calling to air out my frustrations. So … I'm not so good, I'm afraid."

"Why? What's wrong, sweetheart?"

"Well … you'll never guess who I just saw here at the ranch."

"Well, no, I can't imagine. Who was it?"

"Dad."

"WHAT?!?! He's *there?!*"

"Actually, he just left."

"But he told me he was going to L.A. to meet with a few people, and he wouldn't be back until late this evening."

"Well, *that* part is true. He won't be home until late."

"But *what* was he doing there?"

"Wanting me … change that, *demanding* that I pack up and come home with him!"

"WHAT?! Oh, Nicole, I'm *so* sorry! I had *no* idea he was going to do that!"

"Well, he did. And it got really ugly. He was furious that I was standing up to him and then he *really* lost it. My boss, Liam, was right there and stepped in to try to get Dad to back off. You should have seen it, Mom. He was so gallant standing up for me the way he did, but it only got worse. The owner of the ranch, Luke, stepped in and made it clear that Dad was not welcome here, and that he'd better leave, or he would call the Sheriff."

"Oh, no!"

"I had already walked away by then, and of course that *really* pushed Dad over the edge."

"Good for you, sweetie. I'm proud of you for sticking up for yourself like that. I just wish you didn't have to in the first place."

"It's okay. He knows *exactly* where I stand now. And ..." Nicole paused.

"And what, dear?"

"Mom, I'm sorry, but I said something that I shouldn't have."

"What was it?"

"I was just *so* mad at him that I told him I was disowning him as my father, and that he was now dead to me."

Charlotte couldn't reply for a long moment.

"Mom, I'm *so* sorry."

"No, sweetheart, I completely understand," Charlotte replied softly.

"But, saying those words to my own *father?* I ..." and Nicole began to cry.

"Oh, sweetheart. Nicole, listen to me."

"What?" Nicole replied between tears.

"Sweetie, you've been under a lot of pressure, and have had so much on your mind for several weeks. You had just made a decision that you believed was going to bring so much new joy into your life, and you had taken the plunge. The very last thing you could have imagined was to have your father show up and demand, to your face, that you throw all of that away, and return to your old life. He had no right to do such a thing, and I'm *furious* with him for doing so."

"But to say what I did was—"

"It was necessary, Nicole. It may seem like it was harsh, but believe me, it was necessary."

Nicole let out a long sigh.

"Thanks, Mom. I love you."

"I love you, too, dear."

"Thanks again for always being there for me and listening to my problems."

"That's what moms are for!" Charlotte replied gleefully, trying her best to lighten the mood, even a bit.

Nicole laughed through her tears. "Yes, they certainly are. I love you."

"I love you, too, sweetheart."

"I have something I need to do so I better let you go."

"Okay, dear. Take care. And Nicole?"

"Yes, Mom?"

"Be happy."

"Oh! That's reminds me!"

"What?"

"I've sold my condo!"

"What? So *soon!*"

"Yes! Can you believe it?"

"That's *wonderful,* dear!"

"But here's the *best* part! The couple that bought it offered *three times* what I was asking! *And* they want all the furnishings, too!"

"Oh, my gosh, Nicole! That's amazing!"

"They told my agent that they would be glad to have anything I want, like my dishes, silverware, pots and pans, and things like that boxed up and shipped to me at *their* expense! Isn't that cool?"

"Oh, wow! That's so wonderful, sweetie!

Nicole smiled. "Thanks, Mom. At least I have *one* good thing I could share with you after all of the negative."

"And that's what you should focus on, dear. Okay?"

"Okay, Mom. Thank you and I love you!"

"I love you, too, sweetheart. Bye."

"Bye, Mom."

As Nicole set her phone down on the bed, she let out another long sigh, but this one was filled with a gentle sense of relief. Her heart still felt heavy, but having talked with her mother, she was feeling better. Now, to just stay focused on the here and now and not worry about the past!

CHAPTER 66

The Whispers of the Mountain

LIAM WAS RIGHT ON time as he knocked on Nicole's door. As she opened it she was stunned to see not only Liam, but also Wildfire and Calypso!

"Let's go," Liam urged, with a big smile.

Nicole beamed and replied, "Sure!"

Liam helped her into her saddle, then mounted Wildfire, turned, and within a few strides Nicole rode up next to him and they headed for the mountains.

"I talked to Jill, and under the circumstances, she was perfectly fine with you taking the rest of the day off, and Mike is taking care of the rest of my stuff."

"He's a good man."

"The best assistant I've ever had."

"I think Jill mentioned to me that you had worked on another ranch or two somewhere in the past."

"Yes, Montana and Colorado."

"What made you come here?"

"A nice change of scenery and a smaller operation."

"Smaller?"

"Yeah, they were large cattle ranches."

"As large as Silverado Springs?"

"Much larger."

"Really?!"

Liam calmly nodded.

"May I ask how much larger?"

Liam hesitated before replying. "Our family's largest ranch in Montana is over 175,000 acres."

Nicole was momentarily speechless. "Oh, my gosh! That's a *huge* difference!"

Liam smiled and nodded.

Nicole felt a tingling sensation rush over her body. *Liam has* no *idea how amazing he is!*

They followed the trail up to their usual 'sunset ride' spot, dismounted and tied their horses to a nearby tree. They laid out their blanket together, then Liam reached into his saddle bags and pulled out some paper bags and drinks.

"What's that?"

"Dinner," Liam replied with a wink.

"Really? Did you go into town to get something?"

"No. After I left your casita I walked over and asked LuAnn for a favor, and she smiled and fixed up something just for us."

"Oh, my gosh! How nice of her! And *you*, too! Thank you."

"Anytime."

"So, what's for dinner?"

"Roast beef sandwiches with Swiss cheese on sourdough."

"Mmmm. Mayo and mustard, too?

"A dash of each."

"Sounds good!"

Liam's casual demeanor was disarming. Nicole felt so calm and comfortable around him, so … natural. There was no pretense. You got exactly what you saw. Every time. When it was time to work he was focused and on point. And when it came time to relax, he could do that, too. Although, he would usually be found somewhere far away from the center of attention.

When he spoke with anyone one on one, he typically spoke softly. Even when he spoke to a group of people like he did that Monday when she was here on her vacation and introduced the guests to the horses, he did so calmly. She had been especially enamored with him when he was talking with Emma! He was so kind and patient.

And now, here they sat, in their special place. At least, she wondered if it was truly *their* special place. Her curiosity got the better of her.

"So, Liam."

"Yes?"

"Over the few years you've been here, how many other ladies have you brought up here?"

He looked at her and smiled.

She looked right back at him. "What?!"

"Why do you want to know?"

"Because I'm curious. You're a handsome guy, and I'm sure there have been other single women who've come here on vacation that might have caught your eye."

Liam didn't answer, but took a bite of his sandwich instead.

"Come on, no stalling," she teased.

He smiled and pointed to his mouth, as if to explain 'I'm eating!'

Nicole waited patiently until he swallowed, then before he could take another bite she nudged him with her elbow.

"Come on, cowboy. Answer my question." He took a sip of his water, then looked at her and smiled.

"Well, the truth is … "

"Yes?"

"None."

"Oh, come on! You're trying to tell me that a handsome guy like you has *never* brought any other lady up here?"

"That's right."

"Okay, then you must have taken them to some other spot up here, right?"

He smiled and simply shook his head as he took another bite of his sandwich.

Nicole looked at him disbelievingly.

"Truly?" she asked softly.

Liam nodded his head. "Truly."

Nicole pondered this as she took the first bite of her sandwich, and they sat and ate in silence, and enjoyed the beautiful late afternoon view over the ranch and the valley beyond.

When their sandwiches were finished, Liam reached into another paper bag and brought out two freshly baked chocolate fudge brownies wrapped in napkins.

"Oh, my gosh!" Nicole exclaimed. "I *love* brownies!"

"I had a feeling you might. These are yours."

"I don't mind sharing!"

"That's okay," Liam replied as he reached back into the bag and removed two more brownies for himself.

"Aww, very smart man."

Liam looked over at Nicole, smiled, and winked.

That tingling sensation rushed over Nicole again!

They enjoyed their brownies in silence, and when they finished Nicole shifted sideways so she could look more directly at Liam.

"So, I have another question."

Liam smiled. "Okay."

"When you were talking with that little girl, Emma, you said Liam was short for William."

"Right."

"So ... what's the rest of your name?"

"Actually, William is my middle name?"

"Really?"

"Yes."

"Okay, so what's you first name?"

"James."

"James William." Nicole slowly and softly said it out loud and pondered it for a moment. "That sounds impressive."

Liam didn't respond.

"Okay, so, James William, what's your last name?"

"Prescott."

"Wow! James William Prescott?! Now, that *is* impressive!"

Liam politely shrugged off her compliment like it was no big deal.

"You don't think so?"

"I don't really think about it at all."

While Nicole was pondering Liam's comment, he spoke up.

"So, let me ask *you* a question?"

"Fair enough."

"What's your full name?"

"Nicole Renée Hart"

"I like that," he said casually.

"Thank you."

"And now, for my next question … do you ever think about *your* name?"

"No."

"Okay, I think I've just made my point."

"But my name is just ordinary," she politely protested.

Liam looked deeply into Nicole's eyes. "Not to me," he said, almost in a whisper.

Nicole looked into Liam's eyes and smiled as her heart felt deeply touched.

"Okay," she replied softly. "I see what you mean."

Liam reached out and rested his hand on hers, sending a shiver all over her!

"I really *do* like your name, Nicole."

"Thank you, Liam," she replied softly, and they sat there in silence, listening to the whispers of the mountain.

CHAPTER 67

What's in a Name?

J AMES WILLIAM PRESCOTT. NICOLE pondered the name over
and over. *It really* does *sound impressive! But* who *are you, Liam?
You've told me your name, that you worked on cattle ranches before coming here. I know you're the head wrangler here, and that your horse's
name is Wildfire. But … I don't know anything else! And I want to! I
want to know everything about you!*

She thought for a moment, and then had an idea! She reached
for her laptop, typed his name in the search bar, and waited only a
few seconds.

James William (Liam) Prescott

Oh, my gosh! He's in here!! She began scanning over the information listed in an article from *Western Horseman* magazine.

The fourth son of David Allen Prescott and Mary Beth Hastings

Three older brothers – David, Jr., Matthew, and Robert

Two younger sisters – Carole and Melissa

Born and raised in the State of Montana, United States of America

James is a direct descendant of the Prescott family that was instru-
mental in settling the Montana Territory, as well as important aspects
of its growth before and after Montana attained statehood in 1889.

James is named after his fifth great grandfather, William (Liam)
James Prescott, who made his initial wealth when gold was discovered in Montana in 1858. Later, he greatly expanded his wealth after
the discovery of silver in the 1870's.

William started his initial cattle ranching operations in 1865 with 25,000 acres, expanding it to over 100,000 acres by the late 1880s.

The Prescott family has maintained continuous cattle ranch operations in Montana, Wyoming, and Colorado, as well as expanding into lumber operations in Washington and Oregon in the early 1900s.

Today the family holdings include over 500,000 acres for cattle ranches, and over 350,000 acres of forest for their lumber operations, over six states. While Liam is not directly engaged in the family business at this time, choosing instead to work independently, he nevertheless contributes his fair share financially to the family enterprises.

His personal annual income from his family's operations, along with his numerous investments, is estimated to exceed $5 million.

WHAT?! Oh, my gosh!!

Liam Prescott currently resides in Angel Fire, New Mexico where he is the head wrangler for Hidden Glory Guest Ranch.

Nicole sat there staring at her computer! *I don't believe this! This is … incredible! Liam? A multi-millionaire?! Wait a minute … there's a footnote.*

In an interview by Blake Adams for *Aviation Week* magazine, Liam stated that he got his pilot's license after he graduated from college at the age of 22. This allowed him the opportunity to more efficiently check on his family's various expanding operations throughout the northwest.

The article went on to say that Liam's current aircraft was a Deep Sea Blue HondaJet Elite S, which Liam said was co-owned with his friend, Barrett Davidson. They are 50/50 owners, but Barrett has primary possession of the jet in Colorado Springs, Colorado because he uses it so often for his business as a Senior Vice President for a venture capital firm. Liam added that whenever he needs the jet he simply arranges for Barrett to fly to Angel Fire. Then Barrett borrows his car, a Gentian Blue Porsche Panamera 4S Executive, to take care of clients, as well as personal business, between Taos and Albuquerque. Liam generally needs the jet for only a week or two every few months.

Liam said he's more of a 'free spirit' when it comes to the family operations, as his father and brothers prefer to 'stay put' and let Liam do the traveling.

Nicole let out a long sigh, then did a search for both the jet and the car, and was stunned by the beauty of both of them! *This guy really has style!*

I wonder if anyone here at the ranch knows anything about this? I'm guessing Luke and Jill probably do in order for him to take off like that every few months.

Nicole printed out the information and then read it over two more times. Each time she read it she became more and more in awe of the man she simply knew as Liam, head wrangler. *Make that* millionaire *head wrangler!* She shook her head. *I … can't … believe … this!*

Chapter 68

One Dark Night

When Jenson arrived home late Thursday evening the house was dark. It was too early for Charlotte to have gone to bed, and, noticing that her car was not in the garage, he figured she was out with some friends and, would no doubt, be home soon.

He opened the garage door leading into the house and started flipping on lights.

He was thirsty and headed for the kitchen to find something to drink. There, on the island counter, was a note.

Jenson —

HOW DARE YOU!!! I am so furious with you right now! How could you do that to Nicole?! Not only that, but you lied to me when you said you were going to L.A. on business for the day! You've made that trip before, so I didn't think anything of it. But, more importantly, what you did to our daughter is unconscionable!

You're on your own for a while. I won't be answering the phone, so just leave me alone. And LEAVE NICOLE ALONE, too!

Charlotte

Jenson *slammed* his hand down on the island and muttered something under his breath! He sighed heavily, looked around the kitchen, then grabbed a tall glass from the cabinet above the sink. He filled it halfway with ice, got his favorite drink, turned off the lights, and headed for the patio. He shoved the sliding glass door open so hard it nearly came off the track.

As Jenson sat there in the dark he thought back over his day, a day that *should* have turned out very differently, but ended up crashing and burning to the ground instead.

How dare *Nicole stand up to me like that! And how* dare *she walk away from her career like that! And to work on a* stupid *ranch?!*

And where did Charlotte go?! How dare *she go off like this!*

Too many questions ... and not a single answer.

CHAPTER 69

Wondering

IT WAS ONLY NICOLE'S third day on the job, but it appeared that she was blending in with her new surroundings quite nicely. Of course, she was still adjusting to the fact that most of her work was outside, and it was certainly dusty, but at least she didn't have to worry about any allergies.

She had a variety of chores, but she was also able to spend some time with the guests. Having recently been through the very same experience, she was helpful in answering many of their questions. Her bright and genuinely friendly personality, along with her helpful ways, were evident everywhere she went. Several of the staff members were even passing along their positive impressions to Jill. And, each time, Jill's smile grew a little wider.

The one downside to being an employee was that now she was not able to see Liam as often as when she had been a guest, but she also knew that she *might* be able to look forward to them spending some of their evenings together. As many as possible would be just fine with her! Besides, she *still* had so much more to explore about this man who had taken a prominent place in her mind … *and* her heart.

Now that she was here permanently, Nicole was able to get to know many of the other staff on a more personal basis. However, she still made sure to not get too close to either Cindi or Shane. So far, none of her responsibilities had brought her into their proximity, but that could change at any time. She decided that she would simply handle things politely and professionally, and hope that they would do the same.

As Nicole was assisting Brendy with her chores that morning, her curiosity once again got the better of her.

"Hey, Brendy, I was wondering. Do you know much about Liam's personal life, or what he did before he came here?"

"I think I know one of the reasons you accepted this job," Brendy replied with a wink and a smile.

"What? No! Well … maybe. Just a little." Nicole smiled sheepishly.

"It's okay. We all saw a *connection* between you two from the start."

"You *did?!*" Nicole's eyebrows raised as her face began to turn red.

"Yes. There was something about him that changed as the week went on. I think it may have even started when he saw you confronting that guy who showed up and started bothering you."

"Ugh, don't remind me!" Nicole rolled her eyes.

"Sorry."

"That's okay," Nicole replied, shrugging off the nasty memory.

"He's never shown any special interest in any of our single female guests until you."

Nicole hesitated to say anything, but felt like she could trust Brendy to keep a secret.

"Liam and I went for a ride late yesterday afternoon, and I was teasing him, trying to keep things light and casual, and I asked him how many other women he's taken up onto the side of the mountain to look at the view."

"What did he say?!"

"Well, after teasing me back for a couple of minutes, he finally said I was the first and only one."

"I believe it."

"He said it so sincerely that I believe it, too. But don't you find it unusual for a great looking guy like him, someone who *really* knows his stuff, to have not attracted the attention of any other women before now?"

"Well, I'm sure he's attracted other women's attention to him before, unintentionally, of course. The difference is, he just wasn't attracted to them, at least not enough to become friendly with them."

"Hmmm, interesting."

"But here's something else to think about. He always knew they were going home at the end of their week, and he'd never see them again. He probably figured, 'why bother.'"

"Okay, but so was I."

"Ahh, good point. So, there definitely *was* something different about you that caught his eye right from the start."

"*Plus*, knowing that *I* was also going home at the end of my stay, the last thing on my mind was to think about getting interested in someone here, *especially* after having just gotten rid of someone else that first day. I'm not a quick rebound kind of girl."

Brendy nodded in response.

"Now ... getting back to my original question, do you know much about Liam's personal life, or what he did before he came here?"

"Oh, yeah, I guess I got sidetracked again, didn't I!" They both laughed. "Well, all I know is that he came from a ranching background, but I don't know how extensive it was. And I'm pretty sure he was also a head wrangler as well before coming here. Other than that, I don't really know much more about him, at least workwise."

"Do you know if he was married before, or am I getting too personal?"

"Well, I heard that he may have been engaged at some point, but I don't know how long ago that was or why it ended."

Nicole pondered Brendy's responses as they continued to work on Nicole's training list. When lunch time rolled around Brendy mentioned she needed to go to Taos to pick up some supplies for Jill. She asked Nicole if she'd like to go along. "We'll pick up some lunch over there, too. My treat."

"Sounds good! Thanks!"

* * *

As they made their way through the Carson National Forest, Nicole was able to take in more of the scenery that before had just flown past her window as she had driven to and from the ranch. She and Brendy kept up their conversation about Liam.

"So, besides working at the ranch, do you have any idea what else he likes to do, like with his evenings or any time off that he takes?"

"I've heard he likes to go exploring. He'll just take off in his truck and head off to parts unknown. A couple of times I've overheard him sharing some stories with Mike and he really seems to enjoy his time off. I know he lives somewhere in the village, but I have no idea where. He's typically one of the first to arrive in the morning and the last to leave at the end of the day. He's deeply committed to his work at the ranch, and I know he works at the other ranch from time to time when they're a man short. He likes to help things run smoothly there, too."

"Well, his character sure seems to be rock solid, but it's almost like he's too good to be true."

"I know what you mean. I was *so* fortunate to meet a man like Corey who is exactly the same way. Unfortunately, especially from what Beth and a few of my other friends say, it seems like there aren't many guys like that around."

Nicole nodded without responding as her gaze once again wandered off toward the forest passing by.

Once in Taos they picked up the office supplies Jill needed, then found a Mexican restaurant not far away that appeared to be quite busy.

"Quite a popular place, huh?" Nicole asked.

"Yes, there are plenty of Mexican restaurants to choose from in town, but this is one of the best. You'll understand why soon enough."

There was a long line of customers waiting for tables. "It's always like this," Brendy whispered. "But the turnover is fairly quick. It won't take us long to get a table."

"Good, because I'm starved!"

"I know what you mean. That's why I chose this place, because they're always so generous with their portions, and the prices are *very* reasonable."

Brendy was right about the rapid turnover. People were leaving almost as quickly as others were arriving and they had a table in less than twenty minutes.

"Good afternoon, ladies. I'm Maria, and I'll be your server today. May I bring you anything to drink while you look over the menu?"

Brendy nodded to Nicole to go ahead and order first.

"I'd like water with a lime wedge."

"And I'll have a club soda, please," added Brendy.

"Thank you! I'll be right back with your drinks."

"I already know what I want," Brendy proclaimed to Nicole, "but take your time."

"I think I've already found what I want!"

"That was fast!"

"Like I said, I'm starving!"

They both laughed.

"Here you are, ladies," Maria said as she set their drinks down on the table. "I know I may not have given you enough time to decide, but has anything on the menu piqued your interest yet?"

"I'm going to have your chicken enchilada platter with extra sour cream and mild salsa on the side!" Brendy replied.

"Oh, good choice!" Maria replied.

"I know! I've been here several times before, and I love the spicy kick they add to the sauce!"

Maria smiled and nodded, then turned her attention to Nicole.

"I'd like your crown tostada with ground beef instead of refried beans, and extra sour cream on the side."

"O-o-o, that sounds good!" Brendy exclaimed.

"Believe me, it *is!*" Maria replied.

"Good, because I haven't had one in *many* years!" Nicole expressed brightly.

"I'll be back with your meals before you know it!"

"Thank you, Maria!" Brendy said, as Nicole nodded in agreement.

"Oh, Maria?" Brendy caught her attention just after she had turned to go. "One more thing. I'll take the check when we're ready to go."

"Very well. Thank you for letting me know."

* * *

Liam continued to be the main topic of their conversation while they enjoyed their meals and on their way back to the ranch. Nicole enjoyed learning more about the guy who had found his way into her heart so unexpectedly. She knew beyond a shadow of any doubt that she wanted to get to know Liam better, but she also knew she needed to be careful and take it slowly.

CHAPTER 70

Paying the Price

JENSON STARTED HIS DAY in a horrific mood. The house was empty and painfully quiet, and he was sporting a powerfully splitting headache. He had been angry when he went to bed the night before and his mood had only gotten worse.

He called the other men in his foursome and, not caring to disguise his mood, explained he would not be joining them on the links that morning, but gave no explanation.

Where are you, Charlotte. We need to talk, so you need to come home now!

He was in no mood to prepare anything for breakfast, so he went straight to his office. Once his computer was ready, he looked up the details about Hidden Glory Ranch once again. If his daughter *insisted* on working there, he was going to find out everything he could about the place.

Near the bottom of the page, he noticed a link to a related story about Silverado Springs Ranch. As he read the article, he noticed the connection between the two ranches: Luke and Jill Masterson owned them both.

Despite his anger and reluctance, the more he read the more he became impressed with this couple and what they had accomplished.

Silverado Springs Ranch was a highly successful cattle operation and had been in the Masterson family for several generations. It was Jill Masterson who had the idea to create the guest ranch, and Luke had backed her all the way.

The headache he had woken up with had turned into a migraine, and now every move he made seemed to make his head want to explode. However, the more Jenson read, the more his headache seemed to ease ever so slightly, but it still was not fast enough.

When he finished reading about the Masterson's and their ranches he slowly sat back in his chair, closed his eyes, and tried his best to relax. Unfortunately, no matter what he tried, he couldn't diminish not only his migraine, but also the thought of Charlotte walking out on him.

Where are you, Charlotte? Please come home to me.

CHAPTER 71

Questions Unanswered

THAT EVENING, WHILE LIAM and Nicole were relaxing in their favorite spot on the side of the mountain, Liam looked at Nicole without saying a word.

"What?" she asked, wondering why he was looking at her in a peculiar way.

"Just wondering."

"About?"

Liam paused for a long moment, looked out over the valley, then turned back toward Nicole.

"Come on, Liam, what are you wondering about?"

He smiled and half-laughed.

"I was just wondering … if you would mind very much if I called you Nicci?"

Nicole's eyes grew wide. "Really? Hmmm, why?"

"Just because," he replied with a shrug.

"That's not an answer," Nicole replied with a wink and teasing nudge.

"Well … what little I know about you, um, you had a very serious and important career, right?"

"Well, it *was* important to me but I don't know how serious it actually was."

"Compared to what I do, I consider it quite serious. You weren't just drawing sketches of homes and buildings, you were *designing* them right down to the smallest detail. Correct?"

"Yes."

"Okay, so … let me put it this way. You were in a profession where you went to an office every day, dressed professionally, and conducted yourself in a professional manner. At the same time while you were there, I'm guessing that probably had a rollover effect on friendships, and places you went, like nice restaurants."

Nicole still could not figure out where Liam was going with this line of questioning, and the look on her face let Liam know he needed to get to the point.

Liam cleared his throat.

"I guess what I'm trying to say is, this is a much more casual place to work than an office. Now please don't get me wrong, because I like your name, but it kind of seems a bit on the formal side to me, while Nicci sounds more informal, more … casual."

"Okay," Nicole began, "now *that's* a good reason."

"So, is it okay for me to call you Nicci, or would you prefer that I still call you Nicole?"

Nicole smiled and looked gently into Liam's eyes. *Just call me yours*, she thought.

"I would *love* for you to call me Nicci," she replied softly.

"Then Nicci it is!" And with that, Nicci leaned into Liam's arms and got lost in their first kiss.

* * *

As dusk approached and the stars were making their presence known, Liam and Nicci continued to ask each other questions to learn more and more about each other.

Liam avoided asking her about either Chandler or her father, but focused more on her interests and friends. Nicci did likewise. Liam was forthright while chatting about loving sports, especially in high school, although he bucked a little when Nicci asked him if he played any team sports. However, she managed to get him to open up a bit and admit he had played on the football, basketball, and baseball teams. She was dutifully impressed. He made absolutely no mention of his being a three-year letterman in all three sports, nor the state championships their teams had won along the way.

She, likewise, also mentioned playing sports in high school, but played it coy, causing Liam to drill a little deeper to get her to give more details. She didn't mention anything about her being selected as Homecoming Queen or her class valedictorian. That, she thought, would be going too far.

Nicci asked him if he had had a high school sweetheart, and he shared a bit about her. That her name was Marcie, and they had met when her family had moved to town when she was a sophomore. They stayed together until they graduated and Marcie went away to college. Liam chose to stay close to home and attended Montana State University in Bozeman, majoring in psychology.

"Did the two of you write to each other or call once in a while just to stay in touch?"

"Yes, but after a while it felt like she was losing interest. Being so far away from her, and working hard in my own classes, I did everything I could to not get discouraged. Then, during our sophomore year, she met an upperclassman, and they married a year later."

Nicci explained she had earned her degree in Architectural Engineering from USC.

He interrupted her and teasingly asked, "USC? As in University of South Carolina?"

"No, it's the University of Southern Cal—", then she realized he had been teasing her when he started laughing.

"You …!" and she gave him a solid elbow in his ribs as they laughed and then kissed.

"I just couldn't pass that one up."

"Yeah, I'll just *bet* you couldn't!"

Then she told him about attending grad school in Arizona before landing her job back home in Newport Beach.

"So, let's back up a bit," Liam said. "Any high school sweetheart for you?"

His question caught her totally by surprise, although a split second later she realized it shouldn't have, since she had started it by asking if he had had one. She tried her best to swallow the lump in her throat, and then softly replied, "There was one."

"And I'm guessing by your reaction that it didn't go so well?"

"You could say that."

"I'm sorry."

"It's okay. It was … a long time ago."

"Did you ever hear from him again?" *This* question she was *not* prepared for, and her silence made Liam realize he needed to change the subject, and fast.

"Um, so tell me about you mother."

Nicci regained her composure. *Thank you, Liam.*

"My mother is simply wonderful. She's always been very supportive and encouraging, and that's been *so* helpful for me."

"I can imagine."

"And … well, you met my dad. She's been a saint to put up with him all these years. My dad was always so wrapped up in his work. When he chose to retire early, I think my mother was hoping they would be able to have more time together, travel and see the world, but all he wants to do is play golf. I have to hand it to her, though. Once she realized that he just wanted to play golf all the time, she took golf lessons in order to feel like she might one day be good enough that they could golf together. She said the first time she approached him about going with him, he was stunned. Before he could say anything, she led him to the bedroom, opened up her closet, and pulled out her own golf bag with a full set of clubs. She told me he was speechless."

"I can imagine! What did he finally say?"

"She said he stammered out something she couldn't understand, and then a bit louder said, 'Okay. I guess we can give it a try.' She said his lack of enthusiasm or genuine interest just crushed her."

"I'm so sorry. I hesitate to ask this, but … did they *ever* go golfing together?"

"Yes. I guess it took him a while to grasp what she had done, and why, and he finally invited her to go with him one day."

"How did that work out?"

"She said his overall demeanor was grumpy, so it made her feel like all the time, money, and effort she had put into learning how to play, hoping it would be something they could enjoy together, was a complete waste. She thought about joining a ladies golfing club, but her heart just wasn't in it. She never went golfing with him again, and eventually sold everything and went back to simply doing whatever she wanted while he was golfing."

"And she was okay about you making this change in your life?"

"Oh, my gosh! At first she was so surprised, but in a good way, and then she became so supportive and excited for me! Like I said, she's simply wonderful!"

Liam nodded, grateful that Nicci's attitude had not soured.

"So," Nicci said with a smile, "tell me about your family."

"What would you like to know?"

"Everything! I want to know *everything* about you, Liam!"

"Why?" he replied with a reserved smile.

"Because … I care about you," she replied softly.

He looked into her opalescent blue-green eyes, then put his arm around her shoulders and pulled her close.

"Thank you," he replied, almost in a whisper.

Nicci snuggled in a little closer.

"Well, there's not really much to tell." Nicci definitely knew otherwise, but she was curious just how much he would be willing to share with her.

"I grew up in Montana. I come from a large family."

"Large? How large?"

"Three older brothers and two younger sisters."

"Are your parents and siblings all still alive?"

"Yes, they are, thank heavens."

"Thank heavens? Did something happen to someone?"

"No, no, I'm just grateful that everyone is healthy and happy."

"Are your siblings all married?"

"Yes, I'm the only single one."

"So tell me, how is it that such a handsome and hard-working guy like you hasn't been snagged by some pretty lady?"

Liam simply shrugged. "I don't know. I guess it just hasn't been in the cards for me."

Nicci pondered this for a long moment, but Liam derailed her train of thought as he continued.

"Everyone is up in Montana, except me."

"How come you left?"

Liam shrugged again. "Lots of reasons, I guess."

"Would you care to name just one?"

Liam felt his resistance begin to melt just a bit, but certainly not all the way. Some things were just too painful to share.

"I guess I have more of a wandering spirit. It's hard for me to stay in one place for very long."

This concerned Nicci, and she hesitated to ask her next question, but she needed to know.

"And … how long is that, usually?" She braced her heart for his answer.

"Oh, a few years."

"And how long have you been here at Hidden Glory?"

"Hmmm, just over three years, I think."

Nicci suddenly felt a knot in her stomach. She didn't say anything, she just looked out into the darkness of the valley below … and closed her eyes.

Have I fallen for a guy who's about to walk out of my life? Is this all a rerun of Dusty? The knot in her stomach tightened.

"Liam?" Nicci asked softly.

"Yes?"

"Um … I'm feeling kind of tired. Would you mind very much if we headed back to the ranch?"

"No, that's fine! Let me help you up and I'll grab the blanket."

"Thank you."

As they slowly followed the trail back to the ranch, Nicci had a million thoughts tumbling through her mind. *What's the real reason I accepted this job? Was it truly because I wanted a change? Was it because I felt a need to distance myself from my father? Was it for the challenge of a new experience? Or … or was it Liam?* She let out a long sigh.

"Everything okay?" Liam asked as he looked over toward Nicci.

"Yes, just worn out. It's been a long day. I'm sure I'll be fine in the morning after a decent night's rest."

"Okay. Just checking."

They stopped at the stable and got their horses settled in for the night.

"Good night, Liam, and thank you for a nice evening."

"Wait, I'll walk you back to your casita."

"There's no need. There's plenty of light for me to find my way, so I'll be fine."

"Well, lovely lady, I insist," he replied gently, but firmly.

Nicci lowered her head for a moment.

"Okay," she replied, without meeting Liam's eyes.

"Are you sure you're okay?"

"Yes, why?"

Liam didn't reply right away.

"It's just … it's just that your mood seemed to change after I mentioned my wandering lifestyle."

"No, that was fine, Liam. Like I said, I'm just tired. It just hit me all of a sudden."

"Okay, I just want to make sure I hadn't said something to upset you."

"No, we're good."

They walked in silence to Nicci's casita. Once there, she opened the door, turned to say goodnight to Liam, and something inside her urged her to give him a kiss. Liam responded, but she felt something just wasn't right.

"Good night, Nicci."

"Good night, Liam."

She started to close the door, then opened it again.

"Liam?"

"Yes?"

"Thank you for calling me Nicci," she said softly.

"Sure! I'm glad you don't mind!"

"Well, no one has ever called me that before, so it caught me off guard, but … I like it. A lot. Thank you."

Liam smiled and winked. "You're welcome. Good night."

"Good night."

Nicci closed the door and reached to turn on the lights, but chose not to. Instead, she walked over and sat on the end of the bed, closed her eyes, and let the tears flow.

CHAPTER 72

Figure It Out

NICCI WAS MAKING HER way back to the ranch from her morning walk when she saw Liam in the stable up ahead. A knot started to form in her stomach again, but she took a couple of deep breaths to ward it off. *Maybe I can get passed the stable without him seeing or hearing me.* Just then he looked her way and waved. She returned his wave, but it wasn't as enthusiastic as usual.

"Good morning, Nicci! How are you on this beautiful morning?"

"I'm doing better. I got a good night's sleep last night so I'm ready for whatever the day has to offer." *At least I hope I am.*

"Good! Good! Well, I better get back in there. I just had to come out to say hi after I saw you approaching."

"Thank you, Liam. That was nice of you."

"Anytime!" he replied, as he touched the brim of his hat.

Always the gentleman. But … a gentleman with secrets. Then again … I'm carrying one, too.

"I see you two are getting along pretty well," Pat commented as Liam approached.

"Yes, we are."

"Anything you'd like to share?"

"Such as?"

"Oh, where you two go, what you do, you know, those kinds of things," Pat added with a wink and a smile.

Liam shook his head. "Kind of personal, don't you think," he replied with a smirk.

"Yes, I guess so. I just care about the two of you."

"Yeah?"

"Sure! Why not? All this time that you've been working here and never *once* have I ever seen you show *any* kind of interest in any of the single ladies that have come here for a little vacation. Not once! Even after Beth was hired last fall you *still* didn't change your demeanor. And now look at you! You're head over heels over Nicole, and I think it's wonderful!"

"Well, first off, and not counting Beth, why would I show any interest in any particular single woman who comes here when I know they'll be going home again in a few days, and I'll never see them again?"

"Nicole was in the same situation, but I noticed you keeping an eye on her from the first day. A woman can sense these things. Plus, you can't deny it, because I'm not the *only* one who noticed."

Liam didn't respond. He just kept focused on the work he needed to finish before heading in for breakfast.

"It's okay, Liam. She's here now, and you two should spend as much time together as you'd like. I'm not trying to butt in, but I think the two of you would make a wonderful couple. I truly do."

"I appreciate your opinion, Pat. We'll just have to see how things go, one day at a time. Neither of us is anxious to jump into anything serious right now."

"Are you sure?"

"I know I'm not, and after what we witnessed between Nicci and that rich, fancy guy on that first day, I'm sure she's not either."

"Nicci?"

"Pardon me?"

"You called her Nicci."

"Yeah, I did."

"Did she ask you to? Because that's a sure sign right there she's interested in you."

"Actually, it was my idea."

"Really?"

"When we were together last night, I asked her if she would mind if I called her Nicci, and she said it would be okay."

"Hmmmm. Now see? *That's* a sign that *you're* interested in *her!*"

"Well … I am."

"I *knew* it!"

"Just don't go making a big deal about it, especially to anyone else. Like I said, we're just taking everything one day at a time."

"One word of warning to you, though."

"What's that?"

"Don't go doing or saying something stupid to mess it up."

Liam was surprised by that comment. "What do you mean by that?"

"Just think about it. You're a smart guy. You'll figure it out."

Liam shook his head. "I'll see you at breakfast, Pat."

And in the distance, someone had heard every word.

* * *

Shane quietly eased the door to the tack room closed and thought about what he had just heard.

So, the happy couple is getting nice and chummy, eh? He gets my job, he gets the girl, and what do I get? Nothing!

If Shane didn't have to deal with either of them, everything would be just fine. He'd been able to bury his disappointment, frustration, and anger over Liam being chosen as the head wrangler over him, but every once in a while something would happen that would remind him of how cheated he had been.

Then, along comes a pretty little lady that Liam seemed to latch on to immediately, and that cut off *any* chance he might have had with her. And the closer the two of them seemed to be getting, the angrier Shane was becoming. And, if he wasn't careful, he just might do or say something that would get him fired, and he *definitely* couldn't afford to lose this job, even as rotten as it was most days.

CHAPTER 73

Heart to Heart

NICCI'S MOOD WAS SUBDUED as she and Liam rode up the mountain to their lookout spot. They had gotten a late start that evening because Liam had to meet with Luke and Jill after dinner, then had to go into town for a bit before returning to the ranch to take Nicci on their ride.

She still had so many questions about him, but now she was almost afraid to ask them for fear of what his answers might be.

Would she ever be able to find out about who the *real* James William Prescott was, or would he still skim along the surface of his life? And, other than a high school sweetheart, who undoubtedly broke his heart when she got married, he had not even hinted if he had had any other serious relationships, although somehow, she figured he had. Perhaps that was another reason for his leaving home and exploring new parts of the West; to leave *that* part of his past behind, no doubt for good. Who was she, why did they break up, and how long ago was it? Was it a fresh wound that led him to Hidden Glory Ranch to heal?

Liam had said that he usually stayed in one spot for only a few years, and by her best calculations, it appeared that his time here at Hidden Glory Ranch might be coming to a close at some point in the near future. But when? And where would he go? Did he have a plan? Would he share it with her? *So* many questions!

After they tied up their horses and spread out their blanket they sat down and admired the deepening colors of the evening sky.

"I have to go out of town for a few days," Liam began with a sort of not-a-big-deal attitude.

"Oh? When are you leaving?"

"Around nine tomorrow morning."

The suddenness of it caused the knot in her stomach to return.

"Anything fun?" Nicci asked expectantly, hoping to keep the mood light.

"Not really, I just have to take care of some family business."

"How long will you be gone?"

"About a week, depending on how quickly I can complete everything."

Nicci felt a twinge of sadness brush over her, but she did her best to hide it.

"So, family business? That means you'll be flying to Montana?"

"Yes, and I'll probably be making some side trips, too, before I return."

Flying your jet? Side trips to your other ranches? Why don't you just tell *me all about it, Liam?*

"Well, I hope it'll be a productive trip."

"Thank you. I do, too."

Nicci didn't know what else to say or ask, so she remained silent. Liam noticed.

"Nicci, is everything okay?"

"Yes, I'm just enjoying the view. It's nice having this quiet, private spot where we can spend a little time together." Liam wasn't convinced.

"Nicci?"

"Yes?"

"May I ask you a question?"

Nicci sensed from Liam's quieter tone of voice the question was going to be serious. She closed her eyes for a brief moment and took a deep breath. She shifted on the blanket, brought her knees up to her chest, and wrapped her arms around them. Having earned his degree in psychology Liam recognized the protective move immediately.

"Sure."

"I need to know ... is everything okay between us?"

"Yes, why do you ask?" Nicci asked as she glanced over toward Liam. From the tone of her voice Liam was once again not convinced.

"Maybe it's just my imagination, but I've just felt like the last couple of times we've been together I've either done something or said something that bothered you or upset you in some way."

Nicci looked out toward the darkening sunset. She knew that claiming she'd just been overly tired wouldn't cut it this time. When she didn't deny it right away, Liam knew.

"There *is* something, isn't there? Nicci, please talk to me. Tell me what it is."

"I'd … I'd rather not talk about it tonight, okay?"

Liam pondered her request, but he had to press forward.

"Sweetheart, I'm going to be gone for a week, and I just can't carry this heavy heart, knowing that something's wrong. I love you, and—"

The words stunned her! "You love me?"

Liam realized that he hadn't told her before, even though he'd known it for a while.

"Yes. I love you, Nicci."

She looked away and started to cry. He reached out to hold her, but she didn't lean into him like she had in the past. Now he was beginning to feel like everything truly *was* falling apart. *Pat warned me! But what is it?! What did I do?*

Nicci's gentle crying turned to sobbing, and she buried her face in her hands. It was killing Liam that he couldn't hold her. All he could do was wait and pray that she would explain everything.

Nicci shifted on the blanket again, but this time she stood up and walked a few feet away. She looked out toward the valley and wrapped her arms around herself. Unable to find any words to say, Liam remained on the blanket.

Nicci took a deep breath to try to ease her sobbing, but it had little effect.

Finally, Liam found his voice and stood up near Nicci.

"Whatever I did, or whatever I said, I'm sorry, Nicci. I'm really, deeply sorry."

"You have nothing to be sorry about," Nicci replied softly.

"Then I'm completely confused."

"You've been honest with me, so there's nothing for you to be sorry about."

"Then why are you crying?"

"Because … I love you, too, Liam."

"And that makes you sad?"

Nicci took a deep breath and let it out slowly, once again trying to stem her crying.

"You can't imagine how wonderful it felt to hear you say you loved me. It's been *forever* since someone told me they loved me and truly meant it. I know you do. But … I'm also petrified."

"Of what?"

"Of being hurt so badly again that this time I won't survive."

"Nicci, I promise I will *never* hurt you."

"But … you told me that you only stay in one place for a few years before you move on. You've already been here at Hidden Glory for a few years, so that means you'll be leaving me, and—" Nicole suddenly stopped as she felt Liam move in front of her. He placed his hands on both sides of her face, and looked deeply into her eyes.

"Nicci, I love you. I will *never* hurt you, and I will *never* leave you. And I keep my promises. *All* of them. Always."

"Oh, Liam!"

He kissed her passionately, and then she threw her arms around his neck and returned his passion.

As they loosened their arms ever so slightly, they each leaned back and looked into each other's eyes.

"I love you, Liam!"

"I love you, too, Nicci!"

In an immense release of tension and fear, they each began to laugh as they held each other close once again. A while later they sat back down on the blanket, but remained silent for a few more minutes. They were simply enjoying the sounds of darkness.

"What are you thinking?" Nicci asked.

"That I'd like to ask you another question."

"Do I have to answer it?" Nicci replied teasingly.

"Well, I hope you will." Liam was now the one trying to keep the mood light.

"Well, since you've given me a possible way out, go ahead and ask your question. BUT …"

"Yes?"

"I'm reserving the right to *not* answer it, fair enough?"

"Yes, I guess so."

"Okay, what's your question?"

Liam mentally crossed his fingers. "Would you be willing to share with me what happened the last time a guy broke your heart?"

Nicci had a feeling that question would come up some time, but she definitely wasn't prepared for it tonight.

"Um … I don't mind telling you, but would you mind very much if we wait a little while? Something occurred recently that involved that person, and I need to take care of it before I can tell you anything."

"I don't think I'm following what you're trying to say."

Nicci thought for a moment to see if she could rephrase her comment differently, but nothing came to her.

"Let's just say that when I *can* tell you, everything will make sense, I promise. And I keep my promises, too. *All* of them. Always."

They both smiled as Liam caught the reference to what he had just told Nicci a few moments before.

"Okay, fair enough."

"Now … since we're on the subject, *when* I'm able to share that with you, would you be willing to share with me the story behind who broke your heart? And I'm not talking about your high school sweetheart, Marcie."

"What do you mean?"

"Somewhere between Marcie and right now there was another special young lady, and I want to know the story."

"Why do you think there was anyone else?"

"Oh, come on, Liam. We talked about this the other night. You didn't actually *say* there was anyone else besides Marcie, but plain old common sense tells me that you *had* to have been involved with someone else very special in the past."

When Liam didn't respond Nicci smiled.

"I knew it," she added gently. "It's okay, Liam. You can tell me.

Remember, I love you, and I want to know absolutely *everything* about you. Sweetheart, please?"

Liam looked away and thought about it for a moment, then he let out a long sigh.

"Fair enough," he said softly. "When you're ready to share your story, I'll share mine with you."

"Thank you, sweetheart. That really means a lot to me." Then Nicci leaned up and gave Liam a tender kiss on the cheek.

CHAPTER 74

Face to Face ... Again

AFTER BREAKFAST THE NEXT morning Nicci got permission to take Calypso for a ride and rode to the far northwestern corner of the ranch. From there she could see the airport about a mile north. She had not asked, and Liam had not said that he would be flying out of Angel Fire, but she remembered reading the article about him being a co-owner of a jet. She knew that whenever he needed to check out his family's operations his partner would fly into Angel Fire and take Liam's car for business. She wished she had a pair of binoculars to get a closer look, but she would just have to make do and hope she could see *something*.

At ten minutes after nine she heard the sound of a small jet approaching and looked further to the north and saw it over Eagle Nest Lake. After it landed it was over thirty minutes before she saw it take off again, presumably with Liam at the controls.

Bye, my love! Be safe and come home to me SOON!

* * *

As she was returning to the stable Nicole noticed Dusty's truck parked nearby and let out a long sigh. *Oh, great! Just what I* don't *need this morning!* She dismounted and walked Calypso into the stable and saw Dusty talking with Pat near the other end. They saw Nicole and both waved. Nicole politely waved in return and hoped that would be the extent of their contact.

She removed Calypso's saddle, blanket, and tack, brushed her down, and returned her to her stall. She then spent a few extra minutes quietly talking to Calypso and stroking her head. It was clear their bond was growing stronger. She finished, and as she was exiting the stable, she heard footsteps rapidly approaching from behind. *Oh, no.*

"Good morning, Nicole!" Dusty called as he came closer.

Nicole turned and braced herself for what might be coming, and did her best to be pleasant but not overly inviting.

"Hi, Dusty," Nicole replied somewhat politely.

"Beautiful morning, isn't it?"

"Yes, it is."

"Um, I was wondering if I could steal you away for a bit?"

"Sorry, I have an extra-long list of chores I need to get to."

"Actually, I just talked to Pat, and she said it was okay for me to take you away for—"

"Take me away?!"

"Well, what I mean is, I'm hoping you'll go for a short ride with me and—"

"Why?"

"Because ... we need to talk."

"I truly have nothing to say to you, Dusty."

"But I have something to say to you."

"Well, why can't you just say it here and now?"

"Because, it's ... it's private."

Nicole eyed Dusty carefully.

"What do you mean, 'private'?"

"Just that. We have things to talk about—"

"*I* don't have *anything* to talk about with you."

"Nicole, please ... okay, *I* have some things I need to say to you, but I don't want to say them around here, okay? And Pat has already told me I could take you off the ranch for a bit so we can have that privacy."

Thanks a lot, Pat!

Nicole hesitated before saying anything.

"Where are you wanting to take me?"

"Just for a short drive."

"How long will we be gone?"

"I'll make it as quick as possible."

"You'd better, because I have lot to do today."

"I understand, and I promise I'll have you back as quickly as I can. Thank you."

Nicole reluctantly walked with Dusty to his truck. He opened the door for her, which she was hoping he wouldn't, then walked around and climbed in his side. He started the engine and a moment later they were passing the nearby paddock where Brendy and Beth had been watching. Nicole made a halting effort to return their wave, barely raising her hand. When they reached the highway they headed north.

"And you're not going to tell me where we're going?"

"It's not far."

As they passed the airport a couple of minutes later Nicole thought *Why did you have to leave today, Liam? I wish you were here to save me from this.*

A few miles further up the road they turned into the entrance to Eagle Nest Lake State Park, and pulled into an area where they could have a nice view of the lake. Dusty rolled down the windows so they could enjoy the cool morning breeze, and turned off the engine.

"Why did you bring me here, Dusty?" Nicole asked in a tone bordering on contempt.

"Listen, I'm sorry if you're upset, Nicole, but with you working at the ranch now, and the fact that I'm the vet that takes care of the Masterson's ranches, it's inevitable that you and I are going to see each other from time to time. I just want us to have a chance to start fresh with a clean slate."

"And you somehow think that's possible?"

"Yes, I do."

Boy, are you *delusional.*

Dusty could see that this might take longer than he had hoped.

"Nicole, I can't say I'm sorry enough for what I did to you in high school."

"*That's* for sure."

Dusty felt the dagger in his back and knew he deserved that.

"I was stupid, I was a fool, I … I just didn't know how I was going to tell you. And then it suddenly came out that night. I promise I hadn't planned it that way, it just—"

"It just tore my heart out, is what it did!"

"I know, I know …" Dusty replied sullenly.

"And, almost worse, you never even tried to say you were sorry, or to write to me, or—"

"Would you have written back if I had?"

Nicole hesitated. "I don't know, probably not."

"That's what I thought you'd say," Dusty replied glumly.

"All that time I spent sharing my plans about college and a major, and wanting to stay close by and not go away for college, you never said one word about your plans."

"That's because I didn't have any."

"Why not?"

"I don't know, I just didn't."

"You had not thought about college, or what you wanted to do with your future after high school? Nothing at all?"

"No, I was just living in the moment and doing my best to enjoy it."

Nicole sat quietly for a long moment, letting her thoughts tumble in her mind.

"I guess … I guess I should have seen that coming. Up until that point we had been so in tune with each other, or so I thought. But when I was talking about my future plans, I should have noticed that you were somewhere out in left field, but I didn't."

"I'm sorry, Nicole. I really am."

Nicole sighed heavily. "You're fourteen years too late."

The dagger went deeper.

Silence took over as they both just stared out the windshield toward the lake. A minute passed, then two. Finally, Nicole couldn't stand the silence any longer.

"Look it … I almost didn't accept Luke and Jill's offer because of you. Everything else about this felt so right. *Everything!* But the thought of seeing you, even rarely, was almost too much for me to think about.

"But then I thought, 'I'm not going to let him spoil a wonderful opportunity'. So, when I decided to accept their offer, I also accepted the fact that I *might* see you from time to time. However, I also knew I wouldn't need to be nearby while you visited the ranch for any reason, professional or personal. And if, by chance, we did have to deal with one another, then I would be professional about it and leave it at that."

Dusty looked out the windshield as he pondered Nicole's statement.

"I'm glad you didn't let me stand in the way of making that choice," Dusty replied, as he looked at Nicole. "And ... I, too, will maintain a strictly professional attitude around you at all times, regardless of why I visit the ranch."

"No bringing up the past?"

"No, I promise."

"And no trying to start anything new, because I guarantee *that* won't be happening."

Dusty half smiled. "I promise."

"You promise what?"

"I promise to not try to start anything new, because you *guarantee* that won't be happening."

Nicole held it in as long as she could, but then started to laugh.

There it was. The smile Dusty had been hoping to see. Relaxed and friendly.

"Shall we head back to the ranch?"

"Yes, thank you."

The ride back was quiet, but the tension was gone. As they arrived, Dusty left the engine running as his business at the ranch was complete. Nicole opened her door and jumped out. She paused for a moment, then turned to look at Dusty.

"Thank you, Dusty," Nicole said softly. "This helped ... a lot."

"You're welcome, Nicole. I truly am glad you're here, not for anything to do with me, but for you to experience this wonderful life in the country. Not that there was anything wrong with our growing up in the sun and the sand, but there's just something enriching to the soul here that you can't find anywhere else than places like Angel Fire."

Nicole smiled. "Excuse me, did you say that you majored in philosophy?"

Dusty laughed. "No, but it's true."

Nicole nodded. "I believe you."

Dusty tipped his hat, smiled, and said, "See you later, Nicole."

"Bye, Dusty."

After Dusty drove away Nicole walked into the stable where she saw Pat and Cindi chatting. After Cindi left, Pat walked over to Nicole.

"Everything okay?"

Nicole gave Pat a half smile.

"It is now."

"That's good to hear."

"Um … did Dusty say anything to you about … us?"

"Yes, on the last day you were here on your vacation. After you left the stable so hastily, I approached him to see what was wrong. He told me enough for me to understand that the two of you had been together in high school, and he admitted he broke your heart. He then told me he wished he could find a way to make it up to you. But you were leaving to go home so he figured that it was a bridge he had burned that wouldn't be rebuilt.

"But then, after he found out that you had returned and were going to be working here, he knew he had been given a second chance to talk with you."

Nicole nodded. "Well, we talked."

"And?"

"And … things are okay now."

"So, you won't be running for the mountains when his truck approaches anymore?" Pat asked with a wink and a smile.

Nicole laughed. "No, I'll be okay."

"Good. I'm glad to hear that."

Nicole began to walk away, but then turned around.

"Pat?"

"Yes?"

"Thanks for giving me a little time off so Dusty and I could talk. When Dusty told me you had said it was okay, I was not very happy with you, but it turned out okay."

Pat smiled. "Not a problem, Nicole. Now, get to work!"

"Yes, ma'am!"

CHAPTER 75

Losing Ground

AFTER LUNCH **C**INDI **WAS** working with Shane in the stable.

"So, I wonder what's going on with that new lady," Cindi asked.

"You mean Nicole?" Shane replied.

"Yeah, Nicole."

"I couldn't care less."

"Ouch, you're in a sour mood."

"What else is new?"

"What's going on, Shane? Does it bother you that she came back to work here?"

"No, why should it?"

"Well, I knew you were interested in her when she came for that week, and for the most part you wisely kept your distance. However, since she returned, it seems you're doing all you can to completely avoid her."

"And you're surprised by that?"

"Frankly, yes."

"Well, you shouldn't be."

"Why not?"

"One word … Liam."

"What's Liam got to do with anything?"

"Are you blind?! They're practically married!"

"What?! You're crazy!"

"Wow, you *are* blind! They spend every possible minute together after work, and during the day they can't wait to see each other, even if it's from a distance."

"Yeah," Cindi replied sadly. "I've noticed, but I was hoping it was just my imagination."

"So I'm predicting that it won't be long before they're tying the knot."

A lump formed in Cindi's throat.

Shane didn't notice that she was becoming upset by their conversation, or that she walked away without saying another word.

* * *

It was true. Cindi could see it as plain as day. The man she had been in love with for so long was falling for another woman, and there was not a single thing she could do about it. No one knew, not even Shane, and she had always been able to open up to him about anything. But not about Liam. She felt so alone. If only she could figure out a way to make Nicole quit. Maybe then she could make Liam see her for who she really is … someone who is madly in love with him.

CHAPTER 76

DEFCON 3 and Rising

JENSON WAS ALREADY SITTING on the patio as the sun rose over the mountains, spilling over into the desert below. On any other Sunday morning he would be meeting the other men in his foursome at one of the dozens of beautiful golf courses in the valley. This morning it was Rancho Las Palmas Country Club, but not for him. He had called and let the others know that he wouldn't be joining them for a while. One of them asked if he were ill, but Jenson just said he was fighting a tough headache. In truth, the migraine that had hit him Friday morning was nowhere near to easing up.

He hadn't talked to Charlotte since late Wednesday night. She was still asleep the next morning when he'd left for the airport in Palm Springs to start his journey to Angel Fire. Reading the note she left, excoriating him for what he had attempted to do to their daughter, he wasn't sure when he might see or hear from her again.

He was beyond exhausted, not having slept more than a total of five hours over the last three nights. By Friday night he had finally come to understand the error of his ways in flying to Angel Fire and trying to convince Nicole of the huge mistake he thought she had just made in her life. Somewhere during his tossing and turning the night before he succumbed to the realization that he had been wrong about so many things as a husband and a father. As the temperature rose along with the sun that morning, he was sure of only one thing

… he needed Charlotte to come home, no matter what the cost. If only he had a way to reach her.

To make matters worse, in addition to his sleepless nights, he had barely eaten anything since Wednesday. He had been in a hurry Thursday morning as he headed to the airport in Palm Springs. He had only grabbed a quick sandwich as he hurried to the charter jet after arriving in Albuquerque. After leaving the ranch in anger that afternoon there had been no time to get a meal in Angel Fire. Once again he only had time for a sandwich in Albuquerque on his trip home. Plus, there was *no* way he felt like eating anything after reading Charlotte's note that night. And now, between being so tired and so hungry, he became aware of how much he needed his long-suffering sweetheart. He just wanted her to come home to him.

There wasn't even a whisper of a breeze as the sun continued to get higher and the desert morning air was getting hotter. Jenson got up and went inside, easing the patio door closed behind him. He stood in the kitchen trying to decide if he might try to fix something to eat, or go back to bed and try to get some sleep. Or should he just go lie on his recliner in the family room. Despite his foggy brain, his body moved toward the family room.

After slowly leaning back on his recliner, he reached for the remote and turned on the TV, searching for *anything* to take his mind off Charlotte's absence. Channel after channel, from old TV series re-runs, Sunday morning news shows, classic movies, and infomercials … he couldn't find a thing that might hold his attention. The fogginess in his brain caused his mind to drift aimlessly, his eyelids got heavier, and before he knew it his exhaustion took over. In no time at all he was off somewhere in a deep sleep.

When Jenson awoke it took a long while before he recognized the sound of footsteps in the kitchen. He felt completely disoriented, but somehow managed to sit up, his migraine slightly eased. He slowly turned and saw Charlotte carrying in grocery bags from her car. He started to get up in order to offer to help, but he moved too fast and felt an electric jolt shoot through his head. He collapsed back on his recliner. Charlotte continued bringing in more bags without saying a word, even though she could see that Jenson had stirred.

Charlotte touched the power button for the garage door, and as it began to close, she turned and headed down the hallway, presumably to their bedroom. A minute later she returned to the kitchen and began to put the groceries away.

"Hi, Charlotte," Jenson said weakly, fighting his pounding head. He wasn't sure if Charlotte hadn't heard him or if she had chosen to ignore him. He tried again, a bit louder this time. "Hi, Charlotte."

She stopped in the midst of turning toward the refrigerator and looked his way.

"Jenson," she replied with no emotion.

He sighed heavily. *No 'Hi' or 'Hello'? She's* still *mad at me. Just great.* He sat back in his recliner and pondered what he would say or do next. He steeled himself for the pain he was about to experience, then stood up and began to walk toward the kitchen.

"What time is it?"

Charlotte looked at the clock on the wall. "Five-thirty."

"What?" Another jolt shot through his head, less powerful than the last. Charlotte noticed his distress.

"What's wrong, Jenson?" she asked, still with little to no emotion.

"Migraine," he responded feebly.

"Take some aspirin." This sounded more like a command than a compassionate suggestion.

Jenson sluggishly walked toward the master bathroom, reached for the bottle of aspirin on the counter, and swallowed two with a glass of water. He felt dizzy so he walked into the bedroom and sat down on the end of their unmade bed.

After finishing with the groceries Charlotte walked back toward their bedroom and stood in the doorway.

"You look like you haven't slept in days," Charlotte said, still with little to no emotion in her voice.

"I haven't," Jenson replied glumly.

"Why not?"

"I couldn't."

Charlotte pondered his answer, then turned back toward the kitchen without responding.

It took a few moments as Jenson fought back the pain from his migraine, but he finally followed her. He took a deep breath, and steeled himself for her response, and then asked, "Charlotte, can we talk?"

She looked at him without saying a word for several seconds. "Are you up for it?" she asked with a bite in her voice.

"Yes."

"Are you sure? Because this is not, I repeat *not*, going to be pleasant."

"I understand. And, if it's alright with you, I'd like to go first."

"Fine. What do you have to say?"

"May we sit down in the family room?"

Charlotte looked at him and began to ease up on her attitude as it appeared that Jenson was hurting from more than just his migraine. Truth be told, he looked like a broken man.

Jenson sat down in the center of the sofa, giving Charlotte the option to sit on either side of him. She chose to sit in a chair nearly eight feet away. *She really hates me right now. I guess I can't blame her.*

He cleared his throat, then took a deep breath and let it out slowly.

"Okay, let me start by saying how sorry I am for what I did to Nicole on Thursday. It was completely uncalled for and unforgivable."

"And?"

Jenson looked at Charlotte, confused by her question. He had to think for a minute because his brain was still not clearing quickly enough. Fortunately, Charlotte was not rushing him, but sat stoically waiting for him to figure out the next thing he needed to apologize for.

"And I'm sorry for how I've treated Nicole for so long."

"And?" Charlotte was now beginning to lose her patience, but seeing her husband in such a different state than she'd ever seen him, she was still willing to cut him some slack, but not much.

However, with Jenson finding it difficult to think, much less try to apologize for everything, including breathing, he was about to erupt on Charlotte. He impatiently took a deep breath, but this time he let it out hard and fast.

"And what?"

"Think, Jenson."

"Oh, would you give me a break, Charlotte? I'm wracking my brain here, trying to figure out what else I've screwed up on and—"

"Okay," she interrupted, with an attitude, " I'll give you a hint. Last Wednesday night."

"Last Wednesday night?" Jenson was completely befuddled by this.

"Yes."

"What about it?"

"Oh, for crying out loud! Think about our conversation!"

"Which one?!" He was now definitely at DEFCON 3 and rising.

Charlotte sat there staring at him and was seriously thinking about getting up and walking off. *Perhaps I came home too soon!* She gritted her teeth. "Our last one."

Jenson sat back and looked away, and Charlotte could see the wheels begin to slowly churn inside his head.

Finally, humiliated by not being able to figure out what Charlotte was referring to, he shook his head.

"I'm sorry, Charlotte," he replied, feeling completely and utterly defeated. "I just don't remember."

Observing what appeared to be Jenson's genuine contrition, Charlotte eased back on her anger.

"Jenson," she began calmly, "you lied to me when you told me you were going to Los Angeles the next morning. You had no intention of going there. You had apparently worked everything out to fly to New Mexico and confront Nicole. Doing either one would have fried me, but both? That's why I left, and I hope that note I wrote did its job to stab you in the heart, because that's what your actions did to mine.

"I've put up with *so* much from you over the years, particularly in regards to our sweet Nicole, but this ... this horrendous action of yours broke my heart. How *dare* you try to control our grown, adult daughter. She has a life of her own. She's been making her own decisions since she left for college, and she's had the world by the tail. Now she's simply grabbed a different tail, and she's going to ride it like the wind."

"Charlotte, I'm so sorry for lying to you. Can you ever forgive me?"

Charlotte looked deep into Jenson's eyes.

"This was serious, Jenson. *Very* serious. And it's going to take a very long time before I'll be able to forgive you for it."

"I understand," Jenson replied meekly.

"Now, here's what's going to happen. I'm going to get my phone, and I'm going to call Nicole, because I know, beyond a shadow of *any* doubt, that she won't answer a call from you. Once I have her on the phone, I'm going to hand it to you, and you're going to plead for forgiveness from our daughter. Do you understand?"

"But—"

"Do you understand?!"

"Yes, I'll talk to her."

"You're going to do a *lot* more than just talk to her!"

"Yes, okay, I know. I know."

* * *

Nicole was chatting with Brendy while they sat in rocking chairs on the patio in front of the hacienda when her phone rang.

"Oh! It's my mother! I haven't spoken with her in a few days!"

Brendy stood up to leave. "I'll give you some privacy, then."

"No, Brendy. You stay and relax. This will probably only take a few minutes and I'll be back."

"Okay. Thanks!"

Nicole walked off toward the closest paddock and answered her phone on the fourth ring.

"Hi, Mom!"

"Hi, dear. Did I catch you in the middle of something?"

"No, I was just relaxing and talking with a friend of mine."

"Oh, well I won't keep you very long then, but someone wants to speak with you." She handed the phone to Jenson.

"Someone? What? WAIT! NO!"

"Nicole?"

Nicole froze.

"Nicole, are you there?"

"What do you want?" Nicole replied tersely.

"Nicole, I ... I want to apologize."

"Apologize?" She replied, disbelievingly.

"Yes, for everything."

"Do you mean for coming here last week and embarrassing me while demanding that I return home with you like I was a little girl who had run away from home? Is *that* what you want to apologize for?"

"I guess I deserve that," Jenson replied meekly.

"You *guess*?! Do us both a favor and put Mom back on the phone!"

"Nicole, wait. Please?"

Nicole *did* hear something different in his voice. Different than she had ever heard before.

"Nicole?"

"I'm still here." Her patience was razor thin.

"Nicole, I've had a lot of time to think over these last few days, and … and I realize now what a horrible father I've been to you."

He waited for any kind of response, but when none was forthcoming he continued.

"Nicole, I'm so very sorry for everything I've done or said that has hurt you, and—"

"Going all the way back to when I was six?"

"Yes, *especially* for what I said when you were six. It just tears me up inside that I could have even *thought* that, much less said anything about it to anyone."

"I have a question for you."

"Anything, Nicole," Jenson replied anxiously.

"Where is this coming from?"

Jenson paused. "My heart," he replied humbly.

Nicole definitely did *not* expect *that* answer, and when she didn't respond, he got worried.

"Nicole? Are you still there?"

"Y-yes," she replied, fighting back the tears. "I'm still here."

"Nicole? Sweetheart? I love you!" Tears were rolling down his cheeks, and Charlotte began sobbing. Nicole bent over, bracing herself on the rail of the paddock with one hand. Brendy noticed and kept a close eye on her.

"Oh, Daddy …" Nicole couldn't continue as her crying became deep sobbing.

"Nicole, I've been holding on too tight for too long. You're your own woman and I see that. I'm so proud of you, sweetheart, and I want so much for you to succeed in *whatever* you choose to do with your life, so I'm … I'm letting go."

Nicole was still fighting her tears, but she knew she had to respond to this incredible revelation.

"Oh, Daddy! Thank you! And I love you, too! I'm *so* sorry for what I said to you last week, and—"

"Don't be sorry, Nicole. I deserved it. You had every right to shut me down like that."

"But Daddy—"

"No buts, sweetheart. I was completely out of line, and you did what you had to and said what you had to, to make me eventually wake up and see the horrible mess I've made of things." The tears being shed by Nicole and her parents were probably enough to end the drought in the southwest.

"I love you, Daddy."

"I love you, too, sweetie. Now, what can I do to make everything up to you?"

"I can only think of one thing."

"Whatever it is, I'll do it. I promise."

"Just love Mom and me like you never have before."

"I promise, Nicole. I truly promise."

Even though Nicole was over eight hundred miles away, she could hear the smile on his face.

CHAPTER 77

Friday, late afternoon

RECONCILING WITH HER FATHER had lifted a huge weight off Nicole's shoulders. Her days flew past in a blur that week because she was better focused at work; however, even though she was keeping busy at night checking out the nightlife in Taos with Beth, her nights still seemed to drag along too slowly because she was missing Liam.

While Nicole had disowned her father in a rage the previous week, she couldn't get over her feelings of guilt and desolation for having done so. He was her father, and even if he hadn't shown her the kind of love she had always wished and prayed for, she still loved him. And now, after all these years, she had hope of their truly being a family like she had wished she had from early in her childhood.

Liam had called her every night since he'd been gone, and last night he had given her the best news she could have heard from him … he was coming home! The timing was such that he would arrive while dinner was being served at the ranch, so she decided she would surprise him by showing up at the airport. She would no doubt meet his friend, Barrett Davidson, who would be there to make the switch. He would wait for the jet to be refueled and fly back to Colorado Springs. She would follow Liam to his house so he could drop off his car and bags, and then steal him away for the rest of the evening!

Nicole arrived at the airport, noticed a beautiful dark blue sports car, and wondered whose it was. As she pulled closer, she noticed two things, it was a beautiful Porsche, and there was a handsome gentleman about Liam's age, sitting behind the wheel. From what she had read in the past she put two and two together and figured this was Liam's friend and co-owner of the jet, Barrett.

Nicole pulled up next to the car, passenger side to passenger side, so the Porsche would be between her and the airstrip. The gentleman behind the wheel looked toward Nicci and nodded, and as he rolled down the window she did the same.

"Barrett?"

"Yes, and you must be the beautiful Nicci that Liam has been raving about."

Nicci smiled and briefly looked away, her strawberry blonde hair flowing down across the side of her face, hiding her blush.

"Frankly, his description doesn't do you justice. You're far more beautiful in person."

Nicole caught her breath, and her heart skipped before she regained her composure. She brushed back her hair, tucking it behind her ear, and looked back at Barrett.

"And just how much did Liam pay you to say that?" Their laughter eased the moment.

"It's truly a pleasure to meet you, Nicci. Liam has been nothing but a downcast, wandering soul since, I mean, um, for quite a long time. I hope I'm not speaking out of turn, but from what he's been sharing with me, you've brought him back to life. As one of his best friends, I have to thank you."

Downcast, wandering soul since what? Or, when? Or, most likely, who? She needed to change the subject, and fast!

"Beautiful car, Barrett."

"Yes, it is. Not only does Liam have great taste for the special lady in his life, he also has quite the eye for choosing a great car!"

"Wait! This is Liam's?"

"It's all his!"

"Oh, my gosh! As I was pulling up, I noticed it was a Porsche, but it wasn't until just this moment that I realized it might be his!"

"Yes, he bought it fairly recently."

"So, this makes me wonder ... what's a cowboy want with a car like this?"

Barrett laughed. "You'd have to ask him."

"And I believe I will!" *Hmmmm, I wonder what other surprises he has up his sleeve?*

Nicci was about to say more when Barrett's attention was drawn to the airstrip.

"Here he comes!"

Nicole listened and thought she heard the sound of a small jet coming in for a landing. She looked north toward Eagle Nest Lake and saw it about to land. Her heart began to race! She debated whether to keep it cool and remain in the car until he got close, or jump out and fly into his arms the moment his feet hit the tarmac. She chose to stay in the car. Even though her car was higher than Liam's, she knew he wouldn't be expecting to see her here, and she wanted to hold on to the surprise for as long as she could.

Somehow, Barrett must have read Nicci's mind, because he got out and leaned against the driver's door, providing the perfect shield. Liam had radioed ahead and made arrangements for the fuel truck to be on-site so Barrett would be able to take off as soon as he chose.

As the jet engines wound down, the hatch opened and Liam stepped out and descended the steps. Nicci leaned forward ever so slightly to catch a glimpse of Liam as he approached.

"Hey, buddy! Did you have a good trip?"

"Sure did! And did my car turn heads again like you hoped it would?"

"Yeah, a few," Barrett replied, nonchalantly.

"Cool."

Nicci couldn't wait any longer. She opened the door and slid out, trying to stay as low as possible until the last possible moment. As Liam and Barrett continued to chat, she stepped into Liam's view. He froze.

"Nicci?!" He couldn't believe his eyes!

She smiled demurely.

"NICCI!" he yelled as he ran around both cars to reach her and gave her a big hug! She was thrilled by the look on his face and how excited he was to see her!

"My gosh! What a great surprise!"

"Hi, darling! I thought you'd like it."

"But, how … how did you know—"

"About the jet?"

"Yeah!"

"I've known for a while," she replied casually with a wink.

"But how—"

"It doesn't matter," she sweetly interrupted him and left him speechless.

"Ahem. Hey, you two lovebirds," Barrett interjected.

"Oh, sorry, Barrett! Um, Barrett, this is Nicci, and Nicci—"

"We've already met, buddy."

"Oh, yeah, of course."

"Man, you are one flustered guy," Barrett said, and the three of them had a good laugh.

Liam looked back at Nicci. "I'm *so* glad to see you!"

"Good!" Nicci replied with another wink.

"Um, listen, let me finish up with Barrett, and then we can take off, okay?"

"Sure, take your time."

Liam briefed Barrett on some flight conditions he had experienced over Colorado. Barrett assured Liam that he had been keeping an eye on a storm that had been working its way eastward over Utah on its way to Nebraska. He had determined that it would already be east of his flight pattern by the time he would be approaching Colorado Springs. They slapped each other on the back, then Barrett grabbed his duffel bags and took off to wait for the jet to be refueled. He also wanted to give Liam and Nicci a little extra private time together. Liam picked up his bags and tossed them in the trunk of his car.

"So, what's the plan? Are we headed back to the ranch?"

"No, I'm kidnapping you!"

"Seriously?"

"Yes, sir!"

Liam looked deeply into Nicci's eyes.

"I love you, Nicci," he said softy.

"You better, mister, because you are stuck with me, you hear?"

"Promise?"

"Promise. And I *always* keep my promises," she added with a wink.

"Okay, so how are we going to do this, since we both have our cars here?"

"Easy! I'll follow you to your home, where you can drop off your car and your bags, and then I'll be driving to our getaway location!"

"And where would that be?"

"It's a surprise."

"Hmmmm. Well, I like surprises, but I need a favor?"

"Okay."

"I hope you don't have a specific timetable for this evening because, besides not only dropping my car and bags off at the house, I would also like to shower after my long flight."

"Fair enough!" Her enthusiasm was bubbling over.

"You know, you sure seem to be in a good mood this evening."

"Aren't I usually?"

"Well, yes. But this evening you just seem to be … even more so."

"That's because you came home!"

Liam smiled and winked. "Okay. Let's go!"

Nicci winked back at him. "Okay!" she replied excitedly. *I feel like such a teenager!*

One of Nicci's favorite pastimes was watching Liam walk, and he was doing a fine job of it as he walked around her car. He checked to make sure the trunk of his car was latched tightly, got in, and started his car with a muted, but still powerful, roar. As the engine eased up, he put the car in gear and they were off.

This was the perfect plan, because now I get to see where he lives!

____

Chapter 78

Top of the World

LIAM AND NICCI DROVE south on the highway for just over two miles before he moved into the turn lane to make a left turn onto North Angel Fire Road. They passed the signs for Angel Fire Resort on the right and headed up the mountain. They traversed many winding streets through the trees before he finally prepared to turn left onto a street that had a *Private Road* sign posted. Immediately there was a large gate where Liam punched in the code. *Where is he taking me?!* She looked at the street sign as they made the turn and passed through the gate. *You have* got *to be kidding!!*

As they approached Liam's home on the right, Nicci's jaw began to drop. Her eyes also grew large as she took in the view of his beautiful home! Liam stopped before approaching the driveway to a four-car garage on the far side of his home, got out and walked back to talk with Nicci.

As she lowered the driver's window, Liam could see the look on her face and smiled.

"Liam, where *are* we?!"

"My home," he replied, casually.

"Oh … my ……. I think you mean your *mansion!*" Nicci was simply in awe.

"Go ahead and pull into the circular drive. I'll pull into the garage and meet you at your car in a moment."

Nicci was still too shocked to say anything, but pulled into the circular drive and stopped just beyond the wide stairs leading to the expansive porch.

Liam hit the control for the garage door opener, and as the door began to rise she saw his pickup truck that she was so used to seeing him drive at the ranch. There was also a bright red all-terrain vehicle in the far side of the garage. Liam pulled his Porsche into the right side of the garage, removed his bags from the trunk, and locked the car. Then he exited the garage and set the alarm.

"Okay, come with me."

Nicci was shaking her head, still disbelieving what she was seeing. But, she hadn't seen *anything* yet!

As they walked up the steps, Nicci noticed the wide and very tall front doors. Liam opened the right door, motioned for her to enter first, then followed and disarmed the alarm system.

"So, you have two alarm systems? One for the garage, and one for your home?"

"Three, actually. My property is lined with sensors to alert me if anyone tries to climb the fence. I have cameras that sense wildlife that occasionally come near, but no alarms go off. But if someone were to try and scale any part of the fence, lights and cameras will catch them in the act, and they'll scatter."

"Has anyone ever tried it?"

"Only once. I guess the word got out that my property was sufficiently fortified, so no one else has tried since."

Nicci just shook her head in amazement.

"So, I noticed the name of your street as we were passing through the gate."

Liam turned and gave Nicci a smile out of the corner of his mouth.

"Top of the World Drive? Seriously?"

"Well, it is, isn't it," he replied as he swept his hand across in front of him causing Nicci to look further into his home. The floor to ceiling windows surrounding the great room presented her with a view that surpassed anything she had ever experienced from her condo or her office.

"Oh, Liam!" She walked toward the windows, her eyes scanning the full view Liam had of the Moreno Valley below. "Your view is magnificent"

"Thank you. I was fortunate to find this property shortly after I came to work for Luke and Jill and took my time to design and build this place."

"What?! You designed *and* built this home?" Nicci asked incredulously.

"Yes. With this perfect view I had to make sure my home could match its surroundings."

"Well, I am *seriously* impressed!"

Liam smiled nonchalantly.

"There you go, being Mister Cool and Casual about something so amazing!"

"I'm just grateful for the blessing of living in such a wonderful place."

Nicci looked at the man that, day by day, was capturing her heart so completely and felt so lucky to be the woman he chose to fall in love with.

Liam broke the moment by clearing his throat.

"Where I've lived and worked before was pretty much just the wide open plains. Oh, sure, I could see mountain ranges in the distance, but here they're right outside my door!"

Nicole sighed. "It's simply breathtaking!"

"I know you're familiar with the Carson National Forest to the west, since you've driven through it several times. And off in the distance is Wheeler Peak, the tallest mountain in New Mexico at just over 13,000 feet. The peak is within the Sangre de Cristo Mountains, which make up the southernmost range of the Rocky Mountains."

"Well, my kind gentleman, thank you for the geography lesson!" Nicci quipped with a wink and a smile.

"Anytime! Now, why don't I fix you something to drink, and then you can sit on the deck and enjoy the view while I take a quick shower."

"Sure, that would be wonderful," Nicci replied, still feeling like she was in a dream.

Liam grabbed a tall tumbler from the cabinet to the left of the sink in his kitchen, filled it halfway with crushed ice, and added water. Then he reached into the refrigerator and removed a lemon. He cut a slice, squeezed only enough to add a hint of taste to the water, plopped the slice into the tumbler, and brought it to Nicci.

"Thank you, sweetheart."

"My pleasure," he replied as he reached past Nicci and unlocked the sliding glass door to the deck.

"Make yourself comfortable and I'll be ready in no time."

"Oh, please, don't rush on my account. I could spend the rest of the evening right here."

"I thought you were stealing me away for some kind of adventure."

Nicci looked over her shoulder and saw her handsome sweetheart standing in the frame of the doorway, the approaching sunset reflected in the window next to him.

"How about if we take a raincheck on that adventure? I'd rather stay right here and enjoy you and this view."

Liam smiled. "Whatever the lady wishes."

Nicci smiled in return, took a sip of her lemon ice water, and gave Liam a nod. He retreated inside, walked over and grabbed his bags from the entryway, and carried them to the master bedroom. Before closing the door, he stepped out and walked quietly down the hallway and looked toward his deck in time to see Nicci lift her long, shapely legs up and rest them on an ottoman.

"Perfect!" he thought.

CHAPTER 79

More Questions

"SO, DID YOU MISS me?" Nicci asked as the refreshed Liam joined her on the deck, sitting nearby in a matching chair and ottoman.

"Yeah, kinda," Liam teased.

Nicci playfully pouted. "Only kinda?" she asked, trying to pull a fake tear.

"Well ... I *did* cut my trip short by two days."

"Really? Why?" Nicci asked, genuinely curious.

"Because ... I missed you."

That answer brought the real tears. She tried to think of something to say that would take her mind off of how emotional she was feeling at that moment.

"So ... when were you going to tell me you aren't just a poor cowhand?"

"Well ... since you've already discovered the jet, I was thinking as we drove here that tonight would be the best night to share a few more things with you."

"Only a *few* more?"

"Yeah. I need to keep a few surprises held back for the future, don't I?"

"No," Nicci answered coyly." Remember, I love you, and I want to know *everything* about you."

"Oh, you will, I promise. However, it's like a seven-course meal, you don't serve everything up at once."

Nicci looked at him out of the corner of her eye. "Hmmmm …
I see your point."

"Good," he replied with a vocal swagger. This made Nicci laugh
out loud. Liam smiled and sipped his tumbler of lemon ice water.

"So," Liam began, "when did you discover I wasn't just some
poor cowhand?"

"The night you told me your full name."

"What did you do, go back to your casita and look me up on
your computer."

"Actually, that's *exactly* what I did!"

"Really? And I was in there?"

"Oh, yeah! I read articles about your family, how you were named
after a distant grandfather, how many greats I don't recall, where you
earned your bachelor's degree in psychology, and that you got your
pilot's license shortly after you graduated so you could help your
family with their *huge* business empire. Another article mentioned
you co-own a jet with Barrett, and even mentioned your car."

"Seriously? I had no idea!"

"What? You don't remember doing interviews with magazines?"

"Well, I remember a couple of people asking questions occasionally but I guess I forgot they were print journalists."

"So, you don't have copies of the articles they wrote?"

"No, I sure don't."

Nicci thought about that for a moment. "How is it that you can
be so wealthy and still so humble?"

"I guess, for one thing, I don't think about my financial status. I
just concentrate on doing my job well for Luke and Jill and also for
my family."

"So, what do you do for them? Besides fly around in your beautiful jet?"

"Would you like to go up with me sometime?"

"Don't change the subject."

"I wasn't trying to. I was simply curious if you would like to take
a flight? Or, do small jets make you nervous?"

"Can we please talk about that another time?"

Liam could sense that the idea of flying in a small jet, even if she knew the pilot, made her uneasy, so he dropped the subject.

"I'm guessing the articles you read gave you an idea of what my family does?"

"Yes, you have ranches and lumber operations all over the northwest."

"That's pretty accurate."

"So what do you do?"

"Well, because I don't mind the traveling, I fly to each of the ranches and lumber facilities on a regular basis to monitor how everything is going and check to see if there's anything they need."

"And no one else in the family wanted to do that?"

"No, everyone has specific duties we each need to fulfill to make the whole operation run smoothly, and I volunteered to do the travel part."

Nicci thought about that as well, and then asked, "If I can get away from the ranch sometime when you have to make those rounds … may I go with you?"

"Really?! Sure, I'd *love* to take you along!"

"Thank you, Liam," Nicci replied softly. "That means a lot."

"Oh, absolutely!" So … now I have a question for you."

"Okay," Nicci replied exuberantly.

"It's a serious question."

Nicci eased up on her enthusiasm a bit.

Liam paused and let out a long sigh.

"Are you uncomfortable about my having a little 'extra' in the bank?"

"Define 'extra'."

He paused again, a little longer this time.

"Well … let's just say … I'm worth a few million dollars."

"Actually, I knew that, too."

"Seriously? How?! Oh, wait. One of the articles you read online?"

Nicci nodded. "Yes."

"So, I'll ask again … are you uncomfortable about my being what some would call wealthy?"

"Liam, I fell in love with you *long* before I knew anything about that. For all I knew, you were a wrangler who drove a pickup truck. And you have a killer smile."

And there was that smile!

"Yes! That's what I'm talking about!"

Liam chuckled.

"Um … I have a confession, too," Nicci said hesitantly.

Liam looked at Nicci with wide eyes.

"You? Have something to confess? What could *you* have *possibly* done to have to confess?"

"Well … when I left California to move here … I sold my condo in Newport Beach. And … now I'm also a millionaire," she said shyly.

"Seriously?! Oh, Nicci! That's wonderful! I'm so happy for you!"

"I'm still trying to come to grips with the idea of having so much money. I mean, I made a nice salary as an architect, but living in California, especially *Southern* California and up north in the San Francisco Bay Area, is *so expensive* compared to most anywhere else. I guess with the exception of New York City and places like that."

"So … isn't it nice that we both fell in love with each other *before* we found out about the money side of things?"

"Yes, it sure is!"

Liam reached over and gently squeezed Nicci's hand.

"I love you, Nicci."

"I love you, too, Liam."

They sat there in silence, enjoying the exquisite view of another amazing sunset over Angel Fire.

After a few minutes Nicci laid her other hand on top of Liam's and gently squeezed it.

"Now," she began, "there's a matter of something else we need to discuss."

"What's that?"

"That someone in both of our pasts who has been a ghost that's kept haunting us and keeping us from truly moving forward with our lives."

"You're so right."

"So … when shall we do that?"

"Tomorrow night?"

"That works for me."

"Where?"

"Well, if it's okay with you, you've introduced me to this enchanting place, so may we do it right here?"

"I'd like that very much."

CHAPTER 80

Secrets

BOTH NICCI AND LIAM put in a long day wrapping things up for another successful week assisting guests to enjoy their stay at the ranch. All of the guests had left by early afternoon, so LuAnn prepared a light dinner for the few staff that chose to stick around a little longer. Liam and Nicci had decided to finish up early, but he stayed around while Nicci went to her casita to shower and change. On their way to Liam's, they stopped at Lowe's grocery store and bought steaks and all the trimmings for a perfect barbeque dinner.

The mood was different than the night before, more somber. Both Liam and Nicci had a lot on their minds, and they *still* were not sure how much they might divulge to each other that evening. If nothing else, they would enjoy the view; the approaching, gloriously colorful sunset. They would also have some quiet time together away from the busyness of the ranch.

They had agreed that tonight would be the night they would open up about their past, but neither was particularly looking forward to it. Sharing stories about their friends or their families was one thing, but these were secrets that had been buried for years. The thought of them not only rising to the surface again, but to actually share them with someone else, even someone they loved with all their heart, was inching toward a possible meltdown for either or both of them.

After clearing the table they quickly took care of the dishes, then returned to the deck and sat next to each other on the love seat.

They had each tried their best to keep the mood light during dinner. However, knowing what was yet to come was affecting even their laughter when a joke or funny story was shared. Liam was particularly dreading the idea of dredging up his past, but he had promised Nicci that if she would open up to him, he would do likewise. He cleared his throat and took a deep breath, letting it out as slowly as he could.

"I'm caught between a rock and a hard place," he confessed.

"How so?"

He let out another short sigh. "Whether to be a gentleman and 'let the lady go first', or to be valiant and take a bullet for the lady."

Nicci was stunned by that remark. "Take a bullet for me? What are you talking about?!"

"I just meant going ahead and sharing my story first."

"Whew! You had me scared for a second."

"Sorry, I didn't mean to worry you."

"It's okay … now, anyway." Nicci leaned toward Liam and lightly elbowed him in the arm, and they both laughed.

"So … who's it going to be, me or you?" Nicci asked.

"Flip a coin?"

"Oh, no. I want you to decide, and we'll go from there."

"Are you sure?"

"Quit stalling, Mr. Prescott!"

Liam looked at her and smiled. He was truly loving this lady more and more each day, and somehow Nicci was able to sense that.

"I'll go first," she said softly.

"Are you sure?"

"Yes, I'm sure." She looked out over the valley, took a deep breath, and let it out.

"It's about Dusty."

"Dusty? You mean the vet, Dusty?"

"One and the same."

"What does *he* have to do with anything?"

Nicci paused for a long moment before replying. "We were high school sweethearts."

"What?!"

"Are you upset?"

"No, I'm just totally surprised! I had no idea he was from California. I just assumed that he was from somewhere like Colorado, Texas, or just from around here."

"No, he was quite a surfer, born and raised near the sunny beaches of Southern California, just like me."

"Hmmmm. Okay, um … go on."

Nicci explained everything to Liam, including how the emotional abuse she had suffered from her father had made her so completely focused on being the best she could be at whatever she attempted. That also included not getting into any serious relationships with boys. That is, until Dusty stole her heart at the beginning of their senior year.

She also shared the details of their sudden breakup and her subsequent swearing off of any future serious relationships. She avoided anything more than just a fun friendship during college, and also managed to keep Chandler at an emotionally safe distance throughout the five plus years they were together. Finally, she filled him in on the conversation she had with Dusty the previous Sunday, and assured Liam that everything was now fine between them.

"So, the next time Dusty shows up for a vet call—"

"I'll be just fine. If I happen to be near, I'll wave and say hi. If the situation presents itself, we might even chat. He fully explained everything and shared his apologies. We talked and I shared everything I had to say, so we've come to a mutual understanding that it just wasn't meant to be back then. We have each moved on with our lives and we'll fully support and encourage each other as good friends. That's it."

Liam nodded and smiled. "Thank you for sharing all of that, Nicci. I know it wasn't easy."

"Actually, it was. Although, when you and I first approached this subject, there was *no* way I could have handled it. But with Dusty and I having the chance to talk things over, something that we had never had the chance to do before, it really helped. I just needed to understand the whys and wherefores, and without them, I had simply barricaded my heart all those years ago."

"That was a long time, though."

"Yes, it was, but I just *had* to do it."

"I understand. So, I'm guessing Chandler never knew about Dusty?"

"No one did, with the exception of my mother. Well, I mean my friends knew all about us, and I confided in my best friend, Chelsea, about the break-up, but it was my mother who helped me through everything."

Liam smiled and nodded again, then looked off into the distance without looking at anything in particular. It was now his turn, but he was not looking forward to it. However, a promise was a promise.

In the midst of the silence Nicci looked over at Liam.

"Are you okay, sweetheart?" she asked softly.

"Yeah," he replied unconvincingly.

Nicci hooked her arm in his and gave it a gentle squeeze. She knew what was on his mind.

"Sweetheart, if you'd rather wait until—"

"No, it's okay. Thanks anyway, but … I need to get this over with."

Nicci laid her head against his shoulder.

Liam let out a long sigh. "Her name was Tori. We initially met in college but things never got serious, and we lost touch after we graduated. We met up again a couple of years later at a dance after a rodeo I was competing in."

"So, you're a rodeo man too, huh?"

"I was."

"What was your event?"

"Saddle bronc riding."

"Sorry, I didn't mean to derail your train of thought."

"It's okay." His wink and smile melted Nicci's heart.

"Anyway, we danced a few times that night and talked about old times, even though it had only been a couple of years. At the end of the night, she said she had a new phone number and gave it to me. She asked me to call her sometime soon, with the emphasis on *soon*. I didn't call her right away because I had to go out of town for a while. However, a couple of weeks after I got home, I saw her number and a few days later I called her. We talked for a while, maybe an hour or so, that first time. Something told me things were different than in college so I called her again a few days later and we talked for a lot longer, but I still didn't ask her out."

"A little slow on the uptake, huh?" Nicole chided Liam with a smile.

"Yeah, something like that. Anyway, a couple of days later I called her again, and this time I asked her out for dinner."

"How did it go?"

"It was nice. In college things seemed to be a lot more casual. You know, football games, parties, dances, going out for pizza at midnight, all that crazy stuff. But that night was different. She was different, and I liked what I saw and heard and felt. So, we kept dating and things kept getting better and better."

"Did you continue to rodeo?"

"Yeah, occasionally. I was never a serious contender; I just enjoyed it for the thrill of that eight second ride. Tori always went with me and it was nice knowing that someone was there to cheer me on."

"I'll bet. Did you ever get hurt?"

"Just the normal aches and pains that come with the territory, but never anything serious."

"Why did you stop?"

Liam became quiet and stared off into the distance. Nicci felt she must have hit a nerve, so she remained silent, allowing Liam time to think things through at his own pace.

The knot eased in Liam's throat. "For the same reason I broke off the engagement."

"Oh, I'm so sorry, Liam," Nicci whispered.

"It's okay." He paused a moment before continuing.

"We were together for two years before I proposed. We were, as they say, 'head over heels in love', or so I thought.

"His name was Derek and they met at a rodeo I was in. We had been dating for just over a year at that point. It turns out he rode bulls so we didn't compete against each other. But my event always came first with a few other events in between until the bull riding event. We had always stayed until the end of each rodeo. Little did I know that after they met, she had a different reason to stay until the end than to just be with me.

"At the time we got engaged we set a wedding date six months out so she would have plenty of time to plan the perfect wedding which she had dreamed of since she was a teenager. I was doing all that I could to help out, but I was also busy with our family business.

"We were together as much as possible, but not every night. Somehow, in the midst of planning the wedding and being with me, she also found time to spend time with Derek. Or should I say she *made* time to spend with him."

"How did you find out she was cheating on you?"

"A fellow bronc rider tipped me off. He said he thought he had seen something fishy going on between the two of them during the last couple of rodeos. Once he was certain he wasn't seeing things that weren't there, he pulled me aside after our event and told me what he thought was going on. He wondered if I had noticed anything myself."

"Did you?"

"Well, I hadn't before, but later that day I saw something. Instead of watching the rest of the events, I was keeping a closer eye on Tori. Sure enough, when the bull riding event was about to start, I noticed her pay a lot closer attention. And when Derek was up, I noticed her tense up, and during his ride she cheered him on. She didn't call him by name, probably thinking I'd wonder why she was paying so much attention only to him. She had cheered for a few of the others riders, but nowhere near as enthusiastically as she did for Derek."

"What did you do?"

"Nothing right away. She always noticed when I was in a quiet mood and would ask if I was okay. During our three-hour ride home the next day she never noticed that I was mostly silent the whole way. That's when I was nearly sure.

"Over the next couple of weeks everything seemed to be like normal between us, but going into the next rodeo I noticed she changed again. Instead of watching all the events like we had in the past I noticed her eyes wandering, apparently looking for any sight of Derek. Somehow, I managed to hear her voice cheering me on during my ride. I don't know if it was just my imagination, but it seemed different than in the past. Maybe a bit less enthusiastic.

"Later, during the bull riding event, I watched her even closer, and sure enough, I knew that it was over between us. Later that night Derek was bold enough to approach her and ask her to dance. She was just about to jump up and go with him when she froze and sat down, apparently remembering that she was with me. She asked me if I minded and, knowing that it was all over between us, I just waved my hand to say it was okay. I didn't want to make it too obvious by leaving immediately afterward, but later that night when I walked her to her room, it was again clear to me that it was over.

"The drive home the next day felt like the longest trip home from a rodeo I had ever experienced. After I carried her bags to the porch, she turned to give me a kiss goodnight. That's when I told her I never wanted to see or hear from her ever again."

"Oh, my gosh! What did she do?"

"She stood there completely bewildered, not understanding what I was saying. That's when I told her I knew all about Derek, and that I couldn't marry a woman who would cheat on me. I knew I'd never be able to trust her to not cheat on me after we were married. I held out my hand and she looked at me like she had no idea why. It was then I told her I wanted my ring back *now!* She started to cry and reached for her hand to remove the ring. Her hand was trembling as she placed the ring in my hand. She said she was sorry. She promised she would never talk to Derek again, and pleaded with me for a second chance. I told her no one gets a second chance after they cheat on me. Then I turned and walked back to my truck. She was still on her porch crying as I drove away, and to this day I've never looked back."

Liam and Nicci sat together in silence. The sun had gone down as they had been sharing about their loves of long ago. He had choked up several times as he was explaining everything, and Nicci had cried during most of it.

"I love you, Nicci."

"I love you, too, Liam. And … I promise you that you will *never* have to worry or wonder about how true and faithful my love is for you."

"And I promise the same to you." But Nicci heard something in his voice that made her look closely, and she noticed that Liam was fighting back tears.

"Liam, sweetheart! What's wrong?"

Liam looked away and took a deep breath, then looked back and saw such love in Nicci's eyes that he just couldn't hold it in any longer.

"It scared me to fall in love with you," Liam confessed.

"Why?"

"Because I … I had fought *so* hard for so many years to steel my heart so it could never be shattered again. When I found out that Tori had cheated on me, I plunged deep into depression. I hated that feeling and what it was doing to me, so I fought my way out and turned to being angry instead. However, that wasn't the solution either, because I was not only angry at Tori, but I was also angry at the world. No one, and I mean *no* one, wanted to be anywhere near me. Finally, my older brother, David, smacked some sense into me."

Liam became silent as he relived the moment.

"How did he do that?" Nicci asked. When he didn't answer right away, she looked up at him and his chin was trembling and tears were falling down his cheeks.

"I'm sorry, Nicci," he said between tears. "I didn't want you to see me like this."

"Why not, sweetheart. I love you, and that means I love everything about you, even your tender side."

"Maybe so, but …". He let out a long sigh. "I guess I've just built this wall around me, and kept it up for so long that it's hard to feel it crumbling down."

"Isn't that a good thing, though?"

"Yeah, it is, since it's you that broke through."

"I'm just so glad you let me," she said tenderly.

"Oh, my gosh, Nicci, so am I."

"So what was it that David said or did to help you?"

"He took me for a long drive, and we ended up at a lake where our family went camping a lot as we were growing up. It started raining as we were driving up into the mountains. When we got to a stopping place near the lake it was raining so hard we just stayed in the car.

"I asked him why we were there and he said it was because it was too far for me to get out and walk home."

Nicci fought the urge to laugh, but Liam noticed and a smile crossed his face. He sighed and shook his head as he felt his spirits lifting a bit.

"There you go again!" Liam said with a slight smirk.

"What?"

"You just have a way of changing my mood."

Nicci smiled. "I love you," she whispered.

"I love you, too," he replied softly.

"I'm sorry I distracted you. Please go on."

Liam cleared his throat. "I knew what David was going to say, or at least I *thought* I knew. But … instead of railing on me for being such a jerk around everyone, including our employees, he …"

Nicci saw the tears return to Liam's eyes and remained quiet.

Liam caught his breath. "He told me he loved me." The tears were now streaming down his cheeks, and Nicci put her arms around him and just held on.

"Falling apart like I am right now is the same thing that happened to me that day at the lake. Prior to that moment, my defenses had been up because I just *knew* he was going to say something like 'snap out of it!' But, instead, he caught me completely by surprise, and I just lost it.

"You see, I *knew* my family loved me. We've always been close, so it was just a given that we loved and supported each other, no matter what. But when David told me he loved me, it was just … different. I had been so crushed by Tori's betrayal. My family understood and supported me while I was suffering through the aftermath, but when I changed from being depressed to angry, David said it really scared our mother. No one had ever seen that side of me. I mean, *I* didn't even know I had that in me, so while I was getting angrier with every passing day, I was also losing sight of who I was deep inside. My world seemed to be spinning out of control. But, when David told me he loved me, it was like I had just driven into a brick wall and the shield I had erected around me was smashed and gone. I knew at that moment that I wasn't worthless, and that even though Tori no longer loved me, I was still loved by others, and in the end *that* was what truly mattered."

"But you've still kept that protective barrier up since then?"

"Yes, and no. I let go of the anger, but just told myself to not rush into another relationship too soon. You know, the old rebound factor."

"Oh, yes. I know it well. I felt the same way with Chandler, but ..."

"Yes?"

"I have to confess that I just couldn't resist you."

"That's *exactly* how I felt about you!"

"Really?"

"Yes! The moment I saw you I felt something come over me that really shook me up. I was *not* expecting someone like you to come along ... *ever!*"

"Seriously? I'm not that different or special."

"You are to me."

As Nicci leaned up to kiss him, Liam slipped his hands behind her head, cradled her neck, and held her close for a soft, passionate kiss. As if on cue, and as a sign of good luck, shooting stars raced across the star-filled heavens.

CHAPTER 81

Three Months Later

THE PEAK SEASON AT the ranch had passed quickly. Only singles and couples would be coming for the next month or so, as families had returned home so their children could return to school.

Nicci's week as a guest had been near the end of the off season and, for the most part, everything remained calm when she returned to stay soon after. By the end of May she had finished all her training and was now a full-fledged, permanent employee. She was loving every minute of it, dust and all.

Since all of Nicci's furniture and other furnishings had been sold with her condo, Beth had talked Nicci into moving in with her. On the *rare* occasions when she wasn't spending her evenings with Liam, she could be found with Beth at a few of their favorite night spots in Taos.

The peak season kicked off as May arrived, and in early June a scorching heatwave hit that lasted for three days and made things miserable for one and all. But that was life on a ranch. More than half of the guests that week had stayed inside, enjoying the air conditioning. However, the staff was always prepared for this with indoor activities for one and all. The horseback rides had been moved up earlier in the daily schedule so those who wished to still participate would be able to return prior to the grueling heat settling in.

The indoor activities came in handy once again when, three weeks later, a major thunderstorm hit the valley and lasted for two days. The next day was hot once again. However, it took that day and half the following day for the ranch to become dry enough to make horseback riding and other outside activities safe and pleasurable once again.

Liam and Nicci continued to grow closer, spending as much of their off-hours together, either at or near the ranch. They also spent some evenings dancing at clubs in Taos or Red River.

It took a while, but Liam finally talked Nicci into going flying with him. Even though he had asked a long time ago if she would like to go up with him, she had asked twice for a raincheck. While she trusted Liam implicitly, her serious concern was just being in such a small aircraft. She had previously only flown in large, commercial airliners.

Liam made arrangements with his friend, Barrett, to fly into Angel Fire on a Thursday. He spent the evening with them at Liam's, talking and laughing well past midnight. While Barrett settled in to spend a couple of nights at Liam's, Liam drove Nicci back to Beth's. They both had to be up early to be at the ranch, but the fun stories she'd heard from both Liam and Barrett had been well worth the late night.

On Friday afternoon, Liam and Nicci wrapped up their work by three-thirty, headed to their respective homes, and then Liam picked Nicci up for their flight. He had told her they were going somewhere "nice" but didn't get more specific than that. After helping her climb on board, and making sure she was properly strapped in, he settled into the pilot's seat, and started the engines.

"Oh, my gosh!" Nicci exclaimed. "I can't believe I'm really doing this!" she added with a nervous smile.

"You're going to be just fine. Trust me," Liam reassured.

"I *do* trust you, sweetheart. It's just that … well, never mind. I'll be fine."

"Yes, you will." Liam's wink and smile seemed to calm her, if for only a moment.

Liam radioed the flight control center and waited for clearance to take off. He was given the okay to approach the runway where they idled for just over five minutes. Finally, the control center gave Liam the go-ahead. He increased the thrust to the engines, then glanced at Nicci, who smiled and gave him a thumbs up. They were off!

Rising slowly as they headed toward Eagle Nest, they caught the updraft from the winds coming off the mountains to the west, aiding the ascent over Eagle Nest Lake. They then headed west a short distance before turning again to head south toward Albuquerque. Liam reached over and placed his hand on Nicci's left leg and she reached down and held his hand.

"Doing okay?"

Nicci's initial anxiousness had turned to excitement. "Yes!"

Liam gently squeezed her hand and then returned his hand to the controls.

"So, when will you tell me where you're taking me?"

Liam gave her his well-known sly smile. "You'll find out when we get there."

Nicci let out a knowing sigh. *I sure love this man!*

* * *

After arriving at Albuquerque International Sunport, Liam secured a taxi, handed the driver a card with the address of their destination along with a fifty-dollar bill, and off they went. The driver hit I-25 heading north and then merged onto Coronado Freeway / I-40 heading east. A short distance later the driver took an offramp and within minutes they were approaching the requested destination.

On the card Liam had added a notation, 'Please pull in from the side street', and the driver did as requested. As he let them out Liam nodded to the driver and thanked him. The driver, in turn, raised the card with the fifty-dollar bill and smiled broadly as he thanked Liam for his generosity.

Liam's plan had worked perfectly, as Nicci still had *no* idea where they were. It was certainly a nice area, a prosperous commercial district with clean parking lots and attractive, well-trimmed landscaping. Next to a seven-story parking garage was the Japanese Kitchen restaurant and Nicci looked up anxiously at Liam.

"Are we having Japanese this evening?!"

Liam smiled but didn't reply, giving Nicci the impression she'd figured out his plan. But, when they weren't walking directly for the entrance she looked at him again.

"Okay, now I'm *totally* confused."

Liam shot her his sly smile. "Just be patient."

"What if I don't want to be?" Nicci asked with a little girl pout. Liam chuckled.

As they continued to walk through one courtyard and toward another, Liam stopped.

"What?" Nicci asked, curiously.

"I want you to keep holding onto my arm and close your eyes."

She played along, but before they took another step Nicci peeked out of her left eye.

"Come on. Play along."

Nicci let out a playful sigh. "Okay-y-y," she replied with a pouting lower lip, followed by laughter.

Once he was sure Nicci wouldn't peek he began to lead her toward their destination.

"Are we close?"

"Only fifty yards to go," he replied, doing his best to stifle a laugh.

"What?! You're kidding, right?"

"Would I kid you?"

"You do it all the time!"

They were both fighting valiantly to stifle their laughter.

"Well, maybe it's only forty."

Nicci gave his arm a tight squeeze.

Liam eased Nicci to the right to pass through another landscaped courtyard, then eased her back to their left just a bit.

"Oh, my gosh!" Nicci exclaimed.

"What?"

"Something smells so *good!* We *must* be getting close, right?"

"If you say so," he replied, teasingly.

"You are such a brat."

They passed four large windows on their right, with broad red metal frames, displaying posters of special savory features available at their destination. After passing the windows, they took a few more steps before Liam eased them to a stop, and gently turned Nicci to her right.

"We're here!" Liam announced triumphantly.

"May I look now?"

"Yes!"

While still holding onto Liam's arm, she opened her eyes and looked straight ahead at a large red door. But, there was no sign on or near the door to indicate the name of the restaurant.

"Where are we?" Nicci asked hesitantly.

"You're about to find out, sweetheart."

Liam then reached in front of Nicci, took hold of the door handle, and as he began to open it, the delicious aromas that had gently overwhelmed them a few moments earlier came wafting out, even stronger.

"Good evening and welcome to Ruth's Chris Steak House! My name is Alaina and I'm your hostess this evening!"

"Hi, Alaina. My name is Liam Prescott, and we have six o'clock reservations for two."

"Wonderful! Let me check you in!" Alaina looked down her seating chart and saw Liam's name and the notation "Table for Two".

While Nicci was taking in the layout of the beautiful interior of the restaurant, Liam leaned forward and slipped Alaina a fifty-dollar bill. "If it's available, we'd like a table in a quieter area," he whispered. Alaina nodded and winked.

"You've arrived at the perfect time, Mr. Prescott. There will be no waiting, as the table you requested is available."

"Thank you!"

"Susanne? Would you please escort the Prescott's to table twenty-three?"

"Twenty-three?" Susanne asked, raising her eyebrows.

"Yes, twenty-three," Alaina replied politely, nodding her head.

"Right away!" Susanne acknowledged, nodding her head in return.

"Please follow me," she said to Liam and Nicci with a smile, and escorted them to a remote area of the restaurant.

"Here you are, Mr. and Mrs. Prescott, and here are your menus and the wine list."

"Thank you, Susanne, but you can keep the wine list. We won't be needing it," Liam responded while holding Nicci's seat for her.

"Very well, sir."

After Liam took his seat, Susanne asked them if she could get them anything to drink. They both asked for ice water with lemon. After she left, Nicci leaned forward and whispered, "Mr. and *Mrs.* Prescott? Do *they* know something *I* don't know?"

Liam smirked. "I guess they thought we looked like a happily married couple, and they were merely being polite."

They shared a wink and a smile, and Nicci thought to herself, *It does have a nice ring to it.*

When Susanne returned with their drinks they placed their order of an appetizer of crab cakes, and for their entrée they decided to share a thirty-ounce Porterhouse with loaded baked potatoes, and each chose a lobster tail to complement their meal.

As they were casually waiting for their meal, Nicci looked around and noticed that, in their area, not many tables were taken. She brought this to Liam's attention and he explained that he had asked the hostess for a quieter area of the restaurant.

"But … don't you find it a bit odd that it's not busier for a Friday evening?" she asked.

"I'm sure it will get busier very soon, but I was hoping to have as much quiet time with you as I could, before the rush hits."

"That's sweet of you, Liam. Thank you."

"Would I be guessing correctly that you've been to a Ruth's Chris Steak House back home?"

"Yes, a couple of times, but never with as wonderful a man as tonight," Nicci replied with a wink. Liam reached over and squeezed her hand.

"I love you, Nicci."

"I can sure tell. And I love you, too, sweetheart."

Their crabcakes were delivered and Susanne assured them their dinners would be served soon. Liam and Nicci thanked her and she was off to take care of another couple who had been seated toward the entrance to their section.

While waiting for their dinners to arrive they shared plenty of small talk, mostly about the ranch and how Nicci enjoyed her first full peak season.

"Brendy and Beth have certainly been very helpful," she said, "and Luke and Jill have been so supportive. But ...," Nicci paused and reached for Liam's hand, "it's all been *so* much more wonderful ... because of you."

Nicci noticed that Liam looked like he was about to say something so she paused before saying anything else. When he didn't, she looked closer and noticed her big, strong, rugged cowboy was starting to tear up.

"Sweetheart, are you okay?"

Liam nodded. "Yeah," he replied, barely in a whisper. "It's just that ..." Liam looked away, trying to compose himself. When he looked back, and into Nicci's eyes, he had to take a deep breath before he could speak. Nicci waited patiently.

"I've never known anyone like you, and sometimes I just can't believe I'm so lucky to have you in my life."

"Oh, sweetheart, I feel the same way," Nicci replied softly, leaning closer. "Before I met you I was petrified to ever fall in love again. But there was just something about you that made me feel like ... like everything would be okay, that it would be different than anything I'd experienced before in my life, and that it would be the best thing to ever happen to me. And it is!"

Susanne had just begun to approach with their dinners when, from a distance, she could see this tender moment unfolding so she paused, waiting for a better moment to continue. A moment later she saw them share a tender kiss and then sit back in their chairs. As she saw Mr. Prescott raise his glass to take a drink, she picked up the tray from the table she had rested it on, and proceeded.

"Oh, my *gosh* that smells so wonderful!" Nicci exclaimed, as Susanne placed the Porterhouse between them. She then set down another plate in front of each of them that had their lobster tails and loaded baked potatoes.

"And that sizzle from the steak means we are in for a treat!" Liam added.

Susanne smiled. "I'll be right back to refill your glasses."

"Thank you, Susanne."

They were each beginning to carve away at the Porterhouse when

Susanne returned with fresh glasses of ice water with lemon wedges.

"May I get you anything else?" she inquired.

"Not at this time. Thank you!" Liam replied.

"You're welcome! Enjoy your dinner, and just let me know if there's anything else I can do for you."

"Thank you, Susanne," Nicci added. "This all looks *so* delicious!"

"Wonderful. Enjoy!"

"We will," Liam and Nicci replied in unison, then laughed at their perfect timing.

They took their time enjoying their sumptuous meal and continued their loving banter and sweet thoughts. Then later, for dessert, Nicci chose the creamy cheesecake with fresh berries, and Liam ordered a slice of the chocolate mousse cheesecake topped with whipped cream.

As they were getting ready to leave, Liam placed a call for a taxi then requested the bill. A moment later Susanne handed him the credit card holder and he slipped two one-hundred dollar bills inside and told her to keep the change. Nicci noticed the grateful look in Susanne's eyes, and as she walked away Nicci looked at her handsome cowboy, reached over and squeezed his hand.

"You are simply wonderful, Liam," Nicci said, as a tear or two appeared in the corner of her eyes, "and I am one *very* lucky woman."

Liam simply smiled and replied, "*I'm* the lucky one here." He then helped his sweetheart up from her chair and said goodbye to Susanne as they passed her while she was delivering another couple's dinner. They also said good night to their hostess, Alaina.

Their cab arrived ten minutes later, and in less than an hour they were airborne and heading back to Angel Fire.

* * *

"Oh, my gosh, Liam! Just LOOK!"

It turned out that Liam's timing had been impeccable, for on their flight back to Angel Fire he treated Nicci to a sight she had never beheld ... a sunset from eighteen thousand feet in the air! He glanced over toward her and noticed tears flowing down her cheeks. He reached over and rested his hand on her leg, and she reached down and squeezed it.

"I love you, Liam, so *very* much!"

"I love you too, Nicci, even more than I could possibly have imagined before this moment."

"Promise me you'll keep surprising me with special moments like this."

"I promise, sweetheart."

They flew in silence for what seemed like an eternity, but was only ten minutes. They began chatting about the ranch and their plans for the rest of the weekend. Then Nicci mentioned Barrett.

"So, what do you think Barrett is up to tonight? Enjoying the nightlife in Taos, thrilling all the women in your Porsche?"

"No, he told me he was actually looking forward to kicking back and relaxing this weekend. His schedule has been really packed for the last few months. He was extremely grateful I called him and asked if he could fly into town so I could take you out for the evening. He's been to my place many times, so he knows his way around. I'm guessing he's sitting on the deck, watching this very same sunset, and enjoying the quiet."

Liam had one more surprise in store for her. As they were approaching Moreno Valley, he dimmed the lights on the control panel.

"What's going on, Liam?"

"I'm about to call out to the control center to announce our approach to Angel Fire, but I wanted to show you something first."

Nicci looked down into the darkness of the mountains and forest but saw only scattered lights.

"No, look out there."

Nicci raised her eyes and caught her breath! "Oh, Liam! It's *beautiful!*" was all she could say before the tears began to flow again as she saw thousands of stars surrounding them. She had thought it several times before, but this evening made her even more sure. *I'm going to love this man forever!*

CHAPTER 82

***

Saturday Evening

THE EVENING SKY WAS turning toward dusk as Liam and Nicci were saddling up their horses for what Nicci thought was going to be another beautiful sunset ride. The plan was for them to take a casual ride toward the top of the mountain, spread out a blanket, and watch the fading glow of the sun disappear over the mountains in the west. Then they would gaze at the stars for a while before heading back down the trail to the ranch. However, part way up the mountain Liam led them in a different direction.

"Um, Liam? Where are we headed?"

"You'll see," Liam replied with a sly smile Nicci couldn't see.

Nicci smiled to herself, knowing Liam liked to surprise her from time to time with little things. *I wonder what he has up his sleeve this time?* She also knew she was in safe hands and trusted Liam with everything.

This different trail switched back and forth gently. At least it seemed that way from their casual pace.

"So, why haven't we taken this trail before?"

"Because." Liam was *definitely* being difficult, but in a sweet way. She liked how he kept her guessing about what he was thinking or about to do; his mysteriously spontaneous side. What's his name had become too predictable during their time together, and perhaps that's why she may have gotten bored with him. They had reached the point where there was nothing to really look forward to. And on those few times when he *was* spontaneous about something, it was about something *he* wanted to do or someplace *he* wanted to go. In the beginning he had won her over by caring about her and her desires, but that flame had blown out long ago. *Why did he never surprise me by taking me somewhere I wanted to go? Hmmm ... do I really need to answer that?*

"Doing okay back there?" Liam asked.

"Sure am! Just playing follow-the-leader."

"Good."

"I'm certainly not in any rush, but is it very much further?"

"No."

"You're a big tease, you know?"

"Yes."

"What's with all of these short answers?"

"Nothing."

"LIAM!"

He started to laugh and looked over his shoulder.

"What?!" Nicci asked in gentle frustration.

"You're cute."

"Cute? CUTE?! Mister, I—"

"You're getting cuter," Liam interrupted with a big smile.

"Darn you, Liam!"

"What?"

"You know I can't resist that smile."

"Really?"

"Liam, you're doing it again!"

"What?"

"Your one-word answers!"

"Yeah?"

"There you go again!"

Liam simply looked over his shoulder and smiled. Then he winked!

"Oh, Liam, what am I'm going to do with you?"

Silence greeted her question. *Yes, he's driving me crazy,* she thought, *but in such a wonderful way!*

The only sounds were those from the horses' hooves as they

slowly made their way along the trail. The air was perfectly still. Then the faint sound of laughter broke the stillness.

"Did you hear that?" Nicci asked.

"Hear what?"

"I thought I heard some voices, but they sounded far off."

"Might have been from one of the cabins or houses up here."

"Oh, that's right. Your taking me on this *wilderness* trail made me forget anyone else was around."

Nicci heard more voices but they sounded a bit closer which confused her since they were supposedly riding further away from the cabins and houses. In the continued silence her senses were heightened.

"Oooooo! Oh, my gosh!" Nicci softly whispered.

"What?"

"Someone must be barbequing something really delicious!"

"Mm-hmm."

"Do you smell it, too?"

"Faintly." Liam was absolutely loving teasing Nicci.

"Wait a minute! What's up there?!"

"Where?"

"Right up there!" Nicci was pointing further up the mountain.

"There?" Liam pointed in the same direction.

"Yes. That's weird."

"What do you see?"

"Well, it looks like there's a glow of some sort, but it also looks like it's blocked by some kind of, I don't know … a solid dark shield of some sort?"

"Hmm, that's strange."

"How can you be so nonchalant about it? Do you know what it is?"

Liam didn't respond, he just smiled to himself.

"Liam, what's going on? Does this have anything to do with where you're taking me?"

He remained silent.

Nicci sighed deeply, sweetly frustrated, but at the same time anxious to see what was behind that dark barrier that Liam seemed to be leading them toward.

The voices had stopped, but the amazing aroma of something delicious was becoming stronger as they rode ever closer.

Liam and Nicci had finally reached a plateau on the side of the mountain, and as their path leveled off, they were only twenty yards away from something that looked like several black sheets stretched around poles to block their view. Still no voices, but now they could hear the sizzling of something being prepared over an open fire.

Liam halted with ten yards to go, and Nicci did the same.

"Liam," Nicci whispered. "What's going on?"

"Darlin', you're about to find out."

Nicci was beyond excited!

They slowly led their horses closer to the barrier and tied them to a tree. Liam took Nicci's hand and slowly led her to the center of one side of the barrier. Then he walked to the pole to his left, reached down toward the bottom and unsnapped the three snaps on the lower part of the sheet. Finally, he unhooked the top of the sheet, and pulled it back in one swift motion, causing Nicci to cover her mouth as she gasped!

"Liam! Wh—"

"Surprise, darlin'!"

"LuAnn? Brendy? Mike? What … ?" Nicci was overcome with joy and began to cry. "I don't understand. What's going on?"

"This is all for you!" Brendy exclaimed as she came forward to give Nicci a big hug.

"Oh, my gosh!" Nicci let out a long sigh and looked at Liam. "This is for me?"

"Liam planned it all," Mike said.

"And we all pitched in to do our part!" LuAnn added.

The tears were flowing as Nicci leaned into Liam for a hug.

"Thank you, sweetheart! I can't believe this! How long have all of you been planning this?"

"Liam approached me about it, what, about a month ago?" LuAnn asked.

Liam nodded.

"He wanted to know if it was possible to carry off something like this up here on the mountain. I told him I'd take care of everything, and all he needed to do was to just get you up here."

"And I offered to help LuAnn with all of the dinner prep," added Brendy. "And Mike said he'd take care of fixing up a barrier around this area so no one could see what was going on as you rode up the mountain and to set up the table, chairs and everything else."

"And I went to each of the neighbors who live up here to give them a heads up," Liam explained, "and also notified Chief Baker at the fire station, so we're good!"

Nicci looked up at Liam with complete joy in her eyes.

"I love you, Liam!" and she threw her arms around his neck and gave him a big kiss.

"I love you, too, sweetheart."

As they were kissing Mike cleared his throat.

"So," Liam said as he and Nicci did their best to compose themselves, "how's everything coming along for the dinner?"

"Why don't you and Nicci have a seat and we'll dish it up. Then we'll be on our way so you can have some private time together."

"That sounds good!"

"Thanks, you guys! You are simply the best!" Nicci said graciously.

"Thank Liam. This was all *his* idea!" Brendy said.

"But you three were the ones to make it happen. I just had to coerce Nicci into spending *another* moonlit evening with me," Liam joked.

"Coerced? Ha! I can't stay away from you, so there was no coercion necessary." And with that, Nicci leaned over and gave Liam another big kiss!

CHAPTER 83

Moonglow

LIAM CALLED **MIKE TO** give him the heads up that he and Nicci were about finished with their dinner. They would then wait for Mike to arrive so that the area would not be left unattended.

Mike picked up Kevin along the way and they took a back road up the mountain. Their job now was to clean up the area and return it to its natural appearance while Liam and Nicci rode their horses back to the ranch.

As they entered the stable, Brendy met them with a big smile.

"How was it?" Brendy asked anxiously.

"It was heavenly." Nicci replied. "But it's late. What are you still doing here? And where's your sidekick, Beth?"

"Beth wanted to be here, but one of her friends invited her to some special event over in Taos. She asked me to tell you that she'll be staying at her friend's place tonight."

"Oh, okay."

"And as for what's going on here, well, you should ask Liam that question," Brendy replied with a wink.

"Oh?" Nicci turned to Liam. "So, why *is* Brendy here?"

Liam's smile made Nicci think that there was some kind of conspiracy or secret that had been cooked up between the two of them. She wondered if anyone else knew what was going on.

"You'll see."

"Now you're back to your short answers again!"

Liam only smiled.

"Or none at all!" Nicci let out an exasperated sigh as she let go of Calypso's reins and planted her hands firmly on her hips.

"Talk to me, mister, or I'll, I'll—"

"You'll what?! Huh? What will you do if I don't tell you what's going on?" Liam followed that with a wink and a smile.

"You are driving me *crazy*, mister! Do you know that?"

The smile on Liam's face said it all.

Nicci was feeling so many different emotions at that moment. She was *so* much in love with this man, but he was also so full of mystery. Just another reason she had fallen in love with him! She had come to expect that he might surprise her with something at any given moment, and that kept her guessing about what might happen next.

With the horses now being led away by Brendy, Liam reached for Nicci's hand, held it firmly, and led her out of the stable and toward his truck.

Nicci loved his touch. The way he held her hand made her feel so safe, and there was a sense of peace and comfort that came over her every time he held her in his arms. His kiss was something else again!

Liam opened Nicci's door, and after she sat down, he firmly closed it. He glanced at her through the windshield as he walked around the front of his truck. His smile melted her. *What's going on?*

Liam got in and sat down, put the key into the ignition, but didn't start the engine right away. He pulled his hand back and turned to look at Nicci who was already looking at him.

"Ready?" he asked with another wink and a smile.

Nicci bit her lower lip, a nervous habit she noticed had begun shortly after she realized she was falling in love with Liam not too long after they had met. His attention, his caring and gentle way with her, mixed with his firm toughness as head wrangler, made him the perfect man for her. *If only* ... no, she wouldn't go there. It's way too soon to think about *that*.

"Yes," Nicci replied so softly it was as if she spoke it in a whisper.

Liam turned forward, started his truck, put it in gear, and slowly drove away from the stable and out onto the road that took them from the ranch and toward the highway. Once they reached the highway, he turned right and drove a short distance before making a left turn. From there they made their way up a winding road and passed several homes, until they could no longer go any higher. Then Liam turned right, heading north.

A half mile later, they came to the end of the road and Liam stopped his truck. He turned off the engine, got out, then walked around to Nicci's side, and helped her out. She had been silent since they'd left the ranch, trying to figure out what other surprise Liam might have in store for her that night.

After he helped her out of the truck, he reached over into the truck bed and retrieved a large duffle bag.

"What's in there?" Nicci asked.

"Just wait, you'll see."

He took her hand and they walked further north along an unfinished trail until the tree line to their right stopped and they could see the panoramic view of the valley below.

"Oh, Liam, this view is even more breathtaking than where we had dinner."

Liam didn't respond immediately causing Nicci to look up at him. He was already looking at her.

"It sure is, sweetheart."

Nicci melted into his arms.

"Would you do me a favor?" Liam asked.

"Anything for you," Nicci replied softly.

Liam opened the duffel bag and pulled out a blanket.

"Would you mind helping me lay this out?"

"Sure!" In no time at all the blanket was laid out flat and they sat down to enjoy the view.

Liam laid back and looked up at the stars. The sky was perfectly clear, but because of the full moon there weren't as many stars visible as normal.

"Oh, Liam, this is heaven," Nicci whispered as she laid down next to Liam.

"It sure is." Then Liam leaned over, looked deeply into Nicci's eyes, and they lost themselves in a long, but gentle kiss.

As Liam laid back down, Nicci placed her hand on his chest and her head resting above his heart, hearing and feeling its rhythm.

"The stars and the moon are so beautiful tonight. Thank you for bringing me up here."

"You're welcome."

"So, why haven't you brought me up here before?"

"Because."

That simple, one-word reply hit Nicci's trigger, and she immediately began to tickle the very vulnerable Liam. He tried to tickle her back, but she held the upper hand this time, at least for a few seconds. He rolled her over onto her back, pinning her legs under his, and proceeded to tickle her mercilessly until her laughter and squeals began to turn to breathless pleas for release!

Liam stopped, but held his fingers right next to her ribs, ready to attack again at any second.

"Please," Nicci pled, trying to catch her breath, her arms lying limp along her sides.

"Please, some more?" Liam asked teasingly.

"NO! Please *stop!*" Her heavy breathing, mixed with their mutual laughter continued. Liam eased his hands away from her ribs, rolled his leg back over, and laid back down, completely satisfied that he had won. *This* time.

He looked over at his still nearly-breathless sweetheart. Their eyes met, and once again they shared another long and gentle kiss.

"I love you, Liam."

"I love you, too, Nicci."

They looked at each other for another long moment before Liam laid back down beside her.

Nicci took another few seconds before she rolled back toward him, laid her head on his chest, and wrapped her arm around his waist.

Yes, this is definitely *heaven,* she thought.

"I can hear your heartbeat." Nicci whispered softly.

"Yeah?"

"It's beating pretty fast."

"Well. We *did* just finish tickling each other."

"Yes, I know, but ..."

"But, what?"

"Oh, I don't know. Something tells me there might be another reason."

"Oh, really? I *wonder* why?" he replied with a funny look on his face.

A moment later he reached toward the duffel bag and removed a black object.

"What are you reaching for?"

"I have something to show you."

"What?" Nicci replied excitedly, as if she were a little girl anxious to open up a birthday present.

Liam turned and handed the object to Nicci.

"Binoculars?"

"Yep!"

'Oh, you're going to teach me about the constellations?"

"No."

"NO?!" Nicci exclaimed curiously, her eyes growing wide. "Then what am I going to look at."

"Sit up and you'll find out."

Nicci did as Liam asked. Now, sitting next to each other, Liam pointed across the valley.

"Right over there is the ranch."

"Oh, cool!" She started to raise the binoculars to get a better look, but Liam reached over and gently held her arm down.

"Not yet."

"Why?"

"There's something else."

"What?" That's when she saw a look in Liam's eyes she had never seen before.

"Liam?" she asked in a whisper, her stomach beginning to flip ever so slightly and her heart rate quickening.

"Yes?"

"What's going on?"

"As you look through the binoculars start higher than the mountain range, then ease down into the trees."

"Okay. I'm seeing nothing but tall, dark shapes. Oh, those must be trees. And there's an occasional light here and there."

"Right. Those are the cabins up the mountain from the ranch. Go ahead and adjust your focus until it's as crystal clear as possible. Okay?"

"Okay."

"Then continue to bring your view down even more."

"What am I'm looking for?"

"You'll know when you see it."

"I think I see the ranch now."

"Good. Sharpen your focus some more."

"Okay. Oh, Liam, the ranch looks so beautiful from up here!"

"Keep going."

Nicci lowered the binoculars and looked at Liam. "Keep going?"

"Yes." Liam watched as Nicci's hands slowly brought the binoculars back up to her eyes.

Suddenly, she gasped and leaned forward, as if doing so would bring what she had just seen closer!

Nicci suddenly caught her breath, turned toward Liam with tears rolling down her cheeks, and then looked through the lenses again. She quickly wiped her eyes in order to focus and found her mark again.

"LIAM! OH, MY GOSH!! OH, MY GOSH! What *IS* that?!"

Liam could hardly contain himself. "Can you read what it says?"

"YES, I CAN! And … YES, I WILL!!! Oh, LIAM!!!"

She immediately dropped the binoculars, threw her arms around Liam, and kissed him deeply!

After they came up for air, she breathlessly asked, "Liam, what *is* that? How did you do that?"

"Those are moonflowers, and right at this moment they're reflecting the light from the full moon."

"Really?! So how did you do that?"

"Even though they grow wild, I was also able to bring in hundreds more and just had them set up to spell out my message."

"So, how many people knew about this scheme of yours?"

"Well, first I talked with Jill to see if I could have permission to do it, and she was one hundred percent behind the idea. Then we talked over how much help I'd need to make it happen. She called Maureen into the office since she's in charge of everything to do with the landscaping. Even though at first, she felt overwhelmed with the task, she finally accepted the challenge when we assured her she would have all the help she needed.

"Now, in answer to your question, we only chose those that I *knew* I could trust to keep a secret from you. So there was Maureen, Mike, Kevin, Brendy, Beth, and Sonia working on rearranging them in pots over the last few days. Of course, Brendy was the hardest worker. She's so happy for you and she said she came close to accidentally giving it away a couple of times, but she also insisted on being a part of it.

"From the ground no one could tell what they were doing. The flowers don't bloom until after dusk, and with the clear skies and full moon tonight they're giving off the brightest possible reflection."

"So, how did you know that the moonlight's reflection off the flowers could be seen from up here?"

"I noticed it about a year ago when I drove a buddy of mine home after a party. We passed his house just up the road a bit on our way up here. He was the one that told me about it because he had noticed it one night, wondering what this soft glow was that he could see from his deck. Of course, there was no pattern in the reflection at the time, just something that seemed to be glowing in the dark. I got the idea to do this a couple of months ago and spent a week or so trying to figure out how I could make it happen."

"A couple of *months* ago?" Nicci asked. "How long have you known you wanted to marry me?"

"Truth?"

"Yes, always."

"Well, you caught my eye at dinner the first night you came to the ranch, but I knew I couldn't do anything about it because you were here on vacation. When your vacation was over, you'd go home, and I would never see you again."

"But I'm sure you've seen many other women come and go like me, so I'm sure I'm not the first."

"Truth, again … yes, you are."

"Really?" Not that she didn't believe him, but as handsome and rugged as Liam appeared to her, she was *sure* that someone else would have grabbed his attention *long* before her.

"Yeah, really."

They looked at each other for several moments before Nicci reached for the binoculars and took another look at the moonflowers. While she was momentarily distracted Liam laid back down, resting his head on the blanket. His timing was perfect because just as his head hit the blanket Nicci turned and looked down at him and sighed.

"I love you *so* much, Liam. You've made me that happiest woman in the world tonight."

"I love you, too, Nicci, and I'm glad you're happy, because now you're stuck with me," Liam replied with a wink.

Nicci set the binoculars down beside her, and as she turned to lie down, she saw how vulnerable Liam was with his hands resting under his head as he looked lovingly at her. She didn't need to think twice, and in a flash, she decided to go for it! She was able to tickle him for all of about two seconds before he flipped her over to his left and then tickled her until she was gleefully gasping for a breath once again. He laid back down beside her, and they laughed while they tried to catch their breath. Once they were able to calm down a bit, Nicci rolled over, placed her arm around Liam's waist and rested her head on his chest, listening to his rapid and excited heartbeat.

"So," Nicci began after a minute or two had passed, "You knew from the start? The very first night?"

"Yes."

"You kinda knew, or you *really* knew?"

"The moment I first saw you was like no other moment in my life."

"Really? Why?"

"I don't know if I can put it into words. I just … *knew*. Do you remember that moment when we first met and after a brief chat, I excused myself and had to go take care of something outside?"

"Yes, now that you mention it, I do."

"Well … I had to get outside quickly before I said something that might have embarrassed both of us."

"What?! What were you going to say?"

"It was just something silly."

"Come on! Tell me!"

Liam let out a sigh. "Promise you won't laugh."

"I promise."

Liam looked away for a moment, took a deep breath, and looked back into Nicci's eyes.

"I was going to ask you … if you would marry me."

Nicci's eyes popped! "What?! Seriously?!"

"Yes, but I knew it was so off-the-wall that I had to go outside to get control of myself before I messed everything up for us for that coming week."

Nicci let out a long sigh. "Oh, my gosh, Liam. I can't believe it. You fell that hard and that fast?"

"Yes. I was so shocked at my reaction to meeting you. I've always tried to maintain a calm demeanor, but I literally didn't know what else to say, so I had to leave. Once I was able to get outside and take a few *very* deep breaths, I was able to come back in and sit down for dinner. I'm not sure if you noticed it or not, but I didn't look your way for the rest of the night."

"No, I hadn't noticed that. I think I was just too involved with the conversation I was having with Brendy, Luke, and Jill. In fact, if I remember correctly, the next time I really *saw* you was the next day when you were so valiant in trying to save me from my unexpected and unwanted visitor."

Liam smiled. "I was ready and willing to run him out of town right then and there."

Nicci looked deeply into her handsome cowboy's eyes. "I know." She sat silently for a moment, pondering what she was going to share with him next.

"Want to know when I knew *you* were the one?"

"Sure."

"Well, when we were first introduced at dinner that Saturday night there was just something *so* special about your eyes *and* your voice that I … oh, I don't know how to describe it. I guess it just made me feel something I had never felt before. However, I quickly reminded myself that I was there on a vacation, *not* to find a man, so I had to, just as quickly, disengage my thoughts. Then, the next day when my *friend* showed up unexpectedly you stopped to ask if he was bothering me. And in the midst of *that* fiasco … you called me a lady. You handled that whole situation like a true gentleman, like a knight, almost, ready to go to battle for this fair maiden."

"I was."

"I know. I could tell. And my heart … well, my heart just felt something. Something I'd never felt before. And … and it felt so good." Nicci's thoughts drifted as she recalled the tender feeling.

"But then that jerk completely destroyed the mood and persisted in being a royal pain."

"I was ready to ask him to leave, out of consideration for one of our guests."

"There you go again, my knight is dusty armor."

They laughed, then Nicci leaned over Liam and kissed him deeply. She leaned up, smiled sweetly, then sighed contentedly as she slid back down to his side, her head once again at rest on his chest. His heartbeat was strong, and she felt luxuriously safe.

They laid like that for what seemed like forever, but was actually less than ten minutes. Liam reached over Nicci and grabbed the binoculars, and handed them to her.

"What's this for? Is it find-the-constellation time?"

"No, I'd like you to see if you can spot the brightest stars, and then take a closer look."

Nicci scanned the sky, pointed out three that were particularly bright, then raised the binoculars to get a better look. While still looking through the binoculars she pointed to the one that was furthest to the left and said, "I think that one is probably the brightest star I can see."

"How about the one further down, just above the mountains?"

For this Nicci needed to sit up, and while she was appropriately distracted, Liam slid something out from the left front pocket of his Wranglers, cupping it in his left hand. Next he reached into the right front pocket and slipped something out ever so carefully. Then he sat up near her and slid back slightly.

"Yes, that's definitely a bright one!" Nicci replied.

"Okay, now how about this one over here to the right?"

Nicci lowered the binoculars to see where Liam was pointing, then raised them again to check it out. As she did so, he raised his right hand up in such a way as to block her view.

"Hey, what are—"

At that moment he raised his left hand and flicked a penlight on to illuminate a two-carat diamond engagement ring.

"Is this bright enough for you?"

"LIAM! OH MY GOSH! IT'S BEAUTIFUL!"

She turned to face him as he slipped it on her finger, then threw her arms around him and kissed him passionately!

"I love you *so* much, Liam!"

"And I love you more," he replied with a wink and a sly smile.

"That's not *even* possible!"

"Wanna bet?"

"You'd lose!"

The fun bantering made both of them laugh, then Nicci turned and laid down in Liam's lap with his right arm providing a pillow for her head.

"May I see the light, please?"

He handed it to her and she turned it on to admire the beauty of her ring once again.

"This is just so … so *amazingly* beautiful, Liam! Thank you!"

"You're welcome," Liam replied softly as he raised her up closer to give her a hug and a long kiss.

He held her tight for a long time, and they could feel each other's hearts beating.

"Liam?" she asked almost in a whisper.

"Yes?" he replied as he laid her back down in his lap.

"How soon can we get married?" she asked anxiously.

"Tomorrow, if you want," he replied casually.

"Really?!"

"It's completely up to you, sweetheart."

"I wonder if we could find a minister on short notice, otherwise we'd have to wait until Monday and go to Taos to find a Justice of the Peace."

"Whatever you want. I'm with you all the way, but ... what about your parents, especially now that you and your father have been able to work things out."

"Oh, you're right! Of course! What was I thinking?"

"You're excited, so it's just natural to forget some *minor* details like inviting your parents to the wedding!" He laughed and Nicci knuckled him in the ribs, then started to tickle him. And with that he pulled her tight with his right arm, proceeded to tickle her mercilessly with his left hand, and they collapsed on the blanket in hysterical laughter.

After they caught their breath, Nicci took a deep breath.

"Okay ... seriously now. How about a Christmas wedding?"

"Getting married on Christmas day?"

"Not necessarily, but a wedding at Christmas time. I think it would be so beautiful ... and *magical!*"

"I like the idea a lot! But, as I said before, you choose when *you* want to get married and we'll make it happen."

They continued to talk about it, and as they got up to get ready to drive back down the mountain they gave each other another big hug and long kiss.

"Okay, I've decided. We're going to have a Christmas time wedding, and I'll ask Luke and Jill if we can have it at the ranch."

"I like it! And I'll bet they'll say yes!"

They picked up the blanket, shook it off, rolled it up, and Liam stuffed it into the duffel bag along with the binoculars.

As they drove down the mountain Nicci sat next to Liam with her head resting on his shoulder. As they approached the highway, she raised her hand up because the lights from the nearby businesses made it easier for her to see her beautiful ring.

"Thank you, darling," she said softly. "You've made me *so* happy."

"And you've done the same for me."

CHAPTER 84

The Midnight Call

"Hello?" Charlotte's voice was both drowsy and worried.

"Hi, Mom!"

"Nicole?! Hi, sweetheart!" she replied excitedly as she brushed her shoulder length hair away from her sleepy eyes. Jenson woke up and rolled over. "Why are you calling so late, dear? Is everything okay?"

"Mom ... I'm *engaged!*"

"*What?!?!*"

"What's going on?" Jenson asked anxiously.

"Just a moment, dear," Charlotte whispered to him.

"Yes, I'm engaged! I can't believe it!"

"Is it the man that your father met when he was there?"

"Yes!"

"Hang on one sec, sweetheart," she said, then held her hand over the phone and turned to look at her husband. "Nicole's engaged!"

"What?! To that Liam fella?"

"Yes! Isn't that wonderful?"

Jenson sat up on the bed, his mind in a complete fog.

"Your father is speechless, sweetheart!"

"Um, is that a good thing?" Nicole asked nervously.

"Well, from the look on his face ..."

"Mom? Come on, tell me!"

"Darling, he's smiling from ear to ear!"

Nicole began to cry and that started Charlotte crying as well. Jenson got up and walked around the bed and sat down next to his wife, reaching for the phone. Charlotte looked up at him and he nodded and winked.

"Nicole?"

"Hi, Dad," Nicole responded cautiously.

"Nicole, I'm happy for you, sweetheart."

"Thank you *so* much, Dad! That means the *world* to me!"

"I just have one question."

Nicole braced herself, worried that he might ruin this out-of-this-world moment for her.

"What is it?" she asked, as a knot began to ever so slowly build in her stomach.

"Are you absolutely, one hundred percent certain that he's the one?"

"Oh, Daddy, YES! A thousand times YES!"

Charlotte was looking at her husband and put her arm around him as she saw the tears welling up in his eyes.

"That's ... that's wonderful, sweetheart," he tried to say without giving away his emotions as he handed the phone back to his wife.

"Daddy? Are you okay?"

"Sweetheart," her mother began, "your father is *more* than okay. You should see the smile on his face right now." She looked at her husband who nodded.

"Not to mention the tears running down his face."

"Charlotte!" Jenson whispered, not thrilled that she had exposed this rare tender moment of weakness, even to their own daughter.

"Oh, Mom ..." Nicole's voice trailed off as she looked for a tissue. Or three!

Despite the late hour, Nicole and her mother were too excited to hang up.

"Honey," Charlotte said to Jenson, "I'm going to be on the phone for a while, so you just go back to sleep. I'll give you another kiss goodnight when I come back to bed."

"Okay, Char. Love you."

"I love you, too. Jens."

"Hang on one moment, Nicole."

"Okay."

Charlotte got up, put her robe and slippers on, and headed for the family room where she curled up on the sofa with a blanket.

"Okay, I'm back. I told your father to go back to sleep and I came out to the family room to get comfortable while we talked."

"Oh, good idea!"

For the next two hours they discussed several mother-daughter wedding specifics. Before they hung up, though, Nicole asked her mother to check to see if her dad was asleep.

"He still tends to be a light sleeper, so let me check."

Charlotte walked back into the bedroom, and since Jenson wasn't snoring, she thought it might be fairly ease to rouse him.

"Jens? Honey?" Charlotte half-whispered.

"Hmmm? What?" Jenson replied as he rolled over and looked up at his smiling wife.

"Honey, Nicole asked if you were awake because she wanted to say something before we hang up."

"Oh, sure. Hang on." Jenson sat up on the side of the bed and cleared his throat.

"Hi, sweetheart."

"Hi, Daddy. I just wanted to thank you for being okay with my being engaged to Liam. It means *so* much to me. He's such a good man, and I know he's going to treat me right."

"Nicole, I truly am so happy for you. As angry as I was that day at the ranch, especially toward Liam interfering, I later realized that he had stepped up to not only protect you because he was your boss. I also realized even then that he cared about you in a much more personal way. I think I was angry about that, too, because you're my little girl and I was trying to protect you."

"I know, Daddy."

"Sweetheart …," Jenson took a deep breath and exhaled slowly, "thank you for forgiving me for how badly I treated you, and especially for my huge mistake of trying to make you come home from the ranch."

"Sure, Daddy," Nicole replied softly as tears were on the edge of flowing down her cheeks.

"I promise you're going to have the wedding of your dreams," Jenson said, as he was wiping away tears of his own.

Nicole sighed as the tears were now soaking her tissues. "Thank you, Daddy. I love you!"

"I love you, too, sweetheart. Here's your mother."

"Oh, Daddy, wait!"

"Yes?"

Nicole softly sighed. "Daddy, would you please walk me down the aisle?"

A momentary lump stuck in Jenson's throat, but he managed to clear it. "It would be my greatest honor, sweetheart."

"Thank you, Daddy! I love you!"

"I love you, too, Nicole. Now, here's your mother."

"Bye, Daddy!"

"Bye, sweetheart."

"It's so late sweetheart. Are you going to be okay?"

"Are you kidding, Mom?! I'm too excited and happy to sleep!" Nicole replied.

Charlotte smiled as she wiped her own tears away. "I remember that feeling," she said softly. "It's the best feeling in the world, isn't it?"

"It sure is, Mom! I love you!"

"I love you, too, dear. Good night, and we'll chat some more soon."

"That sounds good. I love you, Mom. Good night."

As Nicci hung up the phone, she got up to wash the tears from her face before deciding whether she would even try to get any sleep. After dabbing her face dry with her towel, she walked back to the bed and sat down. She reached toward the nightstand and picked up her phone. *One more call.*

Liam answered halfway through the first ring.

"Hey, Nicci!" Liam said, his voice sounding happier than Nicci had ever heard it before.

"Hi, sweetheart!" Nicci replied. All of a sudden she burst into tears. "Thank you for making me the happiest woman in the world. I love you with all of my heart!"

"I love you, too, Nicci! And thank *you* for making me the happiest *man* in the world!"

"I can't wait until we're married so we don't have to do this over the phone!" They laughed.

"I wholeheartedly agree! It can't come soon enough!"

"True, true, true!"

"Hey! I have an idea!"

"What?!"

"Are you still dressed?"

"Yes, after you dropped me off at Beth's I called my mother and we've been on the phone ever since."

"Great. Stay dressed."

"Why? What's going on?"

"You'll see. I'll get back to you in a little bit."

Before she could reply, Liam had hung up, almost as if he were in a hurry to do something.

What do you have up your sleeve, Mister Prescott? Hmmmm ... Nicole Prescott! Mrs. Liam Prescott! Nicole let out a very long, sweet sigh. *They* both *sound wonderful to me!*

Fifteen minutes had gone by and Liam hadn't called back. She wasn't worried, just curious what was going on. A half hour went by. *Should I call him? No, he said he'd get back to me. I know!*

To pass the time Nicci decided to grab her diary and add a very special entry. She had written three and a half pages when she heard a faint knock on her door. She glanced at her watch, saw her engagement ring and caught her breath! Another tap on her door eased her out of her romantic trance. She walked to the door and as she opened it, she was excited to see Liam standing there.

"Let's go watch the sunrise!"

Nicci jumped into his arms and gave him a big kiss!

"Lead the way!"

CHAPTER 85

The Announcement

BRENDY AND **B**ETH WERE not scheduled to arrive at the ranch until mid-afternoon, but Nicci had texted them the night before and asked if they would both please come to the ranch for breakfast. She said she wanted to talk to them about something, and fortunately each had texted back and said they would be glad to be there.

They had arrived early, and since no guests would be joining the staff for breakfast, they chose a table near Luke and Jill's and waited. And waited.

LuAnn was just about to bring out the food for the buffet when they heard voices coming from the direction of the front door, followed by the distinctive sound of Liam's boots walking across the hardwood floor.

Liam was holding Nicci closely as they stopped at the entrance to the dining room. He wasn't known to have a broad smile very often, but this morning it was bigger than anyone on the staff had ever seen. And Nicci? Well, she looked like she was about to burst, and everyone stared in anticipation. The happy couple looked at each other briefly, then back at their friends.

"WE'RE ENGAGED!" Nicci excitedly yelled, holding up her left hand to show off her engagement ring. Brendy and Beth flew out of their chairs and ran to the happy couple. Everyone else stood, clapped, and cheered!

Liam almost felt like the odd man out as Brendy and Beth were focused only on Nicci and her ring and all three of them were talking a mile a minute! Finally, Brendy turned and gave Liam a hug!

"You both are *so* lucky to have each other, Liam!"

He smiled and nodded. "Well, I'm the lucky one here."

"No, you *both* are!" Beth sweetly chided.

"And my *gosh*, you did a good job on the ring," Brendy exclaimed.

"I have my resources," he added with a wink.

"LuAnn's ready with breakfast, so come join us!" Beth urged.

Liam and Nicci made their way toward the front of the dining room, and as they approached their boss' table, Luke and Jill stepped forward to congratulate the happy couple.

"So," Jill began as she sat back down, "have you chosen a date yet?"

"Not the specific date, but we're planning it for around Christmas this year."

"Oh, that will be lovely! And are you planning on having it in California?"

"No, we're going to have it right here in Angel Fire. In fact, if it's alright with you," Nicci paused and looked up at Liam who nodded, "we'd like to have it right here at the ranch."

"Really?!" Jill exclaimed excitedly.

"Absolutely!" Luke replied. "We are one big happy family, and Jill and I are *so* excited about the two of you finding love together right here at our ranch. We would be honored to host your wedding, and we'll be sure to make it *extra* special! And, even if we only have water, milk, or juice to do this with, I'd like to propose a toast to the happy couple."

Everyone raised their glasses.

"To Nicci and Liam. Congratulations, and may your love last throughout the eternities!"

"Cheers!" resounded throughout the dining room.

And on Luke's signal LuAnn brought out another wonderful assortment of dishes for the buffet.

* * *

Throughout breakfast Brendy and Beth peppered Nicci with questions about how and where Liam proposed. They had obviously known about Liam's surprise dinner for Nicci the night before, but he kept *everyone* in the dark about the proposal. Mike and Kay and their family were at the next table, and as Nicci described seeing the glow from the moonflowers, and how they spelled out 'Will you marry me?', Maureen said, "So *that's* what all of those plants were for?!"

Liam smiled and nodded his head. "And thank you for all of your hard work that made that surprise possible."

Maureen's eyes became a bit misty. "Thank you for letting me be a part of it."

"You're welcome," he replied with a wink.

Nicci then turned to Brendy and Beth. "Ladies, there's just *no* way for me to choose between the two of you, so … Brendy, will you be my matron of honor, and Beth, will you be my maid of honor?" They both replied "YES!" in unison and the three of them began giggling like they were at a teenage slumber party.

Liam slid his chair back, got up, and walked around the table to stand next to Mike. As Mike looked up and everyone's attention was on the two of them, Liam asked, "Mike, it would be an honor if you would be my best man." Mike quickly slid his chair back, stood up, reached forward to shake Liam's hand and said, "Pardner, the honor is all mine. Yes, I'll be your best man." They each placed their left hands on the other's shoulders, gripped their right hands tighter, and shook them once more with firm intention. A moment later they paused, smiled really big, then gave each other a huge hug and a slap on the back.

"Thanks, Mike."

"Thank *you*, Liam."

* * *

After breakfast it was clear that Brendy and Beth were going to be occupying all of Nicci's attention for quite a while as they went over a myriad of ideas for the wedding. Liam started to sneak in a quick kiss, but Nicci stood up and placed her hands on each side of his face.

"I love you *so* much, James William Prescott!"

"I love you, too, Nicole Renée Hart!"

"Thank you for making me the happiest woman in the world!"

Liam smiled that smile that had melted Nicci's heart from the beginning.

"That! That right there!" she exclaimed.

"What?" he asked semi-innocently.

"Every time I see that smile it just does something to me."

"Well, I guess I'll just have to keep on smiling like this then, won't I?"

"You *better*, mister!"

This time Liam quickly pulled Nicci in close and looked deeply into her eyes. She caught her breath and felt herself nearly go completely limp. She was in love with the most *amazing* man! She knew it, everyone in the room knew it, and soon enough everyone in the world would know it!

As he kissed her, Brendy and Beth sighed softly, and it almost appeared as if Liam's kiss had left Nicci a bit lightheaded. She looked up and smiled at her not-soon-enough-to-be husband.

"I love you, Liam," she whispered.

He whispered back, "I love you more."

And even though she knew she would win that sweet argument, she wasn't going to start anything at that moment. She would save it for when they were alone, later that evening, sitting in their favorite spot, under the stars, up on their mountain.

CHAPTER 86

The Countdown Begins

LUKE AND JILL AND their staff began preparations for closing down the peak season guest operations at Hidden Glory Ranch for the winter, and preparing the ranch for the upcoming ski season. Jill blocked out the two weeks prior to Christmas and the week after on the reservations calendar in order to maintain the focus on the wedding preparations. That would also allow any of the family members and other wedding guests to stay as long as they'd like after the big event.

After Jenson and Charlotte had heard the exciting news, Jenson immediately offered to give Nicci a lavish wedding in Newport Beach, but she convinced him that it wasn't necessary. She told him she would be most happy with a small, intimate wedding and reception in Angel Fire. The ease with which he agreed to his daughter's wishes had proven to Nicci once again how her father had truly changed. Her mother had even shared that they were spending a lot more time together after Jenson had realized how close he had come to losing both his wife and daughter due to his bullheaded selfishness.

Relations between Nicci and her father had continued to grow stronger, and now every time she talked with her mother, her dad also asked for some time to speak to her, just to hear the latest and to encourage her in her new life. He *was* naturally curious what their plans were after they got married, and while Nicci and Liam had discussed it in great detail, they were not divulging their exciting plans until after their honeymoon.

Nicci could not believe how fast time had gone by since she and Liam had gotten engaged. With the days and weeks flying by, the preparations for the wedding were in full swing, and it still seemed like there was so much yet to do! As an architect it was always necessary to make sure everything was perfect, right down to the smallest detail, and she felt like she was putting too much pressure on herself to do the same thing for her wedding. *Was* she demanding too much of herself? Or anyone else?

For his part, Liam had done two things – kept busy at both Hidden Glory and Silverado Springs ranches, *and*, more importantly, kept Nicci sane! His strong but calm and gentle demeanor were *exactly* what Nicci needed! He was her rock.

Nicci had missed him terribly when he had to fly off in early November to make the quarterly trips to his family's holdings. He had been delayed in returning home because of some damage caused by a severe thunderstorm at one of their ranches in Wyoming. He was needed to assist in taking care of that Wyoming ranch, but a snowstorm had also grounded him near Fort Collins, Colorado for an extra three days. He had originally invited her to join him in order to have a chance to take her mind off the wedding plans for a while, but she declined his offer. She felt she needed to concentrate on the wedding in order to assure that all would go perfectly. They ended up both being so glad she had declined. Because of his delays, she would no doubt have become a basket case.

However, besides being busy with plans for the wedding, Nicci was hoping that a heavy blanket of snow would fall around the time of their wedding. With Luke and Jill's permission, she had arranged for the special delivery of a sleigh. It was delivered to Hidden Glory just an hour after Liam had flown north. It had been secreted in a Quonset hut used for storage that was located on the west side of the property, out beyond the casitas. It was one of two Quonset huts on the ranch, typically used by groundskeepers for equipment and supplies during the peak season. However, during the winter this one was simply left closed. Liam's responsibilities always focused on the central and eastern side of the property, so there was never a need for him to even venture close to this particular hut, let alone go into it for any reason.

Nicci's wedding surprise involved her arriving at the wedding in the sleigh, driven by Luke, and led by Wildfire and Calypso. She had shared her dream with Jill in late October, and Jill had rounded up Luke, Pat, and Mike to assist. They informed her that it would take time to train the horses to learn how to work together to pull the sleigh. The training began less than three hours after Liam's jet left the ground.

After Liam arrived back in town, Luke had done his part by keeping Liam busy at Silverado Springs, while Pat and Mike worked on training the horses to work together to pull the sleigh. If all went as Nicci had planned and dreamed, Liam and their family and guests would be completely and wondrously stunned by the breathtaking impression she was hoping to make.

* * *

Nicci and Liam invited their parents to join everyone at the ranch for an amazing Thanksgiving feast, and she and Liam were at the airport in Albuquerque to greet them and fly them to Angel Fire in his jet. Needless to say, Nicci's parents were quite favorably impressed, and both sets of future in-laws got along wonderfully! On Sunday afternoon they all made the return flight so both couples could fly home, only to return again a week before the wedding. During both stays they all had the nicest accommodations in the hacienda.

On the weekend prior to the wedding, Liam flew solo to Albuquerque to pick up their parents, along with Nicci's former assistant, Amanda, and her former boss, Warren, and his wife, Margaret. There was also one more special guest Liam had arranged for as a surprise for his sweetheart. Liam warmly greeted everyone, and once they had gathered their luggage they headed toward his jet. In fewer than thirty minutes they were airborne.

Prior to leaving for Albuquerque, Liam had asked Luke if he would mind helping to drive their guests to the ranch after they arrived. Before they boarded the jet for the flight to Angel Fire, Liam had given Luke a call to let him know they were on their way. Luke was working at Silverado Springs that day and at the appropriate time he headed to the airport and arrived in plenty of time to assist in driving the guests to Hidden Glory.

Liam introduced Luke to Nicci's former assistant, Amanda, and her former boss, Warren, and his wife, Margaret. By pre-arrangement, Liam led Amanda and his special surprise guest to his crew cab, while Luke escorted the three couples to his Lincoln Navigator so he could chauffeur them in stye to the ranch. On their way, Luke thanked Warren for being so accommodating in allowing Nicole to come to work at Hidden Glory, and that started a very cordial and heartwarming conversation about the bride-to-be that also put big smiles on the faces of her parents.

Luke drove away first as everyone was quite anxious to get to the ranch and get settled. Liam had Amanda take the front passenger seat and asked his surprise guest to sit in the back. As they were leaving the airport Liam called Nicci to let her know they had arrived safely, and that everyone was anxious to see her. Less than seven minutes later the two vehicles pulled up in front of the hacienda.

Nicci was already outside greeting everyone as Liam's truck approached. She turned when she heard the sound of his truck approaching and saw Liam and Amanda through the windshield and smiled brightly. Just as they pulled up next to the Navigator, Jill asked Nicci a question which distracted her from running over to greet Liam right away. That gave him and Amanda time to get out and join the crowd.

With the doors closed, the deeply tinted windows hid the fact there was someone else in the truck. After giving Nicci a big hug and kiss, he gently set her down facing the hacienda. With all of the excitement of the moment, Nicci was totally oblivious to the sound of someone else exiting the truck and approaching from behind.

"Sweetheart?" Liam said, gently trying to get her attention.

"Yes?" Nicci replied with a joyful smile.

"There's someone you invited that I tried to make arrangements with to be here today as a special surprise, but Chelsea couldn't make it because she's about to have a baby."

"Oh, my gosh! You talked to Chelsea?"

"Yes, I called and spoke with your mother. She has remained close with Chelsea's mother all these years, so I was able to get Chelsea's phone number. She's *so* excited about your getting married and wished that she could be here, but her baby is due any day."

"Really? I was wondering why I hadn't heard from her in a while."

"However, I have another surprise for you."

At that moment Nicci felt a tap on her shoulder. She looked around and screamed with joy!

"CARLI!!!" Oh, my GOSH!!! I thought you couldn't come!"

They shared a long hug, and then Carli explained. "That was all a ruse."

"What?!"

"Right after you two got engaged, Liam called me, introduced himself, gave me the wonderful news, and told me of his plan to surprise you. We cooked up the story that I had previously made plans to take a trip to Europe during the holidays with some friends of mine. I promised I would send you something special for your wedding, and, with Liam's help, I'm here!"

"Oh, my gosh, Carli! This makes me *so* happy!"

"I'm so glad, and I'm so happy to be here to share this special event with you!"

"Oh, Carli, Carli, Carli. I'm just completely speechless."

"That's quite alright, dear. I completely understand. And that means that Liam's plan worked perfectly."

Nicci turned toward her sweetheart. "I love you *so* much, Liam! I can't believe this! Thank you, sweetheart!"

"Absolutely! After you told me about reading an article about this ranch in a magazine at Carli's, and then Carli showing you the painting she did while she was here and then gifting it to you, I couldn't imagine not having her here for our wedding. When you think about it, *she's* the reason you came into my life."

Nicci turned back toward Carli. "He's right! You *are* the reason I came here in the first place."

"And do you remember what I told you when you said you were coming here?

"Something about my possibly not wanting to leave?"

"Yes, and that you just might find it too enticing to stay away. You came, you saw, and you wanted more!"

Nicci looked lovingly at Liam and sighed. "I *sure* did!"

"Now, even though I'm here several days before your wedding, don't worry about me. I'm going to keep myself busy by taking lots of side trips to get ideas for more paintings."

"Oh, that sounds wonderful!"

"Liam promised to take me to Taos to get a rental car for the week—"

"Of *course* he did," Nicci interjected, looking admiringly at her favorite cowboy.

"And then I'll probably be going all over the place this week in search of great scenes to capture. It will be extra special if we can get some more snow."

"Well, we're supposed to get a pretty good storm later this week," Liam mentioned, "so you'll probably be in luck."

Nicci gave Carli another big hug and then everyone headed into the hacienda to warm up in front of the dining room fireplace.

As everyone was getting comfortable near the roaring fire Luke and Jill approached the group. Then Luke spotted the person he was looking for.

"Excuse me. Carli?"

Carli turned and smiled brightly as she looked into the faces of the couple she enjoyed being around during her previous visits.

"Hi, Luke! Hi, Jill!"

"I *thought* I recognized you at the airport."

"Yes, I'm back! And you remember me?"

"Absolutely! You were our guest, hmmm, what was it? About three years?"

"Oh, my gosh! What a memory!"

Luke just smiled that great smile of his and gave her a friendly wink.

"It's so good to see you again, Carli," Jill added.

"It's so good to be back, *and* for such a wonderful reason!"

"Yes, we're so excited about Liam and Nicole's wedding, too! It's truly going to be beautiful!"

"Oh, I can't wait!" Carli exclaimed.

"Everyone else around here feels the same!" Jill replied.

"Well, you just enjoy yourself here this week," Luke said with another wink and a smile, "and you be sure to let us know if there's anything we can do for you."

"I sure will! Thank you!"

Carli turned back toward the others and joined the joyful conversations.

* * *

A few days after Liam's parents, David and Mary Beth, arrived for the wedding, the rest of Liam's family began to arrive and, depending on the size of each of their families, some stayed in the casitas, and the others in the hacienda.

LuAnn provided wonderful meals for each breakfast and lunch, but the dinner she prepared each evening was a special feast in and of itself!

Liam had a special surprise for Nicci that he had arranged with Luke, Jill, Brendy, and Beth. On the morning of the day prior to the wedding, and braving an approaching snowstorm, three very special and excited guests drove down from Aurora, Colorado. Brendy and Beth had been given instructions to take Nicci to Taos for a "girls get-away" lunch, and then to take their time heading back to the ranch. After Liam's special guests had arrived, he texted Brendy the 'all clear'.

The guests were provided with the last available room in the hacienda, which Liam had previously reserved for them, and when the ladies returned from their lunch, Brendy and Beth casually excused themselves from Nicci and disappeared. Nicci's mother, and soon-to-be mother-in-law, Charlotte and Mary Beth, joined Nicci shortly thereafter, and together they all had enough to do to keep Nicci busy and distracted until dinner.

Throughout the week, Luke had been holding court down at Silverado with the future fathers-in-law, Jenson and David. They had been duly impressed with Luke's sharing the history of his ranches. Then it was Jenson's and David's turns to share about their various enterprises. Even though Luke and David's ventures were similar, they made it a point to make Jenson feel quite comfortable and equal. The initial uneasiness Jenson had felt, since he had no understanding of the ranching business, was quickly allayed, and the three men thoroughly enjoyed the time they spent together. Plus, after he and Nicole had reconciled, Jenson had called and apologized to Luke for his highly disrespectful actions earlier in the spring. Luke had assured Jenson that it was all in the past, and he needn't worry about it ever again.

Jill served as the perfect hostess and offered any help necessary to assure Charlotte and Mary Beth that Nicci and Liam's wedding would be the hit of the town! In the past, the ranch had been host to many families coming to enjoy the wonderful ski season. Hidden Glory had been blessed with much of the overflow from the Angel Fire Resort and other prime lodging in the area. In fact, over the last few years, many parties had chosen to try booking their reservations at Hidden Glory before trying the Resort or the other lodges or cabins.

With their lighter responsibilities during the off season, Mike and Kay and their family would quite often head for the warmer climes of Hawaii around Christmas time and return sometime after the changing of the calendar, but not this year! In one way or another, they had all been a part of this wonderful love affair that was about to come to its crowning glory in fewer than twenty-four hours, and each had participated in the various plans and preparations.

During the busy week following her engagement, Nicci had reached out to Sheri Oneal, the Nashville photographer who had taken her beloved photo of hot air balloons, and asked if she would be their wedding photographer. Sheri had joyfully accepted, and Liam had made arrangements for her to arrive on the Sunday before the wedding. That way she could capture not only the actual wedding later in the week, but also the various preparations everyone was participating in, in order to create a unique memory book for his bride. The plan was for Sheri to stay through Christmas and return to Nashville once the weather cleared enough to make the trip safely. She admitted to Liam that she hoped she would be snowed in for weeks, as her schedule up to that point had been crazy busy. She was looking forward to shooting their wedding and then taking some extended time off and perhaps enjoy some skiing!

Sheri thoroughly enjoyed this unique assignment, and made sure to take in more of the general activities around the ranch, as well as everything to do with the wedding preparations. That included the practice runs with Calypso, Wildfire, and the sleigh. This was definitely going to be a unique wedding album!

As nervous as he knew Nicci was in anticipation of their wedding, Liam was now feeling nervous as well, though it had nothing to do with the wedding. That evening his next special surprise for his sweetheart would be revealed!

CHAPTER 87

SURPRISE!

LIKE EVERY YEAR, THE hacienda was beautifully decorated for the season! The dining room was especially decked out, not only for a warm and cozy place to enjoy meals and other general activities when the outside temperatures dropped, but also for the very special and personal wedding taking place the next day.

Luke and Jill had never had the pleasure of hosting a wedding at Hidden Glory before, and the fact that it was for two of their very own employees made it extra special. On top of that, their generosity knew no bounds as they informed Nicci and Liam early on that they would be picking up the tab for the lodging and meals for all of the wedding guests. That would be their gift to the happy couple.

On the downside, there had been some previous years' guests who had been disappointed that they were not able to secure their normal reservations for the ranch for the weeks before and after Christmas. Kay and Ashli had helped these longtime customers find lodging elsewhere, and the guests had appreciated their extra effort.

In very short order after breakfast that morning, the spacious dining room had been completely transformed into a winter wonderland! Christmas trees with tiny white lights, that had already been up for a few weeks, adorned each corner. A local wedding planning company had been hired to come in that morning to hang white drapes and fairy lights across the ceiling, along with adding special accent pieces along all the walls.

The arrangement of the tables remained the same as always, although the dining room would be completely transformed after breakfast the next day, in order to prepare for the wedding. Then it would quickly be rearranged again for the reception.

* * *

As Nicci and Liam arrived for their 'night-before-the-wedding' dinner, Luke and Jill invited them to sit at their table, along with their parents. Luke and Jill sat in their usual places, where they could have a view of the whole room, and Nicci and Liam were on their left. Liam had requested this particular arrangement in order to have the maximum impact on Nicci for the special surprise he had been planning since shortly after their engagement. And in just a few more moments his surprise would be revealed.

While they were waiting Mary Beth leaned toward her son to ask him a question.

"Liam. Do you know where Luke and Jill came up with the name Hidden Glory?"

"Actually, Mom, I've heard there are a few different stories behind it, but let's ask them."

"Jill, my mother would like to know where the name Hidden Glory comes from."

"Yes, I'd like to know, too," Nicci added.

"Actually," Jill began, "there are two reasons. When Luke and I were building this ranch, we struggled to come up with a special name for it. We initially decided on the name because of how this special place made Luke and me feel after it was built and ready to open. To us it was a beautiful resort hidden away in the mountains that we hoped people would discover. We wanted them to have a wonderful experience and would then tell their friends. Hopefully, the ranch's reputation would then grow.

"Now, Nicole, do you recall filling out a card at the end of your vacation, where we asked you to share a little about your experience?"

"Yes, as a matter of fact I remember using some of the ranch stationery to do it, because that card was too small to attempt writing everything I wanted."

"I remember that very well. Now, because of *hundreds* of those cards, *and* a few letters, that the guests have filled out over the years, the name means *so* much more to us, because they, too, have discovered the hidden glory and magic of this ranch in these beautiful surroundings."

"That's so lovely, Jill," Mary Beth replied. "Thank you."

"You're so very welcome."

Luke looked around, and, noticing that everyone had arrived, he stood to welcome them. As he was finishing his remarks he added, "You may have noticed that there are three empty seats at the table on my right near our wonderful assistants, Brendy and Beth. These have been reserved for a very special reason, but neither I nor my beautiful wife, Jill, have had anything to do with this. So, I'll turn this time over to our head wrangler here at Hidden Glory, Liam Prescott!"

Nicci shot a very surprised look toward her fiancé, and Liam smiled that mischievous smile of his, and then winked at her as he stood up. Before he began to speak he looked toward Brendy and Beth, gave them a nod, after which they rose and walked toward the entrance of the dining room. Brendy left the dining room and closed the double doors behind her. That's when Nicci noticed that opaque white shades had been placed over the glass in the doors so no one could see what was on the other side.

"Nicci and I are so very happy you've all been able to join us here this week, and to be able to share with us in something very special tomorrow.

"Shortly after I asked Nicci to marry me, and we had set tomorrow's date as our wedding day, I put a plan in motion that included our friends Brendy and Beth. I simply extended an invitation to them to participate in this surprise, as well as our three special guests, and Brendy and Beth took it from there."

What have you cooked up this time, Liam?! Nicci still had *no* idea what Liam was talking about, and sat anxiously, waiting for his surprise to be revealed.

"The invitations I extended to Brendy and Beth, as well as to our three special guests, were all met with excitement and enthusiasm! Of course, this kind of secret was very difficult to keep, and before long I found out that nearly everyone working here at the ranch had caught wind of what was going on. However ... I also heard from each of our conspirators that they promised, on their very *lives*, that they would keep this secret from my sweetheart."

Liam glanced down toward Nicci and saw her literally ready to bounce out of her chair, and he smiled and winked at her again.

"I also took it upon myself to make a slight adjustment to our wedding ceremony without consulting my sweetheart, but I believe I'll be forgiven for this one impulsive move on my part once she sees what her surprise is."

While everyone's attention was on Liam, Brendy quietly opened one of the doors and slipped in next to Beth. Nicci thought she heard some footsteps and muffled voices coming from the lobby, saw that Brendy had returned, and shot Liam another questioning look, but he simply smiled.

Brendy nodded.

"And so, without further ado ... because I *know* I've been driving my fiancée crazy by rambling on like this ..."

Everyone laughed!

On Liam's cue, Brendy and Beth opened the doors with a flourish!

"May I present our flower girl, Emma Stafford, and her parent's Adam and Carolyn!"

As everyone cheered joyously, Nicci immediately burst into tears as she rose from her chair and ran to hug Emma and her parents!

"Oh, my gosh! Emma! Sweetheart! It's *so* wonderful to see you!"

"Thank you for allowing me to be the flower girl for your wedding," Emma said politely.

"Oh, Emma, yes! A thousand times yes!"

They hugged and cried happily together for several moments, and then Nicci turned and gave Adam and Carolyn big hugs!

"Thank you *so much* for coming! I'm *so* excited that you're here!"

"Well," Carolyn began, "we were so thrilled that Liam reached out to us, and Emma has been on pins and needles ever since!"

Brendy appeared at Nicci's side. "We know you hadn't planned on a flower girl, but Beth and I made sure Emma has a special dress for the occasion."

"What?! Really?! Oh, you guys are the *best* friends a girl could ask for!" She hugged Brendy and Beth tightly and wiped away more tears as she let out a long, joyful sigh.

"So, did you have any problems with the snow?"

"We anticipated that it would be slow going in some areas along the way," Adam explained, "so we got an early start."

"And when did you get here?"

"The timing was perfect, because Brendy and Beth had taken you to Taos—"

Nicci shot Brendy and Beth a look. "You guys tricked me!"

Everyone enjoyed a good laugh, and then Carolyn continued, "and Liam called to give us the all-clear. We were just passing through Eagle Nest at the time, so after we arrived and checked in we took a quick tour of the ranch to see how different it is during the winter. Since then, we have been in our beautiful room here in the hacienda, just waiting to surprise you!"

The ladies all wiped away more tears, and even Adam fought unsuccessfully to hold back a few of his own.

"Come on! I'll take you to your seats," Brendy said, and while Brendy and Beth led Adam and Carolyn to their table, Nicci gave Emma another long hug.

"Sweetheart, I'm *so* glad you're here!" Nicci whispered through her tears.

"Me, too," Emma whispered through tears of her own.

Their photographer, Sheri, was capturing it all for posterity!

CHAPTER 88

December 23rd

THE ANTICIPATED WINTER STORM had hit Angel Fire with a fury overnight, blanketing the Moreno Valley and the surrounding mountains in four to seven inches of glistening white diamonds. Despite this, spirits were high throughout the ranch!

Mike, Pat, and Cindi had all arrived at the ranch a couple of hours before everyone else and began preparing for the day.

The horses needed tending to, especially Wildfire and Calypso who, in just a few hours, would be called upon to perform their first official tandem mission. Liam was full of surprises, but Nicci, Luke, Mike, and Pat had been working together on this surprise since early November. After all, she couldn't let Liam have *all* the fun, right?

Even though he would be getting married in just a few hours Liam arrived next and was somewhat surprised to see the others there before him.

"You guys are up extra early!" Liam exclaimed as he walked into the stable.

"Hey, good buddy, what are you doing here?" Mike inquired lightheartedly. "You should be home kicking back and not getting yourself all sweaty and smelly. Your bride isn't going to appreciate it very much if you're not one hundred percent ready for the wedding, my friend."

"Oh, I know. But you know me, I'm always here early to make sure I get my jobs done so they don't fall on anyone else's shoulders."

"Well, consider yourself temporarily relieved of duty, pardner. Now, get out of here. Go back home or go hang out in the hacienda while you wait for your sweetheart to show up for breakfast."

"Isn't there something about a groom not seeing his bride before the wedding? It's supposed to be bad luck or something like that?"

"That's after she has her wedding dress on, so go relax, have a nice breakfast with Nicci and the rest of us. Then go home and relax, because the wedding will be here soon enough, and that train won't stop rolling until the lights are turned off after the reception."

"Okay, okay, I'm going." Liam began to turn to go and then turned back around. "Hey, Pat? Cindi? Thanks for everything you've been doing to help us all get ready. Today wouldn't be as special if it weren't for the two of you and Mike."

"You don't know the *half* of it," Pat whispered to Cindi with a big, mischievous smile. Even though Cindi tried not to laugh, Liam could tell something was up.

"What were you saying?" Liam asked, curiously.

"Oh, nothing, nothing," Pat replied, doing her best to stifle another laugh, and also to wave off her last comment as completely unimportant.

Liam paused, contemplating what the two of them might be cooking up, not noticing Mike was standing right behind him and giving the ladies a double thumbs up! He dropped his hands just in time as Liam began to turn around to go.

"I'll see you later, Liam."

"You bet, pardner."

Liam looked at his watch and decided to follow Mike's suggestion and simply head over to the hacienda and relax until Nicci arrived.

* * *

Nicci was rushing around Beth's house, trying to finish the last few things she needed to take care of before heading to the ranch for breakfast. She had already packed her medium sized overnight bag to take to Liam's home, soon to be *their* home, after the reception. They would stop by Beth's later the next day to pick up the rest of her clothes and other belongings.

Nicci and Liam planned to stay in town through Christmas Day so they could enjoy it with their families. They would then fly their parents and Carli back to Albuquerque International Sunport the following day so they could catch their flights home. Nicci's former boss, Warren, and his wife, Margaret, along with Amanda had made other arrangements. They would be staying a few more days in order to explore the area together before driving back to Albuquerque for their flight home.

After dropping off their passengers in Albuquerque Liam and Nicci would be off on their three-week honeymoon. Liam hadn't given Nicci a hint about where he was taking her, and she wasn't sure if they would be flying by his jet, a commercial airliner, or just taking a car to their destination. More surprises! *I sure love this man!*

Nicci finally felt like everything was ready for the day. In a few minutes she would be enjoying a special wedding day breakfast with her not-soon-enough-to-be husband, and afterward returning to Beth's, where she would have time to relax a bit. Then Brendy would help her with her hair and makeup and Beth would help with her dress. As they were getting ready to leave, Nicci asked Beth if she could ride with her to the ranch, adding that Liam would be giving her a ride back to Beth's after breakfast. Beth happily accepted.

"Just think," Beth began, "it was only about eight months ago you were a guest at the ranch, and now you're getting married to the most handsome hunk-of-a-bachelor I've ever known!"

Nicci smiled. "I know," she replied, excitedly. "I honestly can't believe this is happening!"

"You're one *very* lucky lady."

Nicci sighed and placed her hands over her heart. "I know," she whispered. She decided to change the subject before getting too weepy. "So, who are you bringing as your plus one?"

"I actually wanted to tell you before now, and I hope, hope, hope you don't mind ... but I asked Dusty."

"Dusty Clark, the vet? Really?"

"Yes," Beth replied nervously.

"Wow! Do the two of you have something going on that I haven't noticed?"

"Well, it's nothing official, but we've dated a few times. Are you okay with that? I mean, I know the two of you had a history and all—"

"Yes, I'm absolutely fine with it! Dusty and I cleared everything up between us shortly after I came to work here, and we're good. Really good, as a matter of fact."

"Oh, I'm so glad. I *really* like him, and have for a long time. I don't know if anything will ever come of it, but the few times we've gone out we've had a great time. So, we'll see."

"I'm really happy for you, Beth. I *really* am! And, if it's meant to be, it *will* be, right?"

"Yes, it will!"

"Okay, I'm *starving*, so let's go!"

* * *

Liam had been anxiously watching for Nicci to arrive, and as he saw Beth's car pulling in, he stepped out onto the patio to wait for his sweetheart.

"Hey there, handsome," Nicci chimed as she hurried toward Liam's waiting arms.

"Good morning, beautiful!" They shared a brief but tender kiss followed by a long hug. "Let's get you inside where it's nice and warm!"

"Smart man! I don't think you would be too happy marrying an icicle!"

"No, I don't think I would," he replied as he held the tall and wide front door for her. "Although, I can think of some fun ways to warm you up," he added with a wink and a smile.

Nicci gently elbowed him. "Behave yourself, cowboy." Liam nodded, with another wink, in response.

As they entered the dining room they saw Brendy waving from their normal table, and Nicole excitedly waved back.

"Good morning, Nicci," Brendy said with a bright smile. "Are you ready for today?"

"YES! Can we skip all of this and go right to the wedding?!" The four of them, along with everyone else sitting close and able to hear Nicci's comment, all shared in a good natured laugh.

"Oh, my gosh! Was I that loud that everyone heard me?"

"No, not really," Liam replied. "It's just that everyone was already watching you since this is your special day!"

"It's yours too, remember!"

"Oh, I know. But I also know that a wedding always revolves around the bride."

"Well, I guess I'll just have to soak up all the wonderful attention I can get today, then," Nicci added, laughingly.

Liam laughed and shook his head. "That's my girl!"

Liam and Nicci's parents arrived and Brendy invited them to join their table. The rest of Liam's family arrived moments later and sat nearby.

LuAnn's special breakfast that morning consisted of Eggs Benedict with her secret recipe for Hollandaise sauce that all the staff had raved about in the past. She also had various sides, juices, and fruits. Nicci was starving, but she tempered her desire to fill up, knowing that fitting into her gorgeous dress was more important.

After everyone had eaten their meal and light chatter had resumed, their photographer, Sheri, went to work. All week long she had been in the background, capturing every angle of every event, regardless of how big or insignificant they might have seemed at the time. Sheri knew that this would be a once-in-a-lifetime moment for Nicci and Liam, and she was determined to capture it all!

Sheri would also follow Liam and Nicci to Beth's place after breakfast, in order to capture Nicci in the various stages of getting ready for her big day. Everyone had been so kind to her throughout the week and she had grown to love the ranch and all the staff. She was still praying that she would be able to take advantage of the beautiful snow in the mountains before heading back to Nashville.

* * *

As soon as breakfast was over and the dining room cleared, preparations began to transform the room into a chapel setting. With all of the major decorating having been completed the day before, it was quick and easy to clear the tables and set up the chairs for family and friends. After the wedding everyone would retreat to the back of the dining room or into the lobby of the hacienda as, once again, the staff would move the chairs aside, set up tables for the reception, and move the chairs back into place.

Liam and Nicci left shortly after saying goodbye to family and friends, and he drove her to Beth's. Knowing that Beth and Sheri had followed them, they remained in his truck, sharing these last few minutes of quiet together. In a moment he would walk her to the door, they'd share a hug and a kiss, and the next time they would see each other would be when Nicci's father was escorting her down the aisle. They were happy, they were excited, and they were both anxious to get this party started! He walked her to the door, they hugged and kissed, then looked deeply into each other's eyes.

Liam began to smile.

"What?" Nicci asked curiously, wondering what his sly smile was all about.

"Will you marry me forever?"

Nicci raised her hands up and placed them on either side of Liam's face and pulled him close. Through loving tears she whispered, "Yes, and for always."

Their kiss lasted much longer than the last one. Finally, they each leaned back and gave each other a wink and a smile. Then Nicci turned to go in, with Beth and Sheri not far behind. Brendy would be arriving shortly after running home to pick up her dress, shoes, and overcoat. Her husband, Corey, would drop her off, with the plan that she would then catch a ride with either Beth or Sheri back to the ranch.

Sheri had everything she needed in a separate bag in the trunk of her car. For now, all she needed was her camera bag.

As Nicci was closing the door after they were all inside, she noticed Liam was still at the curb with the engine running. She stepped back out onto the porch and blew him a kiss. He reached out his left hand to catch it and smiled. Nicci smiled back radiantly, waved, and retreated inside, closing the door as Liam drove away.

CHAPTER 89

The Final Moments

LUKE PULLED UP IN front of Beth's at the appointed time, and kept his truck warm while Nicci and the rest of the ladies were finishing up. Sheri had stopped shooting long enough to retrieve her bag from the car, get dressed, brush her hair, fix her makeup, and grab her camera again. She continued adding to the hundreds of photos she had taken throughout the week.

When Luke saw the front door open, he jumped out of the truck and walked toward the porch. Sheri, of course, was the first to step out in order to capture the bride-to-be as she exited.

"Oh, my gosh, Nicci." Luke exclaimed. "You look absolutely stunning!"

"Thank you, Luke. But just wait until you see what's under my cape! And besides, you look pretty darn handsome yourself!"

"Well, I don't have many occasions to dress up like this, but I wanted to look good for you. And Jill, of course!"

Nicci laughed. "Of course!" and gave him a wink.

"Well, your carriage awaits! Shall we?"

"I'm ready! Let's do it!"

Luke nodded and extended his arm, and Nicci hooked her arm in his as they descended the steps. They carefully walked down the snowy path toward his truck and he helped her get settled inside. Before they pulled away Luke reached into his coat pocket for his phone and placed a call.

"Hi, sweetheart! Are you on your way?" Jill asked anxiously.

"Yes, we're just about to pull away," Luke replied.

"Wonderful! I'll let Mike know so he can distract Liam. Call me again as soon as you're parked out back."

"Will do, darlin'! See you soon!"

"Bye, dear!"

Luke put his phone back in his pocket and looked over at Nicci who was beaming in anticipation of what was about to take place. He put his truck in gear and they were off, with Brendy riding with Beth, and Sheri joining the caravan back to the ranch.

As they arrived back at Hidden Glory, Luke drove Nicci passed the hacienda and casitas and stopped next to the Quonset hut housing the festively decorated sleigh. Wildfire and Calypso were there as well, but were yet to be hitched to the sleigh. With Nicci's permission, Luke lifted her out of his truck and carried her into the Quonset hut so she wouldn't have to walk through the snow. He set her down on the cement floor inside and closed the door behind them to keep the heat from escaping. Pat, Cindi, and Sonia were there to help get everything ready for Nicci's grand entrance.

"Oh, Luke! The sleigh looks *wonderful!*" Nicci exclaimed.

"And you look lovely!" Pat said.

"Thank you, Pat! And thank you all for everything you've done over these last couple of months to make this day so special for Liam and me."

"You're welcome!" Cindi said. "It's been such fun to be a part of the festivities!"

Luke, Pat, and Sonia nodded in agreement.

"All we're waiting on now," Luke said, "is the signal that the guests are in their seats and everything is set to begin. Then we'll hitch the horses to the sleigh, get you settled in it, and then we'll be off!"

Nicci was a bundle of excited nerves. She had been praying for this day ever since she and Liam had set the date. The heavy snow had arrived, just as she had hoped, and the decorations were perfect! And she was *so* excited for Liam to see her in her dream dress! *Any moment now—*

Luke's phone rang.

"We're all set, dear. It's time for the bride to make her entrance!"

"Thanks, darlin'. We'll be on our way momentarily."

On Luke's signal Pat, Cindi, and Sonia hitched Wildfire and Calypso to the sleigh. Luke helped Nicci up and into her seat and then took his place to her left. Pat pushed the button to roll up the door, and Luke looked over at the bride.

"I'm ready!" Nicci replied, as she took a deep breath and stifled a tear.

CHAPTER 90

Forever and Always

WITH THE EXCEPTION OF Nicci's father, Jenson, the guests were all in their seats as the wedding was about to begin. The only other exceptions were Brendy and Beth, Nicci's Matron and Maid-of-Honor, and their flower girl, Emma. Jenson was out in the lobby, awaiting his daughter so he could walk her down the aisle. Pat, Cindi, and Sonia had been the last ones to quickly and quietly slip in and take their seats, and Luke was waiting in the Quonset hut with Nicci.

A small table, smoothly draped in a crisp white linen tablecloth, served as the altar. Three white 10-inch tapered candles were set in a silver candle holder in the center of the 'altar', the outer two set two inches lower than the center candle. Both were lit.

Liam was in front of and off to the side of the altar. He stood ramrod straight, shoulders back, looking dashing in his black western style suit. He wore a starched long-sleeved white shirt with a top-tie black satin western string bow tie, and his lucky gold nugget cufflinks that had been handed down to him through the generations of his family. His fifth great-grandfather had them made after striking gold in Montana in 1859. Liam had spit-shined his black Dan Post dress boots, and, to top it all off, he wore a perfectly blocked black Stetson hat he had bought especially for this occasion. His best man and pardner, Mike, was also standing tall, straight, and handsome right behind him.

As the clock drew near to the noon-hour, silence fell over the assembled family and guests. Then heads began to turn as the sound of bells jingling in the distance floated through the room.

One of Liam's nieces, who was sitting at the end of a row near the picture windows exclaimed, "LOOK!", and all eyes were focused toward the windows. Even Liam and Mike turned to see what all of the commotion was about. Liam caught his breath as he saw his bride riding in a sleigh, driven by Luke, and led so competently by Wildfire and Calypso, with wreaths of bells around their necks. As they pulled up in front of the hacienda, Luke jumped down and helped Nicci down from the sleigh. He then walked her up to the open doors of the hacienda, where her father, Jenson, offered her his arm. Luke turned and tended to the horses, tying them to a railing and placing heavy blankets over them to keep them warm. Meanwhile, Jenson escorted his beautiful daughter through the lobby and toward the dining room doors.

Liam could not believe his teary eyes! There was his stunning bride, standing in the doorway, her wedding gown protected from the lightly falling snow by a nearly floor-length white cape. Beth ever so carefully eased the fur-lined hood off Nicci's head, making sure not to disturb her hair and veil, and then her father gently eased the cape off her shoulders. He handed it to Beth, who laid it carefully over the back of a sofa in the lobby.

Nicci was wearing a gorgeous western-style dress of satin and lace, with a sweetheart neckline. The dress came to just below her knees with flowing lace covering it to just above her ankles. The back of the dress had four pearl buttons at the neckline that ended at a diamond-shaped keyhole opening with a short zipper to the drop waist. Lace covered her arms to her wrists from the brief satin shoulders. Her white western-style boots, with a two-and-a-half-inch heel and pointed toe, were a perfect complement to her dress. They featured an eleven-inch shaft in front, sloping down to eight inches in back, with lace inserts and hook and eye closure. Her diamond and pearl dangle earrings were a gift from her father.

As the pianist began to play, their beaming flower girl, Emma, began the procession as she gently tossed pink and white rose petals along the red carpet that had been rolled out earlier. Beth stepped forward next, followed by Brendy.

When they were all in place the pianist switched to playing the Wedding March, and Nicole Renée Hart made her entrance on the arm of her father. As she came closer it was clear to all in attendance that she only had eyes for Liam, who was waiting anxiously for her to come to him, mesmerized by her beauty.

The exchange was made from father to groom, each of them giving the other a nod. Then Jenson gently kissed his daughter on the cheek and turned to take his seat next to his wife, Charlotte. Nicci looked back at her handsome soon-to-be husband. They whispered their I love yous and Liam whispered, "You look *so* beautiful!" Nicci whispered, "Thank you!" in return. They each took a deep breath, shared a loving and excited wink, then turned toward Reverend Anthony Rosson, a minister from a local non-denominational Christian church whom they had asked to officiate their wedding.

"Family and friends, ever since Adam and Eve, God has ordained marriage to bring together two to become one, and today we are gathered together to celebrate the marriage of Nicole Renée Hart and James William Prescott, and to bind their love together for all time.

"I've had the pleasure of sitting down with each of them, individually and together, and found them to be wise, loving, considerate, … and *very* anxious for this day!"

Soft laughter floated throughout the room.

"Nicole and Liam have chosen to exchange rings and have prepared their own vows." At that point Nicci turned toward Brendy and Liam turned toward Mike. Each received their ring then turned back to face each other.

Nicole raised her left hand and Liam gently held it as he slipped the wedding band onto her finger. Then he reached out and held both of her hands in his.

"Nicole Renée Hart, with this ring I vow that I will be your rock.

"I will move heaven and earth for you to make all your dreams and desires come true.

"I will protect you and our future family at all times.

"I will laugh with you in good times, and I will cry with you in sad times.

"Our home will be a fortress of safety and protection from any and all forces that may threaten in any way to harm us.

"I will love you, and only you, passionately and faithfully."

Liam then let go of Nicci's hands, reached into his coat pocket, removed a paper, and unfolded it. Holding the paper, he cleared his throat and took a deep breath before continuing. Nicci noticed he was shaking, then looked into his eyes and noticed tears begin to flow. She reached forward and held Liam's arms, close to his elbows, in an effort to help calm his nerves. He looked into her eyes and smiled.

"Nicole, I've written something special for you for our wedding, something I've never tried before. I hope you like it. I've called it "Letting Go".

> *I've let go of so many things in my life,*
> *broken toys and dreams,*
> *and broken hearts from love affairs*
> *that I guess were just never meant to be.*
>
> *But for you …*
> *for you I've let go*
> *of everything and everyone in my past that hurt me,*
> *feelings of regret*
> *for the numberless mistakes I've made along the way,*
> *for they changed the course of my path,*
> *and led me to this day …*
> *and to you.*
>
> *I've let go of it all!*
>
> *And now …*
>   *because of you …*
> *I can love again …*
> *with all my heart.*

"You wrote that?" Nicole whispered.

Unable to speak until he could catch his breath, and wiping tears from his eyes on a handkerchief his best man, Mike, had just handed him, Liam finally nodded. Nicci let go of his arms and placed her hands gently on each side of his face, then leaned forward and kissed him.

"It's beautiful!" she whispered.

Liam smiled, cleared his throat, took another deep breath, and whispered back.

"There's just one more thing I want to promise you …" He took a deep breath and continued.

"At the end of every day … I will hold you in my arms as you fall asleep, safe in the knowledge that our love will last forever … and always."

There wasn't a dry eye in the room.

Now it was Nicci's turn to share her vow. She reached for Liam's left hand, slipped the simple but classy gold and silver wedding ring on his finger, then looked into the eyes of the man who had captured her heart. She took a deep breath, and continued.

"James William Prescott, with this ring I offer you my heart, my soul, and my love forever … and always.

"My darling, I will be your confidant to turn to, and with whom you can share all your thoughts, your concerns, your fears, and your dreams.

"I will always be by your side, each step of the way in our life together.

"When troubles appear on the horizon, I will be there to help you defeat them.

"I will be your wife, your best, closest, and truest friend, and your faithful lover.

"Together, we will bring precious spirits into this world, and we will raise a family that loves and serves God by loving and serving others."

Nicole caught her breath, fighting back more tears.

"And at the end of every day … I will be your soft place to land."

Seeing a very intense and romantic look of love being shared between them, the minister paused several moments before continuing so as not to break the tenderness of the moment.

Finally, taking a step closer to them, he said, "Nicole and Liam, it is now time to light your candle." At that moment, the minister stepped aside as Nicole and Liam stepped toward the altar. They lifted the outer candles from their holders, and together lit the center candle. Then they blew out their candles and replaced them in the holders. The minister then motioned for them to face toward each other one more time.

"James William Prescott and Nicole Renée Hart, by the authority vested in me by the state of New Mexico, I now declare you to be husband and wife. Liam, you may kiss your bride." Nicole joyfully leaped forward into Liam's arms and they kissed briefly, but deeply.

"Family and friends, in the sight of God, these two wonderful lives, are now one, and I'm proud to introduce to you Liam and Nicole Prescott!"

The gathered well-wishers stood and clapped as Nicci and Liam walked hand in hand down the aisle toward the back of the dining room. They were soon surrounded by so much love, with hugs and kisses flowing easily.

CHAPTER 91

Good Times!

WITH ALL THE GUESTS standing toward the back of the dining hall, Mike and several other staff members began moving chairs. They transformed the room back into a proper dining area, allowing room, of course, for a large dance floor in the center of the room.

Three long tables for the wedding party were set up along the wall near the fireplace. Brendy and her husband, Corey, sat on Nicci's immediate right, and Beth and her plus one, Dusty, next to them. Liam's best man, Mike, and his wife, Kay, were to his left, and his brothers and sisters and their families sat nearby. Luke and Jill took their places at another table nearby, with Nicci and Liam's parents joining them.

The centerpieces decorating each table were an oval arrangement of ten-inch white pillar candles, with eight-inch white tapers mounted in silver candle holders on each side. These were all surrounded by sprigs of holly leaves and berries. The lights throughout the dining room were dimmed to add the appropriate romantic atmosphere.

LuAnn had worked closely with a local caterer in order to provide a wonderful meal of steak or chicken along with various sides and trimmings. Bottles of Martinelli's flowed freely, which the children especially enjoyed, particularly when it came time for the best man's toast to the happy couple.

Mike rose, tapped his glass flute with his knife to get everyone's attention, and then began.

"Family and friends, and ghosts of every size, shape, and age," he began, causing laughter among the children, "it is my honor, and *heavy* responsibility …" pausing for effect to draw more laughter, "to *have* to come up with some words to say about this couple. Oops, correction, this *happy* couple!" More laughter. He looked at Nicci and Liam, sighed *heavily* and shook his head for more dramatic effect, then continued.

"It all began just last April, when Nicole decided to invade our beautiful ranch. She stayed a whole *week*, doing everything she could to get Liam's attention and mess with his mind."

Nicci's eyes grew wide and her mouth dropped as if to say *Me?!?!* Then she looked at Liam and joined him in laughing.

"Now, for *his* part, I noticed Liam just wasn't himself that week. He wasn't ill or sluggish or anything like that. No, the exact opposite was the case! I noticed that first night at dinner, as I followed Liam into the dining room, that there was a distinct charge that rippled through the air. I quickly glanced around to try to figure out what it was. I saw Liam notice Nicci and all of a sudden he stood up straighter, threw his shoulders back, and walked like a prancing rooster!" Laughter exploded through the room!

Mike cleared his throat and continued.

"From that very moment on, and throughout that week, I could tell that he definitely had his sights on Nicole, *despite* the fact that she would be going home at the end of the week! I saw him do things that week that I'd *never* seen him do before with *any* previous single guest of the female persuasion. Regardless of whatever activities the guests were involved in that week, he took particular notice of Miss Hart, and made sure he wasn't very far away in hopes that she would have *plenty* of opportunities to watch him strut his stuff!" The laughter continued to roll, and Nicci and Liam were laughing the hardest!

"On top of all that, in the evenings he was absconding Nicci to parts unknown! That is, until *I* figured out what he was up to! Yes, ladies and gentlemen, he was steeling her away for horseback rides at sunset, in order to woo her and try to steal her heart!" Nicci and Liam smiled as they looked at each other, and Liam shrugged his shoulders and whispered, "It's true!", making Nicci laugh and then lean in to kiss him.

"Then … then, as it always does, the next weekend came, and that's right! Nicci literally *shattered* Liam's heart into tiny pieces when she left." By now the guests were playing along with Mike's folly and let out a forlorned, "Awwwwwwwww ……" A few people in the audience even let out noticeable sniffles, drawing more laughter.

"Sunday evening came, new guests arrived, and even though we joined this new group at dinner that night, Liam's swagger was *nowhere* to be found. It was as if … it was as if Liam had lost his very will to live!"

"Oh, NO!" Luke yelled, and the room fell apart.

"Now, ladies and gentlemen, hope was not *all* lost, for there was a rumor floating around that Luke and Jill had offered Nicci a job right here at Hidden Glory Ranch! And when this rumor hit Liam's ears you would have thought he'd just won the nation's richest lotto! Then, the next day, he saw Brendy and Beth running full steam toward the hacienda! I got on my phone and called my wife, Kay, and she told me they were headed into Luke and Jill's office, and a few minutes later the two of them came dancing and prancing out of the hacienda as if they'd just received the news that their salaries had been tripled!

"Of course, Liam had to find out for himself what all the fuss was about, so I watched as he ever so casually walked to the hacienda, and a few minutes later came out looking stunned! I'll tell you, ladies and gentlemen, he stood there on that patio and had to brace himself as he tried his best to comprehend the news Jill had just shared with him. He finally started walking to the stable, or should I say *flying* back to the stable, because his feet barely touched the ground. Yes, siree, he had just found out that the girl of his dreams was coming back to stay! Of course, when she finally showed up a week later, he changed back to the cool, calm, quiet, reserved guy we had all known *before* Miss Nicole Renée Hart had first come on the scene. He tried denying that he was interested in her, but *we* all knew better. We just sat back and watched the show, as day after day they found ways to send little signals to each other. We even started taking bets on when they would get engaged!"

Nicci looked at Liam, who shook his head and shrugged his shoulders, and then turned toward Brendy and Beth who were both trying their best to hide their smiles.

"Seriously?!" Nicci asked, and the ladies couldn't hold it in any longer and burst out laughing.

"So, who won?"

"Well, you and I had grown so close since you first came for your visit," Brendy began, "that to keep things fair I had to disqualify myself. I didn't know ahead of time exactly *how* or *where* he was going to propose, but I knew it was either going to be the night he flew you to Albuquerque for dinner, or the next night. Then, when you came home without a ring that first night, I just *knew* it would be the next night. However, I was surprised when the two of you came down off the mountain after that special dinner LuAnn had prepared, and that Mike and I had helped her set up, and you weren't flying off Calypso's saddle to show off your ring. I thought 'what the heck!' You two were all smiles, but you weren't busting at the seams. Then I saw something in Liam's eyes, and I knew *right then* that the night wasn't over by a *long* shot!"

Nicci sat there gently shaking her head back and forth, taking it all in. Then Beth spoke up.

"By the way, Nicci, I won the bet."

"Really?"

"Yep! And I *purposefully* planned to be away with friends that evening because I just *knew* I wouldn't be able to keep the secret if I were hanging around the ranch."

Nicci reached for her napkin and dabbed tears away.

Just then Mike loudly cleared his throat to regain everyone's attention. "May I have your permission to continue now, ladies?"

Nicci laughed. "Yes, please go on."

"Now, where was I? Oh, yes! I was talking about *big* money changing hands as everyone was choosing their dates for when these two characters would *FINALLY* commit to one another!"

Mike was keeping everyone in stitches.

"So now, with the deed finally done, things got serious. Nicci, Brendy, and Beth were kept busy planning the event of the century, and Liam began to wonder what he had gotten himself into. He started spending more and more time at Silverado Springs Ranch in order to stay out of Nicci's way!"

"That's not true!" Liam said loudly while maintaining a smile on his face.

"Oh, no? Which part isn't true, that you were second guessing your proposal, or that the work down at Silverado Springs was *much* more interesting?"

"I would have *gladly* stayed around here to help you with the work, and be near Nicci, but Luke asked—"

"Oh, *now* you're passing the buck onto our boss?! How *shameful!*" The laughter was growing so loud that it took Mike extra time in between each jab to try to carry on.

"Okay, okay, I know I've been carrying on *way* too long—"

"*That's* for sure!" chimed Liam.

"Hey, do you want me to leave you time for dancing?"

"You'd *better!*" Nicci added.

"Oops! Well, it looks like the little lady has spoken, so I better get it together and wrap this up."

Luke just had to get in *his* two cents worth. "It's about time!"

This time it took Mike a full two minutes to calm everyone down.

"Ladies and gentlemen … ladies and gentlemen, in all seriousness I was honored when Liam asked me to be his best man. He'd never been a groom before, and I'd never been a best man before, so we made the perfect pair stumbling forward toward today."

Mike paused, cleared his throat, and as he began to speak again his voice changed as he tried valiantly to fight his emotions. They were hitting him at the worst possible time.

"Ladies and gentleman, it's time to stand and raise our glasses." Mike waited until everyone's glasses were raised high.

"To Nicci and Liam, may God bless you every day of your lives together … with love, joy, patience, happiness, and eternal vigilance, because you both deserve to have the very best in your lives … forever and always! Cheers!"

"Cheers!" shouted everyone in response. Then, as they took their seats, the DJ started the music, and a festive spirit enveloped the room!

Liam and Nicci finished their dinners quickly and then began to go from table to table to thank everyone for their love and support.

When they were finished, Liam nodded to the DJ who made preparations for their first dance.

* * *

Liam and Nicci finished their dinners quickly and then began to go from table to table to thank everyone for their love and support. When they were finished, Liam nodded to the DJ who made preparations for their first dance.

"Ladies and gentlemen, please turn your attention to the center of the dance floor, as Nicci and Liam will enjoy their first *dances* as husband and wife. It turns out they couldn't decide on just *one* song, so they've chosen two, and Nicci's choice is first."

They walked to the center of the dance floor, held each other close, looked deeply into each other's eyes, and gave each other a big kiss. Then Nicci's song, "Unchained Melody" by The Righteous Brothers began.

All eyes were on the bride and groom as they moved smoothly around the dance floor. At one point Liam completely stopped, throwing Nicci off her rhythm for a moment. She looked at Liam to see if something was wrong, and with that sly smile of his, he winked and started dancing again. Nicci pulled him close and whispered, "Always keeping me guessing."

"Always," Liam whispered back.

Without missing a beat the DJ eased right into Liam's song, Restless Heart's "I'll Still Be Loving You".

Everyone enjoyed the party as the DJ provided a great mix of popular and country songs, along with the occasional standards. Liam and Nicci remained on the dance floor for the first thirty minutes, and then it was time to cut the cake.

LuAnn had worked her magic in designing a large, three-tiered round white cake with white buttercream frosting, and Nicci had chosen the perfect cake topper! It was a silhouette of a cowboy and his bride holding hands, while riding side by side on their horses, just like they had done so many times beginning that first week after Nicci returned to work at the ranch.

Nicci was only slightly tempted to take her piece and shove it into Liam's mouth, and even though she knew Liam liked to surprise her, she also knew he respected her too much to do the same to her. Besides, she could always do it with a piece of the leftover cake when they were in the privacy of their own home later that night or tomorrow.

As it turned out, they were both polite, and gently held a piece of their cake for the other to take a bite out of. LuAnn then took over, removing the top layer to save for Liam and Nicci, and then began cutting pieces for the guests.

The DJ got the music rolling again and it wasn't long before the dance floor was once again packed. Liam and Nicci joined the dancing a while later and stayed on the floor for another forty-five minutes before the DJ announced he was going to take a short break.

As the guests began to filter back toward their tables, Liam caught Brendy's eye and gave her a nod. She, in turn, gave Beth a nod, who then looked toward a nearby table and nodded at Pat. Initially, Pat quietly excused herself from her table and headed toward the doors leading to the lobby. Brendy and Beth followed a moment later, and closed the tall double doors behind them. Their movements went nearly unnoticed, except by Nicci.

"Where are they going?" she whispered to Liam.

He looked at her and answered with only a wink and a smile.

She smiled back and playfully poked him in the ribs. "You are *so* going to get it, mister!"

Liam began to laugh, making Nicci laugh as well.

"Come on, Liam," she whispered again. "What's going on?"

"I guess you'll find out soon enough," he replied with another wink and that killer smile of his.

Nicci looked at her handsome husband and just shook her head in amazement. *Keep on surprising me, sweetheart! Always keep me guessing!*

Nicci looked out among the tables of family and guests and smiled. The conversations at each of the tables had been joyful throughout the reception. She felt so loved, and—

Above the clamor of conversations, Nicci thought she heard some loud noises coming from the lobby and turned to look. Suddenly, all the lights in the lobby went off, but the noises continued. They were heavy, and had a familiar rhythm to them. Nicci looked anxiously at Liam, but the sly smile on his face gave her a sense that all was well. He was definitely up to *something*, but she knew he wouldn't say a word.

The tall double doors slowly opened, but the darkness hid the mystery of the cause of the strange, but somehow familiar, noises. Brendy and Beth entered the dining room and closed the doors behind them. Liam stood and cleared his throat.

"Friends and family, there's one more surprise I have for my beautiful sweetheart, and it's my wedding gift to her."

At the nod of his head, Brendy and Beth opened the doors, and Pat entered.

Emma shrieked! "Look, Mom and Dad! It's Calypso!"

Nicci stood up and hooked her arm through Liam's.

"Liam, what's going on?" Tears were beginning to well up in her eyes, and she grabbed her cloth napkin to dab them away, trying her best to preserve her makeup.

Liam turned to his beautiful bride and looked deeply into her opalescent blue-green eyes.

"From me to you, happy wedding day, sweetheart!

"Oh, Liam!" She wrapped her arms around Liam's neck, kissed him deeply, then lifted up her wedding dress and ran around the tables to get to Calypso as family and friends clapped and cheered! She gave Calypso a big hug, told her she loved her, and Calypso nodded back in her way of saying "I love you, too!" Then Calypso whinnied and Nicci completely lost it!

She looked at Pat who winked and said, "Congratulations, Nicci!"

Nicci could barely whisper a thank you in return.

Brendy and Beth came up and the three of them shared a big hug.

With everyone still watching Nicci, she gave Calypso another hug, then turned toward Liam.

"Everyone?!" There was no doubt that she now had everyone's full attention. Then, pointing across the room at Liam, she exclaimed, "I LOVE THIS MAN!" Everyone cheered, and as Pat began to retreat into the lobby with Calypso before returning the horse to her stall, Nicci ran around the tables again and into the arms of her waiting husband.

"Oh, Liam, Liam, Liam! I love you SO much!"

"Oh, Nicci," he said with a smile and a gleam in his eyes. "I love you more!"

At that, Nicci leaned back, they looked at each other, and started to laugh.

"Oh, Nicci!" came a familiar voice from a nearby table. Nicci turned to see Warren smiling broadly.

"It looks like, now that you have your own horse, you'll be able to use that check to get your own special saddle and all the other accessories."

Nicci smiled brightly in return. "Yes! I can! Thank you again, Warren!"

Warren nodded happily. "You're very welcome, young lady. Enjoy!"

"I most certainly will!"

* * *

The DJ returned, the music resumed, and the dance floor was once again packed. An hour later Liam nodded to the DJ and he again paused the music. This time Liam stepped up to the mic to make an announcement.

"May I have all the single ladies please gather to the center of the room for the tossing of the bouquet? And all the single men stay close, because it will be your turn next to see who catches the garter!"

As the single ladies began to gather close to each other, each laughingly jockeying for position, Nicci headed toward the head table. She turned and looked at the distance she would have to throw the bouquet, and also realized she would have to be careful not to throw it too high, otherwise it would catch in the white drapes and fairy lights hanging from the ceiling. Then she turned back around, and as the crowd counted to three, Nicci closed her eyes in anticipation for her throw.

On three Nicci let the it fly, and there was a brief but mad dash toward the flying bouquet, and a scream of joy came from the center of the throng as Beth held her prize up high. Everyone clapped and cheered, and Nicci and Beth ran toward each other to give each other a big hug.

"You're next!" Nicci exclaimed.

"Well, we'll just see about that," Beth replied with a laugh.

Liam then brought out a chair for his bride to sit on in preparation of his removing her garter. True to his character as a gentleman, he kept everything modest. As Nicci eased the dress to her knees, Liam reached for the garter and gently slid it down her leg. He then stood next to his bride, turned his back to the waiting single men, raised his hands, and shot the garter from his fingers. There wasn't nearly as wild a scramble for the garter as there had been for Nicci's bouquet, but it seemed to sail over the heads of the closest men and landed in the hands of, none other than, Dusty! Not only was Dusty surprised by the results, but Nicci shot a quick look toward Beth and noticed her mouth drop and her eyes pop wide open! Nicci pointed at Beth and they both started to laugh.

"Your plus one went to number one, just like that!" Nicci laughed. Beth raised her hands and began to fan herself, and they both began to laugh hysterically.

* * *

The reception began to wind down ever so gradually after these two exclamation points to the day. Snow had fallen lightly but continuously throughout the reception, but not nearly as hard and heavy as the night before.

While enjoying the warmth and glow from the nearby fireplace Liam and Nicci took their time to chat with family and friends who had come to celebrate this wonderful day with them. Their DJ gladly kept the music playing and plenty of guests stayed on the dance floor.

Since it was wintertime in the valley the sun set early, although no one really noticed because of how much fun everyone was having. The happy couple had each enjoyed another piece of their cake about an hour earlier and then Nicci leaned over to whisper in Liam's ear.

"It's time to go, sweetheart."

Liam smiled and nodded in agreement. He then got up and walked over to the DJ just as a song was ending and asked for the microphone.

"Hey, everyone!" It took only a moment for everyone to quiet down. While Liam was preparing to say a few parting words Brendy was helping Nicci with the cape to cover her wedding dress.

"Nicci and I are *so* grateful that each of you were able to join us today, and actually for this whole week! In one way or another you've all played an important part in making today so special for us and we just can't thank you enough.

"We're going to be taking off shortly but you're welcome to stay as long as you wish and enjoy the music and the refreshments.

"Tomorrow is Christmas Day—"

"No, it's not, sweetheart!" Nicci chimed in. "It's Christmas *Eve!*"

Liam stood silently for a moment, and then the light bulb lit up in his mind.

"Oh, yeah! You're right! See what you've done to me?!" Everyone enjoyed a good laugh.

"Okay, well … as my beautiful bride has corrected me, tomorrow is Christmas Eve, and Nicci and I will be here to celebrate it, *and* Christmas Day, with all of you. Then we'll be heading out for our honeymoon the *following* day."

Nicci walked up next to Liam, slipped her arm in his, and reached for the mic.

"I just want to say thanks to each of you, as well. We love you all *so* much. You've made us feel so loved today and we're deeply grateful for that!"

And with that their families and friends cheered and clapped for the happy couple and then began to gather in the lobby in anticipation of the happy couple preparing to leave.

* * *

Unseen by anyone during the wedding or the reception was a dark figure who remained far off in the shadows, not daring to come close. He had parked his old truck out beyond the paddocks and had stealthily worked his way along the outside of the main buildings until he had a good, but sheltered view. His anger festered as he watched Liam and Nicci exchange their vows, wanting the whole time to burst in and put a stop to it. However, he still had enough sense in him to know that if he *did* make such an attempt, he would most certainly be fired on the spot and possibly even arrested for disturbing the peace and being drunk in public. Part way through the reception he'd had enough and, being nearly frozen, stumbled back to his truck. He somehow managed to drive off the property without crashing into a tree or ending up in a ditch. *If* he made it home in one piece, he would certainly struggle to get inside and make it to his bed. Fortunately, he didn't have to work tomorrow and he could sleep it off.

CHAPTER 92

The Beginning

A S LATE AS THE reception had ended, and with the snow falling, there had been no sunset for Liam and Nicci to enjoy that night. Instead, he had helped her into his Porsche Panamera, put her medium-sized overnight bag in the trunk, and prepared to drive her home.

As they began to pull away, Nicci rolled down her window and everyone who had gathered in front of the hacienda cheered and wished them well. Before rolling the window up she let some snowflakes fall upon her and her wedding gown and cape, making another memory she would later write about in her diary. She leaned back in the seat, closed her eyes, and then got this quirky look on her face. Just before they reached the end of the entrance to the ranch she looked over at Liam. As he pulled to a stop and looked each way to check for any oncoming traffic, he saw her looking at him with a kind of silly look on her face.

"What?" he asked.

Nicci smiled, then stifled a laugh, before regaining her composure. "Home, James!"

They laughed about that half the way home.

* * *

After arriving home, Liam helped his bride out of the car. He retrieved her bag from the trunk, closed the garage door, set the alarm, then held Nicci's hand as they carefully walked up the snow-covered steps to their home. He unlocked the door, pushed both doors open, and turned and swept Nicci up into his arms. He then carried her across the threshold, gave her a big kiss, and swung her around twice, making her giggle. He then set her down before he reached over, closed and locked the doors, and reset the alarm.

Nicci walked over to the picture windows, looked out over the snow-covered scenery and sighed.

"This truly is heaven."

"And I found my very own angel," Liam replied.

They held each other tightly, then kissed passionately.

"Oh!" Nicci suddenly said, breaking the tenderness of the moment. "I have something for you!" She released her hold from Liam and reached for her bag.

"Sweetheart, you're all I need or want."

"Awww, that's sweet, darling, but I was going to give this to you at the reception and completely forgot after you presented me with Calypso. By the way, how did you do that?"

"I bought her from Luke and Jill, and promised to find a new horse to replace her."

"So, Luke and Jill were in on that surprise, as well?"

"Yes, most of the staff knew, and I'm *so* grateful no one tipped you off!"

"Me, too, because it would have absolutely spoiled the surprise! But, I just couldn't figure out what was going on with the strange noises in the lobby. Then the lights went out!"

Liam just smiled.

"And you planned the whole thing?"

"Yes, I sure did."

"And last night's surprise with Emma and her parents? I mean ..." Nicci let out a long sigh. "How did I *ever* get so lucky to find a man like you?"

"Just lucky, I guess," Liam teased with a sly wink, and Nicci quickly went for his ribs as they laughed until they were both breathless.

"Listen," Nicci began in between breaths, "I'll be right out, but in the meantime would you do me a favor?"

"Sure, anything for you."

"Would you please start a fire in the fireplace?"

"Sure!"

"I'll be right back," she said with a wink and a smile.

Liam noticed, looked back at Nicci with a sly grin, then walked into the living room to start the fire. A few minutes later there was a nice, warm glow heating up their home. He sat down on the sofa, loosened his tie and collar, raised his feet, put them on the brown leather ottoman, and let out a long, contented sigh.

His reverie was suddenly broken as the vison of an angel appeared to his right. Nicci was walking barefoot toward him in a floor length white nightgown, and his heart almost leapt from his chest.

"Oh … my …"

"I love you, Liam," Nicci whispered as she sat down next to him, and curled her feet up under her.

Liam was truly speechless as he beheld the beauty of his bride.

"I …" he caught his breath and struggled to start again. "I am absolutely the luckiest man in the world. You … are … *so* beautiful, Nicci." He held her in his arms and kissed her deeply. Then he held her close with neither of them saying a word while the fire continued to grow ever so gradually.

"Thank you for making me your wife, Liam. This has been the most wonderful day of my life."

"Mine, too."

They continued to stay cuddled up on the sofa.

"So, *this* couldn't be what you had forgotten to give me at the reception."

"No, silly," Nicci laughed softly. "It's right here." She reached into the pocket of her nightgown and slipped out a small, very thin item wrapped in wedding-gown white tissue paper. She handed it to him and then turned slightly so she could watch his expression as he opened it.

To tease her, he took his time removing the tape and slowly unfolding the layers of tissues, but she wasn't bothered by this. She had been waiting a long time for this moment, and she could patiently wait a few moments more.

Finally, the last layer of tissue paper was about to be moved aside when Liam stopped, looked at Nicci and said, "You sure wanted this to be secure, didn't you?"

"Yes, I did," she whispered.

He moved the last layer of tissue paper aside, revealing a rectangular bronze pendant on a sterling silver neck chain. The pendant appeared to be just under two inches long and about an inch wide, and had a classy, brushed surface, front and back. He looked closer and noticed something was inscribed across the front of the pendant. He looked up at Nicci who was smiling while holding back happy tears, then he leaned forward just a bit so the light from the fire could reveal what Nicci had had inscribed.

He caught his breath as he gripped the pendant. Nicci reached over and wrapped her arms around the love of her life.

"I'll love you forever, Liam," Nicci whispered.

Liam held up the pendant and whispered back, "And always."

* * *

Jace Carlton

JACE CARLTON has had a diverse career as a freelance writer & photographer, award-winning poet, web designer, author, an Adult Contemporary radio DJ in the San Francisco Bay Area, and twelve years as a popular and award-winning play-by-play football announcer. He also spent many years as a songwriter, including eight years in Nashville, TN. He wrote predominantly for the Country genre, but also enjoyed occasionally writing for Adult Contemporary, Pop, R&B, and Smooth Jazz. While in Nashville he also had his own music publishing and artist management company.

As a freelance writer Jace contributed reviews on new music and singer/songwriters to online publications, and regularly contributed book and concert reviews, along with personal commentary on the music industry, to Nashville's *Songwriter's Connection* e-Zine. He now devotes his time to writing fictional romance novels.

Jace is also the creator of ChangeYourStars.com and its companion motivational / inspirational e-mail messages that have been read by tens of thousands of people all over the world.

Jace's current works include his first romance novel, *The Reunion,* as well as *Breaking the Stillness,* a compilation of Jace's first three books of poetry *Sounds of Darkness, Rainwater Tapestry* (unpublished), and

Breaking the Stillness (unpublished), along with several he wrote over the next few years. A few of his favorite lyrics written during his Nashville years are also included, along with the stories of what or who inspired many of them.

Originally from the San Francisco Bay Area, Jace and his wife, Kathi, spent many years in the Nashville and Memphis, TN areas, and now call Eagle Mountain, UT home.